BREAK SO SOFT

Break So Soft Duet

STASIA BLACK

Copyright © 2018 Stasia Black

ISBN-13: 978-1-950097-13-5
ISBN: 10: 1-950097-13-7

All rights reserved. No part of this publication may be reproduced, distributed, or transmitted in any form or by any means, including photocopying, recording, or other electronic or mechanical methods, without the prior written permission of the publisher, except in the case of brief quotations embodied in critical reviews and certain other noncommercial uses permitted by copyright law.

This is a work of fiction. Similarities to real people, places, or events are entirely coincidental.

CHAPTER ONE

CALLIE

The bass of the club beat vibrates through my feet and up to my ribcage. I close my eyes and everything tight in me loosens as my hips start to sway with the beat.

There's that delicious electricity in the air. Bodies are thick on the dark, crowded dance floor. The music is so loud it drowns out every other thought. I could deep swaying and lose myself out here on the dance floor and I'm tempted.

My eyes snap open again. Because no, I'm not here to lose myself. I've done enough of that over the last four months. For most of June and July, I barely left the house except for work.

Then I went out, very reluctantly, with some coworkers for happy hour one night and discovered something amazing. It's the same thing that's drawn me out tonight.

I'm here to fucking feel alive again. Or as alive as I can with the most vital part of myself amputated from my life—my son.

Not thinking about that right now. Not thinking about any *of it.*

Several people enter the club behind me and I finally move

forward. The stiletto heels I'm wearing force me to walk in a certain way. Back straight. Hips swaying. If I'm honest, I'm fucking strutting.

I own it. This is my catwalk. The club's so crowded, I doubt anyone's looking at me particularly, but I imagine they are. I'm commanding every eye in this place. They are all at my fucking beck and call. I revel in it, the power I have in this moment.

It's not all in my head, either. When I sit at the bar and cross my legs, casually fluffing the wild shoulder-length red hair of the wig I splurged on last month, I don't just feel like a queen on her throne. The people in the sphere around me respond to me as if I am one.

A couple of women look down at their own dresses self-consciously. The man sitting beside me immediately angles his body toward me and away from the woman he was flirting with moments before.

I hide a smile as the bartender, also a man, notices me among several people vying for his attention. He leans in as he asks what I'd like to drink.

"Vodka tonic, please."

"Put it on my tab," says the guy sitting beside me.

I only spare a cursory glance in his direction. He looks to be in his mid-thirties. Far from old but a little out of place for this particular club scene in his business shirt with his tie loose and askew. Yeah, it's a Thursday night, but it's eleven o'clock. He couldn't change into something a little more club appropriate?

I smile at him charmingly but shake my head with a strong no. Number one, it's my firm policy never to accept drinks from men. I'll never be indebted to any guy in any way, shape or form. And number two, he's just a little too eager for me.

"I got it," I say to the bartender and slide some cash over the bar. "Keep the tip."

The bartender grins at me, bright white teeth against ebony skin. I perk up. Now *he* on the other hand could be a possibility. I'm a sucker for a great smile.

He grabs a mid-shelf vodka and pours some in my glass. I lean in, elbows on the bar top, cleavage unabashedly on display in the form-hugging electric blue dress that I'm wearing.

"How's your night going, handsome?" I ask, elevating my voice to be heard over the noise.

His grin widens, though I wouldn't have thought that possible a moment ago. My eyes zero in on his lips. They're so inviting and thick, luscious is the only word that comes to mind. Immediately, my mind pictures his big body underneath mine, those lips sucking on my nipple.

"Better and better since you walked up to my bar."

Oh yeah. This guy is looking like a more attractive candidate every moment. I toss him a flirty smile along as well as an eye roll as he presses the spout to fill up the rest of my glass with soda.

"You know what, I don't even care how often you've used that line," I laugh, then take a sip of the vodka tonic. It's a perfect mix. I nod at him approvingly. "You're cute enough to pull it off."

He puts a hand dramatically to his chest like he's wounded. "Aw man, *cute*, that's the kiss of death. I've been downgraded from handsome to cute?"

I'm about to respond back when he holds up a finger and says he'll be right back. Unfortunately, the bar is swarmed with people wanting drinks as the club really hits its peak traffic. I finish up my vodka tonic, enjoying the slight warmth that settles under my skin from the alcohol. It's the only drink I'll have for the night, but it's brought a lovely looseness to my limbs. I manage to catch Cute Bartender's eye and toss him a finger wave as I head for the dance floor.

I slip, squeeze, and push my way through to the center of the dance floor. Being surrounded by so many people doesn't make me feel claustrophobic. It's actually one of the few places I feel safe.

A Lady Gaga classic blasts out of the speakers and again I soak up the beat through my feet. It's so loud and enveloping, I can feel it throbbing in my ribs. My body can't help but move and I lift my arms up over my head. My movements are barely just a hip sway at first but soon my whole body is in sync with the music. I roll my torso and then pop my hips back on every downbeat.

The song switches to a dark, industrial techno mix and I close my eyes and sink into it even more. It's so awfully sensual. Erotic. My hand runs from my neck down the sides of my body. I feel my nipples pucker and the telltale slickness between my legs.

Yeah. Hell yeah.

I drop down and then slide slowly back up, my hands rubbing the insides of my thighs as I go. Everyone around me is dancing similarly. Grinding. Sex and desire steam in the air around the floor as the dance goes on and on. My arms float back up into the air as I groove deep in the dirty rhythm.

The music swells as electric violins drop in on top of the techno, sending the melody through the roof. Goddamn, I feel like I might be having an out-of-body experience. My head goes loose on my neck as I drop it and continue dancing with the beat.

Until suddenly there's a body at my back.

Invasive hands on my hips.

Someone grabbing me. Not letting go.

And in my head I'm back there. Always in that room. Always hearing his voice: *I'm taking everything from you, you shit piece of nothing.*

Oh God oh God.

Wearing out every hole—

I can't breathe.

No no no no no no no *no no no no NO!*

The word galvanizes me into action. I swing around and bring down my arm in a t-bar action to knock his hands away from me.

The dude jumps back with an *oof* of surprise, rubbing his arm that got the brunt of my fist. "What the hell?" He looks at me like I'm nuts. A stranger. Not Gentry. *He's not Gentry.*

"Crazy bitch." He turns away from me and disappears into the crowd.

And then the noise and crush of bodies that seemed so comfortable and inviting moments ago is suddenly jarring and just way too much.

I gasp in half a breath and then choke it out again. I press my palm against my chest like I can force my lungs to expand correctly.

Dammit, I'm past this.

I'm stronger than this. Goddamn mother fuck shit cunt—

I manage another half a breath but it's not enough. Not nearly enough.

I only feel more lightheaded. So goddamned weak. Something I swore I'd never be again.

I look around and see a couple people watching me. Most are too busy dancing, lost in their own worlds. Men with their hands on women and women grinding right back up against them. Normal. Not freaking out because a guy touched them. Fuck.

I stumble out of the center of the dance floor. I swallow, over and over. Sometimes that helps me breathe again.

It's not working tonight. The guy at my back— It was too much like—

It sent me immediately back to that place—

Hands grabbing me, all those hands.

Almost blindly, I keep stumbling forward. I'm still hiccupping for air. Shit. Fuck.

This is a panic attack. I haven't had one in weeks. Goddammit. Why here? Why now?

Sweat soaks my forehead and I keep staggering forward until I make it to a wall. Somehow I've managed to stay on my feet in spite of these ridiculous heels. I have no fucking idea how. I sag against the wall and bend at the waist, trying to remember what the therapist chick said I'm supposed to do.

Step one: Acknowledge the attack. Right. I'm fucking having it. Got it. Then I wince. She talked about not just realizing it's a panic attack, but acknowledging that there's nothing to do but wait it out. There aren't shortcuts. Damn it.

I. Hate. This.

I try to suck in more breath and fail.

Breathing techniques are next. Belly breathing. That's what I'm supposed to do. I blink rapidly and try to slow down and breathe in the way she taught me. Not these quick shallow breaths from my chest, but breathing in deep from my *diaphragm*. That apparently means from your belly.

After another few hiccups, I manage a breath where my belly expands and I know I did it right. Now if I can just manage another one.

Try to remember your panic is based on a fear about something that's not actually happening in the present. I remember the conversation in the counselor's cozy little office like it was yesterday, even though it was actually several months ago.

I went back to the women's center I'd gone to when I first got pregnant. After that...horrible Day Which Will Never Be Spoken Of, I wanted to get a full panel of STD testing done even though condoms had been used.

My breathing stutters, even letting my mind near the periphery of thinking about it. I close my eyes and take another deep belly breath. I scheduled an appointment with a counselor only because I knew I ought to. I forced myself to keep the appointment because of Charlie. He didn't need a mom any more fucked up than I already was. So I went.

Usually the fear is based on something that's already happened or something that you're afraid will happen in the future. To really get rid of the attacks, we need to get at the root of that fear. Why don't you tell me what you think is driving the panic, Callie?

I never went back. I love my son and will do anything for him, but I can get through this on my own. I know the source of the panic, of course. The Day Which Will Not Be Spoken or Thought Of.

No doubt the nice counselor lady would want me to break a cardinal rule I've set up since then and, you know, *talk* about it. Which would require thinking about it. Both of which are strictly off limits.

It's the past. It has nothing to do with me or my future.

Or it wouldn't if I didn't keep having these fucking flashbacks and resulting fucking panic attacks.

But getting pissed about it doesn't slow the attacks down. I've learned that well enough. There's nothing to do but ride them out.

So I do. I give myself up to it, do my best to belly breathe, and ride it out.

This one isn't as bad as others I've had. Within five minutes I'm able to stand up and I can breathe mostly normally again. Just a few hiccups here and there.

I glance toward the exit to the club. The easiest thing to do would be to run with my tail between my legs. But what then? I go curl in terror under the covers for another week? After all, I'm just a poor little victim. I'm what they fucking made me.

See? Sometimes it takes just one session to break a bitch.

I shudder at the memory of Gentry's voice.

But this time it doesn't bring on another attack. I let the anger burn through my veins. My eyes pop open and I ignore the fact that I'm sweaty and probably look like hell. I glance around the dark little alcove I've been freaking out in. No one's even noticed me back here. This club has lots of dark little cut-outs in the walls. If I squint my eyes, I can just make out some shadows in additional alcoves that I imagine other couples have discovered when looking for a discreet escape from the crowd.

Interesting.

Then I turn back to the dance floor and march my way back out into the mass of people. I start to move to the music, but I don't lose myself in it this time. Every move is calculated. I dance my way through the people, eyes scanning every man as I go. I pass by the ones already attached to a woman.

I see a couple guys working the crowd. They approach a woman dancing on her own, always doing that move of coming up behind her and then putting their hands on her body. *Without* her consent. Some of the women welcome the hands, others don't.

I'm not naïve, I know this is how it goes in clubs. It still makes fury burn in my belly and I want to go stab the pointy end of my stiletto into their instep. I want to yell at them: *ask permission—never touch without asking!* Instead, I ball my hands into fists and pass by.

I edge by a group of women who are all dancing together and laughing. Obviously friends out for a good time. I pause, then smile and join the periphery of their group.

I'm easily welcomed in. One of the girls who's voluptuous with wild, curly hair holds out a hand to me. That's more like it. When I grab it, she spins me. It startles a laugh out of me. I dance with them for awhile.

Wow, I didn't realize how much tension I've been carrying. It works its way out of my shoulders as we dance. It feels good to earn my sweat this way. It's also a good cover to watch the crowd and keep up the hunt.

That's when I find him. My target for the night.

He's medium height and build. Medium's a good word for him all around. Not too handsome, but far from ugly. He's not aggressive in his dancing, either. He approaches women to dance, but he does it from the front. He moves into their space and holds out a hand in invitation to pull them closer. Giving them the choice to accept or decline.

More often than not, the women give him a semi-apologetic shake of the head no. I roll my eyes in disgust. A lot of those same women are fine with the backside grinders, but this guy's a gentleman and he gets the brush off for it. The song changes and the woman he was dancing with moves away from him. I roll my eyes. Idiots.

That decides it. He's the one.

I thought I might have to dance in his vicinity waiting for him to be free, but no, looks like I can move in right away. I head toward him.

The transition to the next song is smooth and it's a sultry beat. The guy is just turning in the crowd, still moving his head with the music a little awkwardly like he's trying to figure out where to go next. I slink up to him, eyes at half-mast and licking my lips for good measure.

I'm not big on subtlety.

His eyes widen when he notices me. A smile lights up his face and he starts moving with the music more. He looks like he's about to do the not-so-smooth-move-into-my-space-ritual I've seen him do with the other girls, but I beat him to it. I step into him and drape my arm around his neck, my breasts crushed against his chest.

"Wanna dance?" I hiss into his ear.

"Yeah," he chokes out, nodding his head at the same time.

I smile, but barely pull back. Instead, I drop my face into his neck. He smells good. Well, he might have overdone it a little on the cologne, but at least it's not one of those obnoxious smelling ones. He didn't douse himself in Axe or anything. It's a fresh, cool beachy smell. It feels like everything else about this guy—a little overeager, but really kind of sweet.

I slide my leg in between his so I'm straddling his thigh. Then I dance the fuck out of the song.

And when I say fuck, I do mean fuck.

I'm all but humping his leg as I writhe my hips back and forth to the beat. I keep my arm hooked around his neck but let my upper body loose. I throw my head back and arch my body, breasts thrust up, held up only by my grip on the back of his neck.

I can feel his absolute focus on me, how completely I've captivated him. To him, I'm a goddess who walked out of nowhere and chose *him*.

Oh yeah. My blood heats. I feel the beginning of the rush I've been seeking all night.

I roll my torso once, twice, then I pull myself back up toward him in a dramatic whip so that my fake hair flies and a little bit of the light-headed feeling comes back.

It only feeds my high. I grab Mr. Nice Guy's face and kiss the fuck out of him. I don't bother with the tentative, questioning kisses. No, my tongue immediately goes for the invasion. And after one stunned second, he's reciprocating.

His hands drop to my waist.

My *waist*.

He's so fucking *adorable*. Even with me mauling the hell out of him, he doesn't go for the ass grab.

Now that's a gentleman.

I pull back from the kiss, taking his bottom lip in between my teeth in a way that elicits a low groan from him. I can feel from the tent in the front of his pants where I'm pressed fully against him that this isn't just a one-way street of sexual interest. Good.

I give his lip another nip and then move to his ear again. "Come with me." I have to shout to be heard over the music. I back away from him, but not before I've firmly grabbed his arm to pull him behind me through the crowd.

An upbeat song with a techno beat blasts through the speakers and the crowd is going nuts. The hour has grown later and later. Bodies grind against one another. The raw sexual energy charges the floor. Instead of it making me squeamish, I absorb it. This club isn't one of those super classy joints. I picked it for its mix of grunginess, clientele, and secluded corners. Finding all those alcoves earlier was just a bonus. Even more dark little spots than I thought.

Which is exactly where I drag Mr. Nice Guy. Except that as I'm heading to one of the alcoves, I spot something even better. Along the back wall there's a small hallway that leads not to the bathrooms, but just to a couple closed doors—probably some offices or the janitorial closet.

Absolutely perfect. Private enough for what I need, but still public enough that I can feel safe. Still, I don't lead him down into the shadowed depths of the hallway just yet.

My shoulders are still moving to the music when I slam Mr. Nice Guy against the wall right where we are and press my entire body against him. My lips are immediately on his as I push my pelvis up and into his groin and give several swiveling hip rolls against him. I feel the rumble of his groan through his chest even though I can't hear much because of the noise in the club. He tastes like stale cigarettes but I don't care. Kissing isn't especially about enjoyment for me anymore. It's about getting where I need to go. Establishing an order to things.

My hand snakes down the front of his stomach and I reach for his crotch. I squeeze unashamedly when I get to his dick. He's nice and hard. I can't feel too much about the size of him through his jeans, but he's definitely not a shrinking violet. Always nice, though I'm not actually picky. It's not about that for me.

His body jolts a little when I make contact, but he doesn't pull away. With all signals go, I slip my hand down the top of his pants. He shudders when I make skin-to-skin contact and his breath hitches while he kisses me. I don't bat an eyelash.

I suck his tongue further into my mouth as my hand closes around him. I wasn't wrong. He's got a fair size to him. Aw, a sweet guy with a good package. Jackpot. I wrap my fingers around his girth and grip him firmly, then rub up and down. He leans more heavily into me, pushing himself into my palm.

I roll my eyes. *Slow down, buddy. There's only one driver on this train and it ain't you.* He'll learn quick enough.

I brace my arm against his chest and press him back firmly against the wall. He allows it for a few moments but then his hips are thrusting forward again into my hand. I shake my head and pull firmly away from his body. His face goes all desperate and his questing lips try to follow me, as do his hips.

I just wave my finger in his face. Ah ah ah. Nope.

"My way or the highway," I shout in his ear.

In the dim lights from the dance floor I can see the disappointment coloring his face. But that's all it is. Disappointment, not anger.

Which is all the confirmation I need to take his hand and draw him further down the hallway to the darkest corner at the very back. There I push them to the floor, reach into my bra for a small foil packet, and then sit down on top of his thighs.

In the dimmest light of an exit sign, I can see his eyes are wide as proverbial saucers. He swallows hard, watching every move I make.

The music is only slightly muted back here, but I don't bother saying anything. His dick is still out from a moment ago, so I rip the packet with my teeth and don't waste any time rolling the rubber down over his length.

His hands jump to my hips as I reposition myself to hover over him. I pause there for a moment, about to double check he's cool with all this. He's just staring at me all shocked looking. I'm the last person to want to take advantage of anyone if they're on the fence at all—

But then his hands on my hips grip tighter like he's trying to drag me down onto his cock. Alrighty, I'll take that as a confirmation.

I smack both of his hands away hard, though. "I run the show, remember?"

He jerks back in surprise and that's when I sink down on him.

His hands immediately try to come back to my hips but I grab them mid-air and reposition them, pinning one against the ground and lifting the other to my breast. His cock twitches inside me as his thumb braises my nipple.

Finally. The rest of the tension twisted tight in the core of my body starts to unwind at the sight of this fucker held down underneath me. I squeeze my hips tighter around him, pinning him in place.

Then I fucking ride him. His dick isn't that big after all. Apparently he's more of a show-er than a grower. But whatever. When I lean forward and grind my pelvis against him, my clit rubs at a good enough angle.

"That's right, you dirty fucker." I glare down at him. "You just lay there and take it like the dirty *fucking* bitch bastard you are."

I slam down on him and it feels good. Not great. But good enough.

That desperate sensation starts to spark low in my belly. I throw my head back and ride him with more fury. It's been too long. God, way too long since I've been able to feel this.

I thrust down on him especially hard, grinding my ass to his pelvis back and forth. I writhe back and forth before lifting off and slamming back down again.

"God. Fuck. *That*. Yes. *Right there*." Yeaaaaaaaah. Fuck, this is nothing like when I use toys at home. Those just can't do it for me anymore.

I look down at the man below me. Even with the little bit of light from the hallway, I can see the awed expression on his face. How I am blowing his mind. I'm just some stranger who came up to him and now I'm dominating the fuck out of his dick, his pleasure, his fucking world.

I lift my hand to my mouth and bite down on the side of my palm to muffle the high-pitched whine of pleasure that I can't hold in. Damn, this is what I've needed. Not wanted. Needed. The knot has been winding tighter and tighter inside me, fear and panic threatening to choke me every time I leave my house. I need control.

So I take him faster, land harder, but it's not enough. I need more. I need fucking more.

"You fucking bastard." I slap him hard across the face but never for a moment stop riding him. I tighten my inner walls and feel him swelling inside me.

His hand clamps down on my breast, so hard I bet it will bruise. I slap him again and I'm closer than ever to the edge. Oh Christ oh Christ, almost there. The noises coming from my throat are uncontrollable and I lift my hand to stifle myself again. I can't be too loud in spite of the cacophony of the club. A scream of pleasure will pierce through even that noise.

But oh God, I'm on the edge. Riding that fucking edge.

He starts thrusting harder into me from below.

What. The. Fuck??? Red rage flashes through my pleasure. Hasn't he learned his goddamned lesson by now? I say *how*. I say *when*.

Why do guys always fucking assume they can just take over? What the hell is wrong with them? Even Mr. *Supposed* Nice Guy? Fucking piece of shit.

I drop even further away from the edge, and when he grabs my hip like he's going to flip me over—like he thinks *he's* going to be the one thrusting into *me*, I just fucking lose it.

I use one of the tricks I learned in self-defense to heft all my weight up into my chest and shoulders to keep him pinned in place. He lands back where he was with an *oof* that I can feel more than hear.

He got dislodged during this process, so I grab his dick, shove him back inside me and pump up and down even more furiously.

I glare at him and don't bother hiding my wrath. This is rage-fucking now.

Bastard must have a death wish. He obviously has no idea where my head's at, because he grabs my thighs again. His fingers knead my flesh. I don't knock his hands away this time. His eyes are closed, his head back thrust against the cold concrete.

He doesn't notice me slip the knife from the garter belt tied at the very top of my thigh.

But his eyes sure as hell pop open when I lean over and hold it against his throat.

I keep pumping on him just as furiously, but my face inches toward his. "I'm on top, got it motherfucker?" I say loud enough so he'll hear it.

He nods but just the barest bit so he doesn't come in contact with the knife. His eyes are wide with sudden terror. What a little bitch. I don't even have the knife right up against his throat. There's a good half-inch of clearance. Still, it's close enough. As long as he's a good boy, we can both get what we want out of this exchange.

He still an iron rod inside me but he's learned his lesson. His hands drop flat to the floor like he's afraid to move.

A momentary pang of regret hits.

I didn't mean to scare him. I just needed. I needed—

I move the knife a little further back from his neck, but still close enough so that if I need to, I could strike.

Then I look down at him and take in the whole tableau—him prone and at my complete mercy. A shudder goes through my body and my back arches in pleasure.

Oh God, yes, yes, right there. I grind down on him deep and rub my breasts against his chest. I lick up his neck and suck on his bottom lip, relishing in his filthy, cigarette taste. I hear his pained groan and feel the tension in his body as he struggles not to move.

Oh very, *very* good boy.

I have fucking mastered him. This realization plus all the stimulation finally sets me off like a rocket. I come quick and sharp and hard.

It's gone far, far too soon for all the work I've done to catch it.

Mr. Nice Guy's face scrunches in concentration and anticipation. If I was a super bitch, I'd just leave now, maybe even wave my knife at him and forbid him to get off. But in the end, even if he had a few unruly moments, he pleased me. So I continue grinding on him, clutching my walls tight around his dick.

I lean over and speak loud enough so he hears. "You've been such a good boy for me. You may come now."

Almost immediately his whole body stiffens and his pelvis pushes up into me once and then twice more. His eyes open in fear right after, like I'm going to punish him for it. The rush of power the very thought shoots through my veins surprises me. I climb off him, leaving him to deal with the condom situation.

I feel shaky all over now that the adrenaline high is wearing off. The knife is still in my hand and all the sudden it's like, what the fuck did I just do?

Did I just really think it was okay to hold a weapon against a guy's throat? He could fucking call the cops on me. *I* would call the cops on me. What if anybody had stumbled on us back there and seen me? Oh my God. Holy shit.

I hold a hand to my forehead, then realize it's the hand holding the knife and drop it back to my side.

I lift my skirt and shove the knife back into the mini-sheath in my garter. It was only supposed to be for extreme situations. If I was in danger.

I back away from the guy who is struggling to get to a sitting position and pull up his pants. He looks like he's trying to say something, but I turn on my stiletto heel and high tail it out of there.

CHAPTER TWO

CALLIE

Beep, beep, beep, beep, beep, beep, beep.

God. What the fuck? No.

I sleepily lunge for my alarm clock and slam the snooze alarm. I'm about to let my heavy eyelids drop closed again when I glimpse the red numbers of the clock.

7:39.

SHIT. Holy shit, holy shit, holy shit! I almost fall off the bed, I sit up so fast. How many times did I hit the snooze button this morning. Damn it!

I scramble off the bed and trip on my dress from the night before that's on the floor, barely catching myself on the wall. "Fuck!" I yell as I kick the stupid dress out of the way and haul ass to the bathroom.

What greets me in the mirror isn't as disastrous as I feared it would be. Only a mini-nightmare as opposed to full on Walking Dead extra.

I tried just falling into bed when I got home last night, but within ten minutes, I was crawling out of my skin with the need to get clean.

A thirty-minute shower later and I finally felt like the club was scrubbed off me. Or at least I was too exhausted to care anymore. I fell into bed without even brushing my hair.

Yeah. It shows. I've got a serious case of bed head going on. Even without the oh-so-sexy mattress/pillow styling I'm rocking, the image looking back at me is strange. I went in for a makeover midsummer. Gone are the long natural blonde locks I've sported my whole life. For the first time, I started coloring my hair—a nice but unspectacular auburn shade. I also cut it to just below shoulder-length. My natural wave gives it some body, but I don't do anything else to it except let it air dry most of the time.

Since it's flat on one side and poofy on the other today, I brush the front and pin it back with some bobby pins. A quick glance with a side mirror shows my solution fixed the poof situation. I brush my teeth quickly, one eye on the clock the whole time. Shit, shit, shit.

I'm going to be late.

I'm never late. My boss, Marcy, gets pissed whenever anyone on her team comes in even a couple minutes after eight. The thought has me jogging back to my room and grabbing the first outfit I see in my closet, some pants and a simple blouse. I don't have time for anything complicated today. Like something with buttons. I don't have time for fucking buttons today. I barely give myself time to pee.

Marcy gives people who are late *the glare*. The I'm-dissappointed-in-you-and-don't-think-I'll-forget-this-when-quarterly-review-time-comes-around glare. Plus all week that team member gets assigned the shitty tasks like debugging everyone else's code.

I slip on my fancy ballet flats and then I race to the kitchen to grab a breakfast bar. I snag one and also a banana. I swing around to scurry from the kitchen and—

"Fuck!" I look down to see what my hip banged into—and then my throat closes up.

Charlie's highchair.

All the air is knocked out of my lungs. Everything else disappears. Needing to rush to get to work. Marcy being pissed if I'm late. Everything that went down last night.

Charlie.
Charlie.
Charlie.

My head drops backward so that I'm looking up at the ceiling. I give myself a moment, just this one single solitary moment to feel it. The absolute gaping hole in my heart. Where is he this morning? Is that woman who is pretending to be his mother treating him right? I don't even let myself count to ten. Ten is too much. I'll be paralyzed if I let myself get all the way to ten.

I bring my head back down and start moving again. I realize belatedly that I've been squeezing the banana so hard it's gone squishy in the middle. I'll have to eat it fast or it'll bruise. Guess it'll be breakfast instead of part of lunch. I grab my purse that's by the door and then I'm out.

I hurry to the light rail station, checking my phone for the time as I go. Seven fifty-one. I should be freaking out about how late I'm going to be. No way morning transit is going to get me there in nine minutes, in addition to walking the three blocks to the CubeThink building.

Fuck it.

Stressing about it won't change anything. I keep my steps hurried, but I don't jog. No point in showing up with sweat stains only to save a minute or two. The shit will hit the fan with Marcy either way. Besides, my head is too full of Charlie.

My baby boy. While I don't let myself linger on the feelings of self-pity that could overwhelm me and keep me in bed for weeks on end, thinking about Charlie himself is what keeps me going.

And I get to see him today. Every Friday, I get supervised visitation. That thought brings a smile to my face even as I weave in and out of several homeless men yelling at morning commuters for change. I slip onto the light rail just before the doors close and breathe out, heart racing from my frantic race here.

I lean against one of the poles to steady myself as the train rattles forward. The car is packed just like it is every weekday morning.

The visits with Charlie might be in the most unnatural setting possible—a fancy child psychologist's office with someone watching my every move and noting every word that comes out of my mouth—but I still get to see my baby. Even if it's only for two hours. Once a week.

My hands go white-knuckled around the pole.

Oh hell, calm down. This is more than I got in the beginning. I just have to remember that. Right after they took him away, I didn't see him at all for six weeks.

Even then, the only reason I got supervised visits was because I went along with the bullshit court order to get outpatient substance abuse treatment, along with taking parenting classes. Fucking *parenting* classes. I think that one pissed me off even more than having to be in outpatient rehab for the drug problem that I didn't have.

My new lawyer was busy sending off the paperwork to get the initial sample retested and asking for a new drug test that was far more reliable, a follicle hair test proving not only had I not been on drugs the day of the hearing, but I hadn't even been in the *vicinity* of people doing drugs for the last six months. Still, I'd see my son a lot faster if I did all the other bullshit in the meantime.

So I did. And yeah, occasionally I had violent feelings toward some of my fellow peers in the parenting class. There were some in the class who seemed like they genuinely wanted to reform and were desperate to do anything it took to be better people in order to get their kids back.

But some of the others, God, they didn't deserve kids. At all. In fact, I thought the class should be pass or fail. If you failed, then you not only didn't get your kids back, but you also got neutered at the end. Not PC to say, but fuck that. Case in point: there was one guy who was a disgusting lowlife, watching porn on his phone instead of paying attention to a lesson on current behavioral theory and effective ways to discipline one's children that weren't verbally or physically abusive. We'd all gone around and told why we were there at the start of class. Lowlife had lost custody of his kids for abusing them and his wife. Or as he put it, "ya know, I'd kinda get pissed sometimes. I'd come home after a long day of work and my wife was being a bitch and my kids wouldn't stop whinin' and it would all just get out of control, ya know?"

Yeah. I wanted to take his phone, break the screen, and stab him in the eyeball with it. Toward the end of class, he came in grinning and told us that his wife had taken him back. He was moving in with her and the kids again. He never came back after that and I still feel sick thinking about those kids.

The fact that I was lumped in with the same category of parent as him in the court's eyes... I can't even.

The double beeps of the train announcing the arrival at a station break me out of my thoughts. I look up and see that it's my stop. Shit. Today's not the kind of day to space out and miss my stop by accident. Thankfully, I'm close to the doors.

When they open, I move with the crowd and am expelled out onto the platform with all the other commuters, half of whom are staring at their phones. I don't even bother to check the time. I'm sure it's already past eight o'clock. I jog off the platform, only now remembering my breakfast bar. I unwrap it and shove half of it in my mouth, chewing as I go.

It's at least another ten minutes before I hurry into the building that houses the CubeThink offices. I swallow down the last bit of the bar and now my mouth feels like the Mohave Desert. Must. Drink. Water.

No time though. I make a beeline for the elevator once I'm inside. My heart rate speeds up as I cross the threshold into the small boxed-in space and I look around. It's fairly packed and I quickly scan each face. It's only as the doors close and I've finished looking everyone over that I let out a breath.

No Jackson.

Then I shut my eyes, kicking myself for even letting his name cross through my head. I'm usually so good about it. I don't let myself think about him. His face. His touch. What might have been...

God, here I am doing it again.

I force my eyes back open. There's a reason I take the stairs every day. I don't need to fight through these mental acrobatics each morning, worrying about running into him in the one space we might accidently encounter each other.

That day I told him I'd accept a job with his company and his lawyer's help with Charlie's custody hearing but not a relationship with him was the last that I saw him. I started working here at CubeThink the following Monday, but it's been the unspoken agreement between us that he stays on his executive floor and I never leave my workspace three floors below.

My foot taps impatiently as the elevator rises. I want to scream each time the elevator stops to let people out at what feels like *every* floor on the way to the CubeThink offices. Which naturally take up the top five stories of the high-rise. I check my phone when the elevator finally slides the last bit up to my floor.

8:14. *Fuck.* My whole body winces right as the doors open and I step out.

"Glad someone felt like showing up today." Marcy's sharp voice is the first thing that greets me. She's walking by the lobby, her assistant at her heels holding a tablet and a folder stuffed with printouts.

"I apologize for being late," I say, my voice coming out slightly croaky through my dry-as-fuck throat. I try to compensate by standing up as straight as I can.

"What? No excuses about traffic? Or let me guess, your cat chewed through the cord of your alarm clock?"

"No ma'am. I do apologize, though." I feel my cheeks redden. Marcy might be a hard-ass, but she's a woman I respect the hell out of. I hate being in this position. "It won't happen again." I'll set three alarm clocks if I have to from now on.

She snorts, turns away, and continues walking. "It better not," she says. Then when she's almost to the door, she looks over her shoulder, irritation on her face. "Well what are you doing now?" She seems absolutely exasperated by me. "*Follow.*"

"Yes, ma'am." I scurry and hurry after her. I only glance longingly to the water cooler in the corner before following her through the door.

"Fuck, fuck, fuck," I whisper under my breath as I race into the psychologist's office. It was 5:01 when I last checked my phone in the

Uber as we fought traffic to get from San Jose, across town, then to the office in Menlo Park. Fucking Menlo Park. Only David's stick-up-her-ass wife would be able to afford actually living in this area and demand the custodian for the supervised visits be at a place like this. Yeah, I got to put forth some names as options too, but David and the Shrew were always going to fight anyone I recommended. In the end my lawyer independently checked out this psychologist and agreed she's one of the best, unlikely to be biased one way or the other. I just have to eat the outrageous costs, which I can halfway manage because of my new job.

Not that a fifty-dollar Uber ride to get here on time is helping my finances. Usually I take public transit, but there was a team meeting at the end of the day today. After being late to the office, there was no way I was asking to be excused early. But every minute that ticked by after four o'clock, I felt like my guts were being twisted.

I swear internally again as I yank open the office door. Then I get into the actual psychologist's office, I note the wall clock behind the secretary's desk. 5:04. Shit. That's four precious minutes that I lost with my son. At least David and the Shrew aren't in the lobby to see and take satisfaction. They usually drop Charlie off for a half-hour appointment with the psychologist at four-thirty, then I come for the two-hour supervised visit. Me being late will also go in the recorded notes the court gets. Double fuck.

"I'm here for the visit with my son," I say quickly to the secretary. She's new, not one I've seen before. "Calliope Cruise." The words that just came out of my mouth feel ridiculous. I have to ask this woman to see my son. He's behind walls and doors and I have to make an appointment to get access to him. It makes me furious if I think about it for too long. Later. I can be pissed later.

The woman looks up at me with a slightly bored expression. "What did you say your last name is again?"

"Cruise. I'm here for my five o'clock appointment with Dr. Rodriguez and my son, Charlie Cruise."

She clicks her mouth several times. "Then she frowns. I have a supervised child visitation for a Charles Kinnock. But no Cruise."

That motherfucking bitch-faced bastard—

I squeeze my eyes shut so hard it almost gives me a headache before I breathe very slowly in and out a couple of times. "That's my son," I say, jaw tight. "But his name is Charlie Cruise. My ex's last name is Kinnock, but that's not on Charlie's birth certificate. David made the appointment with the wrong name just to get to me."

The secretary frowns. "Well, I don't know what to tell you. I have an appointment for a Charlie Kinnock. There seems to be an error here and you should call during regular business hours to talk to a nurse to reschedule—"

"Just let me go see my son," I lose my cool and get right up in her face. "I've been waiting all week to come here and see my son. Just push whatever button you have to so I can go and see my son."

I realize my mistake as she backs away from the desk and grabs the phone, looking for all the world like she's about to call security on me.

Fuck! I wasn't shouting but my voice was definitely elevated.

I raise my hands and immediately quiet my voice so that I'm abjectly conciliatory. "I'm sorry. I apologize for raising my voice. Maybe you could just call Dr. Rodriguez and let her know that Miss Cruise is here." I make my voice absolute sugar and honey. "Would that be possible?" I smile my gentlest smile at the incompetent idiot and take a step back.

She eyes me like she's waiting for me to go all super-freak on her but I stand patiently like Molly Mc-DoGooder and after a moment, her posture relaxes and she gives me a smile in return.

"Yes, all right," she finally says. She pushes a few numbers on the phone and repeats what I said. She gives several nods as something is said on the receiver and then looks back at me.

"I'll buzz you through. You can go directly back. It's the last door on the left at the end of the hallway." She's still eyeing me like she can't quite trust me, so I make sure to walk at a perfectly steady pace even though I want to flip her off and run down the hall to see my son.

I give one last glance at the clock before she buzzes the door to the office. 5:12. Damn lady just wasted another six minutes of Charlie-time hassling me.

Then twenty seconds later, none of it matters because I open the door and there he is. My baby. My Charlie. I open the door and he runs straight into my legs.

"Mama!"

I drop to my knees and pull him close. His pudgy little arms close around my neck and I breathe him in.

"You're so big," I say, choking up. The tears come almost immediately like they always do, even though I swore to myself I wouldn't cry this time. Charlie doesn't understand why Mama is always crying when she sees him. I tell him they're happy tears but sometimes it makes him sad and he told me once that he cries a lot too.

He doesn't understand why all the sudden he can't see me every day. I've talked with the psychologist and it's the only way I know the little I do about what's going on with him. Charlie's started having behavior problems. He was always such a happy boy. And now he's acting out and also having trouble sleeping when he never had problems before.

She assured me that there are no signs of abuse, though. As much as I might hate David's wife, Regina, since she was the one who was the catalyst behind all of this, Charlie's incorporated her into his little world. He makes stick figure drawings that include her, David, and me as if we're all one big happy family.

I squeeze him to my chest a little tighter. If only I could protect him from the real world and how horrible adults actually are to one another. If only he never has to know.

"Play, Mama." He wiggles to get out of my embrace. It makes me want to hold him even longer. It's so like my little man. Never satisfied with being still for long. He keeps squirming and I laugh and let him go. But not without tickling him.

He squeals with laughter and the sound fills up my empty soul. God, I should have gotten out my phone to record the sound. Maybe it could get me through the week between visits. A shot of Charlie's laugh to help me ride out the rough patches.

I don't have even a moment to get melancholy, though, because Charlie's little hand is holding onto mine and pulling me toward the corner play area where the trains are. He grabs the wooden tracks and even manages to fit some of the links together correctly. I'm amazed as I help him make a simple circle and then some more difficult designs.

He's developed so much even in the four months since he last lived with me. Grown so much bigger. I swallow hard. How much am I missing in the week between these ridiculously short visits? How many little daily moments when Charlie learns new words, new skills? When he has new revelations about his world and I'm not there to see his face as he takes it all in?

"Mama?"

Charlie crawls into my lap and puts his hand up to my cheek where I only now realize a tear has fallen.

"Mama sad?"

I shake my head and paste on a big smile, swiping at the errant tear quickly. "Sorry, sweetie." I don't want to lie to him and say I wasn't crying. "No more crying."

"Why Mama cry?" His low eyebrows are furrowed deeply.

I kiss his hand that touched my cheek. "Mama was just thinking about how much you're growing. I'm sad I miss getting to see you grow every single day, that's all. But I'm so happy that I'm with you now. Let's focus on that. You want to make the train go around the track?"

But Charlie keeps frowning. "I want you to see me grow. Why can't you live in the house with us?"

Talk about breaking my fucking heart.

"It doesn't work like that, baby. Mama and Daddy live in separate houses. You stay with Daddy sometimes and eventually you'll be able to stay with Mama again sometimes."

He crosses his arms. "No. I want us to live in *one* house. *Now*."

"Well, babe," I tell him prosaically, "there's what we want, and then there's what's gonna happen."

"I want to live in one house." He even stomps his foot.

I can see where this is going. He hasn't changed *that* much. A tantrum is a tantrum, though from what the psychologist says, he's having them more often and to further extremes.

I cut it off at the pass. I stand up and grab him underneath his chest and legs, then swing him up into the air. "Look who's flying!"

Whoa, either he's heavier or my arm muscles have gotten way wimpier.

He tries to stay stubborn, but after a few swirls in a circle, he gives in and giggles his head off. Good thing too, my arms are about to give out. I swing him around a couple more turns and know I'm still going to feel it tomorrow.

I lower him so that he's propped on my hip and drop my forehead to his before sticking my tongue out at him and making a funny face. He giggles more and I feel confident that I've distracted him from the previous subject. At least for now.

I don't glance to the corner where I can feel the psychologist watching us. I'm not sure if distraction is a Psychology 101 approved method for dealing with tough subjects, but any mom knows that any and all tricks to avoid tantrums are one hundred percent super bueno.

"Want to read a book now?"

Charlie nods and we head over to an area that has a plush carpet and pillows set up. I pick up a stack of board books and Charlie settles onto my lap, his sweet head nestled on my chest. I close my eyes for one quick moment, trying to memorize the feel of him against me.

Then I start to read, exaggerating my voice to be all the characters. Anything to hear my baby boy's laugh again.

My hands are on my phone as soon as I'm back in my Uber on the way home.

I text my new friend Lydia who I've gotten really close with over the past few months after meeting her in my self-defense class.

ME TO LYDIA: I need to get PISS ASS drunk tonight. Wanna make a girls' night out of it?

I hit send and then slump my head back against the seat with my eyes closed. It's Friday and it's been a long as hell week. But my sister and also roommate, Shannon, is gone to a week-long conference and I know if I go home to that empty apartment, I'll just drive myself fucking insane.

David and the Shrew were in the lobby when I came out. I avoided eye contact, but still. If only I had made David sign away his parental rights when I first told him I was pregnant and his response was an envelope with two hundred bucks and staunch instructions to "Get rid of it."

I kick the seat in front of me. The driver looks back at me with a glare.

"Sorry," I mutter. A girls' night will make everything better. After last night, I don't exactly trust myself to try going solo again. Plus, I just wanna get *drunk*. I might feel that same itch, the one that wants to… go on the hunt like that. But shit, after last night I can see how fucked up it is.

I'll just be normal tonight.

Normal. I can do that… Right?

My phone pings and I look down. I have two texts. A response from Lydia but also one that I missed since I had my phone turned off while I was in with Charlie. I check Lydia's first.

LYDIA: Sure. Where you feel like going?

Then I check the one I missed. It's from Bonnie, a chick I work with and part of the happy hour group I join sometimes.

BONNIE: Wanna go out tonight? I got VIP passes to Chandelier. I'm thinking like @10?

I perk up. Chandelier is a total hot spot.

ME TO BONNIE: Do you have an extra pass? Love to hit Chandelier with you but just made plans with BFF.

ME TO LYDIA: Checking on something, back to ya in a sec.

Only another minute passes before I get a ping and it's Bonnie.

BONNIE: Totally! Bring her along, Jamaal scored a bunch of VIP passes through this guy he knows who's friends with the owner.

Jamaal is Bonnie's live-in boyfriend who she's been going out with since high school. He started working at CubeThink because she did, though in a different department, sales or marketing or something. She keeps waiting for him to pop the question so they can, in her words, "settle down and start having a ton of babies." Jamaal on the other hand, keeps talking about all the trips they can take traveling around the world once he saves up to buy a catamaran.

Yeah. The rest of us at work can't decide if we should have an intervention to introduce Bonnie to the real world or if it's better to let her keep living in fantasyland. Otherwise, she and Jamaal are totally, completely happy and compatible.

ME TO LYDIA: I just got the hook up to VIP passes for Chandelier!!! You gotta come!!!

It's only a few seconds before I get a response.

LYDIA: Shut the front door! Of course I'm in. You want to come over to get ready?

ME TO BONNIE: Awesome, meet you outside the club at 9:45?

ME TO LYDIA: Abso-fuckin-lutely. Who else would I trust to glam me up?

BONNIE: **Perfect.** See ya then!

ME TO BONNIE: See ya!

LYDIA: Haha, no one. Lord knows what you'd end up looking like on your own. Probably the same ducking thing you wear to work.

LYDIA: duck auto-correct

LYDIA: ducking

LYDIA: FUCKING! Fuck auto-correct

I'm almost pissing myself I'm laughing so hard. The Uber driver probably thinks I'm a crazy nutjob. Oh my God, I love Lydia. My self-defense instructor turned best friend is seriously my saving grace in the shitstorm that is my life lately.

ME TO LYDIA: Omg, LMFAO. You are my special snowflake.

LYDIA: Fuck you. Get your ass over here.

I'm still laughing as my screen goes dark.

Several hours later Lydia and I are glammed up and looking fab as our ride nears Chandelier.

"Stop that," Lydia lightly swats my hand as I tug down on the bright red miniskirt she chose for me from her closet.

"It's just so short," I whisper back.

"You've got great thighs. The world wants to see them."

I feel my cheeks heat up. Does she not see the Uber driver glancing back at us in the mirror every few minutes? He's totally listening in on everything we say.

"The knee-length maroon dress would have worked just fine," I say, continuing my argument from earlier when she was picking out my look for the night. I should never have given her carte blanche to choose my outfit.

"Booooring," she sing-songs. "What's the point of torturing yourself at CrossFit if you don't get to show off your hot bod?"

I bite my lip, glancing down at my bared thighs and tugging down on the miniskirt and the sparkly halter Lydia paired with it. The truth is, the outfit is hot and I look hot in it. I also don't know why I feel so embarrassed since I've been going out in outfits that reveal just as much if not more for weeks now.

But that's different. I'm not... *me* when I do that. It's like I'm playing a character. I'm The Vixen. The Siren.

But now?

I'm just me. Out with my friend. But I'm wearing *Siren Callie's* choice of outfit.

I pull my silken wrap a little tighter around my shoulders. Finally, we pull up in front of the club.

It's a newer place on the outskirts of downtown San Francisco, a refurbished theater built during the late twenties that was bought by restauranteur Kennedy Benson. He turned it into one of the hottest hot spots anywhere in the Bay Area. I watched this whole Netflix documentary on Chandelier and Benson a while ago and have been in awe ever since. A real rags to riches story, he's also the owner of several very popular restaurants in town.

Lydia pays—I already gave her my half of the fare—and I step out onto the sidewalk. I've always wanted to come check out this club, but looking up at the sparkling lights of the façade and the line that goes around the block, I'm reminded of the reason I never have before.

"Callie! You made it!" Bonnie's high-pitched squeal is hard to miss and when I turn around, I see her grinning as she stumbles toward me on heels that seem too high for her to handle. I look down to inspect more closely and shit, those skyscraper heels would be too tall for anybody.

"Damn girl," I laugh as I catch her in a hug, stabilizing her as she battles for balance. "You gonna be able to stay upright in those ankle breakers all night?"

Lydia steps up beside me and lets out a low whistle, checking out Bonnie's footwear.

Bonnie just laughs me off. "That's what Jamaal is here for." She gestures back to her boyfriend who just caught up with her. She grabs his arm and leans into him. He's tall with crazy-wide linebacker shoulders. Even though the rest of him is pretty thin, those shoulders give him a hulking appearance. He stands almost a head taller than Bonnie. She grins up at him. "He'll hold me while we dance."

"I told you before we left the house." Jamaal shakes his head. "You'll break your neck. Don't say I didn't warn you. Those things are deathtraps."

She turns her head and glares at him. "That's not all you said. And I quote," she drops her voice and gives it a slightly growly quality to imitate his, *"but damn, baby, you look sexy as fuck in 'em."* She looks back at the rest of us. "And then he proceeded to—"

Jamaal covers her mouth with one of his large hands and turns to Lydia with a bright smile. "I don't believe we've been introduced." He holds out the hand not covering Bonnie's mouth.

Lydia laughs and it's her throaty, bighearted laugh as she shakes his hand. Bonnie yanks away from Jamaal's grasp and smacks at him. He pretends to wince in pain, even though beside him, she looks like a tiny kitten swatting a bear.

Finally she turns back toward us. "Hi Lydia, I'm Bonnie. This caveman over here," she jerks a thumb toward Jamaal, "is my boyfriend, Jamaal. You can ignore him, though. It's what I do."

"Oh no you don't, woman," Jamaal growls before wrapping his arms around her waist and lifting her off her feet, swinging her in a circle. Bonnie's shrill giggles fill the night.

I roll my eyes at Lydia. "Yeah, they're disgustingly adorable like that pretty much all the time."

"Aw," Lydia says, still watching them over my shoulder. "It's sweet."

I make a choking noise with my finger down my throat. Lydia laughs and smacks me on the arm.

The next moment, though, Bonnie's back and waving our VIP passes at us. "Come on, I'm desperate for a drink. These passes let us skip to the head of the line too. Isn't that epic?"

Lydia shoots amused eyes at me and I grin. Bonnie and I are the same age—maybe it's being a mom, but I feel about a decade older than her. Lydia *is* a decade older than both of us, so she and I click perfectly and I find myself making fun of my generation to her regularly.

"Totally," Lydia says with a wink at me after Bonnie's turned around.

We each take a VIP pass and then Jamaal is ushering us all toward the bouncer.

For a second when the bouncer eyes each of our passes, I'm sure they're fakes and we'll all get rejected. After all, how reliable is it that Jamaal just *happens* to be friends with a guy who knows the *owner*? Now that I think about it, it seems pretty sketchy to me. Not to knock Jamaal, but this place is super swank.

But within seconds, the bouncer has the velvet rope raised and is ushering us through.

"Sweet," Lydia says as she heads into the club. Totally echoing my thoughts. Way to go Jamaal.

"I have a good feeling about tonight," she continues.

"Maybe you'll meet somebody," I lift and drop my eyebrows at her several times.

"Ha," she says, then holds her hands up dramatically. "Oh please, ye club gods and goddesses. Let the perfect single woman be inside looking for love just like me. And let her have a thing for small, athletic women with sub-standard hair weaves and half a college education!"

"Oh shut up. You make a great living doing what you love," I shoulder bump her. "And your hair looks fabulous. YOU are fabulous."

Lydia just got the weave done a couple weeks ago, after a recent breakup. She said she felt like the extensions she previously had looked cheap. I thought she looked great, but God knows I get how refreshed a new look can make you feel. We all need it sometimes. It still seems crazy to me the always kick-ass Lydia could feel self-conscious about anything.

I'm not lying either about her looking fabulous. My girl looks hot with glossy, layered hair down to her mid-back, perfectly applied makeup and bright, intelligent brown eyes. And oh yeah, did I forget to mention the kick-ass minidress that shows off her wickedly toned arms and thighs? Teaching self-defense and kickboxing classes at the local gym will do that for a gal.

She closes her eyes and then looks back up at me. "You know what? You're right. I am fabulous. And screw anybody who can't see that."

She grins at me, her genuine smile that shows all her teeth. There's the Lydia I know and love. It just threw her for a loop when she and her girlfriend of eleven months broke up a few weeks ago. We've had several Ben & Jerry's action movie binge nights. No chick flicks for these ladies. No, the more blood, guts, gore, and explosions the better. And Lydia's not the kind of girl to spend hours doing postmortems of everything she thinks went wrong with the relationship.

Which was good because then she might have expected me to reciprocate. Lydia knows there was a guy who I thought for a while might be *the* guy. And that things went bad right before she met me. She got super pissed when I mentioned him and started crying one of those nights when the wine had been flowing, bullets were flying on screen, and I broke down.

She thought he was the reason I showed up in her self-defense class. No matter how much I tried not to think about Jackson, I couldn't bear to have her believing that. Not about him. He was so good and amazing and—

I cut off the train of thought. How the fuck did I start thinking about this anyway? My sister Shannon is always talking about meditation now that her boyfriend's this Zen master guy. She says the hard part is stilling your thoughts because they're not only running a hundred miles an hour, they're chaotic like a puppy. One second here, the next there. You can barely grab hold of them and then they're gone again.

Trying as hard as I have these past few months *not* to think about certain shit, I wonder if there's not something to what she's saying. Well, I don't know if frickin' meditation is the answer.

Me? I go for the grown-up version of shiny toys. Distraction. Get my mind off it. I take Lydia's hand and drag her farther into the club.

Already I can see the flashing lights. Bonnie grabs my arm and starts jumping up and down. I don't know how the hell she manages on those heels she's wearing, but there she goes, making her boobs bounce with great effect. This is not lost on Jamaal, who's staring at his girlfriend's chest like all the answers to the questions of the universe can be found there.

Aww, even him ogling her is cute. They've been together how many years? And he still can't take his eyes off her.

When the small, dark entryway finally opens into the main club area, it's fucking insane. Laser lights flash out from the raised platform at the front of the room where a DJ spins. Music blasts from a speaker that feels like it's right above me.

People dance everywhere, illuminated only by the flashing lights and columns throughout the room that are studded with tiny neon lights like constellations of stars. The lasers scatter across the crowd in patterns that match the beat of the music. More lights spin and flash from the giant chandelier that hangs over the center of the dance floor.

Even with the alternating lights, though, the atmosphere is dark. Heavy. Sensual. Immediately, it makes me want to go on the prowl.

But damn, that's not what tonight is about.

"Isn't this great?" Bonnie grabs my arm and screams to be heard in my ear.

I wince and shrug out of her grasp. Suddenly I wish I hadn't taken her up on her offer, VIP passes or not. My eyes keep getting caught by everyone dancing on the floor. Yeah the line was long outside, but I could've handled the wait. This place... My gaze continually wanders back to all the bodies pulsing on the dance floor to the music.

Like that hot guy over there, dancing by himself. I bet he wouldn't mind following me to a dark corner... My gaze strays to the wall. The club is huge and from what I've heard, even has multiple levels.

So many places to get lost—

"Cals?" Lydia asks loudly. I jerk my gaze away from scanning the edges of the dance floor to look at her. From the expression on her face, it seems like she might have been trying to get my attention for a while.

Fuck. What am I doing? This is exactly why I didn't come here alone. I didn't want to deal with any of my messed up shit tonight.

"Yeah?" I zero in my attention on Lydia.

"Jamaal said the VIP section is up there," she shouts, pointing to some roped off stairs that lead to the extended loft-like balcony that circles above the first floor. I saw all about it on the documentary I watched last year.

It's a VIP section with a smaller dance floor and small exclusive rooms that can be rented out. All of it overlooks the central dance floor and whoever's performing or DJ'ing for the night. As we head toward the stairs, I realize just how crazy it is that Jamaal got these passes.

At the top of the stairs are more columns lit with dotted neon lights. They aren't an obnoxious neon, just a barely-there scattering of light. Without the laser light show flashing directly in your face like it is downstairs, these columns make it almost feel like you're dancing among stars.

The pumping music rattles through my entire being more up here on the suspended platform. I know it's safe. There might be empty space underneath the floor beneath my feet, but the columns beside me run all the way through, from the ceiling above down through the platform all the way to the floor below that. You know, as columns do. I'm sure we're very secure and it's all an illusion of danger. But still, when the floor shakes beneath your feet with every beat of the bass, it adds a sense of wildness and thrill to each moment.

A waitress in a pair of silver glittery mini-overalls and high heels that rival Bonnie's in death-defiance pauses when she sees us standing at the top of the stairs. "Would you like to open a tab?"

Jamaal starts to pull his wallet out of the back of his pants. Lydia and I do the same, though we grab our credit cards from our bras.

"Nah, ladies, I got this tonight," Jamaal tries to say.

Lydia and I both shake our heads firmly.

"Thanks," I say, "but I've got a policy, even when it comes to friends." I smile so I don't come off looking like a dick. I hand my card to the waitress. "Double vodka tonic."

Lydia rolls her eyes at me and orders a Sex on the Beach.

"Seriously, you have got to start ordering better drinks," she says, eyeing the people around us and not bothering to hide that she's sizing them up. "You think anyone overhearing you ordering a vodka tonic is gonna think, now damn, there's a girl who lives on the wild side?"

I roll my eyes right back at her. "And you've got to stop ordering drinks based solely on their names. Do you even like how that thing tastes?"

Lydia cracks a grin and raises her hand in a so-so gesture. I shake my head at her and we all head to the banister to look down at the revelers below while we wait for our drinks.

It's just a few minutes before the waitress is back with our cocktails. Gotta say, service in this place is impressive. Maybe it's just for VIPs, but still. I've never gotten my drink so fast.

I take a sip and it's good. I raise my eyebrows and nod at Lydia. She seems similarly impressed with her drink. She certainly downs it fast enough.

I laugh at her, but I drink mine just as quickly. The club soda is just enough to take the bite off the vodka. I did come here with a plan tonight after all.

Get drunk. Dance. Forget my life for a while.

Have fun.

I know, a fucking foreign concept for me.

Bonnie and Jamaal must be on a similar page because in the blink of an eye, their drinks are gone too. We pile our empty glasses on the tray of a passing waitress and then Bonnie throws her arms around Jamaal's neck and starts grinding her body against his in what I can only call a *loose* attempt to mirror the beat of the music. The next minute they disappear into the thick of the crowd.

The dance floor here isn't large—it's just built on an extended rectangular platform that overlooks the light show below. It's not as packed as the downstairs, but it's busy.

Lydia laughs at Bonnie and Jamaal and then grabs my hand to pull me in after them. I give in to her tugging and follow her. Already, I can feel the vodka lighting up my veins and loosening me. My limbs feel lighter. More liquid.

Lydia starts dancing and she's fabulous. Like, she's actually taken lessons. Started out with ballet when she was a little girl and then when she got older, she did contemporary and jazz. Now she just does whatever the hell she wants. Hip-hop, whatever. She does Lydia.

At the moment, she's bustin' it all out. I dance beside her, just appreciating the beauty of her movement. She embodies the music. In her hips. Up to her torso. In her chest and out through her arms. She pops her hips back sharply and drops to the ground. The next second she's back up and a sensuous wave works through her entire body, shoulders to knees. I whistle and clap and I'm not the only one.

She does a three-sixty spin on her heels before brushing some non-existent lint off her shoulders and continuing on. I laugh more and it feels so good, so goddamn good that I throw my head back and dance and dance and dance.

We keep at it for another twenty minutes. Several guys try approaching Lydia and she smoothly shuts them down each time, most often by coming over to me. We start dancing seductively together for a while and most guys get the picture. They aren't welcome.

Well, except for a couple that just start whistling louder. One actually tries to move in between us like he thinks he's gonna be the meat in our girl sandwich. Lydia not-so-accidentally stomps on his foot. She's a self-defense instructor, so she knows exactly where to land to make it hurt. He jumps away from us so fast, shouting something we can't hear above the beat of the music. Probably a good thing if he wanted to leave with his balls intact. Things stay copacetic after that.

God, I love Lydia. She's always so kick-ass.

A redhead who's been dancing near us pulls out some sweet moves. She sidles a little nearer and starts to breakdance. There's just a small space that opens up in the crowd, but she still manages to show off some wicked skills.

Lydia slows down her own dancing, bobbing her head to the beat as she watches the redhead. Red culminates with a headspin and then does one of those body flips to get back to her feet. Day-um. I clap fervently. Most people in the surrounding circle are equally appreciative.

Red's only got eyes for Lydia, though, her crop top covered chest heaving hard. She grins at my friend and then dips her head, hand held out.

A challenge.

Lydia's grin deepens further than I swear I've ever seen it. She steps forward into the small, empty circle as the redhead retreats into the crowd.

Lydia starts dancing and absolutely kills it with some crazy-ass moves. She's wearing combat boots but fuck me if she doesn't go up on the toe of the damn things and do a fuckin' pirouette like she's a prima ballerina.

Then she drops down into the splits. Oh, damn! My inner thighs hurt just looking at her! Good thing she opted for sparkly leggings underneath her oversized T-shirt dress. She's got that crazy-ass giant grin on her face as she somehow slides up from the splits and keeps on dancing.

The small crowd around us bursts into applause when she finishes. The redhead looks similarly impressed. And if I don't miss my mark, Red also looks completely turned on. I smile as the crowd melts together again and everyone starts dancing.

Lydia approaches Red and they begin talking. Good for Lydia. Maybe tonight's the night she'll meet the great love of her life after all. Or at least get a fabulous hook up out of it. Red looks just as athletic as Lydia.

I laugh to myself as I move away to give them space to get to know each other. The DJ transitions into an upbeat dance track and my body starts to move with the beat. I don't make the mistake of closing my eyes like last night. No, I'm ever aware of all the people dancing around me. If I see any guys eyeing me who look like the kind to approach uninvited, I flash them Angry Bitch Face, which pretty quickly switches off the light of interest.

And really, it's not that bad, not in an uptown crowd like this. I watch others lose themselves in the way I wish I could. Sweat-slicked bodies grind against one another. Just to the left of me, a dark-haired man holds a woman to him, her back to his chest, his one hand slung around to caress her bare stomach while he grinds into her from behind. She's totally into it. This is not an unwelcome position to her like it would be for me. Her head is thrown back on his shoulder, mouth open, arm lifted and hand buried in his hair as she slithers back and forth against him.

My mouth dries just watching them. They're all but fucking, right here on the dance floor. I turn away from them but everywhere I look, couples dance in similar positions. Knees nudged between thighs. Hands on asses. Bodies hunting for friction. And below it all, the music—a sensual, rasping vocal over a deep bass that rings through every speaker and up through the floor.

My panties get slicker with each passing moment. I glance behind me. I can't see Lydia or Red. My head swings back around and before I even realize what I'm doing, my gaze searches out men who aren't coupled up yet. The ones who don't look like douche bags or overly aggressive assholes.

Immediately, I see a couple potentials.

That slim blond guy who's laughing while he dances with some friends. All his friends are paired up, but he's alone. Then, a little bit further out toward the fringes of the crowd is a dark-haired guy who's a really bad dancer. He keeps bopping his shoulders slightly after the beat. He looks awkward as hell, but in the occasional flashes of light from below, I think I can make out that he's good looking. I'd have to get closer to really tell.

I glance back and forth between him and the blond guy. Hmm, blond guy seems good-natured and he's with friends so that means he's not too creepy. But dark-haired guy seems nervous and awkward, and that's always endearing as hell. I could be his equivalent of a knight in shining armor. Or, you know, chick in a tight mini-dress who'll give him a hot fuck in the dark corner of a club. Po-*tate*-o Po-*tah*-to.

I start to head toward the dark-haired guy when my step falters.

Wait. What the fuck am I doing? Tonight's not supposed to be about this. At all. *Remember last night? How quick that went from zero to super fucked up?*

I stand in suspended animation, wracked with indecision. Tonight is supposed to be low key. Fun. Just hanging with friends. No stress. Just spending time with Lydia and Bonnie. Maybe I get a little plastered. Laugh my ass off. Share an Uber on the way home.

My chest vibrates. What the—?

Oh. Right. My phone.

I pull it out of my bra and see a text from Lydia.

LYDIA: Hitting things off with Shayna. You mind heading home solo?

Wow, that was fast. Lydia's usually pretty cautious about who she lets into her life. At the same time, just the other day she was telling me how sex-starved she was, so maybe she just really needs that itch scratched tonight.

ME TO LYDIA: No probs. Have a blast and be safe, gorgeous.

LYDIA: You too xx

I smile and shake my head at the phone, then drop it back in my bra. Even before I've really decided what to do next, my eyes start searching out Mr. Adorably Awkward.

But dammit—I frown and crane my neck—he's not there anymore. I mean, not that I was definitely going to go try something with him. That's not what I was about. Really. It wasn't. But now that Lydia's got a hook up and Bonnie is with Jamaal, well...

I stretch my neck, trying to peer over people's heads to see if I can find him again. I work my way through the crowd, halfway dancing to the music so I don't look super weird. But when I get to the spot that I'm sure Adorable was standing in, there's no dark hair. No cute awkward body bopping slightly offbeat.

I deflate a little.

It wasn't like I was married to the idea or anything.

I dance for a few minutes, halfheartedly.

My mind keeps spinning thoughts. It's just, maybe getting with guys is *my* way of letting off some steam. And there's nothing really *wrong* with it. It's a Friday night. I'm single. I have a stressful life. People hook up all the time. Even Lydia. So what?

And okay, so maybe Lydia doesn't like, get off on doing it in public, but people have all kinds of, you know, *things* they like with sex. So what if that's my thing?

It's fuckin' hot. Lots of people think so. And sure, maybe last night got out of hand. But I can keep that from happening again. I'm the one in control. Nothing bad would've really happened with the knife. A girl has to protect herself. It was all fine.

I shake my head and focus on the music. The moment. Enough with the internal debate. I look hot tonight. The music is hot. I'm at a hip as hell club. I want what I want and there are plenty of guys here tonight who are up for the same thing. I scan the crowd again. I'm further away from the other guy I scoped out, the blond one, but I think I can just barely make out his group from here. I start heading in that direction.

When I get closer, I happily note that the guy I first spotted is still dancing alone. I note that his hair is slightly reddish as I get closer. It's a night for redheads, apparently.

A slight dusting of freckles dot his nose and cheeks. Sweet. His eyes are closed as he dances. He has much better rhythm than Mr. Awkward. He's not trying any crazy dance moves but has a decent back and forth shuffle/shoulder roll thing going on. I move into the space in front of him and start to dance.

I don't put my hand on him or anything. I'm not a hypocrite. I won't touch or invade his space until I'm invited.

He keeps his eyes closed though, and I can't help the smile breaking out on my face. He's totally lost in his own world as he dances, a slight sheen of sweat on his brow that produces little curls at the front of his hairline and the base of his scalp.

When he finally opens his eyes, he jerks back in surprise when he sees me there. I laugh and then cover my mouth with one of my hands.

"Sorry!" I shout over the noise. "You just looked really into the music."

He quickly recovers and flashes me a bright, white-toothed smile. Damn, good orthodontia gets me every time.

He holds out a hand. The angle he does it makes me think of a handshake, but I give my hand over anyway. His nice smile gets even wider and we start to dance. After a few moments, he uses the hand he's holding to spin me, then roll me back into his chest. It's like a salsa dance move or something, but I gotta say, crazy impressive. He just positioned me, applied force, and there I went, twirling and spinning.

Oh yeah, Blond Dancer is definitely the best choice for the evening. I'm all smiles as we keep it up for several more songs. It's rare that I actually want to stay on the dance floor with a guy for longer than a single number.

I'm usually all about getting down to brass tacks. Well, for the whole month that I've been at this. I have needs. A guy can fill them. Ensue mutually beneficial exchange.

Speaking of, this has been nice and all, but I'm not big on foreplay. I take a quick glance around. VIP or not, the crush of bodies is at a good enough density to be inconspicuous. I lean up and into Blond Dancer's chest, sling one arm around the back of his neck and push into his body. It'll look to anyone watching like we're just dancing intimately.

I lean in. "How we doing, big boy?" No one should notice my hand traveling down his chest to the front of his slacks.

I'm not disappointed. It's only a semi and I have to follow him when he jerks back in surprise. But he quickly perks up to full mast in my hand. The bold junk-grab rarely fails.

I move my body with his and look up into his eyes, eyebrow arched. Who the hell is this femme fatale inhabiting my body at the moment? I don't know, and I don't question it. It feels fucking amazing.

His pupils dilate and his hand on my hip grips harder almost reflexively. Oh yeah, he's into this. I stroke him a couple times through his slacks so he really gets the gist.

Then I turn on my heel and start walking through the crowd of dancers toward the stairs. When I look over my shoulder, he's still just standing there with a kind of dazed expression on his face. I give a slight huff and crook my finger so he gets that he's supposed to follow me.

A slow, lazy kind of smile comes over his face and then he's quickly at my side, a hand possessively on my hip. I brush it off but grab the front of his shirt so he knows it's not a rejection.

I lead him down the stairs. The VIP floor might be a little more upscale and all that, but I'm looking to get lost in a much larger crowd. The darkest of the dark little forgotten corners. The constant light show is briefly blinding once I get to the bottom of the stairs, but I can already see an area that'll be perfect. The neon lasers project from the central DJ platform down and outward toward the middle of the club. There's an area off to the back right that barely gets any light at all.

I'm not really bothering with the polite dance-my-way-through-the-crowd thing this time. I make a beeline in the direction of the dark corner. I'm in heels, but Blond Dancer is the one struggling to keep up. Sheesh, I'd think he'd be more motivated by the promise of a hot piece of ass. If he doesn't think a little hustle is worth it, I'm sure there are plenty of other candidates out there who would.

My brief irritation fades when we get to the corner of the club and I realize the space isn't just a tiny alcove, but a whole room. In fact, there are little rooms all over the place between the dimly-lit columns back here.

I look around and grin. Damn, this place is my new favorite spot. They know what a club is really for.

I grab Blond Dancer's forearm and drag him to an unoccupied couch in one of the small side rooms. In seconds, I've got him down and I'm straddling him, rubbing back and forth. The thin pieces of fabric of my thong and his slacks provide excellent friction for me. I want to throw back my head and revel in my arousal—

But no, there are still too many unknowns about the situation.

Instead, I ride him and look down in satisfaction at the man beneath me. Completely at my mercy. They shoot pornos from this angle but it's always the dude holding the camera. I get the appeal now, though. Being on top and mastering another person.

Dancer Boy reaches around and tries to get a hand on my ass but I swat him away before he makes contact. My eyes adjusted to the dark a while ago and I can see his startled expression. I don't bother hiding my glare, but at the same time I dip down and kiss him hard. I don't care if he feels like these are mixed signals. They really aren't.

I'm in control here. Why is this difficult for them to understand? His hands can only go where I put them.

The kissing is nice—he's even good at it. His tongue stays pretty much put. He's not trying to shove it down my throat. He lets me guide the kiss. Good. He's learning. I feel like he deserves a reward.

Again, my hands snake down the front of his chest. Past his abs. He's not overly built, but his stomach doesn't have a paunch either. I can definitely work with this. I grab his cock and give it a good stroke through his pants.

He's rock hard and bigger than before. I give him a wicked grin. Oh yeah. He definitely knows where this is going and he's on board. I also like the non-verbal thing we've got going on. Compliant and non-talkative. He's turning into my perfect gentleman.

I kiss him deep again while stroking him. It's dark in the room and the couple making out in the corner up against the wall is too busy to bother noticing us.

I've got a condom in my bra—never leave home without 'em is my new motto. A girl's gotta be prepared. Now I just need to figure out how to smoothly grab it and get his pants down far enough so that I can—

"That's *enough*."

The deep voice doesn't shout, but it's so loud in my ear and completely unexpected that I fall off of Dancer Guy's lap.

Strong hands catch me. Hands on me. Some big fuck of a stranger has his hands on me.

"Let go of me! Get the fuck off of me!" I yank out of his grasp and stumble backward.

My hand immediately goes for the knife at my thigh garter belt but fuck, I'm not packing because tonight was just supposed to be a girls' night.

And here I am in a dark corner where no one will hear me scream over the music with this giant towering over me. I look frantically to the couch for Dancer Guy but the fucking bastard took off as soon as we were interrupted. Gentleman my ass.

My gaze shoots back to the giant and I shift my weight to the balls of my feet, hands forming into fists. Run. Don't fight. Lydia's instructions from self-defense class ring through my head, but the fucker's blocking the exit of the little room.

My blood pounds in my ears and I open my mouth to shout *FIRE* at the top of my lungs but the giant holds up his hands and takes a step back. In an extra bright flash of the laser lights, the side of his face is lit up.

Holy shit.

It's my ex. Jackson Vale.

CHAPTER THREE

JACKSON

I see the moment she recognizes me, the surprise, the shock.

"Wha—" she starts to ask but I cut her off.

"I'll be the one asking the questions here."

Fuck but she's beautiful. So beautiful. She always laid me out. Shaped like Venus and smart, too. The only woman I ever met who wasn't interested in me for my money or what I could do for them career-wise.

She never wanted anything from me except me.

Until she didn't anymore.

And that would be fine. Okay that's a fucking lie. I barely had a taste of her but I'm not sure I could ever get over Calliope Cruise. But I don't think it was just that she fell out of interest in me.

He did something. Bryce Gentry. I don't know what, and I don't know how, but he did something to her that set her spiraling. Matthews did his research on her before I ever approached her at that Korean café months ago. Single mom. Before working for Gentry she worked long hours at a bar. She didn't have a car so more often than not, she slept on a worn out couch in the back office. Matthews interviewed one of her fellow waitresses. She never had boyfriends, never slept around.

No, this out of control behavior is new.

Like she can see what I'm thinking, Callie's eyes flick back to the couch where that bastard had his hands all over her and her cheeks flame.

"What the hell are you doing, Callie?" I step close because I can't help myself and her eyes drop briefly closed. At first I think it's in shame but then her nostrils flare. Like my nearness is affecting her as much as hers is me.

Because she is. Even though I only briefly touched her earlier to pull her away from that fucker, Jesus, touching her. Her skin. Her scent. She's imprinted so deep I don't think I'm ever getting her out.

Which makes me even more pissed about what she's been doing.

"So?" I demand.

Her face hardens and I can see her stubborn coming out. "Are you stalking me?"

I wouldn't call looking out for her safety stalking but she takes my silence as confirmation.

"You are, aren't you?" She just stares at me, open-mouthed for a moment.

But she finds her voice quick enough. "You fucking stalker!" She shoves me in the center of my chest. Not just a small shove either. It's like she uses all her momentum and aims it just right, so even though she's tiny and I'm over six-foot-four, she knocks me off balance so I'm forced to stumble backwards.

She stomps past me.

"Calliope, stop," I call after her. She is not going to just leave now. Not when we're finally having this long overdue conversation.

But she just scoffs and gives me the finger over her shoulder.

I've never wanted to take her over my knee more. Or grab her up in my arms and never let her go. I can't decide which.

I follow her either way but I don't make the mistake of grabbing her.

"Callie, you need to talk to me." I catch up to her, my long legs easily covering the distance. It helps that she can barely stay upright in those heels. They might make her legs look fucking fantastic but luckily for me, they aren't ideal for a quick exit.

"I'm not talking to a fucking stalker," she says, eyes on the exit.

"Technically I'm your host," I say.

"What?" she pauses, obviously confused before shaking her head and starting forward again like she's just reminded herself that she's ignoring me.

"Where do you think Jamaal got those VIP passes?"

She freezes again at that and bingo, finally looks my way. "What are you even talking about?" She lifts a hand to her temple. "You know *Jamaal?*"

I shrug. "He works in marketing and we got to talking after the last niche market strategy session meeting." I smile because I've been told I have a charming smile and I'm not above using any weapon at my disposal if it means getting through to her.

Apparently she's immune, though, because she just turns and starts walking again, making a beeline for the exit.

But when I continue beside her, she starts talking. "And you just *happened* to chat up my best work friend's boyfriend? And get him a bunch of VIP passes to a club where you also just *happen* to show up? What, did you hint that he should get his girlfriend to invite a bunch of her friends from work?" She shakes her head. "Did you get buddy buddy enough with Jamaal to mention me by name?"

That's exactly what I did, except for mentioning her name. Give me a little more credit than that. But I'm done beating around the bush. None of this is addressing the real problem here. We're almost to the club exit and she can't leave before I say what needs saying.

"It's not safe. What you're doing." I gesture behind us in the general area of the dark corner we came from. "With random men like that. These…" I shake my head. Jesus, I don't even know the word for what she's doing. "These hookups. Men you don't know, circumstances you can't control."

Even saying it out loud has my fists clenching. She's been putting herself in such danger and I've had to stand helpless from the sidelines. Maybe tonight was extreme—making up the excuse to give Jamaal the

VIP tickets in an attempt to run into her in a setting outside of work —but I had to do *something*. I couldn't just let her keep—

"Oh my God, you *have* actually been following me," she whispers in horror. "Not just tonight." Her eyes are wide with the sudden realization.

We're finally at the club exit and she slams her whole body into the door to shove it open. She's obviously furious, closing it in my face when I try to follow. Shit. This is going all wrong. I had a plan. I was going to be so suave. Why am I such a shit when it comes to people? Code, I get. Code, I understand. But people? I've learned to occasionally fake it over the years, but I've always been shit at people.

"Callie, wait," I call after I get the door open and follow after her.

She was stomping away in those damn heels of hers but she spins and stabs a finger in my direction.

"You don't know what the hell you're talking about. I am in control." She pounds her chest with her palm. "*I* say when. *I* say where. *I* say who. *I* say how. Nothing happens that I'm not in control of."

I don't care about the audience—the bouncer standing only a few feet away by the entry door or all the people lined up outside the club.

I face off with her. "Bullshit."

I point angrily back at the club. "*That's* not safe. You think you're in control because it's public, but that's *bullshit*. I know for a fact that ten feet from where you and that low life were there was an unlocked door to a hallway. What if a couple guys see you and decide to fuck with you? You think you're in control and then *boom*," I slap my hands together and she jumps from the noise but I don't care. Maybe I'm finally getting through to her. "They drag you in there with the doors shut so no one can see or hear you."

"So I'm just supposed to be scared all the time?" She throws her hands in the air. "Or feel ashamed? So it's my fault if I get attacked?" Her voice takes on a hysterical edge. "It's my fault, huh? For dancing suggestively? For daring to tempt the guy because of what I'm wearing? Because I've got big tits? Is that what you're fucking saying?"

She goes to slam me in the chest again but I catch her wrists before she can. My chest roars at the contact and all I want to do is pull her into me. Instead I let her go even though it takes everything in me to do it.

She's in so much pain. I hear it in her voice. I see it in her face and it is fucking killing me. Killing me.

What happened to you, Callie? What did he fucking do to you?

"No," I say firmly. "Christ, I hope you know me better than that." Then again, who am I kidding? I run a hand through my hair and mutter, "Not that we had that much time together to get to know each other beyond the basics."

Was that it? Was that Gentry's plan? Just to dangle the best thing of my life in front of me and then snatch her away? I don't understand. I don't understand any of it.

All I know is that when Calliope Cruise came into my life, I realized I'd been asleep for years. Numb. I had my routines and I had my company and I thought I was happy. Well, maybe I've always thought true happiness was a myth but I was content enough anyway.

Only to find out I was actually sleepwalking through my life.

Because she woke me up.

Nerves gone numb from not firing in years came back to life. It was like Dorothy going to Oz. Everything was suddenly in vivid, heartbreaking color.

Things *mattered* again.

And maybe the Tin Man could find his heart again after all. The thing is, I *did*. But it's beating in her chest.

I'm staring, I know it, but she's not looking away either. And I feel it again—the connection that's like a fucking hammer to the chest. I'm looking at my future. The only future I'll ever want.

And she deserves the truth. I won't play games with her. I'll never be anything like *him*. I don't know what he did to her and maybe she'll only be the ghost of my future. A future that could have been but never will be.

Maybe that's what I deserve and maybe it's a mercy because though she deserves the truth, there are some things about my past I don't think I could ever bring myself to tell her.

"Maybe I have been *stalking* you—" her eyes flare at my words "—if by stalking, you mean having one of my security guys shadow you when you go out on your own."

She gasps and looks furious, her mouth opening like she's about to go off on a tirade but I hold up a hand.

"He always stays a respectable distance away. Nothing invasive is involved and he only follows you when you're in public."

"So you had some guy fucking watching me? And what, like reporting back to you my every move?" She looks both furious and mortified and for the first time I second-guess my decision to have her followed. I only wanted to keep her safe. More than anyone, I know *exactly* how dangerous Bryce Gentry can be. It's why I never wanted her working for him in the first place. Some part of me knew the security guard was an invasion of her privacy but her safety mattered more. It was all I could think about.

Even if it was too little too late.

I hold up my hands again. "He never got close enough to see anything. But when you went off alone with certain... individuals," I swallow to hold back how I *really* feel, "he felt that they were unsafe scenarios. He just stayed within earshot in case he heard you in any distress. But he never saw anything," I hurry to add.

She makes an exasperated noise and I hurry on. I need to make her understand. "I'm worried about you, Callie. Something happened with Gentry. Don't even try to deny it."

Her gaze drops at the name and I watch her closer than ever. She swallows and then I notice her hands are trembling.

Jesus, no. She looks afraid. I've hoped that whatever he did, it was just threaten her. But what if he hurt her, physically? I'll kill him. I'll kill the fucking bastard.

She starts to fidget with her hands and her chin juts out as if she realizes too and is upset about the fact.

"Something happened, something bad, and you changed." Everything in me wants to reach out to her. *Please, Callie, just let me hold you. Let me make it better.*

But I also know that sometimes nothing makes it better. It's a lesson Gentry himself taught me.

If only there were a way to take on some of her hurt myself. To bear it for her. If only she would let me.

She rubs her temples with both hands, looking tired. Looking overwhelmed. Clubgoers stream by us, in and out, voices chatter, cars honk, and the beat of the music from inside the club thunders on and on in the background.

For a second when she looks at me, I can see indecision in her eyes and I think, maybe this is it. The moment she opens up to me. Maybe we can fix this and we'll be stronger together. Maybe both of us can heal from the wounds Bryce Gentry inflicted on us.

Because the truth is I need her to save me as much as I want to save her.

But then she crosses her arms over her chest and glares at me. "So? What the fuck is this?" Her tone is scathing. "An intervention? Are you here to show me the error of my ways and lead me to the righteous path?"

I can't do anything but let out a dark, self-deprecating laugh at that question. "I'm the last person in the world to know anything about righteousness." Our eyes catch again. "But I do know a little bit about finding my way back to sanity after Bryce Gentry blows up a person's life."

She squirms a little under my gaze but she doesn't look away.

"I'm not suggesting that I know what you've been through," I say, "whatever happened. I'm not saying that you should tell me what it was or that I have some great wisdom I can impart."

"What the hell are you saying then?" She throws up her hands.

Okay, here's the pitch I've been leading up to all night. Stay calm. Don't let her see how much I want this. "There are safer ways to get the same—" I cast about for a word, "—*effect* as what you've been doing."

She blinks like, *okaaaaaaaaaaaay*. And?

So I press on. "There are ways to do it safely. In controlled environments. One possibility is to do it with a partner that you have an established agreement with, no other attachment or strings." My eyes briefly drop at this. Of course that's what I'd want more than anything.

Mainly because the thought of her with anyone else makes me want to put a fist through the wall.

But by the look on her face it's clear that's not going to be on the table. Like she thinks I'm saying all of this just in an attempt to get her back in my bed. Which I'm not.

At least I think I'm not. Jesus, I just want what's best for her. In the end, I swear that even if I do want her, I want what's best for her *more*.

"But that's not the only option." I rush the words out. "There are groups of people and places, and I'd like to introduce you. It's a world where *safe, sane, and consensual* are the most important tenants."

Her eyes widen like that phrase rings a bell. My breath quickens and yeah, my cock stiffens a little at the thought that she's even passingly familiar with the idea of what I'm suggesting.

"As in... *BDSM?*" she clarifies, eyebrows at her hairline. "Like Fifty Shades?"

I look around. Jesus, say it a little louder. Then I lean in.

"Okay, first of all, those books and movies got a lot of things wrong. A *lot*. And second, it doesn't have to be seedy and sleazy." My eyes search hers. "Most of us who live the lifestyle have perfectly normal lives on the outside. And like I said, all play is safe, sane, and consensual."

Her eyes went wide as saucers when I mentioned the 'most of *us who live the lifestyle*' part. What is she imagining in her head? Whips and contracts and ball gags? The Fifty Shades version of an emotionally distant, overly-manipulative dominant?

Her eyes are darting every which way and she's backed up a couple of steps. Shit, am *I* the one scaring her now?

I frown and don't go any closer. I don't move back though, either. "I can't tell if that face means wow, how interesting or, wow, how can I distract him because I need to get the hell out of here right now."

"It's just..." she trails off. "A lot to take in?" Then she nods and repeats, "A lot to take in." It's a statement this time.

And she's not running. All good signs. "I understand. I do. I didn't mean to," I wave a hand, "ambush you like this. I was going to suavely run into you in the VIP lounge, buy a round of drinks for your group..."

I shake my head before thinking about why plan went awry before I go looking for walls to put holes in. Just the image of her in that guy's lap—

"Yeah." My hand goes to the back of my hair and then I drop it. Jesus, I've never met another woman who gets to me as much as Calliope Cruise.

But better to leave it here than to press for too much too fast. "Well. You have my number. So."

I pause, waiting for her to say something. To give some indication of whether she'll call or not. To stop me from leaving and declare her undying love for me.

Yeah. She does neither.

Time to go. I give her a half smile. "I'll see you, Callie."

I stop myself from reaching for her as I pass by her to head for the town car. But only just barely. Where is all my normal discipline and iron control?

I lock my jaw and start down the sidewalk.

Okay.

But I never could leave well enough alone. When I reach the corner, I turn back around. She's just standing there on the corner, and God knows what could happen to her if—

"My driver, Sam, is just around the corner," I call back, "and I could—"

She shakes her head quickly and holds up her phone. "My Uber's coming. I'm good."

Of course. Callie is nothing if not self-reliant, or haven't I learned anything after knowing her for four months?

I flash her a smile, linger looking at her for only a moment because I want to memorize the way she looks tonight, and finally turn to go.

CHAPTER FOUR

CALLIE

The bottle of wine I drank after getting home from that showdown with Jackson didn't really help and only results in a monster headache on Saturday morning. Seeing him again after all these months...

He was as gorgeous as ever. The firm jaw and the rough stubble on his face. His strong eyebrows and the flat, arrow shape of his nose. At one point when we were arguing, he stepped so close I could smell his aftershave.

The familiar woodsy pine brought on a rush of memories I can't help losing myself in: the stubble of Jackson's cheek rasping on my neck as he kissed his way to my ear. Breathing him in while I clutched him close as he thrust into me, over and over again. *Him* mastering *me*...

But he's been fucking *following* you.

I snap my eyes open and then go to wash my face with cold water. No. I will *not* be thinking about Jackson Vale anymore.

I spend the rest of the weekend marathoning the second season of *Outlander* with my sister, Shannon. Thankfully Shannon is addicted to two things in life: strong coffee and immersive TV shows. When we have marathon TV sessions, she gets more lost in the story of the on-screen characters than anyone I've ever met. Perfect for me since it means she's too caught up to concern herself with what's going on in my life. So I spend the weekend watching TV, eating ice cream, folding laundry, and texting Lydia.

What I do not do, however, is let myself think about any of the things that came out of Jackson Vale's mouth.

Nope. Not happening. I'm officially checked out for the weekend. The only drama I can handle is of the 18th-century Scottish variety.

And, in small doses, Lydia's. Lydia rarely has drama, after all. She's really into the redhead from Friday night, Shayna. Turns out they didn't hook up that first night. Instead they hung out and walked around downtown San Fran in what apparently turned into one of those epic all night get-to-know-you sessions that ended after sunrise and pancakes.

She only slept a few hours before waking up and immediately blowing up my phone with texts about every detail of the night. After more pings coming in before I can even text back, I finally just call her and we talk for about an hour.

I've never heard her so excited about a girl. When we finally hang up I feel the briefest stab of something in my gut. Jealousy? No, I don't think that's it. Maybe just the hurt of a memory when I'd been similarly happy at the beginning of what I imagined might be a great relationship. Which leads back to thoughts of Jackson and the confusing tangle of thoughts and emotions and...

"Come on," Shannon calls. "How long does it take to go to the bathroom? They're about to land back in Scotland. That means we'll get to see Jamie in a kilt again. Get your butt back in here!"

Yeah. Time to check out of my own life again. I hurry back into the living room. "Just let me grab another pint of Ben & Jerry's."

Now it's Monday and I'm heading into the CubeThink offices with no better idea of what I would say to Jackson's unorthodox proposal if I ran into him in the elevator. Not that I usually see him in the office. But what if he's waiting in the lobby for me, ready to ambush me as I head into work?

When I get there, though, the coast's clear and I let out a small sigh of relief as the elevator climbs to my floor.

I check my phone. 7:51. Good. I'm going to be conscientious to be early for a while so Marcy doesn't hold the one time I was late against me for too long. No one can hold a grudge like that lady. So far I think she's satisfied with my job performance, but you can never really tell with her. It's not like she gives out compliments. She just seems to berate me less than others on the team.

My immediate coworkers are a small group of four fellow coders. When I started, we were just scrubbing code that comes down to us from above, debugging and scrutinizing it for errors, and then setting up experiments to check run times. Wash, rinse, repeat.

But lately, I've been getting to *write* some code. The algorithms we were working on in the middle of summer were dubbed too slow for product viability. We were given a shot at increasing data-run time with our own code, not just quality testing other people's work.

I was determined to prove myself, and I've actually come up with some solutions that seem to be working. It's the first time in my life where I feel like I'm accomplishing something that I can be proud of. Something that I'm earning *for real*—not just because I have a pretty face and a big rack.

My thoughts are full of the project as I grab a coffee and settle into my cubicle. It's your basic workspace, small but not claustrophobically so. Some people plaster the thin divider 'walls' of the cubicles with hundreds of pictures of their kids or their cats. I don't see the point in that. I'm here to work. I don't want anything else distracting me. Sure, I have a picture of Charlie that I keep taped to the left-hand side of my desk, but that's all. This is not my home away from home. This might be a very *good* job, but at the end of the day, that's all it is. A job.

The morning is all clear too, so I can get straight to work. Marcy likes us to come off the weekend and jump directly into whatever we're supposed to be working on. She calls it *starting off the week right*. Weekly meetings are usually on Thursdays and Fridays. I think the whole Friday meeting thing is to try to get us to obsess about work all weekend.

Might work with some of the more anal types but her mind games don't work on me. Not after working for the master of mind-fuckery. Plus, I like not having to socialize on a Monday morning when I'm not in the mood.

Like today. Another plus to being a little early? No one's congregating around the coffee like they do when everyone gets here right at eight o'clock. The last thing I need is anyone wanting to do postmortems about our respective weekends. It's bad enough when Bonnie sends me an IM to ask where I disappeared to on Friday. I just shoot a quick message back that I'm deep into working on something. It does the trick. She leaves me alone for the rest of the morning.

It's about an hour till lunch time when I lift my arms over my head and stretch my neck back and forth that I hear a throat clearing behind me. I swing around in my office chair. A guy stands behind me who looks barely old enough to be in college, shifting awkwardly back and forth from foot to foot.

"Um, hi. Are you," he looks down at the paper he's holding in his hands, then frowns, "Cal-ee-o-pee Cruise?"

I roll my eyes at the complete butchering of my name. "Who's asking?"

The kid looks up at me. "It's Mr. Vale. I'm interning for him this semester." He looks very proud of the fact.

My stomach goes tight just at the sound of Jackson's name. What the fuck? What's he up to? We don't see each other at work. That's our deal. I told him that before I ever agreed to work here. This job wasn't supposed to come with strings. Does he think just because of whatever Friday was that he suddenly has the right to—

I shake my head and hold out my hand. "Just give me the note."

The kid's eyes widen and I realize how clipped my tone was. I force a smile I don't feel and add, "please."

He hands the note over and I realize it's not just a note, it's a small envelope. I roll my eyes again, this time at the ceremony of it. Why not just send me an interoffice IM like a normal human being? I shove my thumb in the corner of the envelope to rip it open. Inside is just a folded piece of paper with only a few words written in Jackson's neat handwriting: *Please come up to my office. I need to talk to you about something. It's extremely important.*

That's all. No hints as to what he's talking about. My foot starts tapping in frustration. Is this just about what he brought up on Friday? Because so help me God, if he tries to push me about his genius plan of becoming my fuck buddy or whatever, his balls are going to be black and blue by the time I'm done with—

"Miss?" the kid butts into my thoughts.

"What?" Again my voice comes off too sharp. But hell, what do I care if I come off like a bitch? Men in offices are short with their employees all the time.

"What should I tell him you said?" the intern asks, seeming intimidated by me. The thought makes me sit up taller and I can't help myself from smirking a little at him. I bite back what I really want to say just in time—*run along little puppy and tell your master that I'll answer his summons.*

I glance at my laptop screen and then click to lock my station. I head to the elevator without another word. The intern follows at my heels. I push the up arrow.

"So how do you know Mr. Vale?" the kid asks.

Silence. I don't have any use for inane conversation with some barely legal guy I'll never see again, so I don't bother.

The elevator dings and I step inside. The kid moves to follow, but I smile and give a head shake. "You catch the next one."

I push the closed-door button before he can say anything else. I roll my shoulders and relax as the elevator starts to move up. Damn, I never realized before how good it feels to be a bitch. I think I missed my calling in life.

I smile to myself as I step off onto Jackson's floor. His middle-aged cardigan-obsessed secretary only nods and waves me through the door from the lobby that leads to the back offices. I've been here on the top floor just once before, but it's enough to remember that Jackson's office is the last one at the very end. The corner office. Naturally.

The old world elegance hits me all over again. The part of the CubeThink's offices where I work is perfectly modern. More industry-standard—brightly lit, fake plants around for ambiance. Ours has nicer furniture and desk spaces than I might expect at most office jobs. Other than that, though, it's fairly sterile.

But up here in the executive offices, comfort and elegance seem to be the watchwords. Even more so when I knock and I enter Jackson's space. A hulking cherry wood desk dominates the room, complimented by comfortable leather chairs and a plush beige carpet. Not to mention the intimidating man himself who immediately stands and comes toward me as I enter.

He tries to wrap his arms around me in—oh God, is that a hug? Is he seriously trying to hug me? Does he know me at all? I'm not a hugger.

Then I try to recall some of the anger I felt when his little intern was sent to fetch me and cross my arms over my chest. "Desperation isn't a good look on anyone."

I take a seat in the chair across the desk from him. "What's so important that you decided to drag me here in the middle of my workday?"

His expression was open when I'd come in the room, but it's shut down now. He strides back around to his desk chair and sits, immediately steepling his fingers under his chin. His features have gone all flat and serious.

Okay. What's going on here? I sit up in my chair, suddenly on alert. I thought this was just his super unprofessional way of getting my attention, but maybe—

"Charlie," I sputter. "It's Charlie okay?" I'm half out of my chair before Jackson holds up a hand.

"Charlie's fine." He looks startled. "Of course nothing's wrong with Charlie."

I put a hand to my chest and then glare at him. "What the fuck then? You just scared the crap out of me."

Jackson rubs one of his hands on his knees as if it's sweaty. "I don't know how to tell you this," he confesses.

"Just spit it out," I say. "That usually works for me. Stop with the bullshit suspense and spill."

He gives a jerky nod of assent and then starts to talk. "I've just learned that your lawyer, your previous lawyer that is, Don Maury, was paid off by David and Regina."

I'm so startled by the intro of my former custody lawyer, and then my ex and his wife into the conversation that it takes me a second to process what he's saying.

"That's why he didn't defend you as well as he could have at the last hearing," Jackson continues.

I freeze. I can't—what? I mean, I was disappointed when David's attorney's kept attacking me and we didn't have anything to volley back with, but Don said we shouldn't stoop to their level... that my case was strong enough without it...

I lean back in my chair and put a hand to my head.

"That's not all. Not nearly the worst of it."

My eyes flick to Jackson's face. Worse? There's something worse than my own lawyer working against me?

"The day before your hearing," his jaw goes tense as he talks, "Don had pastries set out during your prep session, correct? Bagels and some small cakes?"

I scrunch my brows, trying to remember. That whole period of time before the hearing is pretty much just a blur. "I don't know. What does that have anything to do with—"

"Think." Jackson's voice is hard. "Did he have, say, poppyseed bagels that he gave you? Or everything bagels that have poppy seeds mixed with the other seeds? Or poppyseed cake?"

I close my eyes and struggle to remember. Bagels? Cake? I hadn't been able to eat anything the day of the hearing itself, I remember that. But the day before?

Oh my God. My eyes flash up to Jackson's. "Yes! At the strategy session with my lawyer, the day before the hearing. He had bagels set out, but I didn't eat those. It was the poppyseed muffins. I ate two of them, I was so stuffed when I was finished. But I was stressed out and carbs are my downfall when I'm stressed." Then I frown, confused. "Are you saying he spiked the muffins? Like with pot or something so I'd test positive for drugs the next day? But I didn't feel high or anything—"

Jackson shakes his head and for a second I'm only more confused before he clarifies, "It was the poppy seeds themselves. They set off drug tests—a false positive—because they read as opioids. You know, poppy? As in, what opiates have been made from throughout history?"

I blink several times before finding my voice. "And that can affect the outcome of a drug test?" My voice goes high-pitched in disbelief. "So let me get this straight, you're telling me I failed because of *muffins*? They took away my son over a couple of fucking *muffins*?"

"Calm down, Callie."

It's only when he says it that I realize I totally shouted that last one and that I'm standing with my hands clenched into fists.

I push back my chair as I start pacing his office. "You mean to tell me," I stab the air with my forefinger, "that that fucking lawyer set me up to lose my son before I ever entered the courtroom, by fucking poisoning me? With. Fucking. *Seeds*. In. Some. Fucking. *Muffins*."

I throw my hands up in the air and let out an enraged growl. Then I'm nodding my head.

"I'm gonna kill him. String him up by his balls and dangle him on the wall where his law degree used to hang. Motherfucker is gonna be so sorry he ever decided to fuck with me, I swear to fuckin' God."

I'm striding back and forth furiously across Jackson's office. I note that he's approaching and I'm two seconds from ripping into him to when he starts nodding with me. "I completely agree. And I'm going to help you do it."

That brings me to a stumbling halt. "You are?"

"Fuck yes I am." It's only now that I realize his face is mottled with fury. He might not be as angry as I am about all this, but he's close. "I've never in all of my years and interactions with sleazy lawyers, and believe me, I've dealt with some really *sleazy* motherfuckers, come across anyone *this* low, this willing to shit all over his client, the law, and simple human ethics." Jackson's voice is passionate and I've never heard him use so many swear words at once.

"Damn right," I say. We just stand there, face-to-face. It's a position that anyone else looking in on us would see as a standoff.

My chest heaves. There are too many thoughts zooming through my head to focus on a single one. Jackson's standing so close I can see the tiniest cut on the edge of his jaw from where he nicked himself shaving this morning.

Fuck, why is that hot?

I grab him by the tie and yank him toward me and then I kiss him. If he's startled, he reacts quickly enough that it doesn't show.

I kiss him hard, but this is Jackson. Within seconds, his mouth demands control of the kiss. Which only pisses me off more.

I flip my left foot back, lean into it for a moment and then shift my weight forward again so that I can use my momentum to push Jackson backward toward the wall. I'm not sure if the element of surprise makes him stumble or if he just allows it, because, momentum or not, there's no way I'm moving him that far, at least while we're on our feet. Either way, the next moment I've achieved my goal. His back is against the wall exactly where I wanted him. The idea that he might have just willingly submitted to me sends a gush of wetness into my panties.

I run my hands through the back of his hair, up to where it's slightly longer on top. Then I bring his head down to mine. I take control of the kiss, going deep. When he tries to take over and master me with his tongue, I pull back so that he's forced to chase me. That only makes me move away again.

He growls in frustration when I retreat for the third time. I just cluck my tongue at him and shake my head. He narrows his eyebrows at me and I laugh and swoop down again to tease open the seam of his lips with my tongue. This time he lets my tongue do the leading and only engages after I initiate each time, meeting the tip of my tongue with his in a way that shoots electric pulses straight to my clit. That's right. Let me direct the show.

I can't help letting out a most unladylike moan and sagging against him. He makes my body feel liquid. And goddamn him, he was right, this does feel better since I don't have to worry about grabbing for a knife every other second. There's no danger here.

I continue kissing him as I hike one of my dress-pant clad legs open around his hips. Well, he's so much taller, it's really his upper thigh, but all that matters is that I'm achieving some friction now. I rub my body up and against him hard once, twice. Oh *God*, that feels *amazzzzzzzzzing*.

Apparently Jackson feels the same way because he reaches under both my thighs and hikes me up to his waist, then carries me toward his desk.

For a moment, everything's perfect.

I'm taken back in time to when he carried me exactly like this from his bathtub to his bed. Today, just like then, I revel in his strength and marvel at how easily he lifts me.

Then, exactly like in the movies, he shoves all the papers and a cup of pens off his desk onto the floor without any care and sets me down on the edge. He kisses me and for a moment, I'm all consumed. There's only Jackson, his body, that scent of pine and spice and male. There's only want and the insistent pulse between my legs. He kisses me deep and I even let him.

Then he presses me down on the desk with his body. He's gentle. He doesn't slam me down. In some sane part of my mind, I realize he even cups the back of my neck and is careful to keep all of his weight on his hands so no part of him crushes me.

But the rest of my brain goes to a very *not sane* place.

It's his tie. It flops down into my face as he lowers me. And when I look up, I don't see Jackson. I see the fluorescent lights in the office ceiling tiles.

I'm on the conference table again.

A hard surface underneath me, bright blinding fluorescents overhead. Men in business suits. I'm staring at the ceiling as man after man violates me. Oh God, is it over yet? Why isn't it over yet? How is this even happening? It shouldn't be happening. This is an office, for God's sake. It's supposed to be safe here. These kinds of things happen in the dark back alleys of East San Jose, not the conference room of a well-lit fifteenth floor office building.

Next in line, Gentry says, pointing to the box of condoms someone set out beside the coffee tray. *You don't know where that filthy cunt's been. Better safe than sorry.*

I scream and struggle to get away, but Gentry holds my shoulders down and the other man, Carl, has a bruising grip on my hips to keep me still. The next man in line, a middle-aged Japanese investor, puts one hand on my knee and with the other, rolls on the condom.

"NOOOOOOOOOOOOOOOOOO!" I shriek at the top of my lungs. I strike out in all directions.

"Callie!"

Suddenly there's nothing holding me down anymore and I scramble off the desk. I bolt toward the wall. Run! I have to run! My heart is hammering a thousand beats per minute and I look crazily back and forth for Gentry and the rest of—

But—

None of them are there.

There's just one very freaked out looking Jackson, hand to his bloody lip.

Fuck. Me.

I'm not in the conference room at Gentry Tech. I blink rapidly as my head jerks back and forth in disorientation. But I was just— They were just here—

I put a shaky hand to my forehead. It felt so real.

Goddammit. I thought I was getting better, the more time passed. This isn't the first waking flashback I've had, but it's the most intense one ever. I thought I was getting control. Getting past it. God, I'm so dumb. I want to laugh at how dumb I am but mostly I just want to cry.

"Callie," Jackson starts to say but I hold up a hand.

"Don't."

He opens his mouth to try again but again, I cut him off. "Just don't."

I try to gather what little dignity is left to me and I leave the room. Jackson must realize what's good for him, because he lets me.

CHAPTER FIVE

JACKSON

I check my phone for the millionth time. It's 5:05pm. Where is she?

Sitting here in the back of my towncar waiting for her to emerge from the front entrance of CubeThink is starting to make me feel like exactly what she accused me of being—a stalker.

Does the fact that it's *my* building make it any better?

Probably not.

I'm just trying to find a way to approach her on neutral territory.

After what happened this morning... I shudder and curl into myself remembering the look on her face, the absolute terror as she shoved me off and fought and shouted *NO* like she was a trapped animal with the butcher's knife raised overhead.

As if I was her rapist.

The shaking that's hit me on and off all day comes back and I clench my fist. And I know now for certain. *Almost* for certain. Did Gentry do it himself or have someone else do it? I know he's capable of it. I *know*—

My eyes clench shut along with my fists. Even the idea that someone... that someone *violated* Callie... Fuck I'm going to be sick again. I already lost what little bit of lunch I managed to get down earlier.

"Sir?"

At Sam's voice, I look up and there she is. Beautiful as ever even with brunette hair like she's trying to dim her shine. It doesn't work. Not even Bryce Gentry could diminish the burning star that is Calliope Cruise for long.

I step out and stand. Will she approach or hurry away? I give her the choice. I won't chase her. Jesus but I'll always give her the choice. I swear I'll never take that away from her ever again.

For a moment I think she will run. But then she lifts her chin, head high, and comes toward me. So brave, always so brave.

She starts talking the second she's within hearing distance. "Kissing you this morning was a mistake and I don't want to talk about the other—"

"I don't want to talk about that either. Now get in."

I get in the back seat and move over, gesturing for her to join me inside.

Another choice.

She glares at me like I'm the most high-handed jerk she's ever seen.

"Please, Callie," I entreat, voice softer. "I think you'll find the place I want to take you very... *enlightening*." I can't help a slight smile at the last word, imagining her many possible reactions to the place I want to take her.

"Where?" she asks reluctantly.

I lift an eyebrow. "It's a surprise." Maybe I can tempt her with curiosity? Jesus but I want this for her and it's taking everything in me not to show my hand with how bad I want it. She's drowning, I can see it, and I want to put some solid ground underneath her feet. I need to. I need it for her. I need it for me.

She rolls her eyes and lets out an unimpressed huff of air, glancing at the sidewalk that would take her to the nearest light rail station.

"I promise, Callie. Come with me just this once." I won't beg but I do need her to hear me. "If you don't like it, we'll go back to the way we were."

This earns me another glare. "What, with you stalking me?"

I hold up my hands. "With you never seeing my face."

"And the guy you have following me?"

"We can discuss the security detail."

"There's no discussion. It stops. Immediately."

I wish it were that simple. "I'm not comfortable leaving you unguarded while your ex has some sleazy barely licensed P.I. following you around, trying to catch you in compromising photos."

She leans against the car like she's suddenly winded. She must not have known that her ex still had his PI following her.

"I thought the lawyers got a restraining order against their PI." She looks freaked out, really freaked out. Maybe at the thought of their PI potentially catching her at some of her less than wholesome activities. Her ex would have no compunction about using it in court, but she doesn't have to worry.

I get out of the car and join her where she's leaning against the car, her breath coming in quick, panicked gasps.

I want to reassure her but at the same time, she needs to know all of it. "They just hired a different P.I. and once or twice even used lower associates within the law firm. As soon as we slap a restraining order on whoever they hire, they're onto someone else. Even a restraining order only restricts them to a distance of a hundred yards from you. That's nothing for a telephoto lens."

She puts a hand to her stomach. "I think I'm going to throw up again."

"No," I shake my head vehemently. "Callie, listen. My security guards have made sure none of them have even gotten close to you. If you enter an establishment, my guys pick them out of the crowd and they don't follow you in. You've been safe."

"Are you sure?"

She's so panicked and I hate it. I nod emphatically. "I promise. No one got past my guys."

"Guys?" she squeaks. "As in, plural?"

I try to move toward her but she steps away, shaking her head. "I guess in some messed up way, I appreciate what you've done?" It's clearly a question she hasn't made up her mind about. "But no more." She meets my gaze straight on. "I refuse to have men I don't know following me around." The shiver that goes through her this time is visible.

I nod. "I completely understand." And I do. I really do. It was insensitive of me not to consider her feelings from the beginning.

She breathes out audibly. "So you'll cancel the service."

"No."

She tenses and glares at me. "What?"

"I won't cancel the service," I say calmly. "Earlier today I requested a change in your detail so that you'll only have female bodyguards from now on. You can meet them and have as much contact with them as you like so you're comfortable with the situation."

Her mouth gapes open and then closes. Then opens like she's thought of something else to say but then she closes it again.

I'll quit while I'm ahead.

"Excellent. Now that that's settled to your satisfaction, shall we go?" I hold out a hand in the direction of the town car's open door and move aside so she can step in. *Please, Callie. Please.*

She huffs out a breath of frustration and her eyes dart from the door to me to the sidewalk to the door again. She's about three seconds from telling me to fuck off, I can tell.

But then her mouth purses and she points a finger right in my face. "Don't think this means you're off the hook. Stalker."

She squeezes past me and slides into the car.

Yes. I breathe out and chuckle. "Anything you say. Anything you say."

Classical music plays quietly through the speakers as we drive. Chopin, Prelude in E Minor.

I don't say anything. Now that I've got her here, I'm content. Just having her close is enough to soothe that beast that lives inside me. Because just like everything else, her arrival in my life woke him up too.

He's the part of me that's always hungry and restless and mad at the world. I've never gone to a shrink but I know enough to guess that he comes from my screwed up childhood. Mom died having me and my biological father was a loser in and out of jail so often all I ever knew was foster homes. But dear old dad refused to give up his rights to me when I was still young enough to be adopted and by the time he decided he was done with me, I was six, too old and too wild for anyone to want to adopt. The beast was already born by then.

Nobody wanted me? Fine. I didn't want them either. I'd never want anyone.

And I'd *take* all the things the world had refused to give me.

I was right on track to end up just like my father, in jail by the time I was twenty. I'd already come close to going to juvie twice and I was barely eleven.

Until the Kents.

Until Saul Kent, the only man I'll ever call Dad.

Callie's relaxed into the seat beside me, head back and eyes drooping closed. The mere fact that she can do that with me, that she feels safe enough with me, Jesus, it soothes those raw nerves that have been frayed ever since this morning.

And it means I can watch her in peace. Which probably makes me even more of a stalker, watching her while she sleeps. But it's too rare an opportunity for me to pass up. My security guards don't take pictures of her. It's not surveillance, only security, and going all these months without even a glimpse of her... Jesus, in my worst moments, I wondered if she was even real.

Because it wasn't like I could just go back to sleep. No, after her I was wide, wide awake. So I felt every single second of every single day without her. Torturing myself worrying about what Gentry had done. Fearing the worst and those fears only getting worse when the security reports came in of her out of character behavior.

I vacillated between wanting to go smash Gentry's face in and ruining his business so badly that he'll never be able to show his face in this or any other city ever again. Antonio and Murray assure me the later will be the smarter plan in the end and that we should stay the course, but that does nothing to pacify the beast who wants vengeance now, and wants it bloody.

I get angry even thinking about it all. Deep breaths. I close my eyes and try breathing deeply but it doesn't do shit, so I open them again and look at Callie. Instantly the tightness in my chest loosens. The beast curls up and goes to sleep.

I want her in my life. In my bed. At my kitchen table each morning sharing breakfast.

But for now, I have this. Maybe it's all I'll ever have.

And it's enough.

If I repeat the lie over and over to myself enough times, maybe it'll become true.

Callie doesn't wake up until an hour and a half later when we're in busy downtown San Francisco traffic.

My driver, Sam, weaves expertly in and out of traffic until we pull into a small semicircle in front of a tall brick building with a red awning. There aren't any identifying markers on the building, but I know it well.

A valet quickly appears as Sam gets out and hurries around the front of the car. A moment later, Sam opens my door and hands me my small black duffel bag. I step out and shoulder the bag, then hold out a hand for Callie.

She rolls her eyes and opens her own door. I chuckle as I walk around the back of her car to meet her as she steps out.

She does take my arm when I offer it, though. The beast gives a roar of approval.

"Is it really necessary that you have your own driver?" She asks as we head toward the front doors.

I smile and struggle not to laugh. I lean in and speak low in her ear. Is it a shameless excuse to get close to her? Yes. Yes it is. "If you saw my driving, believe me, you'd know the driver is necessary."

That startles a laugh out of her. "Really? The famous Jackson Vale, admitting to a flaw?"

No one takes the shit out of me like this woman. "I didn't get my license until I was eighteen and the first year I had it, I got in three car accidents. Then when I was twenty-four and made my first ten million, I totaled a Bugatti."

"Shut up." She grabs my shirt sleeve right as I reach for the front door to the building. "You did not."

I incline my head. "I'm afraid so."

"But don't those cars cost, like, two million dollars?" she whispers.

I lean in and whisper back. "Two point four million, actually."

"Oh my God." She shakes her head. "Fucking rich people." Then she looks back up at me. "But you had it insured, right?"

Ah, she always knows how to go straight for the jugular, doesn't she? "I was in a bad spot in my life." I shrug. "Not really one for thinking things all the way through at the time. The dealer tried to insist I set up insurance before I drove it off the lot but I assumed he was just trying to sell me a bunch of extra crap I didn't need. I knew I had liability and I could set the rest up myself." I pause. "And then I just kept meaning to get around to it…"

"Stop talking." She starts to put her hands over her ears. "This is literally the most painful conversation I've ever had in my life. Two point four *million*, you said?"

She's so damn adorable, I can't help laughing. "I survived the accident, thank you for caring so much about my welfare," I tease.

She waves a hand as if it's unimportant, but the next second her eyes are flicking my way. And I have to say, I do like the feel of it. Jesus, I've missed her.

"So you can see now why I use the services of a driver from time to time. Besides, this city is full of crazy motorists. Did you see those streets?" I gesture behind us at the traffic. As if to make my point, a Tesla cuts off another car and then switches lanes, barely squeezing in between two other cars in time and eliciting honks from everyone around them. I wince. "I prefer to have an expert at the wheel if I can afford it."

"And obviously you can." She crosses her arms and raises her eyebrows. "There are less pretentious ways to get around, you know. The light rail and the bus suit the rest of us just fine."

"I never said I'm a revolutionary. I can afford the creature comforts." I come close again, so close I'm just a breath away from her ear. "So why not *indulge?*"

At her sharp intake of air, I pull back and drop my hand to the small of her back, urging her inside the building.

———

Her eyes dart all around from the second we step inside, her curiosity clear on her face. If she's trying to guess where we are by the entrance area though, there aren't many clues.

It's just a small room portioned off by floor to ceiling black velvet curtains. The slow thudding beat of club music rumbles from far away.

Stephanie is manning the hostess station today. She has her customary red leather bustier on, along with a gold collar around her neck that is definitely a new accessory. I'm glad for her. She always wanted a full-time partner. More than I could ever give her.

"Jackson." She smiles wide at seeing me. "It's been quite a while."

"I have the back room reserved."

She looks on her computer and types a few things in, then comes around from back behind the hostess station with my keycard, head lowered and lashes flashing.

"Martin thought it would be amusing to make me work up here for several hours," she hands me the keycard, her hand lingering long after I've taken the little card, "but I'll be free later and I'm sure Martin would be happy to invite you to join. Just like old times."

She keeps fluttering her eyelashes—something I bet she practices in the mirror for as much as she's doing it—and I'm about to tell her how happy I am that Martin made it official when Callie suddenly steps in between us.

"You got something in your eye?" she asks Stephanie, crossing her arms over her chest.

"What?" Stephanie glances over at her, the first time she's acknowledged her existence since we walked in.

"Your *eyes*," Callie says, pointing overexaggeratedly at her own eyes. "You just keep blinking them so fast. Seems like there's some kind of problem there." Callie scrunches her face in pretend sympathy. "Maybe you're starting to develop a pink eye situation."

Stephanie makes an offended noise and looks like she's about to start saying something, but I lose the battle and start chuckling. "Stop being a brat, Steph. Martin might put up with it, but I never did. I'm not about to start now."

Stephanie shivers and drops her eyes. Dammit, the last thing Callie needs to see is one of my exes *Yes, Sir*-ing me.

"Follow me," I say to Callie as I push through one of the curtains and head down a narrow hallway, the walls also painted black. Red bulbs mounted on the wall give the hallway an otherworldly glow. I wince, thinking how all this must look like to Callie.

I can't remember what I thought the first time. Miranda didn't bring me here, but it was to a place like this.

Gentry had used her up and tossed her out, just like he did everyone and she'd sought me out because he'd told her about me. Bragged about what he'd done to me. She thought we could be good for each other and she was right. More than she knew, in my case.

I glance over my shoulder and thank Jesus, Callie's actually following and hasn't bolted for the exit.

Doors line the black hallway and a little way down, I stop and open one to a changing room.

Callie lets out a breath like she wasn't sure what she was going to find behind the door. But it's just a small room that's empty except for a large black wardrobe with rounded silver stud ornamentation and hinges.

"We'll both need to change clothes. There is a certain..." I wave my hand in a so-so gesture, "...dress code that's generally expected in this club."

"And exactly what kind of club is this?"

Stephanie and the leather and collar didn't give it away? "Haven't you guessed?"

"How about you spell it out for me?" Callie puts her hands on her hips. Even in her loose, bulky work clothes, she still looks delicious enough to devour and for a second, it's difficult to think.

I wanted to introduce her to this world as slowly as possible, but I guess this is it. Time to lay my cards on the table.

She's still standing by the door like she hasn't made up her mind about staying or bolting so I cross the distance. "I told you I could introduce you to a safe way of playing out your desires. This is the first step."

I gesture around us. "This place. It's a safe space. There are extensive background checks on all members and beyond that, I have my security monitoring everyone who comes in and out."

"So this is a sex club?" she cuts to the chase.

"It's a social space for like-minded people."

She narrows her eyes at me. "A sex club."

I can't help smiling at that. She never lets me get away with any of my shit. "Don't knock it till you try it."

But her head's shaking firmly back and forth. "Any dude tries to put a collar on me, I'll fucking castrate him." She's glaring now. "Even you."

"No, Callie." My voice is solemn. I don't want her thinking I'm treating this like a joke. "I don't think that's what you need at all. That's not why I brought you here."

"Then why *did* you bring me?"

"It's easier if I show you." It's the truth. I could try to explain it till I'm blue in the face but it would do nothing compared to showing her a scene.

"But first we need to change." I walk over to the bag I brought. I might find her perfect in whatever she wears but here, what you wear speaks volumes.

I pull out her suit and hold it up for her.

Her mouth drops open. "You gotta be fucking kidding me. I'm not wearing that... that *catsuit*."

I sigh. How do I explain? "What you wear gives certain signals to the other patrons. No one will ever touch you here without your consent," I hurry to assure, "and tonight, no one should approach you since you are with me. But first impressions are always important. This outfit sends the message that no one should fuck with you."

She looks startled that I cursed. I generally don't, at least not out loud. I rather think the world could do with more civility, not less, so I do my part.

Callie eyes the garment up and down for several long moments before snatching it out of my hands. She holds it by the shoulders and lets it unfold again.

Then her eyes narrow in my direction. "And what exactly are *you* wearing?"

I smile and pull out my leather pants that match her suit, shaking them out so she can see them.

She bites her bottom lip as she tests the leather of the catsuit in between her fingers and goddammit, I swear she's trying to kill me. My own leather pants are going to be a *tad* difficult to put on if I've got a raging hard-on.

We're here for *her*, dumbass, I remind myself.

Her eyes shoot my direction. "Turn your ass around. If you take even one peek," she picks up the high-heeled boot, "this heel is landing right here." She jerks the shoe forward and stops the pointed heel half an inch from my forehead right between my eyes.

"Yep," I squawk in what *might* come out in slightly less than a manly pitch. "Got it. No peeking. Scout's honor."

She scoffs. "As if you were ever a Boy Scout."

My mouth tips up as I step back. "What gave it away? The part where I once spanked your ass in a limo so you came harder than you had ever before in your life? Or bringing you to a sex club where I'm going to put so many fantasies in your head, you're not going to be able to sleep for a week?"

With that I turn around and start loosening my tie. I pull it off over my head, then my shirt.

Is she watching? I haven't heard any shuffling to indicate she's turned around to start undressing so I go a little slower as I reach and tug my undershirt off my head.

With nothing else to do but go insane worrying over her, I've spent more than a little time in my home gym letting out some aggression on my heavy bag.

Finally I hear noise indicating movement and I grin. She was totally watching. But shit, now that I'm listening for her movements, I can't stop thinking about what each noise means. Is she slipping that skirt down those luscious legs of hers? Taking off her shirt. I close my eyes and my head drops back a little when I remember her fucking *amazing* breasts. I've never in my whole life touched a more perfect pair of breasts.

Are you a tits or ass man?

Jesus, I about died on the spot when she whispered those words in my ear the first time we were together. She's lucky I don't have a heart condition. Single hottest moment of my entire damn life.

Annnnnnnnnnnd now I've got a stiffy to rival all stiffies. Great.

I shove my pants and boxers down and grab the leather pants. I've got to figure out how to get the damn things on and hide this hard on.

But can I stop thinking about her naked? Nope. Can't keep my big mouth shut, either. "Make sure to get completely naked before you put on the suit."

I shake my head as I step into the leather pants. It's practical advice but now there are a million images of her flashing through my head even though I only saw her naked a handful of times.

There's a sharp gasp from behind me and I freeze.

Shit, did I freak her out by saying the naked thing?

... Or is she breaking the rules and peeking at *me*? The pants are only up to one thigh and my ass is out for all to see. Well, just for *her* to see. I don't hear any noise for a long while and I grin. She's totally checking me out, isn't she?

Maybe there's hope after all?

I can't help messing with her. "Callie? I don't hear the suit rustling anymore. Did you get stuck or are you done putting it on? Can I turn around now?"

I pull the leather pants all the way up and there's suddenly a flurry of noise behind me. "No!" she squeaks. "Don't turn around."

Then follows all manner of grunts and curses. Getting the suit on is obviously a struggle.

"Callie?"

"I'm fine. Don't you dare turn around."

More grunting. More cursing.

"Is there a mirror somewhere?" she asks a full five minutes later.

"Can I turn around now?"

"Not yet." Her voice bites in the quiet room. "Is there a mirror?"

"Cabinet in the corner of the room, on the door." I hope that sounded less impatient than I feel. Cause I *really* want to see her. Yeah it's the attire of the club but I'm still a damn man.

"You can look."

Is it just me or does she sound excited?

I turn around and holy shit. I try to swallow but don't do it right and end up coughing. Jesus but she looks—

Fuck, I'm just standing here gawking. But the suit hugs every one of her curves and she has *so* many curves. It zips up the front but she only zipped it midway up her chest so that her ample cleavage is on display and, oh shit, I'm *still* standing her gawking. *Say something.*

"You look good," I finally manage. Oh wow, genius. Say something *smarter*. "I mean, very good. Great. Beautiful." I cringe. Beautiful? That's all I could come up with? Besides, that's not the point tonight.

Because I wasn't kidding earlier when I said that clothes have a message here. This entire place is about power. Who holds it. Who gives it up.

The suit Callie is wearing screams power.

And I'd swear she can feel it. It's like she's standing taller. Or maybe she's realized it. Why I've brought her here. Not, as she put it, to wear a collar. No, that's not what she needs at all, I don't think.

Gentry took her power away.

It's time she got it back.

It was the gift Miranda gave me years ago and now I want to give it to Callie.

Callie glances at herself one more time in the mirror and then nods. She looks back at me and holds up the wicked spiked stiletto boots. "Help me with my heels?"

———

Usually walking into the main galleria of the club calms me down. It means release is near. But not right now. I'm wound tight as a steel guitar string.

I can't keep my eyes off Callie. What's she thinking? What's she expecting? We walk inside and everything is familiar to me but I try to see it through her eyes. We pass by the bar area and continue into the main communal room.

The walls are a varnished wood so dark it's just a shade lighter than black. The black tile floor gleams in the ambient yellow light given off from chandeliers studded throughout the ceiling. They're not the only things hanging from the heavy beams running the length of the room far above our heads, though.

I watch Callie's eyes as they follow chains linked to pulleys connected to the beam and then trace back down on the other side to attached cuffs and swings. Her eyes widen and then shoot around to the stations set up all around the room. Several spanking benches. A few small areas where scenes can be staged. A St. Andrew's cross.

The club is mid-level busy tonight. Naked and half-naked bodies are strung up in one corner, spread-eagle over a pommel horse in another, bent on their knees in yet another. A blindfolded naked man with a ball gag in his mouth stands handcuffed to a second St. Andrew's cross in the other corner, wrists and ankles cuffed to the large wooden X. Another dom brings down a flogger on the first man's back. He spasms and an inflamed pinkish spot joins other similar marks on his reddened shoulders.

Callie's eyes grow even wider though I wouldn't have thought that was possible.

Shit. Maybe bringing her here was a bad idea. It's rare that I second-guess myself but with Callie I never feel like I'm on solid ground. But it might have been better to discretely invite a few people I trust to scene at my house and shown her that way rather than tossing her in the deep end like this.

I just thought that a public place might make her feel more at ease. *Or made her more likely to run for the hills and never talk to you again.*

Jesus, her hands are trembling. I reach out to take one without thinking. The second I make contact, though, she yanks away from me.

Right.

Because I've totally fucked any headway I was making, bringing her here. But it's already done and there's no stuffing this genie back in the bottle.

"Do you need another moment?"

She shakes her head no. Vehemently.

"Do you want to go?" I ask roughly. "We can leave."

She takes a deep breath, eyes still darting everywhere around the room. "Is there a reason you brought me here? I mean, something in particular you wanted to show me?"

"Yes. In the back rooms. Mistress Nightblood is doing a scene tonight and she said we could come observe. She's a friend."

Callie's eyes finally come to me. "Mistress..." She trails off and her eyes pause on a woman wearing an outfit not dissimilar to her own, leading a man crawling on the floor by a leash.

Callie blinks a few times and expels a big breath before nodding. "Okay, show me."

I gesture for her to follow me and she holds her head high as we continue through the room. We're almost to the back hallway leading to the private rooms when I realize Callie's no longer beside me.

I turn and see she's stopped by a scene several feet back where a woman is strung upside down. She's strapped into a pair of boots that are chained to the ceiling. Her hands are also cuffed and chained to the ceiling so that her back is parallel to the ground, stomach up. Her head hangs backward, mouth open.

A dom steps in front of her and then without ceremony, grabs her blonde braid, adjusts her head slightly, shoves his cock into her mouth and down her throat. She chokes on it and spittle almost immediately starts to pour out the sides of her mouth, rolling down and into her hair.

Callie's mouth falls open and she looks horrified.

Without breaking stride, the dom fucking her mouth signals with his hand to another man. The second man, in black latex chaps with a cutout where the crotch area should be steps forward. He's already erect and he moves calmly to the other end of the woman and grabs her hips. He's clearly about to penetrate when Callie jumps forward.

"Stop it!" she shouts.

"Callie." I put a hand on her arm to stop her as the two doms look over at us. Shit. I hate to restrain her but she just doesn't understand what she's seeing.

"They aren't doing anything wrong." I speak as quietly as I can to her. I can tell she wants to argue back so I continue hurriedly. "This is a BDSM club. Nothing goes on here that isn't consensual. Completely *consensual*. Do you understand what I mean? They aren't doing anything except what that girl has expressly given them the go-ahead for. What she *wants* them to do."

"She can't even talk!" Callie yanks against my grip and nods toward the man who has the girl's head in a tight grip as he feeds his cock down her throat. When the other man enters her from the other end, I can tell Callie's about to lose it.

Her eyes go distant and she makes a gagging noise. Gagging like it's her with the cock down *her* throat. She's shaking. Her whole body is shaking. Like it's *her* being held in place and unable to move.

What. The. Fuck. Does that mean—?

I have to get her out of here. Right fucking now.

But the way she yanked away from me earlier— Jesus, I don't want to even touch her right now and make it worse.

The next moment though, she's not frozen anymore. She takes a step forward like she's about to charge the man at the woman's head when he suddenly calls out, "Break light," and pulls out of his sub's mouth. The man on the other end pulls back immediately as well. It's only then that I notice the strung up girl is snapping her fingers rapidly.

"Brake light, brake light," she gasps as soon as her mouth is free. The dom at her mouth signals with his hand and the next moment, the chains holding her up start lowering to the ground.

He catches her in his arms when she's almost to the floor, cradling her body. He immediately starts undoing the cuffs at her wrists and the man in chaps comes to her feet, working at the combination of chains and cuffs there.

Tears stream down the girl's cheeks. "I'm sorry, I'm sorry," she repeats several times, "I failed to please you."

The man is shaking his head adamantly. "Don't ever say sorry for using your safe word." His voice is commanding and the girl looks up into his eyes, her own large and luminous. "*That* would displease me."

A gentle smile breaks across her face and she nods.

I keep looking back from the girl to Callie, the girl to Callie. Because Callie is frozen again, her features caught somewhere between confusion and fury and looking like she's about to break out in tears herself.

"I told you our motto is safe, sane, and consensual," I whisper. "Nothing that happens here will ever violate any of those three cardinal rules."

"Safe," she whispers. "Sane. Consensual."

She swallows, eyes still on the girl from the scene as she snuggles into her dom's chest. He places a kiss on top of her head, slipping the tie off the end of her braid. Then he runs his fingers through her hair as he continues soothing her.

Callie turns away from the scene abruptly and starts walking in the direction we were initially going, toward the back hallways.

Okay. Apparently we're moving on. Once we get to the hallway, we pass by several windows that reveal more private scenes being enacted.

I glance through each window as we pass before finally stopping. My eyes are on Callie as she takes in the room that's dark inside except for a single spotlight highlighting a naked man bent over a spanking bench and my friend Patricia standing behind him. Callie's eyes are wide but curious. Not disgusted or afraid. We'll call that progress.

I knock twice and Patricia looks to the window before waving at us to come in. I open the door and we step inside.

"Hello, Mistress Nightblood," I greet Patricia formally. It's unusual that I even know her apart from her Domme name, but she's a friend of Miranda's and we've socialized together.

She inclines her head toward me. "Master Sin."

Callie's head snaps toward me, probably at the moniker. But this is a place we come to fulfill fantasies and I'm unapologetic about the fact. I meet Callie's gaze head on but within seconds, her eyes bounce back to Patricia.

Patricia is fuller figured. A respectable lawyer by day, right now she's dressed in a red bustier and latex skirt that barely hits the tops of her thighs.

"May I introduce my potential apprentice, Mistress..." I look at Callie. Hmm, I should have asked her earlier what she'd like to go by but she thinks on her feet, just like always.

"Mistress Lee," she says with barely a moment's pause. The second half of her shortened name, *Callie*. It's strong. A good, dominant name.

"Nice to meet you, Mistress Lee." Patricia smiles at her and it's warm and genuine. I've always liked that about Patricia. She's real. "Always good to see new Dommes-in-training. We need all the help we can to keep these dicks in line, don't we? Speaking of—" Patricia averts her attention and Callie follows her gaze to the man under the spotlight.

He's chained spread-eagled, ass up. He's also completely naked except for a thick leather collar around his neck, a cock ring, and several weighted metal rings around his balls, dragging them toward the floor. Ball stretchers. I can't help shifting uncomfortably just looking at the damn things.

"Had enough yet, slave?" Mistress Nightblood picks up a brown flogger with a ton of little leather straps coming out the end. Patricia has disappeared. She's all Mistress now.

She flicks his ass with it. Once. Twice. Three times.

He barely flinches and his ass only turns a very light pink as opposed to some of the angry red flesh on the butts we passed outside

The man lets out a groan but it doesn't sound like he's in pain.

"Don't you dare come," Mistress Nightblood says in a warning voice. She reaches between his legs and tugs on the weights that are attached to his balls.

"Please, Mistress." The sub sounds agonized. "Please, please."

She smacks him on the ass with the flogger again, this time harder.

"Please, *what?*"

Callie tenses beside me, like again she has the urge to go forward and stop what's happening. But then the sub starts talking.

"Please let me come, Mistress. I can't take any more. I'm a nasty, bad, *bad* little slave." His ass wiggles slightly. Well, as much as he can, constrained as he is. "But please, please let me come."

I watch Callie's face and see the concern morph to surprise.

"Oh, you can't take any more?" Mistress's voice takes on a dangerous edge. "Since when do you think you're the one who gets to determine how much you can or cannot take?"

I put my hand to the small of Callie's back, the gentlest touch, to lead her a little away from the couple so that we're unobtrusive, but still close enough so we have a clear view of what Mistress Nightblood is doing.

She grabs the head of her sub's cock and he lets out a groan as his whole body shudders. Callie's breath hitches and my eyes are locked on her as she swallows hard, eyes furrowed in concentration as she watches the scene in front of her.

She looks riveted. Is she imagining what she could have? Is she imagining what that kind of control might feel like?

Is that what I looked like my first time?

Miranda was a sub. We'd been dating for a couple months the first time she asked me to spank her.

I was horrified. I'd never *hurt* her. How could she ask that of me? Especially knowing what she did about me?

That was when she brought me to my first club. It took awhile for me to get it. Several visits before it finally started sinking in—it wasn't about hurting someone. Okay, for some doms, the real sadists, it *is* about hurting their subs, when they're both into it. That was never me.

No, what Miranda saw I needed, and what she needed to, though from the opposite end of the spectrum, was the control. The power exchange.

The first time we did a scene together—a *real* scene—and she gave herself up to me in total trust that I'd catch her? Well, it started the long road to healing what Gentry had broken. For both of us, I think.

I follow Callie's gaze. Mistress Nightblood rubs the skin of her sub's cock up and down over his shaft, all the while hissing in his ear, "don't you dare come. If you come, I'll be very, very disappointed in you. What happens when Mistress is disappointed in you?" She rubs her cheek against his, her hand still firmly on his cock. With her other hand, she reaches down and pulls on the weight so that his balls are dragged down. He squirms against his cuffs and his face twists in a mixture of bliss and agony.

"Answer me, *slave*," she says in a tone both calm and menacing. "What happens if you disappoint Mistress?"

Callie's breaths grow more uneven the more she watches. She licks her lips and there I go again, hard as rock. Because it's impossible to miss that she's getting turned on by what she's seeing. She shifts in her boots and I wonder if it's because she needs the friction, so she can get the seam of her suit to rub her just where she needs it—

"I— I—" the slave-boy stutters, "I get put in chastity," he finally manages to say even while he thrusts his constrained hips toward his Mistress' palm.

Callie shakes her head like she knows Mistress won't like that.

And indeed, the next second, Mistress tuts, "Ah ah ah," and pulls her hand away. "Stop pushing, slave. I give and you receive. You know that's how this works." She turns her back to him and walks toward the back of the room.

He whines, sounding absolutely pitiful as he turns his head toward her, begging with his eyes and then his mouth when he realizes she's not looking at him. "Please, *please* Mistress. I'll do anything. *Anything*. I'll worship your pussy for hours with my mouth. I'll cook your every meal. I'll make up your bath and give you the most glorious deep-body massage you've ever received." Words pour out of his mouth, one after the other. "Oh God, just come punish me some more. I'm a naughty, bad, bad little cunt boy. Just give me what I need and I'll give you anything. Everything."

His body goes taut with excitement when Mistress Nightblood comes back toward him, closer and closer. Then she detours and picks up something from a table set up along the wall opposite us.

Callie bites her lip and leans in like she's straining to see what Mistress picked up. It's hard to tell in the dimly-lit space outside the spotlight, but I can guess.

When she brings it into the light in front of the man's face, I can see that I'm right.

"It's a ball gag," I whisper in Callie's ear.

She jerks a little at my voice like she'd forgotten I was here beside her. But now that I've gotten close, I can't bear to pull away. And for once, she's not jerking back, so I continue.

"Watch," I say, no doubt unnecessarily.

"No," whines the man. "I'm sorry. I'm sorry. I know you don't like it when I beg. I'm bad. Bad slave. I just want to make you feel good. Mistress, if you would just let me—"

"What's your safe word once the gag is in place?"

"Mistress please—"

"Safe word or it's chastity now, slave," she demands, looking like she's on the edge of getting pissed off. The sub must realize it too because he starts to snap both fingers.

"Good," she lowers the gag. "Open wide."

He looks like he's going to complain again but she gives him a sharp glare and his mouth pops open. She inserts the large ball into his mouth, then buckles the straps into place behind his head.

"Snap once if it's comfortable and you are not in any pain."

The man snaps once.

"Good. From now on only snap if you want the scene to pause or stop."

He nods and she smiles. "That's better, my little naughty cunt-sucker. You know I don't put up with any fucking brattish behavior from my subs."

She picks up the flogger she laid down earlier and moves back around his bent-over body to where his ass sticks out, spotlight right on it.

"I don't know how your former Mistresses operated," she raises an eyebrow and drops her voice, "but I will be breaking that habit."

She brings down the flogger on his ass, working her way down with smacks on alternate cheeks until the whole thing is bright red. She keeps up a running commentary about what a slutty little slave he is, how she wants to fuck him with a giant strap on, what a fucking clit-tease he is, and most of all, how she expects her slave to obey her in thought, word, and action.

I whisper in Callie's ear, explaining that is more than just a one-night encounter like some of the other scenes we passed by. Mistress Nightblood likes to make arrangements with a submissive man to be her weekend slave. She has exclusive relationships with these men that last anywhere from two months to several years.

The more I talk and Callie watches, the more fascinated she seems. She clasps her hands together and I wonder if it's to stop herself from fidgeting. She loses the battle against squirming in her suit, too, and watching her watch Mistress Nightblood is the most erotic thing I've seen since having Callie herself in my bed.

I chose Mistress Nightblood on purpose because she's not just flogging her sub. She stops constantly to touch him, to give a tug to the ball weights, to rub his hip, to caress down his spine. Or to move around and look him in the face to check on how he's doing. Which is generally just looking blissed the hell out.

She's mastering him but caring for his needs at the same time. She's everything I want Callie to see being a domme can be. She's in complete control.

At least she should be.

I don't know how long the whole scene has been going on—fifteen minutes? Twenty?—when everything suddenly comes to a full stop.

"Stop that." Mistress Nightblood's voice is like a bucket of ice water. She's moved in front of us so I can't see exactly what's happening. "Don't you dare—" she says in a deadly warning tone.

She drops the flogger and jumps back.

"Slave!" she barks furiously. Before now, her voice was calm. Dominant, yes, but there was an undercurrent of affection.

That's completely gone now. She just sounds pissed. Did that little bastard do what I think he did?

"Acknowledge your action." Her movements are stiff as she goes around to his head and unbuckles the ball gag.

"Acknowledge. Your. Action."

Silence.

"Acknowledge your action or find another Mistress." She doesn't shout or even raise her voice, even though it's obvious something's happened to make her absolutely furious. On the outside, she's projecting totally calm, but damn.

"I— I came," he finally says in a contrite whisper. Yep, that's what I thought.

It does not move Mistress Nightblood. "Tell the truth." Her voice is like a whip.

The whine is back in his voice. "I—it's just, you're so beautiful and you were making me feel so wonderful for so long and I just couldn't help it—"

Mistress Nightblood walks to him and quietly starts to undo his ankles from the cuffs keeping him spread eagle.

"What are you doing, Mistress? I swear, it won't happen again. Mistress, if you just let me explain..." His words fade off at her continued silence.

She walks around to where his hands are cuffed on the other side of the bench. Without a word she undoes the straps binding him.

"You know your way out, Samuel."

He recoils at the name as if she struck him. It's a response much more violent than any when the actual flogger was coming down on him.

She stands and goes to turn when he cries out. "Mistress." For the first time throughout the entire session, the whine is gone from his voice and it sounds like a genuine plea. He looks absolutely devastated. "Forgive me." Tears stream down his face.

Callie looks confused about what's happening and she glances up to me. "Isn't that the point?" she whispers. "Getting off? This is a sex club."

I shake my head. "Just watch."

Mistress is still as a statue, staring at him impassively as he falls to pieces in front of her. He peels himself off of the pommel bench and drops into a heap at her feet.

She stands there straight as an arrow, but for the first time tonight, indecision crosses her face. Does Callie get how big a deal this is? I know from talking to Patricia that she was really hoping for more with this sub and now it's all breaking down right in front of us. Because he refused to give himself completely.

Callie's eyes are glued to the both of them as Mistress's expression gentles.

"Acknowledge your actions. This is your last chance." Her voice is only the tiniest bit softer, but still hard as nails.

The sub looks up at her like she's just offered him the sun and the moon and the whole wide world. "I made myself come by rubbing myself against the spanking bench. And I did not ask Mistress if I could come."

Mistress Nightblood lets out the smallest breath of relief and then begins to discuss his punishment—two weeks in a chastity cage that she promptly secures around his cock.

I lead Callie out of the room afterwards.

"But I don't get it," Callie says. "She doesn't get to have sex for two weeks either now."

"That's not what it's about," I explain. "And she doesn't just want control. She wants the best for him. She wants for him to succeed."

Callie frowns. "So all those things he offered—worshiping her and giving her all the orgasms she could want, cooking for her, giving her massages... I mean that's the kind of thing you think of when you hear master and slave. But it's not about that, is it? She wanted something," the furrow between Callie's eyes grows, "I don't know, something deeper?"

She looks up at me and I nod.

"I wanted to show you Mistress Nightblood at work because she's one of the best," Jackson says. "The most important thing between a Dominant and their Submissive is the bond of trust between them. When you started watching the scene, you might've thought that she had all the power. But that's deceptive." He pauses in the corridor and looks down at me, those intense dark blue eyes of his. "Her sub truly holds the power."

Callie scoffs. "He was tied up and gagged."

I raise an eyebrow as I lead her to the right, taking us further down the hall of private rooms. We pass by a few more windows, some with patrons outside watching the scenes unfolding with interest, others just idly chatting. We go past all of them without stopping.

"Really? You saw in the galleria earlier—one snap of a finger and it all stops. A Dominant can only take a Sub as far as they are willing to go. I know at first it all just seems like ball gags and whips and paddles, but the really good doms, dommes, and subs know how to take it to another level." I think back to Miranda and all she taught me. "They know how to help you discover parts of yourself you never even knew were there. It's always a learning process. You learn from one another."

Callie shifts uncomfortably and for a moment I wonder if I said something wrong but then she smiles at me. "Are *you* a good dom?"

I stare at her a long moment. That is the question, isn't it?

"We'll see, Callie. We'll see." I start walking again.

It's not until we come to several solid doors that I slow down. These doors are numbered with fancy Victorian script. I pull out my wallet and grab the key card, then swipe it in front of the door. The light flashes green and then it unlocks.

I push the door open and Callie follows right on my heels. I can only hope her enthusiasm from the last scene carries into this. I only hope this isn't too far too fast.

Because if it's not—?

If it's not, I could give her a taste of what it really feels like. The control I think she needs so desperately. I think of her this morning, the terror and pain in her eyes as she screamed no and shoved me away from her.

So I don't turn around and drag her out of the room but I do pause before she can pass by me and see what's inside.

"We can leave at any time. If you're uncomfortable or you want to go, just say the word."

Her frown comes back. "Just show me what's in the room, Jackson."

I breathe out and step back so she can pass by. They spared no expense with this room. Burnished wood floors, brick walls, and lights tucked away in wall sconces that imitate torches.

And in the back?

My friend Daniel shackled naked to the furthermost brick wall, face to the brick.

His arms are stretched in a Y up above his head by chains that attach to anchor points farther up the walls. He's prepared just as I instructed, with only his wrists cuffed. His feet are free but no doubt it's been uncomfortable, standing with his arms in that position for God knows how long.

Not that Daniel would care. The more pain involved, the more he's on board. He and Miranda were best friends, they were both such pain sluts. In the end, it was one of the reasons Miranda and I parted ways. She *did* want me to hurt her and that aspect of the life never appealed to me. No matter how much I spanked her, she always wanted it harder. She wanted me to choke her during sex. She wanted it rougher. Meaner. And in the end that was the one thing I couldn't give.

I watch Callie and she jerks her gaze away from Daniel, cheeks going pink. Because he's chained to the wall or simply because he's naked? But the next second her eyes flicker back to him like she can't not look. Like earlier with Mistress Nightblood, she's fascinated.

All right then. We're doing this. I walk forward toward the wall where the floggers and canes and paddles hang.

I pluck a wooden paddle off the wall and test its weight. I swing it through the air a few times with a quick whip of my wrist, creating a low whistle of air in its wake. That'll do. I nod in satisfaction.

Then I go back to the wall and pick up another paddle. I test its weight and swing as well. I'm being a bit theatrical, if I'm honest. I want Callie to see everything first and have a moment to take it all in.

But finally, I turn back and hold the second paddle towards her. handle out. "Your turn."

CHAPTER SIX

CALLIE

I ignore the paddle and instead grab the fabric of Jackson's shirt, dragging him over to the corner farthest away from the dude that's chained to the wall. "What the hell?"

Jackson studies me with a dark intensity glinting in his eyes—like he's been soaking up the energy of this place and getting his Dom on more and more the longer we stay.

"The *hell*," he emphasizes the word as he steps directly into my personal space and firmly places the paddle in my hand, "is that you are going to take this paddle and spank that man's ass."

He jerks his head in the direction of Chained-Up Guy. Jackson comes closer till his chest is pressed up against mine and his voice is a growl in my ear. "I'll show you how. The best way to learn is through hands-on experience."

Sexual energy sparks off him.

"But—" I scoff at the ridiculousness of his suggestion. It's difficult to think with him standing so close. Why does he always have to smell so damn good? And why the hell am I focusing on the way he smells? There are way bigger things to be focusing on here. Like the chained-up guy in the corner and the paddle in my hand. Yeah. Holy shit.

"You what?" Jackson asks calmly.

"I don't know how to spank anybody!" I finally manage to whisper, taking a step back and tossing my hands slightly up in the air. There. With a little more distance between us, it's easier to focus.

"Which is why I said I'll teach you."

I look back and forth between Chained-Up Guy and Jackson. Of all the—I can't believe the—I make my voice even quieter but say with no less vehemence, "I'm not having sex with some dude who's chained up!" Though, even as I say it the already-moist area between the legs of my suit seems to get even more slick. I look down so Jackson can't read it in my eyes.

"Who said anything about sex?"

Okay, wait. Now I'm seriously confused.

Jackson must be able to see enough of my face even though I'm not looking at him because he says, "Callie, this lifestyle doesn't always have to be about sex."

Okay, now I do look him full in the face. "But," I say slowly, then gesture back in the direction of the main club. "Isn't this a... sex club?"

Jackson runs a hand through his hair, something he only does when he's really riled about something.

"Sure, in BDSM there can be sex," he says, looking in the same direction I am back at the door.

Then his gaze lands back on my face. "But there doesn't have to be. In fact, a lot of Dominants and Dommes work with clients that they meet on a completely nonsexual basis, just for the sake of fulfilling a need. People seek this lifestyle for all kinds of reasons."

At my skeptical look, he crosses his arms. "Yes, sex can be a big part of it for a lot of people, but it's not all there is. Many more are perfectly celibate for long periods of time. Then they come here to find what they can't in the vanilla world for a release every few months."

I'm about to call bullshit, when Jackson speaks again. "Take Daniel here." Jackson gestures at the man chained to the wall. "He's perfectly happy with a session whether it ends in orgasm or not."

Jackson starts to walk toward the man and gestures me to follow.

I cross my arms but after tapping my toe and glancing at the door, I give up and hurry after Jackson. I mean, who am I kidding? Stay and see more of the craziest live porno I could imagine?

Fuck. I shouldn't like this. After what happened to me, I *should* really find every bit of this repulsive. What the fuck is wrong with me that the crotch of my catsuit is so slick with my moisture I'm afraid anyone nearby might hear me squelch if they walk too close to me. I squeeze my eyes shut hard and breathe out a long, hissing breath through my teeth.

But God, if I'm messed up, doesn't that mean Jackson is too? And everyone else in this place?

No. This is all just a game to them. They aren't fucked in the head because they aren't like you. They don't have your past. Your damage.

"Daniel's interest in BDSM is the *M*. Masochism." Jackson's voice startles me. Even more startling? I'm standing right beside him. Guess my feet and subconscious made the decision for me. Then what he said registers.

My eyes shoot to Jackson's. "He likes pain?" I ask quietly. Maybe I was wrong and I'm not the only damaged one here. Or I just need to redefine my definition of normal. Real quick.

"No need to whisper on my account."

I'm so surprised by the chained guy's voice that I almost lose my footing. These fucking heels. And I just, well, I—

I didn't expect him to actually talk to us.

After Mistress Nightblood ignoring we were there, I don't know I guess I just assumed that's how it would be with everyone here. Stupid really. God, what do I think this is, a zoo? Where we just go and stare at the wildlife? Way to be a bitch, Callie.

"Oh?" I ask, hoping he can't read everything I've been thinking on my face.

The chained guy—no, *Daniel*, I correct in my head—laughs. For the first time I really look up into his face. He's extraordinarily handsome, maybe just shy of thirty?

He's got lush, shining brown hair. Defined eyebrows and eyelashes so long they almost look fake. His face is the kind of handsome that makes me think of a beautiful woman. He'd come off as too feminine overall if it weren't for his toned, very male body. But that body—damn, it just doesn't quit. Bronzed skin, rippling back muscles that lead down to a ripe, round—

"Oh yeah, I am a total pain slut." Daniel smiles at me over his shoulder, showing off a perfect set of teeth that'd give a dentist a boner. "Jackson here can tell you all about it."

Is he answering a question? Did I ask one? Oh shit, I've just been standing here ogling, haven't I?

It takes me a second to catch up. When I do, I look between the two men and feel the line start to crease between my brows. Wait? These two? *Does Jackson swing that way?* I mean, not that I have a problem with that. I just thought... I squint up at Jackson, trying to see him in this new light.

Jackson grins wide and then starts laughing, obviously reading my expression. "What did I just tell you, Callie? These situations are not always sexual. I know Daniel because we have a mutual friend who asked for my help sometimes disciplining him when Daniel was her sub."

"I was more than she could handle, you see." Daniel winks at me. Fucking *winks* at me. While he's strung up naked as the day he was born.

A loud thwack echoes throughout the room. I look down and indeed, the blooming pink on Daniel's ass indicates Jackson just spanked the dude. "The problem is," Jackson says, "you enjoy the punishments too much. You intentionally try to piss your Dommes off so you can get more of what you want."

I glance back up at Daniel's face. Is this really what he wants? His eyebrows are drawn together, his mouth open and instead of tensing at the pain, he looks like he's finally relaxing.

Without thinking, my eyes drop to Daniel's nether regions. But there's nothing going on down there. He's not even semi-hard. I glance back up and see he's twisted to look over his shoulder again, eyes trained on the paddle Jackson's holding. Now I recognize the expression for what it is—not lust. It's longing.

He wants this paddling so bad he's almost salivating for it.

"Some Dommes like trying to tame a bratty sub," Daniel says. He shrugs like it's not a big deal, but with the way he can't take his eyes off the paddle, he's not doing a very good job of pretending nonchalance.

Jackson tilts his head to the side and raises an eyebrow, obviously seeing through this guy's crap. "Any good Dom or Domme is going to drop you like a hot potato once they realize you won't stop trying to top from the bottom."

"Well, that's why you and I make such good friends," Daniel finally looks up, adopting the attitude he had when we first entered. Carefree. Fun. "You never tried to be my Dom."

Within moments, though, his eyes track back down to the paddle in Jackson's hand. "Which is great because it means we can do favors for one another." He grins back up at Jackson. "Shall we get started?"

Daniel's gaze moves to me, brown eyes warming. "I hear we're breaking in a new Domme today. You can do anything you like to me, beautiful. Spank me, try your hand with the floggers, there are dildos of all sizes, I'm fine with bull whips and—"

"Enough," Jackson growls. "You can't pull that crap when I'm around. No topping from the bottom. You want what this paddle has to offer, you respect your Mistress while you're with me. Besides, you know this is just a first session."

Jackson snaps his fingers just like Mistress Nightblood did. "Scene begins now. Eyes to the floor."

Daniel's whole posture changes. His eyes drop and his easy relaxed posture goes on alert. I also don't miss the look of intense and focused concentration that comes over his face. I get the feeling that the Daniel I've met so far has been a mask, except for the brief glimpse of desperate yearning after Jackson first spanked him.

I take a step back so that I can't see Daniel's face anymore. This is all just... There's just a lot more to it than I could have ever expected. I mean... bull whips? Holy *shit*.

"What is your safe word?" Jackson asks.

"Red."

"And yellow if things start to become uncomfortable, correct?" Jackson clarifies.

"Yes. Correct."

"Repeat the safe word one more time."

"Red."

Jackson turns to me and demonstrates how to grip the paddle. "Wooden impact implements like a paddle leave fewer marks but cause more immediate pain than leather. So it's perfect for someone like Daniel who wants to repeat the experience as often as possible without having marks. That way he gets the most pleasure-pain out of the experience."

He explains all this so calmly, like a professor discussing a scholarly subject they've put a lot of study into. It's good, though, because somehow it makes it feel easier to ask questions.

"I don't get it." My brows scrunch together. "I mean, I get that some people might want less pain, but can't you just use the wooden paddle more softly? Not leaving marks seems like a good thing."

Daniel snorts and Jackson shoots him a glare. "Not speaking means no extra noises out of your mouth, either, submissive. Show disrespect again and I'll uncuff you. We'll be done before we start." Jackson's voice is a bark, much harsher than his usual measured monotone and nothing like the gentler, passionate voice he uses with me.

Jackson turns back to me. "Some subs like to wear their master's marks," he explains. "Like the collars. It's another sign of ownership."

"Ownership?" I can't help the hostility in my voice at the word. Every time I start to think that all of this is something I could be into, I learn something else that throws up a red flag. "No human being should ever think they can own another person."

Jackson keeps his eyes steadily on mine. "It's called a power exchange. Exchange, as in, *giving willingly*. The most important part of dominance or submission is the bond of trust between the partners. Think of everything we've seen tonight."

He takes my hand and it's a struggle not to startle at the warmth of the contact. It's so oddly intimate. More intimate than what I've done with the handful of faceless men over the past few weeks.

This is Jackson. My stupid breath even hitches. Once he has me positioned behind Daniel, I snatch my hand back. Jackson doesn't comment, he just moves around so that he's right behind me.

Again, the intoxicating scent of his aftershave encircles me. So goddamn masculine. His arm comes around me from behind and he covers my hand that holds the paddle with his. Damn, how am I supposed to breathe regularly with him this close? It's so unfair that in such a short time, I've come to associate his scent with a sense of safety. There was a long while there where I never thought I'd be able to ever feel safe again.

I want to pull away, but Jackson is back in instruction mode. "You want to have a firm hand, but the key to being a good Domme is learning to watch your sub for even the most subtle of indicators. Part of that bond of trust I was talking about is trusting them to signal if it's too much for them to handle."

"The flipside is that they need to be able to trust you to be watching and aware, able to call it if it's getting out of hand, especially if you are playing with more inexperienced subs who don't know their limits yet."

"How will I know if I'm hitting too hard?" I ask, looking over my shoulder to Jackson. I can't stomach the thought of hurting anyone. Not after being on the receiving end.

"That's why I'm showing you. You'll get a feel for it. Plus," he smiles, "Daniel's the most willing victim you'll find. If you hit him a little too hard while you're figuring everything out, he'll only enjoy it."

Okay. I manage a small smile back. I see now why he picked Daniel. I'm still not quite prepared when Jackson's hand, still covering mine, brings my arm back and then lets loose so that the paddle I'm holding whack's Daniel's ass. Hard.

My eyes shoot wide open. I felt that one reverberate all the way up my forearm but Daniel didn't even so much as flinch.

Jackson lets go of my hand. "Just so you know you don't have to be afraid of smacking too hard. That's nothing to Daniel. You don't have to go that hard at first, but you don't have to be afraid either."

I blink rapidly and swallow. Damn, I really wish there was like, a water fountain around here or something. I'm fucking parched. Then I ignore my dry mouth and turn back to the task at hand.

Which, you know, is the ass in front of me.

That I'm supposed to spank.

Ever have one of those moments in life where you're like: how the fuck did I get here? Yeah, I have one of those for a quick second.

And then I get the fuck over it and start paddling the hell out of the ass of a stranger I just met.

CHAPTER SEVEN

CALLIE

I don't start out spanking nearly as hard as Jackson did. You might almost call them love taps at first. The smack of wood on skin still reverberates with a satisfying *wallop* throughout the room.

"You're doing great, but don't be afraid to put more force behind it." Jackson's arm comes around me from behind again and I just now realize that the position isn't setting off all my alarms like it has when other men have approached me that way in the past few months.

"Alternating cheeks like that is a good idea, but remember the paddle is long enough that you can also hit both at once." He demonstrates and then I try.

I smack both Daniel's ass cheeks with the long flat part of the paddle, right in the center. Daniel doesn't flinch—more like a shudder goes throughout his entire body.

I move so that I can check his face and gauge how he's doing. Jackson said that's an important part of all this and I don't want to fuck it up my first run out of the gate. Daniel has his torso pressed into the brick wall, his head is slightly thrown back, and his features are a mottled mix of agonized pleasure.

Okay. Wow. Guess everything's good here. I don't get it but at the same time—I look over at Jackson and the difficult breathing thing—oh yeah, I'm feeling that majorly.

This whole thing is insane, but... Jackson's only got eyes for me and there's a heat that seems to match what I'm feeling. Doing what we're doing... together... Holy shit, this is the craziest, hottest fucking thing I've ever done in my life.

The Sahara Desert in my mouth only seems drier but another part of my body is making up for it with moisture in spades.

"Why don't you try with your own hands now?" Jackson's breath is hot in my ear.

He caresses a hand from my shoulder down my arm, tracing my forearm to my hand where he finally takes the paddle from me. "There's nothing quite like feeling the heat of their skin. Feeling them tremble under your dominance."

He moves to my other ear, the heat of his breath on the back of my neck making goosebumps rise. "Try it. You know you want to."

My breath hitches. I've always found the low growl of his voice sensual. I twist around to glance up at him, but not at his eyes. I only make it to his lips. They too have always fascinated me. The way the top one is a little bit fuller than the bottom.

Unlike Daniel, there's nothing feminine about Jackson. Or the way he's used those lips on me in the past.

Jackson gestures with a head nod back to the naked man in front of us. Startled, I look at Daniel, who's started shifting back and forth on his feet as if to get our attention.

"Submissive, you will stand still," Jackson orders, "Obey or the session ends now."

Daniel immediately goes motionless. I on the other hand feel like I can barely stand still, I'm so alive with too much energy pulsing just beneath my skin.

The command in Jackson's voice. Holy shit. So fucking hot. I want that. Which is... Just confusing. Because I don't want him commanding *me*. So maybe I just want to be *like* him?

Fuck all this thinking.

I rear my hand back and really let loose on Daniel's ass. Daniel lets out a low *oof*, the first noise he's made all night. I don't worry that I've hurt him. Even from the little exposure I've had, I'm pretty sure to him, that felt amazing. And it only sets off another round of crazy fucking adrenaline shooting through my blood.

I glance up at the chains securing Daniel to the wall. I'm completely safe. I could do anything to him. It's a total goddamn rush—even as I know that he trusts me not to hurt him because of these rules we agreed to before we started.

God, that's part of what makes it so good. I feel... free. Finally *free*. At least in this moment. But to even have a *moment* of freedom... there were days I never thought I'd get this.

I can't help the growing grin on my face as I spank Daniel again. This time I go a little softer but only because I want this to last. Daniel's ass has started to turn pink between the paddle and my spanking. I try to work around to areas that are still white as I continue the spanking.

Holy shit. Spanking. Just thinking about what I'm doing as I'm doing it gets me even more excited. This shit is forbidden. Completely taboo. Yet this stranger is letting me do it to him.

"Daniel likes vocalizations too," Jackson says, again in my ear. It startles me and more goosebumps shoot up and down my body. It's been quiet in the room except for the sound of my hand meeting Daniel's flesh. I thought Jackson had stepped back, but now here he is so close again, body warm at my back.

As much as I enjoy his voice, his words puzzle me.

"Vocalizations?"

He leans in, so close that his cheek grazes mine from over my shoulder. If I thought I had goosebumps before, it's nothing compared to the absolute shiver that runs through my body and straight down to my core at his nearness and what he says next.

"This scene doesn't have to be sexual, but it can be if it's what *you* want. Humiliation is what turns Daniel on. You're the Mistress. This scene is whatever you want it to be."

He pulls back and when I look over my shoulder, I see his eyes are dilated.

Jackson wants me.

I'm not the only one completely fucking turned on by what's going on here.

Jackson lifts a finger and traces my bottom lip before dipping it inside my mouth. I let out a small growl and then bite down on his finger. He draws in a quick breath and he yanks his finger back, but his eyes don't move from mine.

Electricity sparks between us. Yet somehow I manage my wits enough to say, "If I'm the Mistress of this scene, stop trying to top me."

Half of his mouth lifts in a smile and he dips his head ever so slightly. "I wouldn't dream of it, Mistress."

I turn my gaze back on Daniel, eyes narrowing quizzically. "Humiliation?" The question is addressed to Jackson.

"Continue with your spanking," he whispers, again in my ear, only this time he ends with a brief bite on my lobe that elicits a sharp gasp before he goes to lean against the wall right beside Daniel. He crosses his arms leisurely as he watches us.

"You pathetic fucking pain slut," Jackson sneers. "Bringing your sorry ass to *me* of all people. What a sad, sad little cunt. What? You're so fucked up you can't even find your own Domme to play with you?"

I pause mid-wallop in shock at Jackson's harsh words. But he just aims a glare my way and nods toward Daniel's ass. I glare back and deliver a smack anyway, but not a hard one.

"That's right, pretty boy. Such a pretty face for such a fucked up little cunt. No wonder no one wants you."

All right, that's enough. I'm about to go slap some sense into Jackson when he nods again. I think he's trying to tell me to keep spanking Daniel but then he continues talking while gesturing.

"That's what makes you hard, isn't it, you twisted fuck? Hearing me call you a cunt-faced pussy."

I move around Daniel's side and see that Jackson's not wrong. Daniel's cock, which has been totally flaccid throughout the whole session is now standing at full mast—red, pulsing, and thick.

My mouth drops open and I look at Jackson. He merely shrugs and then gestures to me like I should start talking now.

I move back to my position on the left side of Daniel and spank him a few more times. Jackson stays quiet and I notice Daniel's dick start to deflate.

Well hell. Here he is letting us use him as a crash test dummy for my spanking skills and if I don't woman up, he won't get anything out of it. That doesn't seem fair.

"What, is your cock that sensitive? It's going to droop because it doesn't get attention for three seconds?" The words are out of my mouth before I can really think it over. I bite my lip, feeling like a total bitch, but when I glance down again, there his cock goes, all the way back up and pointing toward his stomach again.

Jackson moves off the wall and comes to stand beside me. "Shit-talking is part of being a Domme. A lot of subs find it freeing." He raises an eyebrow at me. "Doms and Dommes too. Try it. Let your inner bitch out. See how good it feels."

"Don't be such a God damn mother fucking bastard," I call out as I give Daniel a good wallop, but it's Jackson who I'm staring at as I say it. "Nobody likes a fucking know it all cunt sucker."

Oh my God, I can't believe I just said those things, but that exhilaration I was feeling moments ago? That high is ten times higher now.

Jackson's eyes flare dangerously but if anything, he only looks like he wants to devour me more. He moves away and returns with one of the small floggers.

I spank Daniel a few more times and then Jackson starts to work the flogger up and down Daniel's back. Like Mistress Nightblood, he flicks his wrist back and forth so that the flogger responds in a complicated X pattern. I step back and watch his mastery with the instrument.

At first I think he's going to calmly instruct me in this to, but no, he's just getting into it. Sweat breaks out on his brow as a rose flush rises all over Daniel's back.

"Tell me, you cock-sucking mother-fucker, how did you lose your virginity?" Jackson asks Daniel. "Did you get your cherry popped when you were repeating your senior year at nineteen in a pity fuck? Or was it a prostitute you had to hire because no one else wanted your tiny little cock near them?"

Daniel lets out what I can only describe as a low-pitched mewl and throws his head back even further.

My breath shoots in and out of my lungs in short, stuttered pants. I've never seen Jackson this way. Everything happening is insanely fucking hot, but at the same time I'm frustrated. Jackson took over with the vocalizations because after my first few attempts, I just couldn't keep it up. I got embarrassed or... I don't even know what, but something keeps holding me back.

But as I watch Jackson completely mastering Daniel, it just—I feel —well, Jackson said I got to be the Mistress. Yet somehow over the last ten or fifteen minutes, I've let myself be completely shut out of it.

At the same time, I'm only getting more and more fucking turned on. Which makes all the frustration feel even more acute.

"Oh, now you want to cum, don't you, you goddamn whore," Jackson taunts and for the fucking life of me, even though I know he's talking to Daniel, it seems like he's aiming the barb at me.

That's it.

I'm fucking done with being a spectator.

I walk over to the props table, find exactly what I'm looking for and grab it. I'm about to talk back to Daniel and Jackson when I pause, go back to the table, grab another item, then return to the boys.

Jackson's eyes track me as I approach but I ignore him. I continue ignoring him as I unzip the top of my suit, pull my arms out, then continue unzipping it. Turns out it's a lot easier to take off than put on.

And yeah, okay, I will admit it is satisfying as hell when Jackson's steady flogging pauses and I hear him audibly suck in a breath. I still don't look in his direction. My large breasts are on display but I'm barely aware of it, I'm so focused.

I don't take the suit all the way off. I merely unzip it and push it over my hips so that my ass and pussy are exposed. I suck in a sharp breath as my warm and wet nether lips are freed to the cool air.

I'm so swollen down there and I can't help rubbing my forefinger several times over my clit. I do this with my eyes to Jackson. I'm not disappointed. His eyes are glued to my hand as I massage myself.

I smile. Good. I'm back in control of this show.

Now. I look down at the two-way dildo in my hand and the complicated elastic bands. How the hell do I put this thing on?

"May I assist Mistress?" Jackson's voice sounds funny. Tight and a little high-pitched. He hasn't taken any steps toward me and his posture is very stiff. One glance down and I see his back isn't the only thing that's stiff. I smirk.

Then I'm startled at myself. Because Jackson's not chained up and we're not in public. And I'm not freaked out at being basically alone in this room with him.

I'm comfortable with him. I'm not afraid. And God it feels *so* good not to be afraid.

I nod to Jackson. "Yes." My own voice sounds a little funny.

But I don't tense up as he comes closer. He's quite the gentleman. His eyes don't drop to my breasts like I anticipate they will. Instead, he takes the large black dildo from my hands and I feel a zing at the slight contact of his fingers.

"Put your hands up." He swallows after he says it. Maybe I'm not the only one who wishes they'd brought a water bottle.

My chest heaves up and down even faster as I do as he asks. I lift my arms up and he pulls on one of the dildo's elastic bands. It stretches wide and he lifts it up and over my head. He slides it down over my raised arms, then to my shoulders, then…

"I've got it," I say, taking over when the band gets to my underarms. He steps back as I roll it over my breasts, down my waist and then just below my hips.

Now one end of the two-pronged dildo teases at my entrance and I shudder, rolling my shoulders at the feel of it. I flick my eyes up to Jackson's as I widen my stance slightly. The tip of the fake cock slips inside me.

I stick the tip of my tongue out between my lips and bite down as I grasp the head of the outer dildo and use it to guide the inner one further inside myself.

Oh God, so full, so fucking good.

"Ooohhhhhhh," I moan and arch my breasts out toward Jackson. "It's going so deep."

He takes a step toward me but I shake my head. Then I snap my fingers at him and point to a chair by the wall. "You sit there and watch."

He drops his chin and glares at me, more than a glint of defiance in his eyes. He's a Dom. He's never on the receiving end of orders.

Too damn bad. I stiffen my spine and glare daggers right back at him. I don't care what his normal role is. He. Better. Fucking. Submit.

"Now," I thunder.

He stares at me for only a moment longer before turning and walking to the chair that I pointed to.

I gift him with a beatific smile once he's seated. "Very good. Now take out your beautiful cock and fuck your hand while I fuck him with this giant dildo."

The room isn't very large. Jackson's only sitting about eight feet from me so I can see his nostrils flare.

My blood sings. My pussy clenches around the rubber cock inside me and the outer dildo rubs up against my clit even as I walk the few steps toward Daniel. My steps are constricted because I only slipped the suit off down to the tops of my thighs, but it's plenty to work with.

I pinch Daniel's ass where the marks are the reddest and get a genuine flinch out of him. It makes me ridiculously gleeful.

Fuck. Does it really only take one night for me to become a sadist? I caress the part where I just pinched and then nuzzle my cheek against Daniel's back. I feel a sudden rush of affection for him. He really is doing me a solid favor by letting me use him as my training wheels.

"I've got a treat for you, you dirty fucking pain slut. I'm going to fuck you with this giant strap on, right here. Right in the ass."

I grab his ass cheeks in both my hands and squeeze. My thumbs are close to his asshole and the sudden rush of excitement makes my cunt clench even harder on the dildo inside me. I've never done anything like this before. Ever. I bite my tongue as my thumb inches lower.

There it is. That forbidden hole. It's not hairy at all like I might have expected and I wonder if he waxes it. My thumb probes at the puckered entrance. There's a little bit of resistance, like he's pushing back.

I pause for a moment, feeling a sudden stroke of horror. He said this was okay at the beginning

"Daniel, would you like to use your safe word at this point. Say continue or use your safe word to stop."

"Continue," comes out in a rush, very sure and confident.

My heartbeat slows and my thumb immediately goes back in his entrance. He's still resisting but I get it now. That's part of his thing. I take the lube, the second item I grabbed from the table and drip some over my thumbs. I rub it around the puckered bit of flesh and then lean over to get a better look.

Then I push my thumb in again and this time I start talking. "Don't even try to keep me out, you dumb little fuck. My thumb and a whole lot more are coming for this little bitch ass." I thrust my thumb all the way in and at the same time, my pussy squelches around the dildo buried inside me.

I don't even know how to describe what I feel with my thumb. He just sucks me right in. It's warm and snug but immediately I want more. I use my free hand and rub lube all over the giant dildo sticking out from my body. Then I pour more liberally over the top crack of Daniel's ass.

"That's right, cunt, there's no getting off this train. You're getting fucked by a woman and I'm not taking pity on you. Because you deserve to be punished, you sorry stupid worthless fuck-up. That's how you like it, isn't it?" I jam my other thumb inside him as I finish my tirade. His whole body jerks and he lets out a high-pitched moan of pleasure. His ass relaxes against my invasion and my thumbs are easily working inside his ass now.

It's so hot inside him. Holy shit. *Inside him*. I'm inside a man. I pull out my thumbs and shove two fingers up deep instead. They fit easily so I add a third, exploring the contours all the way around.

Daniel's breathing heavily now. He's *so* getting off on this. Holy shit. Holy *shit*. I twist my fingers around and around, loosening him up even further.

Then I remember that touch alone isn't enough for him. Vocalizations. Right.

"Look at you, you stupid, filthy shithead." I crow in laughter and it isn't forced, but I think that's only because of the crazy high I'm feeling right now. I rock forward and back a little on my heels so the dildo inside me gives me friction. Oh fuck *me*. That's so— I can't even—

"You dirty cock slut," I manage to get out between heaving breaths of my own. I start to twist my fingers in his ass more roughly. "You fucking love this, don't you? Being used. Like the fucking piece of trash you are. Well I'm going to use you good, you dirty little shit. I'm going to use you so hard you're going to wish you weren't such a fucking whore!" I smack his ass with as much strength as I have in me.

Then I grab his hips to brace myself and jam the dildo up his fucking bitch cunt ass. And I fucking ram it all the way home. No fucking mercy.

His whole body jolts forward and the chains above his head rattle. I don't stop there, though. No, I pull out and then slam back in again until my hips are flat against his ass and my breasts brush up against the reddened skin of his back.

And it feels good. I can't deny that. Great even. Everything about tonight has kicked sex up to a level I never knew it could go. But there's still something missing.

My head swings over to look at Jackson.

And I immediately groan in pleasure. He's leaned forward in his seat, pants dropped, cock in hand. He's not pumping furiously like I might have expected. No, he has himself in what looks like a painful iron grip as he slowly drags up and down on his shaft. I can't make out the expression on his face. It looks like a mix of fury, concentration, and being more turned on than I've ever fucking seen him.

"Ughhhh," I groan in pleasure as I pause, jammed to the hilt inside Daniel for a long moment, making slight rolling motions with my hips for friction. All the while staring at Jackson.

Fuuuuuuuuuuuck me. The dildo is. At. That. Perfect. Spot. Without moving my torso, I tilt my hips back so that the dildo slides out of Daniel slightly. Then I jerk up and in again. And again, the motion rubs the dildo against my clit so good and makes the length inside me hit another spot that brings light near to bursting behind my eyes.

Oh shit, I can't be that close already, can I? Oh God oh God *oh God*.

I keep Jackson's eyes in laser focus as I reach around Daniel's chest and pinch one of his nipples. Daniel shudders beneath me and I pull my hips back so I can keep fucking him hard.

But it's Jackson's response rather than Daniel's that ratchets everything up to an even greater intensity. The anger seems to evaporate from Jackson's face the longer I keep my eyes focused on him.

He stands up, hand ever on his cock and he starts jacking off like he's proud of it. Like he's saying, *here's the most glorious goddammed cock you've ever seen in your life. Bow down and worship, then spontaneously orgasm at the sight.*

My back arches, forcing my breasts into Daniel's back as I continue thrusting in his ass. Fucking him. For the first time in my life, I'm the one doing the fucking. It's the most erotic goddammed thing I've ever done.

I watch Jackson the entire time.

"Fucking bastard. You mother fucking bitch-faced cunt sucker," I all but shout.

Jackson only raises an eyebrow and his tongue comes out. He moves it in sensuous imitation of the act I just mentioned. Like he's sucking my cunt.

I start fucking Daniel with an animal fervor. Both of us grunt every time I land, the double headed dildo jamming deep inside both of us and—

"Shitting fucking mother cunt fuck of a whore—" I yell and then there's nothing left except a wordless high-pitched moan that comes from deep inside my throat as I hit a climax so high, *so hard*, that I feel like my heart is about to explode in my chest.

But I don't stop there either. I give myself two seconds to breathe and then I keep going, jerking in and out until I get to a second peak that tops out just a little bit higher than the first.

When it finally comes down, I collapse against Daniel's back, head facing Jackson. Jackson's still standing, cum dripping down over his huge hand.

His eyes are wide and his mouth open. He's looking at me like... like... I don't even fucking know. Any and all brashness is gone.

His expression is a mixture of vulnerability, awe, and confusion—mouth slack, eyebrows drawn together, chest heaving up and down. I feel just as jumbled up. That was just so— God, it was so—

I drop my face so that my forehead is braced on Daniel's back while I continue trying to catch my breath.

Which is when I remember Daniel. You know, the guy whose ass I've still got a dildo jammed up inside. Shit.

"Did you come, sub?"

"No, Mistress."

My shoulders drop.

He seems to sense it because he quickly follows up, "Mistress did not say that I could."

Well, damn. Mistress faux pas. Then I look at the brick wall. It's not exactly friendly for him to rub up against. Maybe I'm expected to jack him off?

But no, that's *not* happening. Somehow, and I know this is totally screwed up, but even though I just fucked this guy in front of Jackson, touching Daniel's dick feels like it would be... a betrayal. Because *that* totally makes sense. I shake my head at myself but figure out a quick solution.

We're close enough that I can wrap the top of my catsuit around Daniel's body. Ha, I can even manage to get one of the arm-sleeves over his cock. Even though his staff is starting to flag. Ah. The work of a Domme is never done.

I'm exhausted and all I want to do is go pull off the bottom half of this catsuit, get off these heels, drink a glass of wine, go to sleep, and process all the shit that just went on at a much later date. Like tomorrow. Or next year.

Instead, I drop my voice and infuse it with disgust. "Rub that pathetic tiny dick against the wall, you sad little shit. I've never before in my life had such a disappointing lover." I wince internally at the cruel words. Even though I felt a much more intense connection to Jackson instead of Daniel throughout the scene, this has hands down been some of the best sex of my life.

But from the way Daniel has started grinding against the wall, his cock safely covered by my suit, my words are obviously doing it for him.

All right, whatever floats his boat. I continue calling slurs and insults at him and even moving the dildo in and out of his ass a few times before ordering him to come.

Which he does on command. Neat trick.

I slide the dildo out of his ass and can only stand there looking down at it for a moment. The top of my catsuit is still wrapped around the front of him, and everything seems to hit me in a rush. Everything that just happened over the past hour. Or has it been longer since we walked into the club? It feels like *way* longer. And also like it's been *no* time at all. The half of the dildo still inside me feels suddenly huge.

I put a hand to my forehead and squeeze my eyes shut. Shit. I swallow and the fact that I haven't had any liquid in so long seems like a big deal now. I'm so thirsty. Like, really really thirsty.

"Water," I say to no one in particular.

"What?"

I look up in surprise to see that Jackson is right beside me. He's retrieved the top of my suit off of Daniel and knotted the 'spent' arm in on itself. That's a good idea. I should've thought of that. It would've been messy otherwise.

I blink at the top half of the catsuit when Jackson lets go of it and it flops down in front of me. My breasts are completely exposed, but again Jackson isn't staring.

Instead he moves with a practiced efficiency. He does something in the corner, pushes a button or engages something, because the chains holding Daniel's arms begin to lower. Jackson goes immediately back to Daniel's side.

As his arms are lowered, Jackson moves behind Daniel, catching him underneath his armpits when he's no longer being held up by the chains. Daniel staggers backward and Jackson helps him to the ground, then he props him up against the wall. Jackson murmurs to him gently while he undoes the padded cuffs around his wrists.

Jackson's so gentle with him. It seems incongruous with the insults he was shouting at him twenty minutes ago. Then I remember how the men earlier treated the woman suspended from chains, roughly fucking her one moment and then taking care of her the next.

I should be over there, helping him with Daniel. This is probably an important part of what it means to be a Domme. What happens after. The things you're supposed to do to make sure your submissive is okay.

My feet carry me a step back instead. I swallow. So thirsty. I'm just so thirsty. I look over to the table. Why didn't Jackson bring water bottles along with his bag of tricks? If only I had some water.

But then I notice something else at the end of the table. Towels.

I glance back to where Jackson is still talking to Daniel. I really should—

I turn away without finishing the thought.

I head toward the towels, wrap one around myself and I open the door as quietly as I can. As I try to slip out without being noticed, Jackson's head pops up and a pair of dark blue eyes meet mine right before the door closes behind me.

Jackson finds me waiting for him in the room where we first changed clothes. I'm back in my work clothes. I don't meet his gaze when he comes in. Tonight was amazing, beyond what I ever could have... just... beyond. That's a good word for tonight. Fucking *beyond*.

That doesn't mean I have any clue about what this is now between Jackson and me. Or how to even describe or... wrap my head around those moments back there when we... I pretended to rub at an invisible scuff on my sensible work flats. No more stiletto thigh highs for me. Which also leaves me feeling oddly bereft.

"Ready to go?" I expect Jackson's voice to be disapproving for how I acted at the end. Disappearing instead of helping him with Daniel.

Instead, his tone is warm. Startled, I meet his eyes. The normally dark icy blues are lighter. His whole expression is soft. He already has his shoes and socks on and is buttoning his shirt. He hasn't bothered changing out of his leathers and the contrast with his work attire is incredibly alluring.

"Callie?" he questions again. "You ready?"

I nod. Shit. I'm totally out of it, aren't I? "Is there somewhere I can get some water?" There's a gravelly quality to my voice and I'm not sure it's just because I'm so thirsty.

His eyebrows go up. "Of course. I'm sorry, I should have brought some bottles along." He shakes his head as if disappointed in himself. "Wait here and I'll go grab a couple before we go."

I nod again and he's out the door. Half a minute later the door opens again. Wow, that was fast. But to my surprise, it's not Jackson's dark head that pops around the door.

It's Daniel's. He just sticks his head in at first, a boyish grin on his face. "Mind if I step in for a moment?"

Uh. Holy shit. He looks so... normal. "Of course." I wave him in.

He slips inside and I don't know what I'm expecting, but the concert tee, skinny jeans and converse all-stars aren't it. No leather or dog collars in sight. He must think the same thing because he smiles and says, "Wow, you look very professional. Bet you're some corporate big-shot like Jackson."

"Not hardly," I laugh as I glance down at myself. It's funny hearing Jackson described like that, actually. I guess that yes, he is the CEO of a huge company, but I never think of him as very corporate. His mind is too creative for the label. He's an inventor first and foremost.

"Anyway," Daniel says, charming smile back in full effect. "I'm glad I could catch you alone. I wanted to give you my contact information in case you ever want to play one-on-one."

He pulls a card out of his pocket. I look down and run my finger over the cardstock. Daniel Parsons. According to the card he's a sculptor. I flip it over and see that he's written his number on the back.

I look back up at him. He's so relaxed and casual. Like thirty minutes ago he wasn't chained to a brick wall and I didn't have a dildo shoved in his ass while I screamed obscenities at him.

I have to shake my head a little at the incongruity of the image compared with the completely normal-looking dude standing in front of me. Already it feels like what went down was too surreal, that it could have only happened in a dream, not the real world.

"So give me a call sometime?" Daniel asks.

I look from the card back up to him. "I don't really know what I'm doing." I gesture around us. "You got that tonight was my first night, right?"

Daniel's smile softens. Then he reaches over and his hands close over my fingers holding the card. "How do you think Doms and Dommes start off? It's just a myth that they all have some wonderful mentor. Most of them have subs help them as they figure everything out. I'm happy to be your test subject any time."

Again with the charismatic smile. "I really enjoyed my time with you tonight and I think you have more potential than anyone I've seen in a long time to be a really powerful Domme." He dips his head down as if he's shy saying this last part.

Then he takes a step away and lifts his head. "Anyway." He shrugs and laughs a little. "Just remember, I'm here if you ever need me."

I nod and raise his card a little for emphasis before putting it in my pocket. "I'll keep that in mind." I mainly do it to make him feel good. I might not have done what I should have earlier in caring for him after the scene, but I'm not going to shut him down when he reaches out.

I doubt I'll ever call him. If Jackson wants to involve him in the future, I could be down with it. But one-on-one? God, I'm not ready for that. Plus, after tonight, the idea of getting together with Daniel without Jackson there... it makes my stomach twist up. Because it would feel like... again I just have that feeling of wrongness.

What the fuck? I don't owe Jackson anything. What the hell is wrong with me? He takes me out on one date... or *whatever* you'd call tonight, and I'm suddenly declaring we're exclusive or some shit? This doesn't make us boyfriend and girlfriend. Far, far from it.

Daniel waves and I manage a smile for him. He goes to open the door, but just as he does, the knob moves and Jackson pushes the door from the other side. The two men stare at each other in surprise for a second.

"I was just saying good night to Mistress," Daniel says, a slight tension entering his voice.

A crease appears between Jackson's eyebrows. His eyes ping-pong between me and Daniel before he nods. "All right. Good night, Daniel."

Daniel hurries out the door and Jackson holds out a water bottle to me. I grab the bottle and head out into the hallway. I have half the bottle drunk before we're outside. Oh blessed water. Drinking also effectively keeps me from having to talk to Jackson. Bonus. Unfortunately, that only works until the bottle is empty.

Jackson holds out the second bottle to me, but I shake my head. "I'm good," I say, gasping a little because I didn't breathe much while I downed the water.

A small smile of amusement curls the edges of his mouth. "Next time, just tell me that you're thirsty."

Next time.

I look at the cobbled stones in front of the building where we stand waiting for the valet to bring the car around. I was already thinking in terms of next time too, though, wasn't I? Just moments ago, with Daniel. I'd thought I wouldn't mind being with Daniel again only as long as Jackson arranged it and was present. Because I was wondering when we'd be doing this again.

Next time. Fuck, what does all this mean? Even as I question it, scenes from tonight flash on repeat. The absolute exhilaration in the moments where I took control of Daniel. Shoving the dildo up his ass and conquering him completely.

But not just Daniel. Jackson too. By the end, I captured his attention so completely, I'd mastered him as well.

The heady sense of exhilaration hits me all over again, even while standing on the sidewalk dressed in my completely sensible business attire.

Next time.

Yes, there will definitely be a next time.

CHAPTER EIGHT

CALLIE

My muscles burn and I seriously contemplate murder as I stare at the clock on the wall that slowly counts down to zero. Fifteen seconds to go.

"Don't start slacking now," shouts the CrossFit instructor. "Every second counts. You're only cheating yourself!"

"She means you," my sister Shannon adds oh so helpfully from beside me where she does another squat with a kettlebell.

I glare at her, groan, then jump onto the knee-high box again. I make it, thank God. My legs feel like jelly after the thirty-minute session. I look to the clock again. Nine. Eight.

"Get those last reps in. I see those of you trying to wait out the clock." The instructor's eyes zero in on me. I'm tired enough that her attempt at shaming only just barely works.

"Told you she meant you," Shannon says, straining to get out of the squat. "Mother of the deity, this damn thing weighs a thousand pounds."

"This is all your fault," I whisper back. "You were the one who wanted another way to wake up ever since your boyfriend got you off coffee." Damn Sunil, her Buddhist boyfriend.

I jump off the box. The instructor's still staring at me. Five seconds left on the clock. Her stare turns to a glare. Mother fucking bag of shit pissing—

I jump up on the box one last time and then the buzzer sounds announcing the end of the session.

Shannon drops the kettlebell and collapses on the floor. "Don't blame me," she huffs, gasping for breath. "I wanted—" she pants, "—the yoga class. CrossFit was your bright idea." She wipes the sweat off her brow with her forearm.

I sit my ass down on the box and dangle my feet as I catch my breath. Mother fucking CrossFit. I push some sweaty hair that's fallen out of my ponytail behind my ear.

"The whole point was to wake you up. Yoga's shit. It would put you to sleep." I take a swig of the water bottle I brought with me. "Besides, this is whipping our asses into amazing shape just like Lydia said it would."

She just makes a face at me. "You suck."

I grin. "What are sisters for? Come on, get your ass up, lazy. Unlike some people, I have to show up at an office on time."

Shannon flips me off and I laugh, then stand and hold my hands down to help her off the ground.

She takes them and I hike her up till she's standing beside me. "Ugh, get off of me, you're all sweaty." She lets go of my hands and pushes me away.

Which only makes me try to hug her.

"You are so gross," she squeals and holds out both hands to keep me at arm's length.

I relent, but only because I'm fucking exhausted. In spite of what I said to Shannon, I agree with her about CrossFit. There are some things that are just wrong to put your body through at six-thirty on a Thursday morning. Especially since I've barely been able to sleep since Monday, tossing and turning in my sheets all night.

I can't stop thinking about it. Constantly running through every second of what happened with Jackson and Daniel. *Jackson.* God. I haven't run into him at work at all. When he dropped me off on Monday, he said the next move was mine to make.

He's respected my boundaries since. Which alternately makes me grateful and irrationally pisses me off. The last thing I need right now is Jackson chasing me, but Monday was... just wow. Off the charts intense. I obviously can't stop thinking about it. Was it not that way for Jackson? How the hell has he not even *tried* to contact me, boundaries or not?

I lean my head back and blow out an exhausted breath. Yeah. Way too early in the morning for this shit. Not that I'd ever let my sister know I regret signing us up for the class.

"Great job, class," says the instructor, flashing a bright, toothy smile. "I'm so looking forward to working with you all next week while Indira is out visiting family."

"Make her stop," whispers my sister. "I can't handle that much pep before seven a.m." She pauses as if thinking, then adds, "Or ever, really. Did you hear how she introduced herself as Brittani with an 'i'? Like when we're cursing her in our heads for torturing us, is it really that big a deal that we're internally misspelling her name?"

I don't do a good job of stifling my bark of laughter as I stumble on my jelly legs for the door. For having such a Zen boyfriend, Shannon's kind of a pessimistic bitch. Which of course makes me love her.

We've never been as close in our whole lives as we have been the past couple months. Well, maybe when we were really, really young. But we were little more than strangers for most of my adolescence and all of my adulthood. Even when she lived with me and was helping raise my son.

Then we reached our make or break moment when I lost Charlie. To be honest, I thought for sure it would break us. Instead, Shannon's stuck with me. We've talked more in the past few months than in the whole decade before. We don't talk about a lot of deep shit, but we talk. We're... sisterly.

She tells me about her boyfriend, her first really serious relationship. I tell her about my new friends at work and my job. She tries not to judge me so harshly and to let up on telling me what to do. I keep half of what's going on in my life—aka, my sex life—secret so she doesn't have shit to lecture me on. I'd say overall she and I are a work in progress.

"Don't forget to stretch," Brittani with an 'i' calls out to the class. Shannon and I ignore her. I might stretch a little bit if I have time. Shannon works from home with her graphic design business, but I've got to get my ass to work.

"If you don't stretch, lactic acid can build up in the muscles and—"

The door shutting behind me cuts off Brittani's perky voice. My legs feel shaky.

"Shit," I say, putting a hand on the wall for balance. "Would it make me a pussy to hold onto the wall all the way to the locker room?"

Shannon looks over at me and glowers. "No, it wouldn't, because that would indicate weakness and *pussies*—a word I don't like at all by the way—are incredibly strong. They push human beings into the world."

I pause and stand up straighter. "Day-um. I'd high-five you if I could lift my arm. You're just full of hidden depths." Then I realize what I just said and start laughing, cracking myself up. "Hidden depths," I manage through a wheezing laugh. "Pussies—they're full of hidden depths. Get it?"

She rolls her eyes and puts a hand on her temple. "You are so juvenile. Are you ever going to grow up?"

I grin at her as I stumble along. "Not if I can help it. Hey look, we made it to the locker room."

She pushes through the locker room door, still shaking her head at me.

"Callie!"

I look up when I hear my voice called and see Lydia coming around the corner of the lockers just ahead of me.

"Oh thank God, Lyd, help me to one of the benches before I collapse!"

She shakes her head at me and looks to Shannon. "I take it you did CrossFit this morning?"

"I told her we should have done yoga," Shannon quips.

My legs give out as soon as I make it to the bench that runs along one wall of the locker room.

"It's your fault," I accuse Lydia. "You said we should take it."

Lydia holds up her hands in a show of innocence. "I said that because Indira's usually the teacher. I don't know anything about this new chick."

"She's the devil." Shannon only barely lowers her voice to relay this bit of information.

"I thought you were Miss Peace and Sunshine now?" I look at Shannon with an eyebrow raised. "We're all connected by universal energy that we can tap into through meditation, blah, blah, blah."

She shrugs. "My worldview doesn't have to include evil CrossFit taskmasters. I can leave her in the Judeo-Christian realm. Therefore, hell and devils. Of which she definitely is one."

I can only stare at her for a second, then I burst out laughing. "You are such a piece of work."

She gives a mocking smile. "All right, I'm off. I've got the meeting with Keller today. See you later."

She gives Lydia a little wave, then she heads off to grab her bag from her locker. She's never one for drawn-out goodbyes or chatting just for the sake of catching up. Since she works from home, she just showers from there.

Lydia sits down beside me and I drop my head onto her shoulder. "Why can't you just teach all the classes? Then you could give me special treatment and everything would be perfect."

Lydia laughs again and pats my knee. "Oh, poor spoiled baby. I'm sorry, are you actually being forced to get in shape? Besides, look at these guns."

She pulls back and grabs one of my arms. I put up no resistance and it's completely floppy under her grasp. She holds it up in a muscle-man pose. Then she narrows her eyebrows at me.

"It doesn't work if you don't flex, bitch."

I make a whiny noise but she just slaps at my bicep without a care. I groan but do as she asks. I flex and she feels around the muscle definition. She makes an impressed noise.

"See? A little torture goes a long way."

I pull my arm back out of her grasp and sprawl more on the bench, doing a total man-spread thing. The bench is plenty long and there's not enough people here for me to be in anyone's way so I'm not being a dick about it. I just don't want to hold any part of my body up.

"Oh my gosh, I have never met anybody more dramatic in my life. Don't you have to get to work?"

I close my eyes and groan. "Don't remind me."

Lydia smacks me in the stomach and stands up.

"Oww," I whine even though it didn't hurt. It's just how Lydia and I are. I sit up straighter as she turns to go. "Wait, I haven't gotten any updates on you and Red since last weekend. What's going on with that?"

Color rises to Lydia's cheeks and if my muscles didn't feel like pudding, I would've jumped to my feet and demanded answers. I wave a hand instead. "Just imagine me jumping up and down and doing the whole girly squeal thing. Now spill."

Lydia's hands start to fidget and she tips back on her heels a little.

"Not much to tell," she hedges. "We've just been texting a lot all week. We may have gotten together last night for a coffee that turned into dinner that turned into late-night drinks at her place..." She trails off and averts her eyes. "That turned into breakfast this morning."

"Oh my God!" I drag my tired ass to my feet and hug her. When I pull away, she's smiling even though she still looks embarrassed as hell. "So it's good?" I search her eyes. "You guys were, you know," I cajole, "compatible?"

"God," she pushes me back. "Don't ask me things like that!"

It's my turn to laugh. "I forget how much of a prude you are."

She narrows her eyes at me. "I'm not a prude about doing the things in the moment. Just, you know," she waves a hand, "I don't want to go through a play-by-play afterward." She raises her chin. "I don't kiss and tell."

I bust out laughing at that. She glares.

"I thought you were too tired to stand up?"

I groan. "Don't remind me." I let out a dramatic sigh. "Unfortunately, I do have to drag this tired ass to work now. What's your excuse? Why the hell are you here so early? Especially if you got to wake up in Red's bed?"

Lydia glances down at her watch. She's quaint like that. She still wears an actual honest-to-goodness watch instead of just her phone like the rest of us. She uses it for other things like keeping track of her heartbeat and timing distance when she jogs and things, but still.

"I'm teaching a spin class in ten minutes. Speaking of, I better go and get ready."

"They all abandon me!" I make an exaggerated smooching noise as I kiss my palm and then pat her cheek roughly with it. "All right, hon. See ya later."

She squirms away from me and makes a face. Now that I think about it, she and Shannon are a lot alike. They've only spent a little bit of time together, but I should fix that soon. I should call for another girls' night. You know... erm, one that's actually about the girls instead of hooking up.

"Remind me again why I'm friends with such a freak?" Lydia asks.

My grin only widens. "You know you love me!" I call after her as she heads for the locker room door.

"Yeah, yeah. Text you later," she calls over her shoulder as she goes.

As soon as she's gone, I start feeling the workout all over again. I think it was those box-jumps that really killed me. Ugh, I need a nap, but instead I have to go to work. No fair.

A quick shower helps loosen up my muscles, but I only feel more like laying down once I'm done. I drag my sorry ass to my locker, turn the combo lock and pull out my gym bag. The locker room is plenty active even though it's so early. Lots of other people have the same idea as me—get in a workout before they start their days. I strip down without feeling too self-conscious since there are half-naked women all around me.

My work clothes hang crisply from the bar at the top of my locker. I quickly dress in the modest blouse and loose skirt that hits below my knees. No more sex kitten tight pencil skirts for me.

I'm just putting up my sweaty gym clothes in the breathable laundry pouch on the side of my bag when I hear the telltale alert tone from my phone that means I just got a text message.

I grab my purse and scramble around inside for my phone. At last my fingers grab onto the small, smooth flat surface and I pull it out. I touch the screen to wake it up and am surprised to see that I have two unread texts.

Usually the only one who texts me is Lydia and obviously, I just saw her heading to class. What if Jackson's self-discipline has finally broken down and the texts are from him?

I click a little too eagerly on the text icon only to see the most recent is from Bonnie asking if I can pick her up some coffee on my way in this morning. She knows I like to treat myself to a mocha from the coffee shop on the corner on days I go to the gym before heading into work.

Stupid, *stupid* to think Jackson would text and get all excited about it. What the hell is wrong with me that I'm obsessing so much about a boy? I try to shake it off.

My thumbs go to my phone.

ME TO BONNIE: Sad u know my workout schedule just b/c it means good coffee for u.

BONNIE: is that a yes? *insert praying hands*

I roll my eyes, but I'm smiling.

ME TO BONNIE: Of course. I'm a sucker for a damsel in distress.

BONNIE: :)

I shake my head again as I look to the first text that initially came in before hers. I ignore the second stab of disappointment when I see it's from an unknown number, not Jackson. It has a video attachment. What the hell? It must be a wrong number. Or some kind of spam.

But in the little window I see the start of the message.

UNKNOWN: We need to meet, Calliope.

My eyebrows furrow. Well, clicking just on the message itself without opening the attachment shouldn't introduce any viruses to my phone. It seems like it *could* be from someone I know—though certainly plenty of phishing scams can find people's first names, so that doesn't always mean anything. I won't click the attachment if it's spam after all. I touch the screen to open the message.

And then almost drop the phone.

UNKNOWN: We need to meet. You pick the time & location. Else this video goes viral. – G

The first frame of the video shows beneath the message. It's of me on my knees in the Gentry Tech conference room table. Conference Room B. My shirt is open and pulled down to my waist. Men are seated all around the table watching the show.

Me, on display.

My hands shake and my knees buckle. I sink to the ground in front of my locker. G. *Gentry*. My former boss and the organizer of and participant in my gang rape. He sent this.

Blindly, I reach for my purse. My hand goes inside and I dig around. I'm hardly breathing as I drag out my headphones. My hands tremble so hard I can barely get the cord in the small jack at the top of my phone.

It takes about four tries before it finally goes in. I bring one of the earbuds up to my ears and jab numbly at the play button with my other hand.

"Tell us, whore, how much you want it." Gentry's voice. Only the bottom half of him is in the video's range of vision.

But me. All of me. There. Completely exposed. The worst day of my life.

On screen, Gentry's hand reaches around and grabs my ass.

But it's the words that next come out that have me covering my face in horror.

"I want it," says the girl on-screen even as she ducks her head in shame.

"What was that?" Gentry asks.

She repeats it louder, "I want it."

No. No no no no no no no no no no—

"And what do you want, whore?"

I squeeze my eyes shut.

"Are you hungry for my cock?"

"Yes."

NO!

"Ah ah ah," he chides, waving a finger in the air. "I want to hear you say it. Are you hungry for my cock?"

There's a long silence and I want to beg the girl in the video to get off that damn table and run for the door. Run. *Run!* Maybe she wouldn't have made it, but at least she would have fucking tried.

Instead, she replies in a stilted, monotone voice. "I'm hungry for your cock."

The video cuts and disgusting manly grunts and the slapping of flesh fills my earbuds. Of course Gentry edited out the part where I said no, where I said stop.

I yank it away from my ear and then run for the toilets. I barely make it there in time before emptying the contents of my stomach. Just when I think I'm done, I'm reliving it again in my memories. All of them violating me. One after another, barely waiting for the last to finish before the next one grabs me.

I throw up again even though there's nothing left in my stomach except acid. It burns its way up my throat. My eyes and nose run. I flush the toilet and then slump back against the stall when I'm finished.

I grab some toilet paper and wipe at my mouth and nose.

My phone vibrates in my hand and I jolt at the feel of it. I drop the vile thing to the ground. I'm shocked I didn't drop it back by my locker. I— I can't—

My mind blanks for a long minute.

Just…

Nothing.

"You okay in there?"

I blink hard and look up at a middle-aged woman peeking in the stall. It's not like I locked the door behind me. I was just aiming for the toilet.

My whole body is still shaking and I look down at myself. Thankfully there's no vomit on me. I had good aim at least. But I'm hiding hunched in on myself on the floor of the bathroom stall in the women's locker room.

"Are you sick?" the kindly woman asks. She's lean and looks to be in her mid-40s with short cropped brown hair that's going gray. She looks down to the phone near my hand. "Is there someone I can call to help you home?"

My hand shoots to the phone and I grab it before she can touch it. I click the button for the *home* screen without looking at it. "No," I bark out too sharply. "I'm fine."

She looks a little taken aback, but her eyes are still soft. She reaches a hand down to help me up. Right. She's just trying to help. I take her hand and attempt a smile. It probably comes out like a grimace.

She walks with me back to my locker. I continue trying to assure her that I'm fine and in a strange way, it helps. Putting on a facade for her helps me pull myself back together. Enough so that when I finally convince her I'm okay, I have the strength to look at the new message that came through on my phone.

God, please just let it be from Bonnie asking for something other than her normal caramel macchiato.

It's not from Bonnie.

It's another message from my rapist.

GENTRY: Who is going to give custody of a child back to a woman who begs for cock and then fucks a room full of men? Message me back to meet or this goes viral.

My legs threaten to give out all over again.

Fucking bastard. He already stole my soul. Now he thinks he can take everything else? What the fuck does he even want from me?

I want to ignore the message. I swore that man would never have any power over me *ever* again.

But he has this video. Goddamn him. I think about what my sister said about hell and devils earlier. She has no idea. I've met the devil in person and his name is Bryce Gentry.

There's no other choice.

Then I shake my head. No. I've fallen into Gentry's traps by that logic too many times in the past. How many stupid decisions did I make because I convinced myself there was no other choice? I won't do it again. I refuse. I fucking *refuse*.

At the same time, I need to know what it is my enemy wants. It won't do to be blind where he's concerned. And so, although it makes me want to go throw up again, I text Gentry back.

Three hours later, I have on the outfit that's the closest thing I own to armor—a black turtleneck, some camo skinny jeans and my steel toed boots—and I go to meet my rapist. I called in sick to work earlier. Which in all fairness wasn't even a lie.

I went straight home after the gym and threw up again. Luckily, today was one of the rare occasions Shannon had a face-to-face meeting with a client who was in town. I have no idea how I would have answered her questions about why I looked so shell-shocked and pale.

Since getting the message, I've been trying to physically and mentally prep myself for this meeting. It had to be today. I couldn't handle putting it off and being tortured knowing it was coming. I'm a rip-off-the-Band-Aid kind of girl.

So I armored up and here I am, walking into a busy open plaza at noon on a Thursday. Oh and of course I accessorized. There's a knife strapped on the inside of my boot. This little lady rarely leaves home without one.

In addition to the self-defense classes I've taken with Lydia, I signed up for a knife training course that a hiking and survivalist group was offering. It didn't take much batting of my eyelashes to get the instructor to show me how to defend myself with the knife along with the survivalist stuff—I played the little woman all alone in the big city card.

As I walk through the plaza and take a seat by the central fountain, I assure myself I'm safe. Perfectly safe. Even if I didn't have the double-bladed knife in my boot, there are tons of people milling around. Gentry can't do anything to me here. All I have to do is scream.

My vocal cords almost vibrate in memory of all the times I've shouted *NO!* in Lydia's self-defense classes. I might have officially graduated, but I still stop by from time to time to help out and brush up on my own skills.

I'm ready for this. I can see the fuckhead face-to-face without pissing myself. Today is nothing like that June afternoon. Hell, *I'm* nothing like that pathetic woman I glimpsed on the video this morning.

And Bryce Gentry can roast in hell if he thinks he's going to somehow control me with it.

But then, unbidden, I hear their grunts in my mind. I remember the bruising grip of Gentry holding me down. I remember how painful it was each time another man—

"Miss Cruise, how delightful to see you again."

That voice. My eyes snap up and there the bastard is. That charming, easy-going grin. He's wearing his expensive gray suit, the one with the slight silvery sheen to it.

He sits down beside me. Too close. I can smell his cologne. Too heavy. Too much.

Oh God, the smell. It takes me back there. I'm back there, choking. Choking on what he's shoving in my mouth. I said no. I said red. I said stop.

But he shoved himself in my mouth and the other man, he—

I can't breathe. I can't—

"Miss Cruise, is something wrong?" Gentry sounds so genuinely concerned. How can he do that? He's a monster but he hides it so well. It's terrifying. That he can just walk among the rest of us and it's impossible to see before it's too late.

I scoot away from him on the bench to put as much distance between us as possible. I'm probably not doing a good job of hiding the horror on my face. I wouldn't give a shit, except I imagine he's enjoying it.

"You're a sociopath," I finally whisper.

He tilts his head to one side as if contemplating my statement. "I don't know about that. I just have certain..." He strums his fingers on his knees, "appetites. And particular goals. Which you are going to help me obtain."

I'm already shaking my head no. "You can go fuck yourself."

His hand slips out and grabs my forearm. "I'd be careful what came out of that mouth if I were you." His voice is cold. He's dropped the Mr. Congeniality act. "Or did you forget I hold your son's future in my hands. I can ruin you with the click of a button."

I jerk my arm out of his grasp even though it takes so much force I know it's going to leave a bruise. "And what exactly do you think I'm going to do for you?" I need to get this information and then get the fuck out of here.

"You're going to get me the navigation algorithms to Jackson Vale's newest drone prototype."

For a second I'm speechless. As in, I genuinely can't come up with any words. Soon enough though, I find my voice again. "You want me to commit corporate espionage for you?" I choke out. "No way." I move to stand.

"I'm hungry for your cock."

I looked down in fury to see he's got his phone out and has pushed play on the despicable video. I smack it out of his hands and the phone clatters to the ground.

Gentry laughs. "Oh I've got plenty more copies where that came from."

"Wait a minute," I cut him off. Fury is warring with rationality right now, but I can still manage a bit of coherent thought. "Why is it so important to get Jackson's drone anyway? You've already got your own under contract with the DoD. Unless…" I look back up at the man I despise and put two and two together. "Oh my God. Do you not have a working prototype?"

The vein in Gentry's forehead jumps and I know I've guessed right.

"But how…?" I'm speechless for a moment, my brain spinning a mile a minute. "The DoD doesn't just give out defense contracts without a demonstrated working model." I feel my eyes open even wider. "Unless you blackmailed or bribed someone there just like you're doing here."

Another vein jump. He did. Holy shit, *he did*. He has a who-knows-how-many-million-dollar deal on the line with the federal government and no product to show for it. Did he initially think he could develop it in time or did he plan on stealing it all along?

"Holy shit," I whisper, sitting back.

Gentry's ice-cold eyes fall on me. "Like I said, I hit send and that video goes viral. With copies specifically emailed directly to your ex, his lawyer, and the judge presiding over your case. Do you really think the judge is going to give precious Charlie to a mommy who participates so enthusiastically in gang bangs? After watching that, it's not a stretch to argue you were involved in prostitution and—" .

I punch him.

It's not nearly as satisfying as I would've liked, but it does feel good. I used good form like Lydia taught me when making my fist so I'm only wincing a little as I shake out my hand. Gentry cries out like a little girl and grabs at his nose, bending over on the bench.

When he pulls his hand away, it's covered in blood. "You broke my nose, you cunt!"

He moves like he's going to grab for me but I'm up and off the bench, ready to scream my head off.

The next second, a loud chuckle comes from Gentry. He's gotten control of himself and settled his civilized mask firmly back in place. The brief glimpse of the real Gentry is buried once again.

He stands up but keeps his distance from me. "I hope you enjoyed that, Calliope. It's the last hit you'll ever get because I own you now."

He waves the cell phone he picked up off the ground in my face. The disgusting video is still playing. I wince and avert my eyes from the screen. Gentry's shark grin widens, white teeth bright in the sun.

"I'll expect regular reports at this phone number. You have two and a half weeks to deliver." He holds a card up right underneath my nose. I jerk back from it and he laughs before tossing it at my feet.

"Two and a half weeks, Miss Cruise, or you lose your son forever."

With that, he turns and walks away.

I go home.

I shower.

I scrub.

I scrub some more.

"Hey," Shannon bangs on the bathroom door. "Stop wasting all the hot water. You've been in there forever."

It's not until I look down and see how red my forearm is from repeatedly brushing the loofa back and forth that I realize just how long I've been showering for.

"Shit!" I throw the loofa against the far wall of the shower like it's toxic.

"What?" Shannon asks.

I grit my teeth, then manage to call back in what I hope is a normal-ish tone, "Nothing. I'll be out in a minute."

"'Kay, well hurry. I made lasagna and it's getting cold."

"Yeah."

I listen and finally there's just silence, which I hope to God means she's left me alone. I lean back and bang my head against the shower wall as the spray of water hits my body. I haven't been reduced to this in so long. Yet with one afternoon, one conversation with *him*, here I am again. Feeling as filthy and disgusting as right after it first happened.

"No." I shake my head back and forth, water droplets flying from my hair. "I'm stronger than this." My tiny voice barely makes a sound in the spray of water.

"I'm stronger than this!" I hiss and slap the wall tile for emphasis.

I reach behind me and shut off the water, then fling back the curtain. The bathroom mirror is completely steamed up and now that I'm stopping to think clearly, I realize how hot it is in here. I can barely breathe.

I wrap the towel around myself and shove open the door that leads to my bedroom, letting in some needed cool air. I grab my clothes from the floor, hating even to touch what I wore in his presence. I shove them in the hamper and close the lid tight. I try to walk away, but feel a nervous tic in my jaw.

It's like I can still feel him *on* the clothes. He was sitting so close beside me on the bench. I swear the odor of his cologne seeped into the cloth and I can smell it even with the hamper lid closed. Which is ludicrous. I'm just making shit up now. Laundry day is on Sunday. That's in two days. It'll be fine just sitting there until then.

I turn away but then pause. Because I know myself. Dealing with the clothes on Sunday would just mess up my head all over again.

I open the hamper and grab my shirt and pants, holding them with the furthest tips of my fingers. As I head toward the washer and dryer at the back of the apartment, I hear his voice in my head.

I own you now.
Two and a half weeks to deliver.

My hands shake and I overfill the laundry detergent cap. "Shit." I pour it on top of the clothes and then slam the lid shut.

Or lose your son forever.

I jam the gooey lid back on the detergent container, shove it on the shelf over the washer, and press the button for wash.

"What are you doing?" Shannon stands in the door to the tiny laundry room looking confused. "Sunday is laundry day."

I avoid her eyes as I squeeze past her through the door. "It had a stain. I didn't want it to set." I make a beeline for the bedroom but she follows.

"Those weren't your work clothes you came home in."

"So?" I keep walking. The blue detergent that overflowed the little cup is all over my hands. *Dirty.* I want to shower again. Just one more good scrub down. That would make me feel better. I just need to get clean.

"So?" Shannon repeats, sounding offended. "So you came home at the same time as normal but you weren't in your work clothes. Why?"

I head into the bathroom and turn on the tap. I put my hands underneath and start scrubbing. I don't know how long I'm doing it before Shannon grabs my elbow.

"Are you even listening to me?" She sounds pissed until I try to pull away and she reaches down to my wrist. "God, Callie, are you bleeding?"

I look down and see that I've been scrubbing my hands so hard together my nails scored the skin over my knuckles and indeed, little beads of blood are surfacing.

My hands clench into fists and I squeeze my eyes shut.

I just stand there, frozen in my bathroom like a frightened animal facing down an oncoming car. Damn it. Goddammit.

I'm past this. *I'm fucking past this.*

He doesn't get to have control over me. There has to be a way. There has to be. I refuse to let that man force himself on me in any way ever again.

I look up, straighten my back, and look at my sister. "Sorry, Shan. I spaced out for a second there." I put my hands under the water one last time to rinse them, then grab a hand towel to hide the damage I've done. "I gotta get dressed now.

She just stares at me for a long moment. "What's going on?"

I smile and shake my head. "Nothing. Just a stressful day at work. I changed clothes before I came home for a more comfortable commute. Grabbed a taco from a food truck and dripped hot sauce on my favorite top. Speaking of, I'm pretty full. I think I'll skip out on lasagna. I'm going out. Save me some leftovers."

With that, I usher her out of the bathroom and then wave her from the bedroom too. "Skooch unless you wanna see the headlights up close and in all their glory." I make like I'm going to drop my towel.

Shannon covers her eyes and hurries out of the room. "You are so weird," she mutters over her shoulder.

As soon as the door shuts behind her, I let out a long breath and uncover my hands from the towel. They're scratched up all to hell.

Which fucking pisses me off. Because fuck that. Gentry doesn't get to make me feel dirty and cower in the shower for hours on end. No. That's not who I am anymore.

No. The word is my fucking motto now.

I head straight to my closet and push all the sensible office clothes to the side. Tonight is a back-of-the-closet kind of night. The secret stash of too tight, too short body-con dresses. I flip through them. There's the plunging red spandex one, or the blue—

My eye catches on the black one with the tags still on at the very back. I bought all of these online, too embarrassed to go into an actual store and try anything so revealing on. The black one was an especially daring buy—it's a faux leather strapless mini-dress. I tried it on when it came and it suckered to my body like a glove. But even for me, it seemed too… much. Too loud, even though it's just black and not an in-your-face red.

It's a dress that you don't just wear, you have to *own it*. You have to have presence to pull off a dress like that. It's the dress that men should bow down before.

I feel a spike in my heart rate.

I aimed straight for my closet because it was habit. I didn't have a particular plan in mind when I told Shannon I was going out. Loosely, that I was headed out to the clubs, I guess.

Then Jackson's voice rings in my head:

Safe. Sane. Consensual.

I can't do what I've been doing. My jaw tics again. But I can't just sit here cooped up in this apartment eating fucking lasagna and watching whatever crime show Shannon will inevitably want to watch either. I've got the itch. I need this tonight. And now I know there's another way.

I drape the black dress over one arm and head toward my purse to grab my phone. I scroll through my contacts in my thumb hovers over Jackson's name.

The ride home the other day was... awkward. At least for me. Jackson didn't seem uncomfortable in the least. He wanted to talk about the session and go over some of the other things we'd seen. During the scene, I thought I'd want that too.

But when it finally came time, all I could give him were monosyllables in response. Everything we'd gone through in the club had hit a little too deep for me to want to dig any further.

Jackson let us continue to drive in silence for a long while before speaking up again. "Control is central to what this is all about. My life felt out of control for several years and this was a way for me to find a center again."

He looked at me and for a second, I allowed the intensity of his dark blue eyes to capture mine. "I found this lifestyle at the point when I really needed it and I guess I hope I can give that to other people."

I scoffed as I looked away out the window. Night was just falling. "BDSM as therapy?" I tried to joke. "Is that what this is?"

"Do you need therapy?" His tone was completely serious.

The question struck a little too close to home. "Are you one of those people who always answers a question with a question?"

"I don't know, am I?" A smile tilted the edge of his lips.

"Ha ha." I was glad he let it go. Maybe he sensed pushing me further wasn't going to get him anywhere. Then at the end he told me the ball was in my court. Where it's been sitting untouched all week.

My fingers drum on my thigh as I stare down at the phone. I've been looking at it for so long, the screen goes black. I make an annoyed noise and click it back to life. Jackson's name shines at me from the screen.

That's the problem with Jackson, though. He always sees too much. It's too intense between us, always has been. He'll just look at me and know something's wrong. And everything he said on Monday about how BDSM is supposed to be about trust and openness between partners...

I click to exit my contacts and grab my purse again. There. In the inner pocket, just where I remember shoving it—the card Daniel gave me.

I glance at the clock on my phone. It's six-thirty. Is that a good or bad time of day to call a sculptor to make a date? And God, my hand goes to my temple, is that even what I'm asking for? It's not like I want to go out for dinner and drinks. More like, I want to tie you up and... A blush rises on my cheeks as I try to imagine what I even want to do.

My mind skitters across all the things I saw in the club but nope, brain overload. Even the... dildo thing... oh my God, my neck is turning red in embarrassment just thinking about it. Yeah. Probably not that either for tonight.

Spanking, though. That I can do.

Just that image, having a man bent over in that position of submission like Mistress Nightblood had her slave—it sends a wave of, I can't even describe it, it's like I can take a full breath again for the first time since I saw Gentry's fucking text this morning. I focus on the image, imagining the powerful back of a muscled man, his wrists cuffed in chains, completely at my mercy. My heartbeat, which has been erratic all day, slows.

Yes. God, yes.

I type the numbers from the card into the phone and save the contact. Then I debate between texting and calling. But a text seems too passive. It's not the tone I want to set.

So I take a deep breath and push call.

It only rings twice before a deep voice answers, "Yes?"

"Is this Daniel?"

"Yes?" He sounds uncertain. Then again, he picked up when an unknown number flashed across the screen. Everybody else I know just ignores those kinds of calls.

"This is Mistress Calliope."

I hear the expulsion of breath on the other end. "How may I serve you, Mistress?" His voice has dropped several tones and become intimate in a way it wasn't before.

I bite my lip but keep my voice confident. Commanding. "You will clear your schedule. Make yourself available for me tonight."

There's not even a moment of hesitation before he replies, "Yes, Mistress. Where would Mistress like to meet?"

Oh. Shit. I should have thought that one through better. We can't exactly meet at my place with Shannon in the other room. And the club, well, Jackson obviously had a membership and signed me in as a guest. Then I brighten. Obviously Daniel has a membership as well.

"Perhaps Mistress would like to come over to my condo," Daniel says. "I have a dungeon with everything that Mistress might need."

Oh. He has a dungeon. Um. Damn. Maybe this was a bad idea after all.

"A dungeon is just what we in the community call our playrooms," Daniel offers when I've apparently been quiet for too long. "The room we played in the other day was also called a dungeon."

Oh. Does that make it better? Am I really ready to go over to some stranger's house and head into his dungeon? Willingly? I bite my lip again. Then again, Jackson seemed to know this guy pretty well. The way they talked, they seemed to have been acquaintances for years.

"Perhaps Mistress would feel more secure if she called a friend and let her know my address? Several of my female friends in the scene do this and arrange a second call at some point in the night."

Of course. Lydia and I have actually done this for each other before. Well, she's texted me when she's hooked up with people. I've never done it because I've always kept my... activities... well, semi-public.

Daniel's still talking. "I'll also chain myself even before you arrive and toss the key out of my reach. I want you to feel completely safe."

My mouth drops open. Whoa. This dude is serious. "Why would you do that? You barely know me."

"I enjoyed our scene the other day very much. And Jackson obviously trusts you." His voice has taken on that intimate quality again. "It would be a privilege for me to have the opportunity to help you explore your dominant nature."

My mouth dries and I quietly suck in a deep breath. "Text me your address. Be ready at eight-fifteen." I hang up before waiting for his response.

I clutch the phone to my chest, breathing hard. Holy shit. Am I really doing this? The phone vibrates only seconds later and I look down to see Daniel's address. He lives in San Leandro. That's about an hour away by public transit. I look to the ceiling again, then down at the dress in my arms.

I own you now.

Fuck that. No one owns me. My jaw tightens. Hell yes I'm doing this.

I'm the only one in control of my life.

It starts now.

CHAPTER NINE

CALLIE

Daniel's place is a townhouse in a nice enough part of San Leandro. It's no mansion in the hills like Jackson has, but all real estate in the Bay Area is insane. I wonder if he's renting or if he actually makes enough as an artist to own a place like this. The building is painted a bright white with pale green accent shutters and window boxes with rows of potted plants along the front. It gives off a very homey vibe.

My phone beeps three times signaling a text right as I'm about to ring the bell.

DANIEL: Key is under the flower box by the front window. Box velcro'd on front left.

Oh. I reach under the window box bursting with flowers and yep, I feel what seems to be a small hide-a-key box secured on the corner closest to me. I tug at it and hear the familiar noise of velcro being pulled apart and the little box comes off in my hand. I slide one side up and then upend it, dropping the key into my palm.

I stare at it for a second. Should I really be doing this? I mean, did he actually handcuff himself in there? And then he's cool telling me, a relative stranger, how to find the key to his house? What if I was a crazy person intent on hurting him? I mean, yeah, sure, Jackson introduced us, but it's not like he gave us full background checks on one another. Doesn't all this violate the *safe* part of safe, sane, and consensual?

More beeps come from my phone and I look down. It's a facetime request from Daniel. I click to accept. Daniel's face comes into view but at an awkward angle. I can't see much behind him except light from the ceiling.

"Mistress, I'm so glad you came." His tone is easy-going but his features don't quite match. He looks tense. Maybe with anxiety, maybe with excitement. I can't tell.

"If you come in, the first door on your left leads to the basement. I'm here waiting."

I hesitate for another moment. Because the same thing that's true for Daniel is true for me. I don't know him at all either. This isn't safe. Just because Jackson knows him doesn't mean Daniel doesn't have some secret life. What if he just plays at being a submissive so that he can lure women to his house in some kind of trap?

I take several steps back from the door. Shit. What am I even doing here? Why am I risking this?

But as if he sees my retreat on my face or in the shutter of the camera as I step back, Daniel's eyes go wide with panic.

"It's safe, I promise. Look." The camera shifts from his face to a close up of his wrists. They are handcuffed to what looks like some kind of large wooden post centered in a well-lit room. Fingers fumble with a small key.

"I trust you," comes Daniel's voice from off-screen. One of his hands jerk forward and the camera shakes, but catches the trajectory of the key as it sails to the ground halfway across the room. Then the camera focuses back on the handcuffs at an awkward close-up angle since he's holding the camera in one of his bound hands. The handcuffs shake and rattle to show that his wrists are indeed secured tightly.

"I'm locked up. You're in complete control. And here, I'll show you the room so you can see that we're the only ones here." The camera jostles crazily again before steadying and doing a slow three-sixty panorama of the room.

In spite of the unsteady cam, I get the picture. It's a bright, clean room and the walls aren't a garish red or anything. From the little I can make out, the cream-colored walls are perfectly plain except for two sections where well-organized implements hang like tools in a garage. Other than that, the room's empty except for the wooden post and a few larger pieces of furniture placed around the room, similar to things I saw at the club.

At the same time, none of it is large enough to obscure anyone's form. Daniel's telling the truth. There's no one else there.

At least not in that room. But what if he has friends hiding just outside the door, waiting until I let my defenses down? A big part of me wants to turn back. Go home where it's safe.

"Please, Mistress," Daniel suddenly abandons his façade of charm. He's turned the phone back to his face and his eyes plead with me. "I need a session tonight as much as I suspect you do. Your call felt like a gift from God."

In any other situation, that line would've sounded too cheesy to believe. But there's something about the sincerity in Daniel's face, a certain need haunting his eyes.

Christ. I bite my lip. What was he even thinking, throwing away the keys like that? What if I decided to turn and leave? He'd just be stuck there for... how long? I guess he still has his phone, but damn. It's reckless. A little insane.

I know the feeling.

Isn't it the same need that drove me to ride the train for over an hour to a stranger's house on a whim?

And I keep thinking *stranger*, but that's not exactly true. It's not like he's just some dude I hooked up with over the internet or at a club —which is something people do all the time. Jackson has spent time with this guy. They have mutual acquaintances and talked like they'd known each other for a while.

Before I can talk myself out of it, I go to the text I already composed to Lydia with Daniel's address and a message about sending in the cavalry if I don't call in three hours. Then I put the key in the lock, turn it, and open the door. It opens easily and then I'm inside the tiled foyer of the townhouse. I close the door behind me and set the key on a side table in the entryway.

It's quiet in here. I look around, my nerves jettisoning my heart rate. Hardwood floors. The place is styled in cool tones. Slate gray walls, white accent trim. Very classic.

There's a stairway to the left and a small hallway to the right leading to the rest of the house. A quick glance shows the door cut into the wall underneath the stairs. No doubt that's the one Daniel was talking about that leads down to the basement. It makes sense. The two stairwells are most likely stacked parallel on top of one another. Slowly I move forward. Instead of opening the door to the basement, I pass it by.

I bend over and slip my hunting knife out of my steel-toed boot as I continue creeping forward. Yes, I'm wearing the mini-dress with my kick-ass combat boots. I actually like the message it sends. I fuck with you, not the other way around.

The hallway opens into a dining room. Framed modern art hangs tastefully on the walls—bright splashes of color that don't form recognizable shapes but draw the eye nonetheless. I take all this in, but not with an appreciative eye. I'm scoping out the territory. Assessing threats. Other than the walls, the house is sparsely furnished.

I check out the whole house to make sure Daniel was telling the truth and no one's hiding and waiting to jump out at me. It all checks out.

I don't put the knife back in my boot, though. Not until I open the door to the basement and head down the stairs. The room at the bottom is just as well lit as it was in the video, and bigger than I expected. It's a full basement, equal to the size of the house.

And there in the center is the large wooden post, thick as a telephone pole, which Daniel has indeed handcuffed himself to. Oh, and he's naked, ass toward me. Considering this is how I've spent most of my time with the guy, it's not as startling as I would have thought.

A quick glance around shows me that there's no one else here, either. No tricks. No traps.

Daniel actually chained himself to a post and has been waiting for me to show up. Daniel's watching me over his shoulder and his eyes immediately zero in on the knife in my hand. His eyebrows go up and his mouth drops open slightly.

"Sorry," I apologize, immediately bending and stuffing the knife back into its sheath in my boot. "Better safe than sorry."

"Of course," he says. When I look up again, I see his eyes are on my left boot where I sheathed the knife. "You don't know me. Safety's the first rule in the lifestyle, after all."

I can't help arching an eyebrow at him. "Exactly. So how is restraining yourself and giving a stranger the key to your house safe?"

His eyes finally come up and lock on mine. "I'm good at reading people. I knew you were someone I could trust. I felt it when we first met."

It's a good sentiment and I can't deny it makes a little something twinge in my chest. I still keep my voice stern when I say, "It's still stupid and reckless. You shouldn't do it."

Daniel casts his eyes down. "Mistress is correct. I was very foolish. I deserve to be punished." His eyes flick hopefully back up at me before returning to the ground.

I look to the wall. All kinds of things hang there. Wooden paddles of all shapes and sizes. Leather paddles too, studded with metal bits. Floggers with thin little leather strips and others with wide leather pieces. Some of the flogger strips are knotted at the end, a few even with little bits of metal tied into the knots. And then there are the whips. Whips of all lengths, material, braids and tassels.

Suddenly I feel like exactly the newbie that I am.

"What does Mistress require of me tonight?" Daniel asks.

Uh, is there some sort of script I'm supposed to be following? Probably so. At the same time, Jackson did say that it's supposed to be a learning process. Daniel knows I'm inexperienced and he gave me his card anyway. I step closer to him.

"You know that I'm new. I need to be in control. I like it when you're tied up." I reach out and give a tug on his bound wrists. It jerks his whole body even closer toward the pole and I smile.

Having him immobilized like this, knowing I can step away and he can't follow... Oh yes, I like that very much. "It made me hot when we spanked you. What about you?" I tilt my head at him. "What do you like? What do you need?"

He's been looking at the floor, but his eyes come back to mine and as I watch, they dilate.

"Pain. I like pain."

Yes. I remember that. Pain and humiliation. I nod and paste on my most confident smile. This is all a little weird still, but I don't want him to feel like I'm judging him.

"All right then. So, the paddle?" I look over to the wall at the assortment of instruments. The wooden paddle is the only one I've used before.

"The whip," he says, his voice certain.

I look back at him sharply and his cheeks color. His gaze immediately jumps back to the floor. "If it pleases Mistress."

I bite my lip and feel bad for a second. Jackson said dominant-submissive relationships should be about mutual benefit. Dommes are supposed to care about their sub's needs before their own but I came here only concerned with what I needed. Damn, I'm failing even before I begin at this. I reach out and touch Daniel's cheek, urging his face back up.

"It's not that I don't want to give you what you need," I say. "It's just that I don't know how to use those yet."

His eyes brighten. "I could teach you. It's easy and a quick lesson would be enough. Then we could play."

He seems so earnest.

"The rubber whips are more like practice ones anyway," he nods toward the wall. "Like that green one. Even if you screw up, they'll barely sting. This is how a lot of mistresses learn. Their subs help them pick up new skills."

I consider him a moment and then look up where he's gesturing. It's easy enough to see the neon green rubber whip. A practice whip. It would be good to learn.

And it'd be good for me if tonight turned into a session practicing my Domme skills, focusing on what Daniel needs rather than stewing in my own shit. Gentry's smug face flashes in my eyes but I swallow hard and force the image out.

Yes. It would be far better to make tonight about Daniel rather than letting Gentry have any more space in my head.

I walk over and retrieve the key to Daniel's handcuffs from the floor where he tossed it earlier. I come back to him and look at his cuffed hands.

His posture is deferent, but he's still a big guy. I bypass his hands and go first to the ankle manacles that lie unused at the bottom of the pole. A heavy chain runs through an iron eyelet screwed into the pole. It's long enough to give the person locked in some leeway to step away from the pole.

I heft the chain in my hands then inspect the ankle cuffs. Unlike at the club, these aren't padded leather cuffs, just regular metal handcuffs like the police use. The ankle ones do look larger, but that seems to be the only consideration given.

Daniel doesn't make a sound of objection as I attach the cuff to his ankle. It's curiously satisfying to hear the small lock click into place and know he can't go anywhere unless I allow it. The feeling only gets more intense as I lock the other ankle in.

I make sure to leave a lot of extra space so they don't close too tightly and chafe. Though I don't imagine the metal cuffs can be comfortable. Really, I'm surprised he doesn't have the leather kind. Everything else in his 'dungeon' seems to be professional-grade equipment like at the club.

I'm slow to stand, taking in his corded legs, high, tight buttocks, narrow waist that leads up to his nicely shaped back. He's not overly muscled. He has something of a jogger's body. I run my hand up his thigh, skip his ass, and then continue up his back, cocking my head to the side as I observe him.

He shudders slightly under my touch and he bows his head. And God. The sight of a man chained and at my mercy—

My breath escapes in an erratic stutter and for a moment I feel lightheaded. Yeah. That high from Monday night? It's back. Maybe not quite as good because it doesn't have as much sexual edge without Jackson here, but the high is still present. I kick at the chains near Daniel's ankles just to hear them rattle and it sends another sizzle running through my blood.

There's a tiny bit of slack at his wrist cuffs. Grabbing the chain, I yank him forward just enough to topple his center of balance. His chest rams roughly into the smooth wood grain of the pole but he keeps his eyes on the floor. It pleases me even though I can't describe why.

Whoa. So maybe this is what the rush is about for me. Everything that happened Monday was all kind of a jumbling flash of sensation. I couldn't separate out what parts especially spoke to me and what was simply happening and exciting because it was the first time I was seeing it. From the reading I've been doing since then, dominants and subs usually have a preference in what they're into. Which letter or letters of the BDSM acronym particularly call to them, or maybe a kink that's even more specialized.

Daniel embraces masochism. And being humiliated.

So what will my thing be? Bondage obviously goes on my preferred kinks checklist. What else? I lick my lips, taking one more long second to enjoy the sight in front of me. I think about the other letters. Dominance. Sadism. Do I like inflicting pain?

A secondary rush hits when it starts to sink in: this isn't just about the sex. I get to... discover myself. Find out what's inside me. My fingers grip around the key in my palm. Do I want to know if a sadist lives inside me? What does that even mean if I do like it? Hurting people?

"If the Mistress frees my hands, I can begin the demonstration." Daniel's voice is soft. Deferent.

Still, he probably shouldn't speak without being spoken to. But I appreciate being pulled out of my thoughts, so I don't chide him. I do make my face stone, though, as I use the key to undo the handcuffs at his wrists. I do a quick inspection of the skin and see red lines from where the cuffs cut into his skin.

"You had them on too tight." I glare at him. "They should have been secured one or two notches over." I made sure to leave space for two fingers when I was tightening his ankle cuffs. He obviously pulled these as tight as he possibly could. And he should know better.

His eyes stay downcast. "I'm sorry, Mistress."

"Don't do it again." My voice is cutting. I'm totally new to this whole deal and even I know he deserves a good spanking for that. Then I remember Jackson saying that for Daniel, that would be a treat. So maybe not.

"What am I going to do with you?"

Daniel dares to look up at me, that charming smile on his face. "Let me train you in the art of whipping a naughty sub?"

I give him a wallop on the ass for mouthing off. His face drops immediately to the floor, but I notice the smile remains. What a little—

Instead of giving him what he wants with another spanking, I order him to stand up straight. I put the key to his cuffs in my bra. He watches, which of course is part of the point. Look, but never touch.

Heading to the wall, I grab the green whip. "Which one do you want to demonstrate?"

Daniel's head pops up and his eyes barely skirt the wall. "Brown braided leather, third to the right from the green."

I locate the one he means and hold the two whips side-by-side. Though they are different materials, they have a similar shape and length. I head back toward Daniel and he gestures toward the far corner. "You see the mannequin bust over there? It's what Dommes usually practice on."

I arch an eyebrow at him. "So I'm not the first you've had to teach these tricks to?"

He ducks his head. "I'm happy to educate when I can."

I half laugh, half scoff. "I bet."

The bust in the corner is heavy, but it's on wheels. Unlike a regular mannequin, it's not flesh-colored, but covered in black latex and when I touch the shoulders, I can feel that it's more heavy-duty than just pieces of molded plastic. I assumed it was just a part of the decor when I first came in.

I roll the bust close to the pole where my—out of nowhere the word *slave* pops into my head—stands chained. Slave. My glance drops to the two whips where I let them fall just out of Daniel's reach. My stomach flips with excitement.

Holy shit. Holy shit holy shit holy shit. What the hell am I doing?

I notch my chin up higher. Fuck it, whatever I'm feeling, I've got to put on a brave face. My sub... slave... might be the one teaching me a new skill tonight, but I'm the one in control. It's not just what's expected. It's what we both need. For the first time all day, I feel like I can really breathe. Inhale. Fill up my lungs with oxygen. And when I exhale, breathe out every toxic feeling.

Because in here, I am a Master and for this small, agreed-upon time, this man is my slave.

"How far away should it be placed, Slave?" Inside my head, my use of the word is tentative, but outwardly, I keep my voice like steel.

Daniel doesn't seem to think I've said anything out of the ordinary. "For these whips, a distance of about eight feet is good. We'll get an even better feel once we begin."

I move back out of the strike zone and then toss Daniel his whip of choice.

"First, we'll start with an easy one, the circle strike." He crouches slightly and with his right hand, he whips the leather in an arcing horizontal circle. At the end of the circle, the tip of the whip strikes the mannequin's upper back.

"It's best to aim for the fleshier areas of the back, at least with new subs. An experienced sub like me can take it really anywhere. I just want to let you know the protocols for when you take your new skills elsewhere."

He repeats the strike over and over several times. I watch the graceful movement of his arm. It's really more about the wrist, though. My eyebrows furrow as I zero in on the way his wrist rotates to create the circular motion. I repeat it with my own whip in a smaller scale and without the intensity to make the whip fly.

Daniel's whip falls to his side and with a nod of his head, he indicates it's my turn.

"Toss me yours." It's a command and I hold up my arm. This situation might seem on the up and up, but there's no way I'm letting him keep anything that can even remotely be used as a weapon near me. He's the only one that, for whatever reason, has agreed to trust me that far. I never said I'd do the same.

He gathers the whip without comment or expression and tosses it in my direction. I let it drop near my feet because me and coordination skills are not best friends. Somehow I think butter-fingering a simple catch wouldn't do great for establishing my dominance. I leave the coil of leather on the floor and walk forward to reposition the bust so the back faces me. Then I step back again and try out the circle-strike.

My first few tries, I'm not close enough and I miss the target completely. I step nearer but the circle I try to make is wobbly and oblong.

"If you lower your stance slightly, you'll get better results," Daniel says.

I do as he instructs, lowering my center of gravity. The first time I get a satisfying *thwack*, a jolt of electricity seems to travel from the impact back through the whip, up my arm and into my chest where it reverberates. Oh yes. That's *quite* satisfying. I do it again and three out of five times get a satisfying whack.

"Now reverse the direction of the circle so you can strike at the other side of the back."

I do is he instructs. It's a little trickier at first to go counterclockwise, but after ten repetitions, I'm getting the hang of it. I practice switching back and forth for another quarter hour. Daniel also shows me a diagonal technique where I flip my wrist to create an X pattern in the air to deliver equal blows on the upper shoulders similar to what I saw Jackson do.

After half an hour of practice, I feel comfortable with both strike patterns.

Jackson.

Shit. Why does thinking about him make me feel a rush of guilt? Like being here alone with Daniel is somehow wrong? God, I'm not even here to have sex with Daniel. This is just a skill- gaining session. What the fuck?

"Mistress is a natural," Daniel says, bringing my focus back to him. I don't know if he's bullshitting me or not, but when I look over at him, his eyes are focused with intensity on the whip in my hand. "Would Mistress like to practice on her slave now?"

My gaze bounces between the bust and Daniel's back. Am I ready? I fight the urge to bite my lip. That's not what a Mistress would do.

Damn, if I overthink this, I could put it off forever. I have a feeling it's like diving headfirst into a pool for the first time. No matter how much you stare at the water, there's no way to get a feel for it other than just *doing* it.

With a decisive nod, I turn toward Daniel. "Yes." I turn my back to him and bend over at the waist, stretching my hands to my toes. Giving him a perfect view of what he'll never have. His intake of breath brings a wicked smile to my face.

"Did I hear the slave say something?" I roll back to standing, then stalk with sure, confident strides toward Daniel. He follows me with his eyes.

"No, Mistress." He swallows hard.

I grab his chin roughly with one of my hands, squeezing his cheeks. "Good." I make my voice menacing. "Keep it that way."

But then I remember another important part of play. "Unless it's your safe word. What is your safe word? Say it now."

"Red."

"Say it again," I command.

"Red." His voice is confident. Okay. He gets the idea.

"Other than that, I don't want to hear a single word out of you. My slave is to stay silent. Is that understood?"

He opens his mouth but then closes it again when I arch an eyebrow. Instead, he nods.

"Good boy," I croon.

I grab one of his unbounded wrists and jerk it back toward the cuffs. Reattaching them, one after the other, I make sure that they aren't cutting off his circulation this time. They are tight enough to make sure he's not going anywhere, but he still has good blood flow.

Satisfied, I step back to examine my work. And God does he looked pretty. So, so pretty, bound and chained there for me to do whatever I want to. He peeks up at me.

"Eyes on the floor," I command roughly. I don't know where the Domme voice comes from, if it's a role I'm playing at or if it's a real part of me. Hell, maybe it's a mixture of the two here at the beginning while I'm still figuring everything out. Maybe I'll become Mistress the more and more I play. And some day I can be this badass version of myself all the time. Queen over all her domain. Never bowing under the heel of anyone, man or woman.

The high is so high I want to stand here, feeling it forever. But like all highs, it's unsustainable without continuing to feed it. So I walk back to the whip. What could be more thrilling than knowing I have the little key to someone else's pain and pleasure?

It's without much ceremony that I swing the whip in the circle movement and bring it down on Daniel's back.

In spite of my determination to inhabit this role, it's a less-than-decisive strike. Okay, let's call it what it was. Weak. The whip barely has the energy to complete the circle and Daniel has no reaction to the impact whatsoever. It might as well have been a fly landing on his skin. I remember his body jolting from the flogger when Jackson applied it last Monday.

Then again, Daniel did say this was just a practice whip. Which is good. I don't need to be marking up anyone's back. But still, a little redness isn't going to do anyone any harm. I make the circle again and strike with a more satisfying hit. Daniel still doesn't move, but the noise that echoes throughout the room is rewarding. A mid-pitched *thwack*. Very, very nice.

I land a few more blows in that direction before alternating counterclockwise for five more. Then I switch back to the other and continue, back and forth until I land twenty more. I pause to examine my work and can't help grinning at the reddened canvas of his upper back.

I step forward and gently rub my hands over his skin. It's warm to the touch. I trail my fingers across his shoulders and down his shoulder blades. When I glance around to his face, I'm expecting to see some of the pleasure like I saw in our last session.

Instead, I only find consternation. I feel my eyebrows draw together.

"What's wrong?"

He's quiet, even going so far as to bite his lip.

"You can speak now. I've asked you a direct question."

His eyes flick up to meet mine. "It's nothing."

I grab his jaw again. "Never lie to your Mistress. It's not nothing."

I feel him swallow but only tighten my grip.

"It's just that, I'm a dirty, nasty, stupid slave. And filthy slave boys require heavier correction. We need to really feel it if we're ever going to do any better. We're stinking, hideous little bitch boys." He strains against his restraints. Not because he wants out of them, I realize. He just wants to feel the pain of the metal handcuffs digging into his skin.

He didn't just accidentally pull the wrist cuffs too tight earlier. It was on purpose. He'll do anything he can to get to the pain.

Which is why he needs me. And I've been neglecting the other half of his psyche. The part that needs to be humiliated.

I toss his chin I've been gripping so hard to the side roughly. "Why am I even bothering with such a pathetic excuse for a slave?"

"Please, Mistress, I'll do whatever you ask—"

"Back to no speaking, you fucking idiot," I force myself to sneer. "You're right about one thing, you are my little bitch for the night." I walk back to the whip and test its weight in my palm. It feels good.

"Is my whiny little bitch boy going to complain about a little pain?" This time when I land the circle strike, it's a *thud*. Oh yeah. That one landed. Fuck's sake, did it land. Daniel's body finally jerks just the tiniest bit and I smile.

"I bet you loved that, you little slut. You're a slut, you know that right? You let me in your house, almost a complete stranger, because you're so hard up for this, aren't you?" Another hard strike.

"Yes," Daniel cries out. "I'm a bitch slut for whoever will give it to me."

"I told you not to say a word." I move to counterclockwise strikes. "Not." Whip swing and *strike*. "A." Swing and *thud*. "Word."

I change up my swings and try out the X pattern. I'm a little rough at first, but eventually get the rhythm of it. These land more on the inner part of the back and I try to distribute the blows so they don't all land in the same place.

"Twisted pain slut," my heart races as I continue shaming him. I didn't think I'd find this part so thrilling, but damn if I don't. "If you could speak, I know you'd be begging for it. But you are my slave and you can't say a damn thing. You're a helpless little bitch."

My next swing is a little off and barely grazes him but I follow it up with another that lands on the target. From eight feet away, I can see his back is growing redder and redder. The session has been intense but awesome. He's probably had about fifty blows by now. Shit. I should have been counting. That's something I bet Dommes do. Or they have their subs count. Right. I feel like I've read somewhere that that's the thing.

Oh well. I won't feel bad about it. Daniel knew going into this that I'm just learning my way around. I let the whip drop to my side and am about to go closer to inspect his back and make sure he's okay when he speaks up. It's bad enough that he's talking out of turn, but then his words register.

"If I'm a slut, Mistress is a slut too. You came over so willingly. I bet your panties are soaked."

His laugh is caustic. "Fucking bimbo piece of trash. As if you're even good enough to suck my cock. You'd be lucky if I wanted to shove my big fat cock down your throat. But if I did, I'd jam it in so far, you wouldn't be breathing for a week. You'll choke on it, you'll—"

The whip is singing through the air before I quite realize what I'm doing. Stop him. Stop him from saying another word. That's all I can think.

But the crack of the whip on his back only makes him laugh. He looks over his shoulder at me defiantly. "Oh yeah, I'd fuck your face so hard you couldn't breathe. I'd make sure you were the one in these fucking chains, locked down here in my basement so I could use you whenever I want. My own personal cum bucket. That's all a bitch like you is good for. And you'd want it. You'd love it."

That's right, you love it, you filthy whore. The words of my rapist, while he was still inside me. Violating me from behind while his co-rapist took from the front.

Oh God, I feel them. Suffocating me from all sides, sickening cologne and rancid breath biting at my breasts. Get them out of me! God help me! God, where are you?

See? It just takes one session sometimes to break a bitch. That's what this is. Intentionally trying to break me. To crush the bits of my soul into pieces smaller than the finest grains of sand until there's nothing left.

"Cause that's how whores like you want it," the voice in the room shouts, taunting and full of menace. "You pretend like you don't, but you just need a man to come and shove it in your cunt, then you're creaming all over—"

I scream and the whip flies. "I'm not broken! You didn't break me!" I bring the whip down again. And again. And again. "You sick motherfucking rapist bastard!" I scream. I bring the whip down yet again with all the force I can manage.

Tears blur my vision as my arm rears back to strike again when the figure in front of me suddenly slumps to his knees.

Wait. What? What's going on?

I stumble back, lose my footing and fall on my ass. I look around, confused and disoriented. Then it comes back to me. Daniel's basement. The scene. Everything was going great until—

I look over at Daniel.

Oh God. I swipe at my eyes so I can see more clearly but the image is still the same. Blood. There's blood on his back. A lot of fucking blood.

"Oh my God." It's a horrified whisper. Did I— My eyes jerk around the room. Of course I fucking did. Who the hell else do I think was here just whipping the helpless man chained to a post?

Oh my fucking God. What did I just do?

I scramble to my feet and run over to him.

"I'm so sorry." The broken whisper barely gets past my throat. I grab for the key in my bra and then fumble to unlock his wrists. I jam the key at the little lock but can't seem to get it in the hole. I shove it again but my hands are shaking so damn bad.

"Motherfucker," I swear to myself as I try yet again.

"It's okay," the hands I'm trying to free grip mine and I look up to find Daniel's eyes on mine.

How can he even look at me? "I didn't hear your safe word. I swear, I would've stopped if I'd heard it." Tears pour down my cheeks. "It's unforgivable, but I'm so sorry, I'm so—"

Daniel just shakes his head vehemently back and forth and cuts me off. "I didn't say it. I, I didn't want you to stop. Please. I'm sorry for the things I was saying. But please. Just a little more. I need it. You don't understand how much. No one else will give me what I need."

"What?" I yank my hands back from him. I want to pretend I didn't hear him right.

His whole face has gone hopeful. "That's right," he nods toward the whip I discarded. "You should punish me for being so disobedient and speaking out when I shouldn't have. Saying such bad things. Give me as many more lashes as you want. I can handle it." There's a manic edge to his voice. He hugs the pole and struggles back to his feet.

I step even further back from him. The blood on his back... God, there's so much of it. It's dripping. I whipped a man bad enough that his back is dripping blood. And he wants more of it. My stomach goes queasy.

"I'll get help," I call over my shoulder as I turn and bolt for the stairs. *Help.* I don't know what that means in this situation, but I just have to get the hell out of here. Out of this dungeon. Away from the man who wants me to injure him more than I already have.

So I run.

What are you doing? You can't just leave him chained up down there. I hiccup as I try to get enough air in before I have to gasp for another breath. Shit shit shit. Running up the stairs like a bat out of hell didn't help the breathing situation. In the hallway at the top, I bend over and put my hands on my knees.

In. Out. In.

My head swims and I finally manage one longer breath for every three short hiccupping ones. After a couple minutes, it seems like there's less of a chance that I'm going to pass out. Great. Okay. One crisis averted.

I look around the narrow hallway. It's full dark outside. I'm in this crazy fucker's house all by myself. The crazy fucker in question is still cuffed to a pole downstairs. In need of medical attention. Should I uncuff him and take him to the hospital? And how exactly am I supposed to do that? I don't have a car and I don't know if Daniel does. Not that it would matter even if he did. My fucking license expired a couple months ago and I didn't see the point of renewing it since I don't have a car.

The image of me trying to drag a bloody and half-delirious Daniel onto public transit pops in my head. He's a foot taller than me and outweighs me by at least seventy pounds. Yeah. Not happening. From my brief glance, it didn't seem like the cuts were serious enough for an ambulance and I don't think an Uber driver would look kindly on me being like, *cool if you take us to the hospital, I'll just put some towels against the seat so, you know, my friend doesn't bleed all over your Honda Fit.*

My breaths start to stutter again and I ball my fists.

No. I'll just head down there, calmly ask him where his first aid equipment is, and… and… Oh shit, I feel sick. I press one hand to my stomach and the other to my mouth.

I turn to try to find a trashcan and almost trip over my purse where I dropped it in the hallway when I first got here. I stare for a long moment. My stomach settles as an idea hits.

Of course. The most obvious solution of all.

My hand is still shaking as I crouch down and paw through my purse. There it is. The hard plastic of my phone case. My hand closes around it and a great whoosh of breath escapes through my teeth. But when I breathe in again, for the first time in fifteen minutes, my lungs seem to expand fully.

I thumb through my contacts and press call. As the ringtone sounds in my ear, I consider the very real possibility that he might not pick up. It's a Thursday. Not Friday, but still. He's undoubtedly a busy man. Probably has a full social life. My stomach tightens unpleasantly at the thought. The phone trills for the third time.

Shit. He's not going to pick up. I'm all alone in this. I press my palm to the flat of my forehead.

God. It was stupid of me to think of calling him in the first place. Never rely on anyone. That's been my motto for years now. What the fuck is wrong with me? I made this mess. I shake my head in disgust and pull the phone away from my ear to end the call.

"Yes? Callie?" Jackson's strong voice is distant but clear even with the phone inches away from my ear.

I stare at the phone, my thumb hovering over the end button.

"Calliope, are you there?"

My mind flashes to the man in the basement. Fuck it. This is about more than just me. I bring the phone up to my ear.

"Jackson. It's me. I need your help."

CHAPTER TEN

JACKSON

I rushed to Daniel's house as soon as I got Callie's call. Miranda met me there. As soon as we assured that Callie was okay—shaken, but okay—we went downstairs and found Daniel.

It didn't take long to uncover what had happened. I was tempted, so damn tempted, to pick up the bull whip and complete the job Daniel was so desperate to trick Callie into doing. He might be the one bleeding but it's her who'll have lasting scars from tonight. I saw it in her eyes when we'd briefly checked in with her. The shame and horror at what she'd done. It was like looking in a mirror.

The only thing stopping the beast from grabbing the whip was how much pleasure it would have given Daniel. It was good that Miranda was there. She uncuffed Daniel while I prowled the basement pacing back and forth, trying to shake off my anger at the man.

He stumbled as soon as he was free and was too heavy for Miranda to catch so finally, I joined them and shouldered his weight to get him up the two flights of stairs to dump him in the tub and turn the shower spray on.

I don't bother waiting for it to heat up.

"Wash yourself," I bark and turn away in disgust.

Miranda gives me a *what the hell* look and passes by me to bend over and help Daniel. Aftercare, yeah yeah yeah. She knows just as well as I do that Daniel did this to himself. I thought about calling one of his former dommes but know that none of them would have wanted to come. Not again. He's pulled stunts like this one too many times.

Daniel swore he was getting better. Going to counseling, and his probationary period at the club's been over for two months.

Then for him to go and pull this shit... I should never have introduced him to Callie. I keep making mistake after mistake when it comes to her.

"Fuck." I run my hands through my hair as I stomp into the bedroom and sit down on the bed. I don't go downstairs to Callie. Miranda might still need my help and I'm not sure I can face Callie yet, not after failing her again.

I guess I thought I'd, I don't know, swoop in like some white knight with all the answers. She'd be my apprentice domme and I'd be her wise teacher in the art of domination. I envisioned long sessions learning flogging patterns and how to lead a sub through the various devices and stations at the club, about all the different toys used in the lifestyle. But nothing's worked out like I imagined. Then again, nothing ever does, does it?

Miranda comes out of the en suite bathroom, eyes shrewd.

I swallow. "How is he?"

"He'll be sore for a few days. Nothing that a little ointment, arnica, and rest won't cure."

"He's got bigger problems than a sore back," I say darkly.

"Oh I know." Miranda says, gaze flicking back toward the bathroom. "But I think he can still come back from this."

I glower at her. As far as I'm concerned, Daniel is done. But Miranda's just shaking her head. "He won't tell me who it was that did it to him."

I frown. What does she mean. Obviously it was Callie who—

"I mean who broke him. Who made him so fucked up." She looks toward the window. The sun has long gone down but her gaze has gone faraway. "At least I'm at the place where I can say the name of my demon out loud. Bryce Gentry."

She heaves out a heavy breath after saying the bastard's name. "I have to know we can come back after what they did to us, you know? I have to know it's possible."

I reach over and take her hand. "You know you can talk to me any time. Have the nightmares gotten any better?"

She attempts a smile but it barely lifts the edges of her lips and makes it nowhere near her eyes. "Some nights I manage to sleep. Which is an improvement, as you know."

It's true. When Miranda and I were together, she could rarely make it through the night in bed beside me. Usually she climbed out of bed somewhere around three a.m. and went outside to smoke. Sometimes she'd come back to bed but more often than not, she'd take her laptop and just go start working.

"Does she make you happy?"

"What?" I sit up straighter. "Oh, it's not like that. We're not— We're just friends."

She arches an eyebrow. Damn that eyebrow. She always could say so much with it. "Sorry but I don't think you'd drop everything and call me and demand I drop everything too if she was *just a friend*."

I scoff and point to the bathroom. "Daniel was in need!"

She rolls her eyes. "You don't give two shits about Daniel."

"That's not fair. I wouldn't have just left him locked down there."

"Ha! You were tempted."

"Nobody could ever read me like you," I grin.

"Oh put away that dimple, pretty boy. You already got your way."

"How are you, Miranda? Really?" I haven't seen her in months and though she's putting up a good front, she looks, I don't know, sad underneath. She's the only ex I've ever stayed friends with after a relationship—genuine friends with. Maybe because I was always more of a project to her than anything else and we were never the right fit to begin with. We moved out of each other's lives but we still call every few months to check in. It's been awhile though.

"I don't know, Jack. You ever feel like you're just spinning in life? Your wheels are going around and around but you're not really getting anywhere?" She looks at me and for once her shields are down. "All I ever wanted was for someone to look at me the way you look at that woman downstairs. But it just might not be in the cards for me."

"Don't say that."

She sighs. "Where can a girl find a man who will whip the shit out of her at night but still be a gentleman in the morning?"

I lean over and kiss her on the top of her head. "He's out there somewhere."

"Yeah, yeah. Why don't you head downstairs, Prince Charming. I've got Daniel."

I frown. "You sure? He might need help getting out of the—"

"I've got it. Go. She needs you more than we do."

I'm not gonna stand around and argue the point. I hurry out of the bedroom and downstairs. Callie's bent over on the couch, her head in her hands.

"Callie."

Her eyes snap up at my voice. Her jaw tightens like she's bracing for something and her eyes drop to the floor.

"Callie, look at me."

She lets out a heavy breath and slowly, like it pains her, brings her eyes up to meet mine. I'm so tall she has to all but tip her head back, so I sit down on the couch beside her.

Being this close to her is as much treat as it is torture.

I can't help reaching for her hand, but like so often lately, she pulls it away.

"Don't." Her voice comes out thick and choked sounding.

Jesus she's killing me here. She's so obviously hurting and I can't fucking stand it.

"Calliope." Maybe she'll push me away but I can't just sit here and not hold her when I see her there looking so devastated. Please, please don't pull away, I pray as I tug her into my arms and pull her against my chest.

When she doesn't resist, I can't help pulling her closer, all but into my lap as I cradle her. "I'm so, so sorry, Callie. This is all my fault. I should never have trusted him or even introduced you. Or at least I should have warned you about him."

I shake my head. "I thought he was better. His probationary period at the club was over and I thought he was recovered." I nestle my chin over her head. I don't know how long she'll let me hold her and I want to give her every ounce of comfort I can while she'll let me. "I'm an idiot to have even risked exposing you to such a potentially manipulative sub. I'm so sorry. Can you ever forgive me?"

And then, all too soon, she's struggling to pull away. I give one last squeeze before I loosen my grasp on her. She tries to back away to the other side of the couch but I just can't let completely go. I keep her hand in mine and she finally stops trying to pull it away even as she keeps shaking her head.

"No, Jackson, it was *my* fault. Daniel was chained to the pole the whole time. I don't know what he told you, but it was all me. I lost control. I've just..."

"I just..." She waves her hands like she doesn't know how to explain it. "... lost it. I kept hitting him and then when I stopped, there was all that blood and I've..." Tears gather and fall down her cheeks. She looks furious that she's crying and scrubs at her eyes, finally pulling her hand away from mine.

But Jesus, she's got it all so backwards. "No," I reach for her again. "No, Callie, you're the one who doesn't understand."

She glares at me furiously. "Stop it! I was the one who was there."

Why is she always so damn stubborn? "Yes you were," I say, trying to be patient, "but you were inexperienced. You trusted Daniel and he lied to you. Did he or did he not tell you that the rubber whip is a so-called 'practice whip.'"

She throws both her hands in the air. "Yeah. So what? He trained me how to use it. And I ignored everything and started going way too hard. That's all on me."

My jaw sets and I can feel the back of my neck heating. The beast is roaring in my ears. "Rubber whips are the most intense impact implements in all of a Dominant's arsenal. Did he tell you that? Leather ones are actually much kinder. Besides which, there was no way you should have been anywhere near a whip at this point in your training. I wouldn't let you near a person with the gentlest flogger until you've had at least three hours of practice. And a *whip*.

For Christ's sake." Calm the fuck down. I drag my hands through my hair.

It takes several moments but eventually everything I've said seems to finally sink in. "Daniel lied to me," she says.

I nod. "He knew what he was doing. He targeted you on purpose because you're a brand-new Domme. He's pushed too far with his previous Mistresses and they've all dropped him for trying to top from the bottom. He's gone outside the club before to find partners who will abuse him. The last time he did, he ended up in the hospital beaten all to hell with broken ribs and internal bleeding."

I cut myself off with a sharp shake of the head. "Some of us at the club had an intervention. This was a couple years ago. We thought it was rock-bottom and that he finally wised up. Then he goes and pulls this shit." I shake my head. Jesus even thinking about what Daniel did tonight disgusts me. I'll make sure that little shit never steps foot in the club again. "Miranda thinks it's just a setback, but I'm done with him. He's through at the club."

Callie's gaze goes to the ceiling. The furrow between her brow deepens as she frowns and her eyes dart slightly back and forth. Whatever she's thinking, it's obviously upsetting. But she doesn't say anything for long minutes. I'm trying to be patient and let her talk in her own time but patience was never one of my strong suits.

"What are you thinking? What's going on in that head of yours?"

"Nothing," she responds in little more than a monotone. "I'm not thinking anything."

"Don't give me that, Calliope Cruise." I grip her upper arms and turn her on the couch cushions so that she's facing me. "Don't you dare slip away from me. Not now."

She shrugs noncommittally.

Dammit, I won't let her do this. She's giving up before my very eyes.

I give her shoulders a little shake. "I'm serious."

She shrugs again, the barest lift and sag of her shoulders, as lifeless as a doll. "I'm tired. I want to go home."

She makes a move like she's going to stand but I don't let her go. Goddammit, I refuse for this to be the way tonight ends. For her to leave here defeated. Maybe this was all my fault, but I'll fix it. *I'll fix it.*

"Listen, the only way a Dom/sub relationship works is if there's complete trust between the partners. That was broken tonight."

As the words come out of my mouth, the solution hits me.

Of course.

"And I can see that I've gone about this all wrong. Trying to mentor you from the sidelines was never going to work. How did I expect you to be able to forge that bond with someone else you don't even know?" What was I thinking? I was forgetting the most basic tenant of the lifestyle. It's all about *trust*.

"I don't know your history, Callie, but from the little I do, I know it's been shit. You need a sub you can trust completely."

She immediately starts shaking her head. "No way. No more subs."

"But there *is* a way."

I can see more denials on her lips so I barrel ahead.

"Me. I'll be your submissive."

Her head jerks my direction and her eyes go wide. "But, but you're a..."

I slide my hands down her arms until I'm grasping her hands, palm to palm. "For you, I'll be whatever I need to be." I nod, everything becoming clearer the more I talk it out. "I've known Doms who've transitioned to switch relationships before. They made it work." I lift my head up. "I can too."

"But, but..." she sputters. "That's crazy!"

I settle against the back of the couch, not letting go of her hands. Nothing has ever felt more right. I might have made a shitload of mistakes, but this, finally, feels right.

"I don't think so at all." I smile and it's never felt so natural. "I imagine it'll be very easy wanting to be at your beck and call. I already want to fulfill your every desire." I wag my eyebrows at her.

"Have you ever done that before?" She looks as surprised by the question as I am, but then she presses on. "Been someone's sub?"

I shake my head. "No."

From the beginning, I trained as a dom. I never wanted to give up control. I always wanted a space where I could exercise it safely.

But for her...

When she tugs at her hands again, I let them go, though not without a reluctant sigh.

"I guess if you're going to be my Mistress, I better start learning to let you have your way. Even if all I want is to drag you into the back of my town car, push that dress up your thighs, yank down your thong, and eat you out until you're screaming my name."

She blinks at me and that gorgeous blush hits her cheeks. It's a good ten seconds of her just staring at me open-mouthed, eyes flicking around my face like she can't do anything but take me in.

When she does finally speak, all she manages to get out is, "Um."

I've never grinned wider. Oh yes, this is going to be good. She's not running. She wants it as much as I do.

Because I do. The idea of being a submissive or switch has never *ever* appealed to me before. But kneeling at Callie's feet? Worshipping *her?*

Yeah, yeah that I'm definitely into.

Callie sits there looking a little stunned but not lifeless anymore. I might even say that she looks hopeful.

She sits up straighter on the couch. "Your proposal sounds..." she trails off before landing on, "intriguing." She nods like she's proud of herself for finding the right word. "Maybe we can get together sometime and talk about it more. For tonight, I think it's time for me to go home and get some rest." She grabs her bag and stands up, and when she does it, she stands with her head held high.

Jesus but she's gorgeous and amazing and resilient and— about to leave. I jump to my feet, too.

"I'll have my town car pick you up Saturday night? Say at six o'clock? We could catch a light dinner and then play."

Her nostrils flare slightly at my words and I don't miss the swift inhale of breath. She blinks rapidly a few times and then nods tightly. "That sounds acceptable."

"Excellent. I'll get you home now. We should both get as much rest as possible the next couple days."

CHAPTER ELEVEN

CALLIE

My chest is tight when the town car pulls into Jackson's rounded driveway on Saturday evening. I can't tell if it's anticipation or anxiety. Probably both. Yesterday I had work and my visit with Charlie to distract me, but today was torture. Having this to look-forward-to-slash-freak-out about all day long? And now it's here.

My heart pumps a mile a minute when I step out onto the brick walkway and head up to the door. Before I can even press the bell, the door opens and there's Jackson.

Immediately my mouth goes dry. He's shirtless, and holy shit, I've forgotten how built he is. His barrel chest is a golden expanse of muscles that cut sharply down in a V below his waist. And yep, ab muscles round out the whole sex god vibe he's got going on. A worn pair of jeans sit low on his hips and my eyes linger on the light dusting of hair that trails from his navel down to—

"You look gorgeous." His voice comes out strained with lust and I look up, startled. I'm not the only one doing some ogling, apparently.

His eyes dart up from my chest guiltily, like he's embarrassed to have been caught staring.

Normally it always turns me off when guys can't stop staring at my rack, but on this occasion, Jackson gets a pass. After all, I picked this dress with the super low corset top for a reason. It laces in the front and I went ahead and laced it tight for full effect, meaning my double Ds are spilling so far out of the top, the top edges of my nipples are just barely covered. Thank God Shannon had an early date with Sunil so she didn't see me getting ready.

I made a stop at Miss Monroe's Adult Toy Expo early this afternoon and bought the dress and stiletto boots. I opted not to go for the obviously latex dress and instead picked out a dark maroon velvet number with a bustier bodice and a small bustle in the back. It looks a little more like a burlesque number than a strict dominatrix getup, but somehow it felt *right*. It all cost a pretty penny, but I figured looking the part would give me the confidence to truly inhabit the role.

The thought of anyone other than Jackson seeing me wear it was crazy embarrassing, but the chauffeur was extremely professional and kept his eyes averted the entire time, even when he held the door open for me. I had to fight back a smile at the thought that he'd make for a good submissive.

Jackson swallows hard and from how intensely he's looking into my eyes, I'm guessing it's taking all his willpower not to glance back down at my chest. This brings a feline smile to my lips. I have no idea how tonight will go.

Since today was Saturday, I spent a lot of it reading up on being a Domme, watching instructional videos online, basically anything and everything I could get my hands on. Despite the disaster of last night, before everything went to shit, there were some good moments. Even just having Daniel constrained and at my mercy felt amazing. But I'm not going to be caught unaware again, that's for damn sure.

I arch an eyebrow at Jackson. "Are you just going to stand there or are you going to let your Mistress in?"

Jackson's eyes widen and he swings the door open. "Of course. Christ, of course, come in."

I smile as I step over the threshold. Jackson Vale, flustered? Oh, tonight is going to be fun.

My stiletto heels make a *clack clack* noise on the expensive tile of his entryway. Jackson's eyes have dropped, but not in deference. He's staring at my thigh-high boots.

I lift my chin and it creates the effect of looking down my nose at Jackson, in spite of the fact that he's taller than me—even though he's barefoot and I'm wearing four-inch heels. Speaking of, my gaze lands on his feet. What is it about a guy's bare feet that is so sexy? Well, not any guy's. My ex, David, had nasty feet. He never trimmed his nails and they smelled so bad when he took off his socks, it was like a family of rodents had died in the walls. So yeah, I either had him wash his feet when he got home or keep his socks on at all times. Which is, you know, less than sexy when doing the deed.

But Jackson's feet are sculpted and manly with neatly trimmed nails and, insofar as I can tell from standing right beside him, no problematic odors. The whole package, him shirtless and with bare feet just makes him look... approachable and vulnerable in a way that I've never seen him before. Usually he's in power suits, in perfect control of everything around him.

But tonight he's handing those reins over to me. A sudden rush of giddiness flushes my skin.

He seems to notice and his dark blue eyes dilate. "Dinner is ready and waiting for us." His words seem to contradict the way he's looking at me. He looks like what he really wants to say is fuck dinner, grab me, shove me up against the nearest wall, and completely ravish me.

But he restrains himself. He's keeping it all leashed inside. I tilt my head sideways at him. Will he actually be able to do this? Submit to me? My fingers squeeze reflexively into my palms. Shit. My hands are sweaty. But fuck it. *No overthinking it. Stay in the moment.* That was the advice from the Dommes in one of the videos I watched and I'm thinking she knew her shit.

"Dinner sounds nice," I say.

Jackson nods his head. "This way." He turns sharply as if fighting some internal battle with himself.

I follow slowly behind him. It's not reluctance that stays my steps.

More curiosity. And again, anticipation. I bite my lip. Just how far can I push him? The question sends a somersault through my tummy. Not of fear, but a thrill. He's offered himself up on a platter and God, I want to bring him to his knees, in all senses of the word.

He leads me to a dining room full of windows and a skylight so that the room is doused with natural light. One window boasts a view of a tree-lined lot and the other, an inner garden courtyard. An antique mahogany table and otherwise simple furnishings make the room elegant without being ostentatious.

Jackson surrounds himself with beauty. I don't know why the realization startles me. I've known since I first met him that he has an appreciation for the finer things. But watching him move around in his home reveals a new layer to him.

Oh yes, I'm going to bring this man to his knees all right. And I'm going to start by doing so literally. He moves to take a seat beside the head of the table, where he gestures for me to sit.

But I shake my head at him. I snap my fingers loudly and point at the floor by my feet. I stare him down and continue pointing at my feet. The message couldn't be more clear. There's a spark of rebellion in his eyes. It's as if I can hear his thoughts: *This is my house. I'm not going to be reduced to sitting on the floor like a lapdog in my own house.*

But he doesn't voice any of that out loud. Other than a tick in his jaw, he gives nothing else away. Instead, he comes over to stand by my chair and bows his head. Then he gracefully drops to his knees before settling back on his haunches, head still bowed.

The thrill I felt earlier races even more forcefully up and down my spine. Oh God, I knew this would be a rush, but I didn't anticipate feeling this *much*. And so quickly. We've barely started. All he's done is sit at my feet and God… I shift in my seat and feel the beginning signs of moisture between my legs.

I can't help from reaching out a hand and stroking it through his hair. It's soft and springy to the touch. There is no gunk or product in it. Like everything else about him today, it's all natural.

Jackson's stripped himself down. For me. All for me. He leans into my touch, going so far as to lay his cheek on my knee. My heart rate speeds up again as I continue running my hands through his hair, caressing down to massage his scalp. I don't stop even when a low groan comes from his throat.

I'm only jerked away from our intense little revelry when I hear a polite cough and then look up to see that a middle-aged woman with a tray of two steaming bowls of soup has entered the room. She's petite with mostly gray hair even though she doesn't seem to be older than her late forties.

"Excuse me." She hurries into the room, puts the tray on the table, and then arranges the soup on the table where two places have been set. Like the chauffeur, she doesn't look directly at us. I feel a little *Downton Abbey* with them serving us like this but at the same time, in this moment it's not like I want a lot of attention from outsiders.

Jackson doesn't seem fazed by her even though he's on his knees at my feet, so I decide not to be either. I can make friends at a more appropriate time. You know, when I'm not wearing a barely-there corset dress with my lover on the floor like an animal begging for scraps.

The thought makes me want to laugh but I only permit myself a smile. Jackson's doing very good and keeping his eyes to the floor, so he doesn't see. I lean over and place a kiss on the top of his head. "Go get your soup and bring it here."

He moves swiftly to do as I ask.

He sets his bowl beside mine and I see his eyes dart toward his chair. Like he wonders if he should bring it as well. I snap and point to the floor at my feet again. I'll make this very clear for him. His shoulders tense briefly like he wants to argue but he masters himself just in time and sinks back to his knees.

"Do you have something to say about this arrangement, slave?"

The tense of muscles at the back of his neck is the only response for a long moment. "No, Mistress," comes his eventual response.

I stare down at the top of his head, a ridiculous smile of gratification taking over my face. Every moment of this is going to be a fight against his natural inclination. Why does that fact exhilarate me? I don't know but I'm too into the moment to think about it right now.

I dip the large, round soup spoon into the thick potato soup and then lift it to his lips.

"Sip," I order, my other hand going underneath his chin in case any spills. He immediately obeys, his wide mouth opening and taking in the entire spoonful. His gaze meets mine as he slowly releases the clean spoon with a sensuous *pop*.

I can't help staring at his lips, the way his top one is ever so slightly fuller than the bottom. He smirks after a second and my brows narrow. Oh, the big bastard thinks he can gain even the slightest bit of power back over me? I've learned my lesson about being topped from the bottom.

With the same spoon I used to feed him, I get another spoonful of soup and feed it to myself. I close my eyes and moan in enjoyment at the smooth buttery flavor of the soup as it slides down my throat. I turn the spoon over and lick it clean, opening my eyes so I'm watching Jackson all the while my tongue plays suggestively over the metal implement.

His pupils dilate and he shifts on his knees like he's trying to adjust himself. Well now. That's better. I'm the only one with power here. I give the spoon one last lick and then give him another spoonful. He takes his time doing his own tongue acrobatics with the spoon, his eyes continuing to smolder. Holy shit, who knew that some soup and a fucking spoon could be such hot foreplay?

I'm not even sure who's winning the battle for dominance at this point. All I know is that I'm turned on as fuck and I don't want it to end. We continue back and forth, me feeding him a spoonful and then myself until his bowl is finished and we're halfway through mine. Then the cook/serving woman comes in with the entrée.

Again I see Jackson shift uncomfortably on his knees. The woman doesn't look overtly in our direction but I don't miss the way her eyebrows go up before she schools her expression when she notices where Jackson is still seated. She obviously sees us out of her periphery. The idea only makes me smile wider and I make sure to feed Jackson another spoonful before she leaves the room. Jackson takes it but scowls at me. I smile beatifically back.

"Something to say?" I arch an eyebrow at him.

He averts his eyes back to the floor and shakes his head. I look over the main course. Shrimp pasta with a light cream sauce. Yummy.

When I reach over the table to Jackson's setting, my breasts all but smother Jackson's face. He inhales sharply but doesn't say anything. My panties moisten even more at his obvious reaction to me.

Still, as much as I want to push everything off the table and order him to lay down so I can mount him, I know I have to exhibit the discipline that I want from him. I can't just *play* at being a Domme. If I'm doing this, I'm fully committing.

I withdraw as I lift his plate and bring it over close to my own. Jackson lets out an involuntary little-frustrated groan when I do.

Excellent, I smile to myself. Right on track. I pick up my fork and use the wide soup spoon to start rolling the pasta. I stab a piece of shrimp on the end for good measure and then put it up to Jackson's mouth. "Open," I say cheerfully.

He does as I ask but again, it's as if I can see the wheels turning in his brain. How much longer of this? How much more will I subject him to? I roll another bite, this time for myself and let out a little moan of my own. It really tastes fantastic. Better than anything I have had at a restaurant in a long time. Granted, I haven't been to very many fancy restaurants in my life. Nor can I imagine the kind of lifestyle where you have a cook who comes to your house.

I feed Jackson another bite and some of the pasta falls out of his mouth. His eyes widen in embarrassment and he tries to turn away, lifting a hand to no doubt pushed the rest of the pasta in. I slap his hand out of the way right before he reaches his mouth. He tries to slurp the rest of the fettuccini using just his mouth and I pinch him on his nipple.

He winces right as I swoop down, kissing him and eating the extra pasta off his lip. I nip his bottom lip with my teeth for extra measure. His eyes are so wide when I pull back that I feel another pulse of slickness coating my underwear.

Enough. After the soup, even a few bites of the plate of the pasta was filling. Even if it wasn't, I'm too turned on to bother anymore with it. I grab my ice water and drink half of it, then lift the rest to Jackson's lips. He drinks eagerly, but his eyes stay clasped on mine the entire time.

I watch his Adam's apple bob up and down as he chugs the water.

God, why is that part of a man so sexy? Then again, I tend to think that about every inch of Jackson. It just depends on what feature I happen to be zeroing in on at the moment. My eyes slide languidly down his chest to his wine-colored nipples in the light tuft of dark hair that circles each one. His muscular biceps. The vein that traces down his forearm and over the top of his hand. Those strong, blunt fingers.

"Mistress?" There's a growl in his low voice. "How may I serve you?"

My cheeks flush. It's probably not very Mistress-ly of me but I can't help it. I'm too fucking excited about what comes next. "We haven't discussed your hard and soft limits." See, told you I did my research. "Tell me now what you are and aren't comfortable with."

"I'm open to almost everything." Jackson's voice is calm and sure. "Obviously no play with implements you haven't been trained on yet. Though I guess I do have a couple hard limits beyond that. No knife play or," he swallows and looks down, "fisting." He says it so quietly that at first I'm not sure I heard him. Then I replay it in my head. Fisting. No fisting. Holy shit. The thought never entered my mind, but now that I think about the implications, my thoughts go there. While fisting is out of the picture, the door is still open for all kinds of other naughty activities. I bite my lip and a rush of adrenaline floods my chest.

"Got it. What's your safe word?"

He meets my eyes. "Red... or *stiletto*."

Oh, wicked boy. "Anything else I need to know before we begin?"

"I'm all yours."

My heartbeat pounds so hard I can hear the blood racing in my ears. "Good. Do you have a room to play or just your bedroom?"

"I have a room."

The woman who's been serving us all evening comes in with dessert cups full of some kind of chocolate mousse.

"She's done for the evening," I keep my voice low so that only Jackson can hear. "Send her on her way. I don't want anyone in the house except you and me."

"Thank you, Marie. The dinner was delicious," Jackson's eyes stay on me the whole time he's talking to her. "You can leave for the night."

Marie looks over, startled. "But I need to clean up and—"

"You can do it tomorrow. Thank you again."

Marie looks like she wants to argue, but then seems to realize the awkwardness of the situation and maybe to pick up on why he might be asking her to leave without cleaning up. Redness rises to her cheeks and she averts her eyes. "Of course, Mr. Vale. Thank you." She turns and ducks out of the room.

A smile blooms on my lips and I drape my arms around Jackson's neck. "I don't think we're being very subtle."

"It's my house. Fuck subtle." He leans forward to try to capture my lips in a kiss and I'm *this* close to giving in. Jackson so rarely curses and it means one of two things when he does: either he's pissed or turned the fuck on. So goddammed hot.

Still, I pull back and wave my finger in front of his face just before his lips make contact.

"Ah ah ah, just because you're the boss at work, don't forget who's running the show here." I withdraw my arms from his neck and stand. "Now show me to this playroom, *slave*." I smirk with emphasis on the last word and see his back straighten. Which makes me laugh out loud. Oh dear, tonight is going to be fun, isn't it? That's only what, the twentieth time I've thought that?

I grab the two cups of chocolate mousse and follow him out of the dining room and through his labyrinthine house. Without him guiding the way, I think I'd get lost in here. I prefer more open-space concept houses than this older style involving a network of rooms, but I can't deny the luxury.

There's still lot of light throughout and I realize that the rooms on the ground floor basically create a circle around the inner courtyard. We head up a flight of stairs and down the hallway. Jackson pauses at the second door on the right and pulls a key out of his pocket.

When he pushes the door open, I smile, realizing I chose my outfit exactly right. It's like stepping back into the nineteenth century. If, you know, parlors in the nineteenth century had floggers, paddles, and nipple clamps hanging on the walls. The floor is covered with an ornate, Victorian-era styled rug.

A huge, antique wooden four-postered bed with an intricate lace and organza canopy dominates the room. All the other furniture looks antique as well, though some of it must be contemporary and just fashioned to look antique. The leather spanking bench, for example. Or hell, maybe the Victorians were into kink, but I doubt it would've survived in such gleaming condition. I walk over to it and run my fingers over the soft leather and down to the ankle restraints. Also leather.

I look up to Jackson. "Fancy."

He inclines his head. His posture is slightly stiffer than normal and I wonder if he's nervous. He's probably used all of this equipment with other people, but he's always been on the giving end. Never receiving.

For a moment, I frown. I don't like the idea of Jackson here with women before me. How many? Was he serious about them? When was his last relationship? Why did it end?

Then I give my head a rough shake. The fuck? I don't care about any of that. That's not what this is anyway. Besides, no matter who's been here before me, this is the first time he's ever let someone else take the reins. The first time he's ever submitted. The thought fills me with intense satisfaction and I feel at least a foot or two taller when I turn to examine the rest of the room. I walk over to a leather-padded table that's about seven feet long and as wide as a twin bed. Ankle and wrist restraints hang on their respective corners.

A smile curls my lips. Oh yes. This will do nicely.

"Slave," I say sharply. "Clothes off. Then up on this table." I snap and point at the table in front of me. "Cock up."

I see just a second's hesitation but then he's doing as I ask. He drops his jeans and I see that he's going commando. A small gasp escapes when I notice that he's also already sporting a semi.

Under my perusal, he hardens more even as he walks toward me. Straight toward me, like he's going to try to brush up against me before getting on the table.

I shoot him a warning glare and move to the other side of the table. "Don't get yourself in trouble. Slaves who don't obey the rules get punished."

His eyes narrow on me. I see the challenge even if he doesn't verbalize it. He's wondering exactly how I think I can punish him.

I lift an eyebrow. "Oh darling," I sneer. "Please. Just try me." I might not have been studying up on this Domme business for very long, but everything I read pointed to one basic truth: men are guided by their dicks. Get control of that and control of the man will soon follow.

Granted, Jackson Vale is certainly one of the most intimidating men I've ever met in my life but that makes mastering him even more of a triumph. He's not some wimpy boy who will bow at my beck and call to lick my boots. No. He's head-to-toe alpha. Can I tame the lion?

Tonight will tell.

He pauses, his hot stare on me with the table between us. I flick my eyes down to the leather surface in silent command. We continue standing for another five seconds. He's told me that he'll submit, but inside, everything in him rebels against it—it's obvious in each inch of his body. I stand taller and make my voice like ice. "On the table, slave." I make sure to over-articulate every word.

His nostrils flare but he finally does as ordered. He turns, hefts himself up, and lays flat on the table. His cock points almost straight up, an arrow to the ceiling.

I smile down at him. "That wasn't so hard, now was it?" Then I glance again at his cock. "On the other hand..." I give him one quick stroke up and down. His dick is hot and hard, and his whole body jolts with the touch, torso lurching up off the table. Another one of those thrills zings through me, but I immediately let go of him.

"We can't have that, now can we?" I quickly move to the head of the table and draw his left arm up over his head. I feel the flex of his muscle as I set his wrist into the padded leather cuff. I smile as I slide the wide buckle into place and secure it. He's not getting out of these babies. There's even more tension in his other arm as I fasten it in place.

As soon as his arms are secured, I grin so wide I'm afraid my face is going to split. Oh my God. Yes, his legs are free, but already, Jackson Vale is so much at my mercy. Helpless before me.

I stroke my hands down his body, starting at his inner forearms, down his arms to his chest, then his stomach. I continue to his hips and skim down to his thighs, completely bypassing his cock.

He lets out a stunted groan of frustration and my smile grows impossibly wider. When I come to his ankle, I grasp it firmly and secure the buckle. Then, before he can pause or overthink it too much, I move to the other side and lock his last limb in.

I look down at my work and the flare of heat that surges in my core is like nothing I've ever experienced. This isn't just any man laid out before me, handcuffed to a table, naked and at my mercy. This is Jackson Vale. Holy fuck. Never in my wildest dreams... I mean, I didn't even *know* to dream for this.

I move up his body, slowly trailing my fingers along his shins, then to his inner thighs. He sucks in a breath as I tease, moving closer and closer up to where I know he longs for me to grasp him.

But I don't. He hisses out his disappointment when instead I start to massage his inner thigh, right below his balls.

I'm fascinated as his cock grows and grows, surging up toward his stomach. The rush of power I feel is insane. I continue massaging, working my way down to his kneecaps and then back up. I can see on his face what he's hoping for every time I inch close to the prize. After all, I gave him a tug once. When am I going to do it again?

I move my right hand a little further north so that my thumb just brushes the outside of his sack. With the little bit of slack he has in the restraints, he tries to press into my hand. I laugh and withdraw completely.

He swears and presses his head hard back into the leather table, arm muscles flexing against his restraints. The chains rattle against the frame and the noise makes me rub my legs together in pleasure. He's turning out to be even more of a caged beast than I imagined. I make eye contact and lick my lips. He swears again and then closes his eyes while he visibly tries to calm his breathing.

I turn on my heel and pretend to ignore him while I head to the wall. The implements seem to be arranged in order of impact. From left to right, there are a variety of paddles and floggers with just a few whips in the very furthest corner.

But right in front of me are all kinds of interesting items. I pick up two brushes. At first they just look like hair brushes, but when I run my fingers over the bristles, I notice that they have different textures, one soft and the other rougher. Interesting.

There's a small cabinet as well and I open it. I find even more fascinating little trinkets on the shelf. Nipple clamps of various sizes with different jewelry and weights attached to them. Several kinds of lubricant. Dildos of all shapes and sizes too, still in packaging. My attention peaks at those. But maybe not for tonight. In the corner sits a fat red candle and a box of matches. *Oh.*

I read about this earlier today. Hot candle wax. It seemed like something that even beginners couldn't screw up. I grab the candle, the matches, and a little pizza cutter looking device that has blunt metal nubs notched along the rolling circle. I read about this too. Like the brushes, it's meant for sensation play.

And sensation is what I'm after with Jackson tonight. I want to make him insane with sensation so that he's strung tight with desire. He thinks he'll bow to any of my wishes now, but I'm going to bring him to the point of begging, no, *weeping,* to serve me.

When I return to him, his cock has flagged only slightly. I put my hands on his stomach and slide them down to his hip again, framing his dick on either side.

I lean over and blow hot air right across the tip. It jerks to life, bobbing half an inch away from my lips. I pull away and slap it lightly with my palm.

"Don't be greedy," I chastise. "You'll get what you get when I determine you're ready."

With that, I start running the soft brush down his chest. He looks confused for a moment and then his eyes slide closed. He relaxes into it.

I brush all the way down his chest and to one thigh. I imagine he thinks I'll move to the next, so I change it up and run the soft bristles down his pulsing shaft. He lets out a groan and his eyes pop open again. They shift down to observe my movement. I brush his cock up from underneath, then back down again.

I lock eyes with his and then bring my mouth right beside his pulsing member. I'm just going to breathe on it again to tease him but when I get close, I'm shocked by my own desire. The rounded mushroom head is so... pretty. Jackson Vale would die if I described his cock to him that way, but it is.

My pussy contracts and my mouth waters as I watch the way it jolts under the ministrations of my brush. I glance up to his face and he's so focused on what I'm doing. Utterly enthralled.

My tongue flicks out and I lick the thick vein that runs the length underneath the shaft. Jackson's entire body trembles and a muted groan comes from his throat.

I pull back and stare at his dick with trepidation. I can't believe I just— I didn't think I'd ever be able to—

Memories rush up. The last time I saw one of these up close, it was being shoved at me. I said no and my rapist forced it on me anyway. Revulsion shudders through me and I move several more inches back.

I can feel Jackson's eyes on me. I don't look up. I don't want to know if he's noticed something change in my demeanor or if his gaze is full of demand that I get back to attending to his cock. Neither would be acceptable.

So I keep my eyes averted while I pick up the second brush with firmer bristles and resume brushing down his legs. I can feel the slight scrape against the skin the brush provides and I smooth my other hand down the flesh after upbraiding it with the comb.

But my mind isn't on the sensations I'm providing. It's back on the bastard who stole so much for me. Who tried to break me. Am I really going to let him steal this aspect of sex play from me forever? It's part of why I got back on the horse, so to speak, this summer. I wanted to prove to myself that Gentry hadn't totally jacked me up. I could still have sex and enjoy it. He hadn't stolen anything from me. I was *so* determined to prove it.

And now, what? I'll never be able to give oral again? Because of what that fucking bastard did to me? Jackson's entire body jerks as I run the bristles along the bottom of his feet.

"Does it hurt?" He hasn't reacted so violently to anything I've done so far except the first time I grabbed his cock.

"Tickles," he manages through gritted teeth.

I can't help the laugh that bursts out of me. I run the brush across the sole of his other foot and he twists in his restraints just as much as with the first foot. God, I guess I am a sadist. I take pity on him after that, but I'm still chuckling.

And that's when it hits me. I feel safe with Jackson. If there's anyone to try it with, it's him. Especially while I have him completely immobilized like this. It won't be anything like it was with Gentry. No one will be holding my head and forcing anything on me. Here, I'm in control. I suck in a quick breath. Shit. Am I really going to do this?

I look around the room and my eyes zero in on the chocolate soufflé cups that I abandoned on a side table when I first entered the room. Oh yeah. I smile and I quickly retrieve them, adding to my little collection on the ground near the candle and brushes. I lift up the soufflé and run it underneath Jackson's nose.

"I have a test for you," I say in a low, sultry voice.

Jackson looks wary. "What is it?"

I use the spoon and put a dollop of soufflé over one of his nipples. Then, leaning over so that he has full view of my over-ample cleavage, I lick and then suckle it all off.

The chocolate flavor explodes on my tongue, but even more pleasurable than the flavor is Jackson's response. His pupils dilate even wider, his nostrils flare and the chest underneath my mouth moves up and down like he's running a marathon. I give the nipple one last teasing bite and then lift up.

"You see, I'm hungry for dessert." I give a coy smile. "And I'm happy to make it an enjoyable experience for you as well. I take the spoon and land another dollop right on the tip of his long, throbbing dick. His eyes flare and I lick my lips.

"But," I hold up a finger and give him a severe look. "The slave only gets the treat of his Mistress' mouth if he does not move a muscle. There will be no shoving, no thrusting, no movement of any kind. Am I understood?"

He nods.

I glare at him. "Am I understood?"

"Yes, Mistress." His voice comes out thick and I smile in gratification.

Now let's see if he can hold up to his end of the bargain. I lean over and put my mouth over the entire head of his dick. The flavor of the chocolate mousse again hits my senses, but as I suck it away, I began to taste something else.

Jackson. His shaft is thick and pulsing in my mouth. I suck him in far enough so that my lips close right over the fat ridge of his head. As I lick the last of the soufflé way, it mixes with his essence, a little bit of pre-cum that has leaked out from how excited I've gotten him even though I barely touched him so far. Just the thought has me sucking even harder.

I bob my head up and down once, making sure to give good suction especially as my lips close over the ridge again. I don't miss Jackson's low, ecstatic groan. Or the way his cock twitches in my mouth and seems to grow even more.

But he's a good boy and he doesn't thrust his hips at all. He doesn't shove himself down my throat. The chocolate flavor, Jackson's scent, and even the smell of the oiled leather from the table are enough to separate this moment from the other so that no flashbacks are popping up.

Thank you God, thank you God, thank you God. I reach over for the cup of mousse and lather him up and down with the sugary treat again. Then I get to enjoying my dessert.

I'm tentative at first about how far I take him in my mouth, but when he continues lying there like a good little slave, I venture sucking more and more of him in.

Christ, I never realized how hot giving a BJ could be before. He's trembling underneath me. When I glance up, his heated stare is enough to send volcanic fire shooting straight to my core. The desperation, the need on his face... My fingers bite into the leather on either side of his hips and I bob my head even lower until his bulbous head hits the back of my throat.

I apply suction and my cheeks hollow out. Then I lazily bring my mouth back up until I let go with a loud *pop*. His eyes go wild with lust. I'm about to start humping the edge of the leather table, this is getting me so hot. I lick the slit at the top of his head and then move to take him in again, inch by slow torturous inch.

And then he bucks up into my mouth, thrusting his cock nearly into my throat, not once, but in and out and back in again before I tear myself away from him.

"Motherfucker!" I yell at him and slap his dick.

He looks shocked and it quickly morphs to mortification. "I'm so s— sorry," he stutters and tries to sit up but is jerked backward by his restraints. "I can't believe I just— I'm so sorry— I didn't mean—"

I glare at him. A riot of feelings battle for prominence in my chest. Disappointment, the lingering flash of fear I felt in the moment when his cock was almost choking me and also, strangely, a savage excitement because he's still locked up and now he deserves whatever punishment I give him.

I turn away from him and stalk over to where a high-backed wooden chair sits on the wall. I drag it over the hardwood floor, enjoying the scrape of the wood on wood as I go. I hope I'm fucking up his floors. I slam it in place right beside his head. I sit down, spread my legs, and hike one calf up over the wooden arm rest of the chair.

"I'm sorry. Callie, shit. I'm—"

"Shut up," I say, proud when I manage to keep my voice calm. "It's *Mistress* to you, and you will not say another word."

He shuts his mouth even though I can see it's killing him. Too fucking bad.

I adjust myself slightly as I work my black lace panties over my ass, down past my thighs and over my thigh high boots. I toss them on Jackson's chest. He watches me with a mix of concern and fear. Good for him, the fucker. Can't even obey one simple set of instructions.

I slouch further down in the chair and lift my dress so he has a good view of my glistening pussy. All the nicer to touch myself. I'm slick and swollen from the buildup of everything tonight.

Rolling my clit between my fingers makes the surge of excitement race that much higher. Jackson's eyes are locked on the movement of my hand. I switch to rubbing my clit with my thumb and drive my first two fingers inside myself. I shudder and sink even lower in the chair.

"Oh God, yes," I moan, rubbing the upper walls of my sex.

"Let me free, I can take care of you. I'll make up for disappointing you, I swear." Jackson's voice is choked with fervency.

My fingers pause their motion and I tilt my head at him. "Oh, you will, will you?" I shoot to my feet. I take the fingers that were just inside myself and rub them over his lips, then jam them in his mouth. He eagerly sucks at my juices, nostrils again flaring.

When I pull my fingers back, his corded neck is taut. "I swear, I'll make you come harder than you ever have before in your entire life."

I lean over so that my breath is hot on his ear. "That does sound delectable." I move to his other ear, letting my hair fall over his chest. "It also sounds like something that only a deserving slave should get the privilege of doing." I bite his ear, not roughly enough to draw blood, but more than a simple nip.

He hisses in a breath and I pull away. His eyes are full of frustration more than remorse now. He's definitely not a natural submissive. Which makes me all the more determined to master him.

Before I sit back down, I walk over to the cabinet and retrieve one of the midsized dildos. Then I take a seat and opened my legs wide. I open the top of the box and pull out the flesh-colored plastic cock. "So pretty," I murmur. I run my hand up and down the length of it, miming jacking it off.

I bite the tip of my tongue as I reach my fingers down and stretch myself a little further. Watching Jackson's furious eyes and muscles flexed against the restraints makes me squelch. Oh yeah, I'm ready.

"I bet you wish this was your sad, neglected dick." I hike my leg even higher on the arm of the chair so he has a picture-perfect view as I rub the crown of the lifelike dildo up and down my slit, teasing my clitoris.

"Oh God, that hits the spot," I moan, tossing my head back. Even from this position, I watch Jackson through slitted eyes. "You tasted how wet I am. I think it'll go in just fine without any lube, don't you?"

Jackson grits his teeth.

"I asked you a question, slave," I snap.

The vein in his forehead pulses. "I'll apologize a thousand more times, if you just let me—"

I shove the dildo home and let out an unabashed cry of ecstasy. "Oh God, I'm stuffed so full. You can't even imagine how full I feel."

When I look back over at Jackson, he's turned his face away so that he's looking at the far wall.

"Eyes on me, right now."

His head doesn't move and I pull out the dildo, enjoying the wet noises it makes even while I'm pissed as fuck at Jackson.

I move until I'm towering over him, directly in his line of sight. "Do you want to use your safe word and end this scene?" I'm dead serious. I want to make this work but if Jackson simply doesn't have it in him to submit, then there's no point to any of this.

A pained look crosses his face. He squeezes his eyes shut for a moment and then he looks up at me. "No," his voice is quiet. He sucks in a deep breath. "I don't want to end it."

"Then stop being a fucking baby." Each one of my words is a stab. "You're a Dom. Would you put up with a sub pulling this shit on you?"

He jolts like I struck him and it finally seems to sink in. "No." He's subdued but nods decisively. "I'd spank them till their ass was black and blue for acting like this." He lets out a breath and drops his eyes. "I'll submit to whatever punishment you deem necessary."

I grab his chin and jerk his head up, forcing his gaze to meet mine. "And you'll obey when I give you a fucking order?"

He swallows but nods, then catches himself and says, "Yes, Mistress."

"Good. Now that we've had this little come-to-Jesus moment," I climb up on the table so that I'm straddling his chest, dildo in hand, "we can continue. You are to watch what I'm doing. Don't you dare take your eyes off me. No matter what."

"Yes, Mistress."

I repeat the teasing ritual I went through earlier with the tip of the dildo before easing it back into my body. It's even better this time, with Jackson's hot body between my thighs. I scoot down so I'm straddling the upper part of his waist right below his chest. I'm high enough that there is no contact with his straining cock. I bet he can smell me, though. I smile at the thought. From the pained look on his face as he watches me, I imagine I'm right.

I prop the base of the dildo against his stomach and ride it. I suck in my breath as I grind down on it.

"Ooo, that's so good," I groan. "If only you weren't such a fuck up, this could be you inside me." With the hand not holding the dildo, I reach up and grab my breast. The ladies are already spilling so far over my bodice, it's little effort to pop one out over the top so that my nipple is exposed. I squeeze my plump breast in my hand and then lift it higher so that I can lick the tip of my puckered nipple.

"Oh *fuuuuuuuuuuuuuck*, does that make you hard?" I ask Jackson, rising up and then jamming down again on the fake dick. A glance over my shoulder shows a stream of pre-cum trailing the side of his pulsing shaft.

I look back to his tormented face. "I wonder if you can come just fucking the air like that," I ponder out loud. "Doesn't seem like it would be very satisfying," I lean into the dildo and come back down at an angle so that it rubs my clit just right, letting out another high-pitched satisfied moan.

"But at least," I manage through gasped breaths, "you won't be left with blue balls at the end of the night."

"For fuck's sake," he curses.

"Did you say something?"

He shakes his head, but his face is red with strain. Fuck me, he's the hottest thing I've ever seen. His arms tense and yank against the restraints. I think it's unconscious, he can't help trying to break out from being held down like this. It's not in his nature.

So why is he doing this? It's obviously more than difficult for him. Every bit of the night has been a strain against his natural inclinations.

"Why are you doing this?" As much as I might want this, I need to understand. "Why did you agree to be my submissive?"

His chest moves up and down underneath my body like a great bellows. He looks a little dazed by my question at first, like he's been so lost in what we're doing that human words take a moment to register. "Because... it's you."

Nice sentiment, but it doesn't tell me anything. "You're a dominant. What's so special about me that you'd put up with any of this?" I gesture at his hands in the restraints.

He's quiet but I'm not having any of that. I turn and grab his neglected cock in my fist. His whole body jerks. I pump him up and down and then let go.

"Tell me what's different about me," I command.

Again he struggles for words, but finally says, "You and I have a bond. We're..." He shrugs as much as he can while being locked up, "... similar. When I first met you, I looked at you and saw a little bit of myself."

I blink in shock. What? I thought— I thought when we first met he saw me as a victim. I thought that's why he pursued me in the first place.

"What do you mean?" My voice comes out as little more than a whisper.

Jackson looks away from me and I can tell by the expression on his face, the way his mouth tightens and his eyes shudder, that he's said more than he meant to. "Just that we've both been too trusting and we know what it's like to have been taken advantage of by manipulative people." His eyes come back to mine. "We've both survived and are stronger for it."

I... This is not what I was expecting. Here I am, lodged on a dildo, still horny as fuck, and Jackson's words are sending me on a tailspin.

Gentry. He's talking about Gentry. He's alluded to his past with Gentry a few times. But always in very vague terms. Something bad happened there. I can't imagine it was anything like what went down with me, but what *was* it?

I grip Jackson's shaft again and he groans. The sound shoots straight through me. "You are so fucking turned on right now, aren't you" I ask huskily. I loosen my grip on him and tease my fingers up and down his length before juggling his balls between my fingers.

"I bet all you can think about right now is what my hot cunt would feel like, squeezing around you, milking you fucking dry." I give him a hard squeeze and rub him up and down again. He hisses and his cock flexes up into my hold.

I hover over him and grasp his shoulders. "Tell me what Gentry did to you."

His eyes had been closed in ecstasy but they shoot open at this. And they're full of fear. Not of Gentry himself, I don't think, but of me finding out... something. What the fuck? What doesn't he want me to know? I dig my fingernails into his shoulder muscles as I lean in, pressing my breasts into his chest.

"Tell me." I've never sounded more like a Domme than in this moment.

Jackson's eyes are wide and wild. "Yellow," he whispers.

Yellow? He's going to fucking yellow me?

No way, buddy. Yellow is meant to be a signal things are pushing a sub's comfort zone too far, but part of the point of all of this is to break through the boundaries of comfort zones. And this is supposed to be about establishing a bond of trust. He's just revealed that what brought us together involves his past with Gentry. And he thinks he can just fucking leave it there?

I pull back, but I'm not nearly done with him. I go back to pumping up and down on the dildo, but it's Jackson that I'm riding. This great beast that I'm determined to subdue. At least I have him leashed for this brief moment in time.

I look down at him, taking him in in all his glory. Muscles bulging. Face and chest glistening with sweat as he bucks uselessly beneath me, his dick thrusting into nothing but air.

My pussy clenches around the dildo inside me. I can't quite pretend it's him. No, Jackson Vale inside me would be an altogether different experience. But seeing the denied want in his eyes is a high all its own. And God, the wave inside me— It's rising, and God, the heat—

"I'm going to tame you and then ride you, you fucking beast."

Oh, oh, it's close. Almost there. Oh *God*. I lean forward and grab onto Jackson's sweat-slicked hair, bringing my face so close to his we're sharing a breath. "Tell me what Bryce Gentry did to you," I demand. "Now!"

"Stiletto," he says, and then closes the gap and kisses me hard. I'm furious and so fucking turned on and—

I claw at his hair as I impale myself on the dildo and come in a sharp bright burst. It's shorter than others I've had, but intense. So intense I feel like I might get a goddamn migraine from it or pass out. I pull away from Jackson's mouth and lean my head on his shoulder, gasping for breath as I come down.

Then what he said registers. Shit. He used his safe word. That means all play is supposed to stop immediately. I scramble to get off him, but my leg cramps up and I almost fall in the attempt.

"Careful," he says. He's breathing hard too. I grab onto his bicep to steady myself as I ease to the floor.

"Got it," I say, my legs shaking. I remove the dildo and then look around, suddenly embarrassed. Shit. This feels awkward now that the scene is over. Like, hey, where's the sink so I can wash my pussy juice off this nice brand-new dildo?

But when I glance over at Jackson, his eyes are averted like he's embarrassed too. He's trying to scrunch his legs together at an awkward angle but it's not working since the restraints are holding him spread-eagled. I move to release his ankle cuffs when I realize what's going on.

His cock's no longer flying at full mast. Nope, instead, there's a small puddle of... Holy shit, he came. Without me even touching him, he came. I mean, I'd heard that could happen for guys if they were stimulated enough, but I sort of thought it was a myth.

And he looks embarrassed about it. I hurry to his face, take both his cheeks and leaned down to kiss him. "You're fucking amazing."

His eyes search mine. He looks so vulnerable. I've never seen his shields down like this before. Like I could crush him or be his everything depending on how I play this moment.

Tonight could be considered a failure if one was just looking at it from the outside. Jackson had a hard time submitting and disobeyed my demands. At the end, he used his safe word. But right now, the way he's looking at me, his fucking heart and soul stripped bare for me...

I bend down and kiss him again. First with the gentlest brush of my mouth on his and then deeper when his lips tug on mine and his tongue seeks entry. God, I've never felt more connected to another human being in my whole life.

I only pull away so that I can release his wrists from the restraints. He immediately sits up and the first thing he does is pull me into his arms. There's no more embarrassment between us. He just holds me for I don't know how long. Eventually we undo his ankles. He wraps the towel tightly around his waist and then, hand in hand, he leads me down the hall to his master suite.

CHAPTER TWELVE

CALLIE

When we get to his room, I'm not sure who is taking care of who. From all I've read, aftercare is supposed to be the dom/domme's job, so I head straight for the large Jacuzzi bath and set the faucets going. But it's Jackson who takes my hand after I've undressed to lead me inside.

Jackson settles his large body behind mine and curls me into his arms as the jets start their magic work. The pumping jets ease away all stress, anxiety, and mixed emotions about what did and didn't work tonight.

I sink into his warm body and his big hands as they start to work shampoo through my shoulder-length hair, massaging my scalp until I'm completely limp against him. He seems pleased by my reaction.

"That's right," he murmurs, cupping one big hand over my eyes while the other splashes water over the suds to rinse out the shampoo. I should probably be doing this to him. From the outside it makes sense for a sub to serve his master like this, but really, it throws off the control dynamic. I ought to be the one taking care of him.

I'm about to say something when he soaps up my shoulders, gently massaging as he goes. But fuuuuuuuck it. That feels so good. And *right*.

Because you know what? Roles were never going to be strictly black and white between us. He's too alpha, and apart from the times when I just need to be in control, I can't deny I love being pampered and taken care of like this.

Still. Aftercare is aftercare. Once he's massaged me all the way to my toes, spending a fair share of time making sure each centimeter of my breasts have been scrubbed squeaky clean, I flip over so that I'm facing him.

His thick member bobs in the water between us. He may have come earlier, but it couldn't have been that satisfying. I press my soap-slicked body against his, his erection sandwiched between us.

Time for a new game. He groans and presses his hips up against me. So predictable.

I pull my hips back. Before tonight, the words I would've used to describe Jackson were disciplined, in control, and—to everyone but me at least—standoffish.

Yet just in this one session, I've broken through to levels of want that bring out the horny teenager in him. I've seen him stripped of the control he values so highly. And it's magnificent.

Because I'm betting I'm the only one who has seen this side to Jackson since he actually *was* a teenager. It's probably something he's ashamed of and thinks he should hide. Just like the many things I have tucked away. Secrets. Including the secrets he won't tell.

Yet. He won't tell me yet. Rome wasn't conquered in a day and Jackson Vale won't be either.

I run my wet fingers through his hair. The bath seems to be doing its magic on him as well. His head is relaxed against the sloping side of the bath and his eyes are lazy in spite of his cock standing at attention.

Maybe he's just accepted this is how it will always be between us. He's not begging, which is very good. I couldn't handle my man constantly begging to get off, like the whiny guy in Mistress Night-blood's scene. But no, Jackson would never demean himself like that.

I squirt some shampoo in my hand from an expensive-looking bottle on the ledge and work it through Jackson's hair. His eyes close and all his features soften. God, he's gorgeous. The heavy ridge of his brow and his sharp, arrow-shaped nose. I could sit and stare at him for far too long if I let myself.

I'd think he was asleep if not for the fact that he bends his head forward for me to rinse his hair. That and the aforementioned boner that has not settled down one bit. I chuckle to myself as I cup water and pour it over his head, working the shampoo out and drawing my hands down his solid back. Just having him under my hands is getting me all riled up again too.

I move myself in the tub and push him forward so that I can scoot behind him. Then I wash his back with long strokes. Once he's clean there, I can't help it. I start kissing his muscled shoulders, then down his spine, vertebra by vertebra.

Even though the bath water is warm, I'm delighted to see the chills on his skin. Such gorgeous skin. Just the right amount of tan so he's not pasty, but not in an orange way where I imagine him spending time in tanning beds.

What is his ancestry anyway? Maybe the olive skin tone has more to do with where his parents or grandparents came from than spending much time in the sun. I kiss up his neck and nip him on the back of his ear.

Oops. That seems to have set off some kind of reaction in him, because the next thing I know, Jackson has pulled me around to the front of his body, cock grinding between us again as he lifts me out of the bath. The Domme in me wants to protest, but the girly girl, Callie, is loving it.

Besides, the previous scene is over and we are just figuring this whole thing out. I don't think Jackson and I are the kind of folks who are interested in a 24/7 power exchange sort of thing. I breathe out in relief at that. I don't think I'd have the energy to keep that up all the time.

And when he lays me on the bed, eyes dark and looking like he wants to make a feast of me? Yeah, I'm on board with that too.

Except that when he leans over, his whole body over mine to kiss me, I'm slammed with a sense of claustrophobia. Can't breathe, can't breathe.

I immediately hook my foot through his inner knee and grab his elbow, then transfer my weight like I learned in self-defense. The next second, I've rolled us so that he's the one on his back with me looming over him. On top.

Breathe. In and out. Looking down, well fuck. That's just hot as hell. Jackson's looking at me like he wants to devour me even more now. I grin, able to breathe again and suddenly growing even hotter by the fact that I was able to not only escape and evade this giant of a man, but captivate him as well. Because when I lean over, letting the low hanging fruit of my large breasts dangle in his face, he seems to have forgotten all about the position and any thoughts of being on top.

I grind down and the length of his cock rubs my most intimate places. My breath hitches. I'm shocked I was even able to get off on that stupid dildo earlier when the real flesh-and-blood thing was so nearby. Fuck teasing him anymore. Fuck preamble and foreplay and any of the rest of it.

I lean over him, open the door on his nightstand and, as expected, I find condoms. There's even a new box, which is appreciated. It's always nice not to open a guy's drawer and find a hundred pack with like, fifty of them gone. None of us want to think about who the rest of the pack got used with.

I tear the packet with my teeth and in the next second it's rolled down over his shaft. He hisses out his pleasure, dark eyes watching me. I can see from how tensed he's holding his whole body he's expecting this to just be another tease. He thinks I'm going to pull back and not deliver. Punishment for some failing from tonight's scene.

I frown a little. We'll have to work on communication in future scenes. Yeah he wasn't perfect, but it was his first time as a sub. I don't want him always off-kilter, afraid of what will or won't happen next. I can see how some Dommes might like that, but it's not what I want between Jackson and me. Sometimes anticipation is fine. But I'd rather have communication and openness.

Still, I can't help smirking at his watchful expression and then I sink down on top of him. His eyelids flutter with ecstasy. His hands aren't bound this time, though, so he quickly grabs my hips. I'm on top, but I can tell that doesn't mean that Jackson plans on being a passive participant.

Using the hold he has on my hips, he lifts his torso off the bed, his ab muscles flexing. "You feel so fucking amazing. I've been waiting all night, hell, for months to get back where I belong."

He jackknifes especially deep and we both groan simultaneously. Oh God. *Fuck.* So much better than that cheap piece of shit dildo.

My hands fall on his shoulders, fingers digging in my nails as I pull him to me. Now neither one of us is really on top. We're sitting up straight, holding tight onto one another and melded together by our fused, rocking centers.

"I'm gonna love you so good," he says and this time it's him who nips at my ear.

I throw my head back, thrusting my breasts forward into his chest. One of his strong hands runs over my mouth, down my chin, then traces my neck down to the valley between my breasts. He continues all the way down until his thumb starts working my clit.

Oh God, it's rising too fast this time. Too fast. We just started but there it is. How does he know just exactly where to touch—?

He starts taking me even harder, rougher. The bed bounces with each thrust. At this angle, the bulbous head of his cock strikes some place deep up inside me I've never even known existed before. Is that what people mean when they talk about a G-spot? Holy hell. Jackson rubs at my clit while he continues ramming at that perfect target.

"Come for me, baby," he growls. "Do it. Come for me now."

And I do. I explode. Fireworks light behind my eyelids and shudders rock me so hard from the inside out I feel like I might rip in two.

An animalistic noise comes from Jackson as he jerks inside me and stills, holding me to him with a bruising grip while shudders continue to wrack my body.

We must have slumped back down to the bed at some point, because when I blink my eyes open, we're laying side-by-side, legs entangled. His cock has slipped mostly out of me. Just the tip remains.

He seems to notice it at the same moment because he turns away, ties off the condom and tosses it in what I assume is a small trashcan beside his bedside table. "I'll clean up more later," he murmurs, pulling me back into him and slipping his thigh between mine again. "I'm not ready to let you go yet."

I'm feeling a bit speechless after that orgasm and even if I could talk, what's there really to say to that?

I make an assenting noise of some kind and then close my eyes and settle into the warmth of his chest.

When I wake up, it's to find Jackson watching me, propped up on an elbow. I startle slightly and pull the sheet to cover my breasts. His eyes stay trained on my face though.

"What are you staring at, you freak?" I mumble, blushing and letting some hair fall to cover my face.

"I want to transfer you so you're working directly with my team on the newest prototype we're developing. Every report I get from your supervisor says your work is head and shoulders above the rest. I need your kind of expertise and out-of-the-box thinking on my team."

"What?" I blink blearily and try to wrap my sleep-fogged brain around what he's saying. Wait, does he mean—?

He reaches forward and grabs one of my hands between both of his. "Come work with me." His eyes zero in on mine, the blue of his irises shining in the morning light filtering in through the curtained windows. "And I mean, work with me side-by-side. No more of this being in the same building but on separate projects crap."

I sputter. "Stop it. You know I never wanted special treatment just because we're..." I wave a hand between our bodies, "... *involved*."

A crease appears between Jackson's eyebrows. "I'm not just suggesting this because I want to spend more time with you—"

"But that is one of your considerations," I butt in.

His eyebrows drop to a full frown of annoyance. "If you'd let me finish—" He moves so that he's even closer to me in the bed, face to face. "—It's not just selfish, it's good business sense. I've been watching the work you're doing. It's phenomenal. Even your supervisor Marcy thinks so."

I draw back from him. No way perpetual-stick-up-her-ass Marcy can have anything good to say about me.

"No way."

Jackson puts a hand to my cheek to stop me from shaking my head. "Have I ever lied to you?"

My eyes flare briefly back up to his.

"She reports that no one cleans code up as quickly as you and that when you discovered Thompson's bug a few weeks ago—the one that wasn't just a bug but a logic error—you coded an elegant solution that made the algorithm work three times faster. She said you're the best on her team."

Wow. Marcy paid attention to that? I mean, I included it in my written report, but I didn't even think she read those things.

Still. "Then why not promote Marcy herself?" She's ambitious as hell and would no doubt be pissed if I was promoted ahead of her.

Jackson smiles at me, head tilted sideways. "A person would think you didn't want a promotion." He shakes his head and laughs. "Not that it's any of your business, but I am in fact promoting Marcy to a top project management position. That's only coincidental, though. Like you, she's earned it. All of my employees know that while loyalty is rewarded, skill is what is most highly valued. There's a reason that we have avenues at CubeThink for bright new talent to rise in the ranks more quickly."

Bright new talent? Is that really what he thinks of me?

This has all got to be a load of bullshit... but his eyes are searching mine earnestly and he looks completely serious.

And fuck, I hate myself for even thinking it, but this is exactly what I'd need if I was going to go along with Gentry's plan—an inside track to Jackson's most exclusive products that he himself is personally developing. Of course, there's no way in hell I intend on following through and giving into what that bastard wants, but... just in case...

Can I really refuse a chance to look behind the curtain? To get my hands on the information that Gentry is demanding so I have all the bargaining power?

Fuck.

I look into Jackson's bright blue eyes, lit up instead of dark for once because of the morning light.

I should continue arguing with him about this 'promotion.' It's too early for such a move. I never wanted special treatment. I was adamant about that from the beginning. And his words might sound pretty, but if he had no personal interest in me, would he *really* be promoting a college dropout so quickly, even if that college was Stanford? I should shut this down. I swore I'd make my own way in the world.

But Gentry... and my little boy. And he *is* promoting Marcy too. I swallow and turn over on the pillow so I don't have to look Jackson in the face.

"Okay." My voice is small. "When do I transition?"

Jackson's hands snake around my waist and his chin nuzzles the back of my neck. "Monday. You won't regret this, Callie. I promise, this is where you belong."

I can't tell if he means in his arms or working with him at his company. Maybe he means both. My chest squeezes hard at the thought. Because what if I can't find another way out of the bind with Gentry? I think of last night and the intimacy we shared. A deep shudder works its way through my body. I was so upset about him keeping a secret from me but...What if I'm forced to betray him?

"Are you cold? Come here, baby. I'll warm you up." I can hear the smile in his voice as he lifts a powerful leg and wraps it around my body, cocooning me even further.

Instead of suffocating me like I might have expected, it makes me feel safe. Incredibly safe.

And the question pings through my head again: oh God, *what if I'm forced to betray him?*

CHAPTER THIRTEEN

JACKSON

Bright and early on Monday morning, I lead Callie down the hallway on the floor below mine to meet the rest of the team. It's hell not touching her. She left my house Sunday morning even though I could have kept her in bed all day long. And all night. And all this morning.

But she said she had chores she'd been neglecting and I'm not that dense. She needs space. I might want to go from zero to sixty in zero point three seconds but I need to be happy she's letting me back into her life at all. And she took the promotion. Take the win, Vale. Take the win.

Didn't mean I haven't been going out of my fucking mind waiting for today so I could see her again. I went jogging yesterday. And had an hour long session on the heavy bag. And went swimming.

Still I could barely sleep last night for excitement about seeing her again.

Callie on the other hand? She looks less than delighted to be here. She's fidgety and her steps are sluggish.

"Hey, is everything okay?"

"What?" She startles at my question. "Of course it is. Just had trouble sleeping last night. Nervous before my big day on the new job."

She flashes a huge smile.

A huge, fake smile.

She nods down the hall before I can question her any more, though. "Come on, I want to see. The sooner you show me what we're working on, the less anxious I'll be."

What is she not telling me? I frown but follow her. As she pulls open the door to the testing lab, she starts peppering me with questions about the live drone trial today. If she's trying to distract me, it's a good technique because I have been excited to show her the new prototype. I can't really remember the last time I was this excited to show off for someone, actually.

And Callie's easy to impress. She looks stunned even stepping inside the state-of-the-art open facility that takes up half the floor of the building. It's nothing like the floor of cubicles where she's been working. It's a sleek white area, well lit, with people buzzing all around as they prepare for the trials.

"If you don't close your mouth, a bug's going to fly inside," I can't help whispering, nudging her on the shoulder.

She snaps her mouth shut and smacks me on the chest. Still, as we enter the space and walk forward, her eyes dart everywhere. We pass several stations with large monitors all scrolling data. In one corner, two quadcopter drones circle one another about a foot from the extra high ceiling.

Her eyes keep searching until they land on the two techs with tablets who are controlling the drones. In other stations, drones lie in pieces, while elsewhere, complicated programing code fills screens.

"Holy shit," she whispers. "This is officially the *coolest* place ever. I want to see it all at once."

I grin and drop a hand to the small of her back, guiding her to the left. Even though it's the slightest touch, I feel like electricity pings through the pads of my fingertips at the contact. Jesus I can't get enough of this woman.

She keeps looking over her shoulder, so much that she almost plows into one of the computing stations.

"Whoa, look where you're headed, Miss Cruise." I jerk her to the side just before she makes impact.

"Oh!"

Do I use it as a shameless excuse to hold her even closer to my side? Yes. Yes I do.

"This place is..." She shakes her head, unable to keep the awe out of her voice, "... amazing."

I smile before leaning in. "I kind of think so too." I pull back but don't miss her contented little sigh before I do.

"Let's go. I want to show you what we're currently working on." I feel my mouth flatten into a line as we head forward the last few feet to the current drone. As excited as I am to show her what I'm working on, I know the prototype is still far from perfect. I'm not at all sure how today's test is going to go.

I lead Callie to a glassed-in room that runs along the back wall of the entire floor, effectively creating a very long, narrow room. I swipe my ID card and pull open the door. There's rubber all around the door so that it suctions slightly when it opens and closes.

The room is full of equipment and my lab techs bustling around making last minute preparations.

"Mr. Vale," says Amit, getting up from his computer and hurrying over to greet us. He's a middle-aged Pakistani man and one of the best on my team. "Just in time for the nine a.m. prototype test." Amit looks from me to Callie and I make the introductions.

"Amit, this is Calliope. She'll be joining the team to work on Falcon Six."

Amit smiles and holds out his hand. "Welcome to the team." Then his attention turns back to me. "Let's see if our latest set of calculations made any difference."

I nod and we head down the makeshift hallway along the window that separates the room from the rest of the floor. Callie follows as Amit continues running through the drone specifications.

"If we use a low-pass filter capture, we can catch large objects on a collision course before they hit. But if we try to use any more complex filters, then the amount of data—" Amit shakes his head and Jackson continues where he leaves off.

"—Becomes too much to calculate for effectiveness in real-time situations," I finish.

"Exactly," Amit responds.

"How do the computer simulations do with the new algorithm?" I ask.

Amit waves his hand in a so-so gesture. "Sometimes the drone is able to respond in time." Then he winces. "Sometimes not."

I grimace. "Let's see how the test goes." I turn to Callie. "Did you follow that?"

"Your unmanned drone can't get out of the way fast enough when things are in its way."

I smile and feel some of the tension ebb from my shoulders. "Exactly. At its most basic, that's our problem. This is why we need some new eyes on the project."

She shrugs. "Just calling it like it is."

"Yes, well, maybe that will all change today and you'll get to join in on an already-successful project rather than a struggling one. Take a seat." I gesture toward several seats that line the wall by the window, then pull out my phone to check the time. 8:57. More and more people file into this side of the long room until a small crowd has gathered. Then Amit begins to lead the meeting.

"You know we've been working on releasing a new and improved version of the Falcon Six BIOS. We're here today to test what we've all been working so hard on over the past month. Hopefully we worked out the bugs and have gotten her up to speed."

He lifts a tablet from a nearby table. "Without any further ado. Falcon Six, solo flight directed only by GPS coordinates. Obstacles to encounter will be wind turbulence, a simulated tree branch and a secondary drone that is our stand-in for a bird or other air debris the Falcon might come across in the real world."

He looks down at the tablet in his hand, finger hovering over a button. "And *go*," his finger descends and presses the screen.

I look to the opposite end of the room along with everybody else. It's hard to even make out the drone at first, it's so far away. But I know what I'm looking for and I quickly catch movement and hear the slightest humming noise.

There it is—my quadcopter prototype speeding in a fairly quick clip in our direction.

Then comes the first obstacle, a loud burst of air like the rush of wind turbines sounds in the otherwise quiet room. Callie jumps beside me, she's so startled by the sudden noise.

It's from the large bank of industrial size fans set up about halfway down the long room. They're stacked three high, five wide, and are each four feet in diameter. We passed by them earlier but Callie must not have been paying attention.

I lean forward in my chair, watching to see if the Falcon can recover from the simulated wind. The Falcon's propellers are about a foot in diameter themselves, but the drone is still blown so far off course by the blast of air from the fans that I worry it's going to slam into the glass wall partitioning the testing room from the rest of the lab.

Just before copter blades meet glass, though, the drone course-corrects and continues on at a steady pace toward us. The collective gasp of the group around me is audible.

Everyone wants this test to succeed. If we could create the first self-guided drone on the market, it would be game-changing.

A lab tech at the halfway mark moves into the Falcon's path and holds up a giant fake bushy branch. The second obstacle. Again, the drone alters its course, moving out of the branch's way with plenty of space to spare.

The people around me clap but I'm shaking my head. The response time was too slow. If these were real life, real time obstacles, those reaction times wouldn't cut muster.

The drone is coming closer, probably still about forty or forty-five feet away when one of the other techs in the group uses a tablet to lift a drone off a nearby table.

Obstacle number three. It rises up in the air with a soft whir and advances toward Falcon Six in a steady path. At first it doesn't look like the Falcon recognizes it or is going to do anything about it, but when the other drone is still a good four feet away, Falcon Six ducks and flies smoothly underneath.

Cheers erupt from the people around me, but I'm stiff. The Falcon *barely* reacted in time.

I stand up and take the tablet from John, taking control of the secondary drone. I've driven these so often it's nothing to make the drone pull a U-turn and start heading back toward Falcon Six.

It trails right behind the Falcon with no response at all from the lead drone. Then, with a few flicks of my finger, I loop the follow drone out in front of Falcon Six. I don't even immediately put it in Falcon Six's path. I give it about two feet lead space.

It's not enough.

Falcon Six crashes straight into the second drone, sending them both to the floor in a loud, unforgiving clatter of impacting propellers and hard plastic.

The reaction from the crowd is similarly audible. Gasps and cries of "No!" as well as a general shift of the group forward, like they could have stopped the calamity from happening in its last moments.

I just stand still, completely unsurprised. But sometimes it's best to make a clear, visual point. Today was not a success and I didn't want anyone walking out of here thinking it was.

"All right team," I say, raising my voice as I step forward and look around the room. "We have our work cut out for us. Reaction time is still far too slow. We need real-time-response capabilities if we want a truly autonomous unmanned aerial vehicle…"

I pause and take time to look each member of the team in the face, including Callie. I want her to know I consider her just as much a part of this team even though it's her first day here. "…which is the *entire goal* of this product. Anyone can make a drone. Hell, you can look up schematics on the internet, order the parts, and build your own these days."

"We're trying to break boundaries." I pound my finger on the nearest desk in emphasis. "To do what has never been done before. I should be able to throw this," I pick up a fist-sized geode paperweight, "at our quadcopter mid-flight," I mime hurling it at top speed, "and it should be able to recognize, react, and evade it."

All around me heads are nodding. Good. I have their attention.

Because while I don't want them leaving here thinking this was a success, leaving feeling like failures won't do anyone any good either. I've learned over the years that being a good leader means knowing when to push for more when I know they can give it. And I know the team around me can.

"So of course it's going to take us more than a couple of false starts. We've already improved reaction time by an incredible amount."

I turn and again I make sure to make eye contact with each person on the team. And again my perusal of the group ends up landing on Callie. I can't help it. She's like a magnet I can't stay away from. All roads lead to Callie.

"But the real world is messy." I hold Callie's eyes for a beat before turning to the room at large. "Still, we need our drones to be able to deal with anything life might throw at them. Literally." I heft the geode in my hand and smile. The energy in the room has shifted. People seem recharged rather than disappointed. Good. That's where I wanted to get them. There's clapping and nodding.

"Let's get to it then," I say. "Meeting with the software engineering group in ten." I make a shooing motion and everyone scatters.

I turn back to Callie. This is going to be some first day. "Hold onto your pants. We're jumping straight into the deep end."

CHAPTER FOURTEEN

CALLIE

Jackson wasn't joking. I spent the morning with my new team looking at code and trying to find ways to shave time off the pattern recognition algorithm.

That's basically what the problem comes down to. The drone's taking in too much data at once to process it all fast enough to be able to react in time. To increase the speed, we need more processing power. I think through possible fixes, but each has problems that makes them not viable as real solutions.

The real world is indeed messy. And why did Jackson look at me when he said that earlier? Does he sense there's something important I'm not telling him? Does he guess about Gentry? Shit, only a few days of this and I feel like I'm going to crawl out of my skin with paranoia and anxiety.

Except for the fact that Jackson's drone not working is really only good news for me. This hit me about halfway through the day and when it did, the vice around my chest *finally* loosened so I could breathe easily again. There's no moral dilemma or Sophie's choice or whatever the fuck to face anymore. There's no possibility of me stealing anything and giving it to Gentry because there's nothing to steal! God, not that I would have done it anyway. Fuck no. But still. Now I don't even have to stress out about it. Jackson hasn't figured out the problem any more than Gentry has.

So when I see Gentry's burner phone number pop up on my screen while I'm coming back from the bathroom after lunch, I duck into a small alcove.

Cold. Just be cold and don't let anything he says get to you.

"Yes?" I'm proud when there's only a small tremor to my voice.

"How's the acquisition coming?"

I put a hand to my suddenly churning stomach. It's a physiological reaction whenever I hear the bastard's voice. I just immediately want to throw up.

I brace myself against the wall and swallow hard. *You can do this, Callie. You're safe. You're in Jackson's building. Gentry has no power over you except whatever you allow him.*

I swallow down the bile, hating that he knows by my silence he's getting to me. "There won't be any acquisition. Jackson doesn't have his next-gen AI drone working yet. He hasn't cracked it."

This time the silence comes from Gentry. "I don't believe you. You're lying."

"I'm not!" I only realize how loud I've spoken when a woman passing down the connected hallway looks in my direction. Damn it.

"I'm not," I whisper again, still with a vehemence I can't seem to keep out of my voice when dealing with this fucker. "I'm not shitting you. He can't get the drone to process data quickly enough. I just watched the prototype crash and burn today."

"I still want that prototype. And the program."

"But I just told you, it doesn't—"

"It doesn't work *yet*." Gentry's slick voice purrs in my ear. "You still have two weeks to—how shall we say?—*encourage* Vale to iron out those kinks. I expect a working prototype in my hands by the end of our contracted date. Just wrap him around your little finger and then *motivate* the hell out of him. After all, we both know you have considerable talents in that area." His tone is so lascivious and full of innuendo that this time I do gag and throw up in my mouth a little.

"Don't forget the consequences if you don't comply," Gentry's voice turns hard. "I bet little Charlie needs his Mama more than ever now. In fact, I heard through the grapevine that he got kicked out of his latest day care program just today for getting into too many fights and biting other children."

What? My heartbeat hiccups in my chest. What is he talking about? How the fuck does he know anything about my son?

"You stay away from my child." My whole body is rigid and my voice goes low and deadly. "I will castrate you and shove your balls down your fucking throat if you or anyone you employ ever comes within even a thousand yards of my son. That's ten football fields, just to be clear. Your balls." I overenunciate each word. "Stuffed. Down. Your. Throat. Are we fucking clear?"

"Relax, mama bear," he says, sounding a little bit thrown by my sudden viciousness. Good. He can fuck with other parts of my life, but if he dares come near my son, so help me God, I will make good on my very bloody threat.

"Many people are in my debt," he continues, "including someone on the Board of Directors for the chain of nurseries your ex enrolled your son in. It's in their best interest to keep me informed is all."

I scoff. "You mean you're blackmailing them too."

"I'm merely illustrating a point. Your son is having a hard time without his mother. You can be so easily reunited. A happily ever after.

It's not a new feeling when it comes to Bryce Gentry, but I have the strong urge to learn how to disembowel somebody. Beyond that, it's finally sinking in what he's saying about Charlie. What if the fucker's not bluffing?

Number one, when the hell did David put Charlie in daycare? Is he even allowed to do that without notifying me? And two, if my baby's having this kind of trouble, how the fuck am I not hearing about it? My chest goes tight and my heart starts racing. I'm furious but at the same time feel completely impotent. Because maybe they don't have to notify me. I don't have custody. I don't have any rights when it comes to my own child's well-being.

"I expect to have the prototype and software in hand within two weeks—"

I click end on the call and rush back into the bathroom. After hurrying into a stall and locking it, I bend over with my head between my knees. I don't know if anyone else is in here with me, but hopefully they'll ignore the huffing gasps of panicked breathing coming from this stall.

Get yourself together, Cals. Breathe in. Breathe out. Shit. No, not breathe *in* again five more times like a hyperventilating chipmunk.

Out. Breathe out. Slowly. Then in. Slow cleansing breath. Fill up the diaphragm. That's right. I manage one full breath, then more hiccupping gulps before catching two complete ones.

I sit down on the closed toilet lid and put my head in my hands. Dammit. How am I gonna hold this shit storm together?

I feel like I'm on a roller coaster that's trundling forward. In two weeks, it's going to hit one of those killer loop-de-loops. I'm going to have to make a choice. There's no way off this ride, no matter how much I beg. I'm speeding ahead, strapped in. No way off. No fucking way off.

The thought threatens to bring back my panic attack, but I close my eyes and continue my deep breathing technique. Freaking out about it won't change anything.

With one last gulp of air, I step out of the stall and go to the mirror. Smoothing down my hair, I check my makeup in the mirror. A slight sheen of sweat covers my face, so I blot it with a paper towel. There. No hairs out of place. My complexion actually looks even more dewy now and the lip stain I applied this morning has perfectly survived my Venti cup of coffee.

I shake my head at myself as Gentry's ugly voice reverberates in my head: *just wrap him around your little finger and* motivate *the hell out of him*. My hands lift, almost of their own accord and hover at the top button of my shirt. If I undid it, let just a little more of my ample cleavage show...

I drop my hands and step back from the mirror, disgusted at myself. Oh my God. Am I actually letting that bastard get in my head? Taking his advice to seduce Jackson to get what I want?

Tears bite at the edges of my eyes. It's the position that men have put me in my whole life until I believed it's all I was good for. That I only had my body to offer. Christ, it's why I took the position with Gentry in the first place when I felt like I was out of options. Even now, I still can't bring myself to believe Jackson really gave me this promotion because I actually *deserve* it. Because he thinks I have skills outside the bedroom that are worth something.

I bite the inside of my cheek and turn away from the mirror. I straighten my back as I walk to the desk Jackson arranged for me among the hive of other top robotics engineers. As I sit down, I notice he hasn't gone back to his office. He told me earlier that when the team is on deadline like this, he adopts a temporary office down here so he can be right in the thick of it. Indeed, I can see him at the end of the open room. His secondary office has walls of transparent glass and the door is propped open.

I pick up my fitted blazer and slip it on, primly securing the two buttons at my waist. Then I turn on my conservative two-inch heels and head for his open door.

"Callie." Jackson smiles when I arrive at his door. "How can I help you?"

"I was wondering if I might visit the machine shop? I'd like to see how the prototypes are made." I shrug and smile an embarrassed smile. "It might seem silly, but I was hoping it might jog loose some ideas for how to improve reaction times if I can fully understand each and every component."

His eyes brighten. "That's a great idea. Not silly at all. Thinking outside the box is the only way we're going to tackle this thing. I'll call down so they know you're coming."

I force myself to smile back. "Thanks. I tend to take things in slowly. My process is to stew on problems." I look down demurely before looking back up and meeting his eyes. "Do you think it would be possible to change my clearance so I could visit the shop whenever I want?"

He holds my gaze for just a second longer than is comfortable before nodding slowly. "Of course. I look forward to hearing any and all of your thoughts." His head dips and his eyebrows go up slightly, as if there's more significance to the words than just talking about drones and prototypes.

I can't keep his gaze. I look at the ground. Shit. What am I doing?

You're doing what you have to, that's what.

Nothing bad, I hurry to assure myself against that other voice in my head. I'm just covering all contingencies. I'm being smart this time. I'm *not* Gentry's marionette. I'm fucking not.

I'll do this my way. But the roller coaster, the fucking roller coaster. There's no getting off it, and in two weeks, I better have figured a fucking miraculous way out of this.

"Thanks again." I turn to leave when Jackson's voice stops me.

"Callie. I also wanted to ask you about something."

I swing back around to look at him. Only to find him running his hand through the back of his hair and looking slightly... Oh my God, is Jackson Vale nervous?

"You know what, never mind. I shouldn't be asking this during business hours."

"Okay, now I have to know." I prop a hand on my hip just inside the doorway.

"It's just that, well..." Red creeps up his neck and he readjusts himself in his chair. "I was wondering if you wanted to maybe, that is, Christ, I really shouldn't be asking this during business hours."

"Just spit it out." It's probably mean, but I can't help laughing a little bit at how uncomfortable he looks.

He narrows his gaze at me but does finally manage to get his request out. "In a completely non-professional manner, not as your boss but only as Jackson, I was wondering if you'd be interested in spending the weekend with me at my cabin about an hour away at a little vineyard."

Wow. Um. What do I say to that? A weekend with Jackson. Alone. Secluded.

"I know they say silence is golden, but you're leaving me hanging here," he says when I've been quiet for what is probably an awkwardly long period.

"Yes."

Shit. Did I just say that?

Dimple appearance alert. "Great. You spend Friday evenings with your son, right?"

I nod, surprised and moved that he remembers.

"So I'll pick you up at nine on Saturday morning." It's a statement. He's so self-assured now after his momentary attack of anxiety. So put together. Which makes it all the more incredible that he debases himself to submit to me.

"Great," I mimic. A smile covers my inner grimace. I shouldn't be continuing whatever this... *thing* is going on between us. Not right now anyway. It's too messy, too complicated with Gentry breathing down my neck.

At the same time, even as I stare at Jackson, all I want to do is walk over there, grab him by his tie, and force him to the floor. A cool sense of calm washes down my body at just the mental image of it. Each tense muscle in my shoulders relaxes at the thought of him on his knees, head bowed before me.

I don't even know quite how to describe the sensation. It's like a kind of euphoria, that instant relaxation and stress relief that sweeps down my body, starting from behind my forehead, down to my shoulders, chest, belly, resonating with extra vibration in my groin, and then continuing down my legs all the way to my toes. And that's just at the *thought* of dominating him. What would an entire weekend bring?

I need it.

I need it now more than ever.

"Callie," Jackson's voice is low and when I look back at his eyes, I can see them dark with obvious lust. He's picked up on my internal thoughts. Guess I haven't bothered masking my emotions as well as I want.

"I have to be getting back to it. Work, that is." I lift an eyebrow and shoot him a sly smile before I turn and hurry out the door. The smile even feels genuine. Which only leaves me feeling more confused than ever.

CHAPTER FIFTEEN

CALLIE

Saturday dawns sunny and only slightly cool. The temperate climate in the Bay Area means that even though it's October, it's in the sixties and will warm up to probably seventy-five by mid-afternoon.

At seven-thirty in the morning, I find myself doing something I would never have believed of myself—I'm waiting at the window for a guy. Of course I don't admit that out loud. I just have the curtain conveniently open while I drink my morning coffee with Shannon. I can't believe that she too is willingly up so early on a Saturday—and her for no other reason than she wants to get an early start on the day.

She's given up giving up caffeine. She's back to drinking the characteristic black sludge she's been addicted to since college. Sunil keeps buying her fancy boxes of caffeine-free tea and even a bag of this organic pretend coffee made out of chicory, but other than that week and a half where she made a valiant attempt, none of it's been able to sway my coffee-loving sister. Thank God. It's unnatural not to have a few vices.

"So," Shannon says, sipping her coffee while flipping through the news on her phone—she's the only person I know who reads BBC News articles in the morning instead of skimming Facebook like the rest of us mere mortals. "A weekend getaway. This is getting serious."

I shrug her off and pour some more sugar and creamer into my coffee. After already watering it down heavily. It's either this or brew a separate pot from the mud she drinks.

"Nah, we just wanted to get away from the noise of the city. He has a place down in wine country and after going all that way, it seemed silly to turn around and come back the same day. Might as well stay the night." Yeah. All of that came pouring out of my mouth *way* too fast.

One of her eyebrows arches.

I ignore her and go back to looking out the window as I drink my coffee. It's still strong, but sweet enough that it tastes pretty damn yummy.

"How are things between you and Sunil?" I ask.

"Because that's not an obvious deflection. You know I never thought it was a good idea to date your boss. That said," she rubs her thumb along the rim of her coffee mug while eyeing me, "whatever relationship you've been having hasn't seemed to impact your work. Whether you guys can manage to keep that up or not, well..."

Yeah. I never told Shannon that Jackson and I stopped seeing each other. I didn't want to listen to any of her *I told you so's*. Nor do I especially want to hear any more of her thoughts on the subject now.

I smile sweetly. "You've been spending a lot of time at Sunil's place. I saw how good you were at CrossFit the other day. As much as you complain, I think you even go on days when I'm not dragging your ass there." I do the eyebrow raise thing back at her. "Seems like someone's concerned with looking good for her man. Things must be getting hot and heavy between you two."

A slight blush stains her cheeks. Shannon and I have never been the kind of sisters who do this—the whole gossiping about boys thing. We're just learning how and it still hits my funny bone every time I see her like this.

"He's well..." she looks down at her coffee, her blush growing deeper. Slam dunk—distraction managed. "There's so much to learn about the Zen lifestyle."

I can't help laughing. "So that's what you do? Spend all your time talking about meditating?" I waggle my eyebrows up and down. Then a thought strikes me and I set my coffee cup down on the table so hard, it almost sloshes over the sides. "Oh my God, is he into that, what do they call it? Tarantula stuff? Like with sex?"

"It's tantric," Shannon corrects and immediately raises her coffee cup to cover the bottom half of her face, clearly embarrassed as hell. "And that's none of your business."

"Oh my God," I slap the table. "You knew the right word for it! You're totally having tarantula sex with your boyfriend!" I grab my abandoned phone off the table. "I'm looking up what tantric sex is now. Is he like downward-doggie-styling you?"

"That's not what it is at all!" She jumps up, completely red-faced and tries to grab my phone as I start typing furiously with my thumbs. I have to put my body in the way so she can't get at the phone.

"Give it to me!"

"Never!" I laugh. "I've got to see what kind of freaky-deeky stuff my sister's getting in to."

"What are you, twelve? Give me the phone." She's all but crawling over my back at this point to get to the phone, but I curl up so I can still see my screen. I manage to type in 'tantric' and hit *search*.

"Oh look, a Cosmo article on eight tantric positions to heat things up in the bedroom," I read off, laughing so hard my stomach hurts. I manage to click the link in spite of the fact that Shannon's hands are prying at my arms to get at the phone.

"Oh my God, look at the Lover's Lap Dance. Or the," I gasp for breath through my giggles, "Penetrative Pretzel. Wow, you've gotta be really limber to manage that one. Maybe you should squeeze in that yoga class after all."

Shannon chokes. "You little—" Then her body straightens up. Still slightly out of breath, she points to the window. "Speaking of lovers."

I uncurl and my head pops up to look out the window like a gopher. A fancy car idles by the curb in front of the apartment building. It's not Jackson's usual town car and driver but a shiny silver Volvo instead.

A text pings on the phone I've got clutched so tight in my hand.

JACKSON: I'm outside.

"Dang," Shannon's voice is more sober. "You're really falling for this guy. You should see your face."

I look away from the window and go for my bag, but not before sticking my tongue out at Shannon.

"Brat," she says.

"Sex fiend."

"I know where you sleep," she shoots back.

That makes me laugh. I stop on my way toward the door and turn back and give Shannon a huge hug. "Love you, sis."

"Oh get out of here," she grumbles.

"Go drink some of that sludge you call coffee," I say as I pull back, just far enough so I can plant a loud smooching kiss on her cheek.

"Ugh." She pulls away from me, rubbing at her cheek.

I'm laughing all the way out the door. This sister thing is actually pretty damn cool now that we're finally trying. Who knew? I heft my weekend duffel bag higher on my shoulder as I jog down the steps of my apartment building toward... my stride breaks momentarily and both my eyebrows raise in question when I get closer.

Sam, Jackson's driver, is nowhere in sight. "I thought you said you didn't drive."

"Sam's been giving me lessons. Only a few traffic cones were sacrificed in the endeavor." He smiles down at me.

I huff out a laugh which seems louder than normal in the quiet morning. Jackson walks around the car and opens my door. He takes my arm before I can sit and pulls me to him.

"You look beautiful this morning."

The low, intense quality of his voice, the feel of his muscled chest against me, and just... *him*... being in his proximity. I meet his eyes and the *zing* hits.

God, the day together just started. How can I already be feeling so much? The butterflies riot in my stomach and I swallow.

I'm wearing dark maroon leggings and an oversized blue sweater, figuring I should go for a comfortable, friendly vibe. But the way he's looking at me, you'd think I was prancing around in the sheerest lingerie.

"Hi." That's the only word I manage to find in the moment. I've had this man on his knees, but he can still just fucking overwhelm me. How is that fair?

The dimple appears. "Hi." He drops down and kisses my nose. Then he grabs my duffel off my shoulder and goes to put it in the trunk.

Wow. I sit inside. I can't believe I'm a little punch-drunk off something as simple as a kiss on the nose. But then I'm distracted by looking at my surroundings, because damn, this is some car.

The leather seat forms itself to my body and I can't help but let out an audible sigh as I sink into it and close my eyes. I couldn't sleep much last night. I was nervous about the trip, yes, but it was also my visit with Charlie that kept me up.

He was healthy enough from all outward appearances. I mean, it seems like he's eating and there aren't any obvious signs of neglect or anything. All the nice feelings from moments ago with Jackson evaporate.

I prop my elbow on the door and rub my temple. Because as far as everything else... I just can't tell. He flipped out with excitement when he saw me but started getting progressively more out of sorts and whiny as our hour and a half together came to a close.

It's frustrating as fuck because I'm not allowed to ask about what it's like at his dad's since the damn supervisor was there standing over us and recording everything I say. Which is so fucking stupid, because it's what parents are *supposed* to do. They help their children transition during difficult periods in life.

How the hell is Charlie supposed to understand what's going on when the parent he's loved and known ever since he was born can't even fully explain why she's allowed only a paltry two hours with him a week? Who knows what the hell David or his psycho wife is telling him the rest of the time? There's no supervisor watching *their* interactions with Charlie.

I blow out a long hiss of air and try to settle my suddenly raging emotions. *Just a little longer.* A few weeks and I'll have my baby back. As long as Gentry doesn't fuck things up.

I let my forehead drop hard against the window. That emotional roller coaster? Yep, that's pretty much every minute of my life these days. Up and down and upside down. I jump only slightly when Jackson's door opens and he slides into his seat. "Ready?"

"Totally." I swallow hard but don't turn his way. I can't quite put on a cheerful façade yet. The next second, I feel the pressure of Jackson's warm hand on my forearm.

"How was your time with your son last night?"

Damn him and his intuitive nature. I can't help the way my body stiffens. Jackson pulls his hand back like a pot has just burned him.

"I'm sorry," he hurries to say. "It's not my place and if you don't want to talk about it, that's fi—"

"No," I turn and face him. "It's not that." Shit. "It's just—" I look out the front windshield at the street lined with apartment buildings and the gas station that's seen better years. Then I let out a long sigh. "I really miss Charlie. I hate not knowing if he's doing okay. Like, *really* okay. He's always upset when it's time for me to leave."

There. At least I found something true to say. I doubt there's a way to come out of this with my integrity intact, but hell if I can't be as honest as I can in the meantime.

The fuck of it is, I *want* to tell Jackson everything. For the first time since David, I think I've found a man I actually trust. That moment of intimacy outside the car? I want more of that, all the time.

Jackson reaches out again, just long enough to grab my hand and squeeze it before turning on the car. "You have some of the best lawyers in the business." His clear blue eyes lock on mine. Usually they're so dark I can barely make out the color of his eyes, but in the morning sunlight, the irises look like the deep blue of the Mediterranean Sea.

Why does he have to look at me like that? God, when all is said and done, we still barely know each other. A few intense fucks and a scattering of days together. But he looks at me like... like he sees me down to my bones and then even deeper than that.

He takes my hand again, like he can't keep himself from going two minutes without touching me. He brings it to his mouth and brushes his lips across my knuckles, back and forth, his breath warming my skin before he finally presses his mouth down in a firm kiss.

Christ. This man. Even a kiss on my hand sends shivers skittering up and down my spine. Not to mention the warmth that immediately rekindles in my lower belly.

It would be wrong to jump him in his fancy car on the curb right in front of my apartment. Wouldn't it? I lick my lips.

When he leans over into my space, I think he's having exactly the same idea and the spark between my legs bursts into full flame. Only to realize that he's just grabbed my seatbelt and is buckling me in. He pulls back just as I was about to reach out and grab his face for a quick kiss.

I drop my hands and let a growl of frustration. "Oh, you're going to pay for that."

He laughs full out as he puts the car in gear. "I have no doubt." He flashes me a grin as we pull out onto the street.

It's a sunny morning as we turn onto the 101 heading south. Even early on a Saturday there's plenty of traffic. That's Silicon Valley for you. Few people slow down long enough to take a breath, much less a day off. And when they do, it's only to play as hard as they work.

Jackson glances my way. "How is—"

"Let's just listen to music for the drive," I cut him off. I don't know what he was going to ask. How is my day going? More about my son? Whether he's aiming for polite car chatter or more meaningful dialogue, I'm not in the mood.

"And coffee," I add as I reach for the dials on his radio. "Please tell me we're getting coffee somewhere along the way."

My hand pauses in front of the dash, where I would normally expect dials and buttons. But fuck, rich people. There's a freaking little flatscreen instead. Because of course.

A little logo in the upper right announces it's satellite radio. Little round images of buttons light up at my touch that I presume are presets. I press number one and screaming metal music rips through the air, assaulting us from all sides at earsplitting volume.

The car jerks slightly in the lane and I swat at the screen trying to make it stop. "Oh my God!" I yell, finally giving up and slamming my hands over my ears.

Jackson rolls his finger in a counterclockwise motion on a circle in the bottom lefthand corner of the screen and the volume goes down. I'm still hesitant when I pull one hand away from my ear, like it's a trick and the eardrum-bursting noise is liable to come back any second. But no, it's all clear.

"Who has hardcore metal as their number one car preset?" I swat Jackson on the shoulder.

He shrugs, his face neutral. "It's good stress relief after a hard day at work."

I can only stare at him like he's crazy. "Are you fucking kidding me? That music makes me want to go stab somebody, not feel calm."

He laughs at this.

"All right, crazy." I give him the side-eye. "Let's see what's behind door number two." I push the little number two preset and brace myself. At first I can barely hear anything, he's set the volume dial so low. Cautiously, I spin the digital dial so it's loud enough for me to hear the music.

Alanis Morissette crooning about irony fills the car. Now I'm the one laughing when I look over at him.

"Seriously? You go from metal to nineties pop music?"

One edge of his mouth quirks up but I don't miss the slightest bit of redness on the back of his neck. "What? I'm a child of the nineties."

Oh. Right. He's thirty-two. Ten years older than me. I consider him, really looking at the lines of his face. There's nothing noticeable that announces his age. But he definitely looks like a man and not a boy.

Even dressed in more casual clothes like he is today, a dark gray Henley shirt that shapes the outline of his muscled shoulders without being *too* tight and a pair of denim jeans that look soft and worn... My mouth waters a little, I shit you not.

Let's just say, if he walked across my college campus, no one would mistake him for a student. My eyes linger longer than necessary on the jeans. Damn, this man can wear the fuck out of a pair of jeans. I get a little lost just watching the way his strong sloping thigh shifts as he moves between the gas and brake pedal.

At least until I notice him watching me watching him. Ahem. I avert my eyes.

The Alanis song switches to one I vaguely recognize but can't recall the band or song name. I scrunch my face as I listen to the lyrics. "What is he saying? She's his wonder all?"

"His wonder wall," Jackson corrects.

"What's a wonder wall?"

"Who knows? The band's British." He says that like it explains it all.

I bark out a short laugh and then press number three. It's NPR. Okay. A bit boring but impressive. Four. Howard Stern. Interesting.

Number five. Acoustic strumming guitar and a man with a ragged voice singing an old folk song. My gaze shoots back to Jackson. It sounds a little bit like the Civil Wars except I get the feeling this is actual original folk, the kind of stuff the Civil Wars took their inspiration from.

"You've got eclectic tastes, my friend."

"Different music for different moods."

I arch an eyebrow at him. "And what mood are you in today?"

He keeps his eyes on the road. "Number eight."

I press eight. It's downtempo deep-house music. Slow but still with a thudding bass that I can feel underneath my seat, resonating… well, you can guess where.

I lick my lips. Eventually a woman starts singing and her deep voice caresses the melody. It's sultry. Sensuous. The excellent sound system in the car makes the music a full-body experience. I kick off my flats and draw my legs up onto the seat. My thighs shift as the singer hits an especially low note that collides with the bass, sending an extra rumble through the speaker underneath my seat.

I look over at Jackson just in time to see him glance away from me, back to the road. The heat blooming inside me spikes. I let out a breath I hadn't realized I was holding.

"You know what? Forget the coffee." I fumble with the buttons on the right side of my seat until I find the one that reclines the chair.

Then I close my eyes and settle into the uber-comfortable seat. "I think I'm just going to rest a little more until we get there."

Jackson doesn't say a thing and I'm tempted, so tempted, to sneak another glance at him. Is he looking at me again? Is the music making him feel the same way I feel right now? Or does it just seem like music to chill out to for him?

Then again, this is the guy who destresses to screaming metal bands.

But I don't even so much as peek at him. Self-control wins the day. Or it would if I were actually sleepy and that damn music weren't making my pussy throb crazily.

I press the back of my head against the seat with force enough it makes my neck strain. God. Well. Jackson said it only takes forty-five minutes to get there. So that means, what? Only another half hour of this torture.

Oh goody.

"All right, just put your thumb there and move it gently in a circle," Jackson's voice is low in my ear, his arms wrapped around me from behind.

I bite my lip and concentrate as I do what he says.

"That's right. Right there. *Perfect.*"

My heart pumps a mile a minute at his pleased praise.

"Not too hard," he says sharply.

"Shit." I struggle to readjust.

The quadcopter buzzing over our heads suddenly takes a sharp nosedive.

"Shit shit shit!" I frantically try to shove the controller back into Jackson's hands but he won't take it.

"Jackson!"

"It's fine," he says at the same time.

My eyes shoot back to the quadcopter, cringing as I wait for it to crash into the small meadow beside the sloping hill of the vineyard.

But the hover copter just sits there, well... hovering. Its little quadcopter blades whir and it has righted itself about five feet from the ground, far from catastrophe.

I look down at the controller in my hand. None of my fingers are touching any buttons. "It's just doing that... by itself?"

I look over my shoulder at Jackson and he's smiling. I swear, when I first got to know him I didn't think smiling was in his repertoire. But now he does it all the time.

At least around you.

The thought warms my chest. Stupid chest. Maybe my first impression was wrong. Maybe he's the smiley-est damn dude who ever lived and he was just having an off couple weeks when I met him. I was in the company of his worst enemy at the time, so it's certainly possible. But no, even when I came to visit him at his office the first time, on his turf, he was the same way. At least, initially.

I force my focus back to the quadcopter. It's still just hovering there. And Jackson keeps grinning, obviously waiting for me to ask the question.

I roll my eyes at his obvious baiting. "So how is it doing it?"

"It's our foolproof design. So amateurs don't ruin their expensive equipment while they're learning. I put it on safe mode so whenever it comes within three feet of the ground, it automatically switches to upright hover."

I narrow my eyes. "All right, you definitely just referred to me as an amateur, but I think you also called me a fool."

He chuckles and his chest is so close to my back, I can feel the rumble of it. "See, that's what I love about you. Anyone else would be too impressed by me and my little gadget to focus on anything I said."

Well I'm sure as hell laser-focused in on his words now. *That's what I love about you?*

Holy shit. No, stop freaking out. It's just a saying. An expression. Because he can't— I mean we've only known each other for like, well, it's been several months, but we weren't talking for most of those and, I mean, it's not like that—

"Here, put your hands on top of mine and try to feel how I'm moving." Jackson takes the controller from me and I wish there was a way for me to shake my hands out without him seeing. Fuck.

"I'll just watch," I try to say but Jackson is already holding the controller one-handed and reaching for my retreating arm. He places my hand, arranging my fingers to cover his on the small joystick. He reaches for my other arm so I lift my other hand and place it on his.

Alright God, you big beautiful dame up in the sky, please don't let him feel how much I'm trembling.

Jackson pushes the left joystick forward. The quadcopter rises straight up into the air. With his forefinger, he clicks a button and the small screen in the middle of the controller lights up. A bird's-eye view of where we're standing comes into focus on the screen. I see the tops of our heads growing smaller and smaller as the drone ascends.

I can't help letting out a little gasp. Of course I know that Cube-Think makes copters equipped with cameras, but I didn't think the one Jackson was letting me practice with would come with such advanced equipment. The image we're seeing is crisp and professional. The vineyards are spread out on beautiful sun-soaked hills and it looks movie quality.

"Let's bring her back down a bit," Jackson says and I swear he pulls me even closer against his body. I split my time between watching the dark speck in the sky and looking down at the monitor. The footage is so smooth, not jerky at all.

I look back into the sky. The whirring object comes closer into view, but instead of heading toward us, Jackson uses the second joystick to veer to the right, skimming the drone right over the top of the plantings in the closest vineyard.

I look down at the screen and it's so beautiful it makes my chest hurt. Greenery bursts from the top of each staked vine. The drone flies straight down the row, slowly lifting in elevation as it goes, panning out to see the vineyard as a whole. It's magnificent to watch.

Jackson's handle of the controls is perfect, even though it's got to be awkward reaching around me like this. The image doesn't jolt but is smooth and continuous as the copter glides back up into the sky. Yet again, the squares of each vineyard and the rolling hills of the larger valley come into view.

"All right, color me considerably impressed." The thing is, I'm not even being sarcastic. He's built a truly amazing machine.

I feel his shrug. I turn my head toward him. "Oh, come on. I didn't think you were one for false modesty."

His mouth is a straight line, though. "It could be improved," is all he says as he brings the quadcopter back in again.

His words surprise me. Then again, I suppose they shouldn't. I haven't gotten to see much of this perfectionist side to Jackson before the glimpses throughout this past week as I've begun working directly for him. He's exacting, constantly pushing himself and his team for better and better. But unlike a lot of people with his ambition and personality bent, he's not an asshole about it.

"Your work is personal to you," I say as the drone comes back in range and lands smoothly on the ground at our feet.

"Sure, I guess," Jackson says. Again I feel the arms around me lift in a slight shrug. The drone is down and I wasn't doing much learning while it was in the air. There's no real reason for him to still be holding me but I don't pull away.

"I don't know how to do it any other way. I feel like," he pauses like he's searching for words, "like the people working for me see that I'm demanding just as much of myself as I'm asking of them. If every project is a passion project, well then, we're all working toward something special. It's more than a job."

I can feel his eyes on me so I twist a little in his arms to look up at him. Those goddamn eyes of his. So intense and piercing.

"But it's also not my whole life," he says, eyes flicking back and forth between mine. "That's actually something I've been realizing only recently." He goes quiet after that revelation.

I don't ask him what's changed. I'm too afraid of his answer. I swallow and bat his hands away from the controller. "Well if I'm going to work on these copters, it's just *embarrassing* if I can't even keep one in the air for more than ten seconds at a time."

He chuckles easily and doesn't try to steer the conversation back to deeper waters.

"All right," he says. "Remember that your left joystick is all about lift and the right one is for directionality. If you get in trouble, just let go of the controls and she'll hover wherever she's at."

I smile as I take over but inside all I can think is, *please don't find a way to fix the problem with the new drone.* If Jackson can't correct it, then no matter what Gentry threatens, there's simply nothing for Gentry to leverage me *for.*

We spend a couple more hours out in the meadow. Once I learn the trick about letting go if I get in trouble and allowing the copter to hover, it's a lot easier. Yeah, apparently the fear of crashing the thing every three seconds was really holding me back. Once I get past that, it turns out the controls are a lot more user-friendly than I expected.

My video is still much more jerky than Jackson's, but by the end of the first hour, I'm definitely getting the hang of it. Jackson brought a second quadcopter and several batteries for each of us so we could have a long afternoon flying together.

After a while all my worries have drifted away and I'm simply having *fun*. A truly shocking concept. Jackson is a master at maneuvering his copter and helps guide me when I lose mine a couple times. They fly so high they seem to disappear into the white clouds.

The sun is warm on my skin when we finally bring them back home for the last time. We're flying low and I see some trees ahead.

"Trees," Jackson says.

"Saw them." I follow the instructions Jackson gave me earlier about what to do whenever an obstruction comes into my path—push forward on the left joystick to lift straight up until I'm sure I've cleared it. The drone is too far away for me to visually track with my eyes, but looking at the screen I can see we're past the patch of trees and I drop altitude again.

"You know, really all your copters need is to know what's right in front of them. All the other stuff on the other sides isn't important. Like us, we just need to know about the trees in front of us and then we correct…"

Jackson's hands drop off his controller, sending his copter into hover mode wherever it may be, as he turns to me, mouth open. "Oh my God. I'm an idiot."

Oh shit.

It just popped out of my mouth.

An offhand comment.

One of those little thoughts you have.

"Of course!" He starts to pace back and forth, one hand to his forehead. "I'm such an idiot. We don't have to process the data for everything on all sides of the copter. I mean, yes," he waves a hand dismissively, "they could have a low-level filter that takes the three-sixty view into consideration, but we really only need a forty-five degree window of what is directly in front of the copter to do more in-depth analysis on. I've been trying for too much. Trying to get the hardware where I want it instead of accepting its limitations and finding other ways to get the job done. It's so simple but I couldn't see it because I was being such a damn perfectionist!"

No.

No no no no no—

An excited frenzied light sparks in Jackson's eyes. "If we focus just on the first few Eigenvalues of the latent space translation, then capture only the most important signal, we'd detect potential objects on a collision course. Then we use that as the first-pass filter and do the in-depth analysis of the field of view. But *only* in the direction of travel." He looks at me, excitement pouring from him in energetic waves.

"Do you realize what this means?" He grabs me by the waist, easily lifting me and swinging me around in a circle. "I bet we can reduce our calculation time by a factor of three. *Three!*"

"Three," I whisper, a watery smile on my face.

Emotion clogs my throat. He's so excited.

He sets me down and grabs his controller to guide his drone back in, but I can see his mind working a hundred miles a minute. He's probably doing calculations in his head, just itching to get to a computer so he can start coding.

If what he's proposing works, he'll fix the problem and then some. Reducing the calculation time by a factor of three means the drone will have real-time reactions.

Jackson will perfect his new drone.

Which is exactly what Gentry wants.

And fuck me, me and my stupid big mouth might have just helped Gentry get it.

There's nothing to do but help Jackson start coding when we get back to the house. He's all fired up to get working. And it's not like I can fudge the code. He's too skilled. He'd recognize it and wonder what the hell I was doing.

So we worked together on two systems he has set up in his computer room, each with three massive monitors. I imagine this is his equivalent of musicians who have studios in their houses.

I've worked with dimensionality reduction data before so he sets me on that while his fingers start flying to restructure the main code to the drone's central program.

It's all right there in front of me. The code that Gentry is willing to ruin lives over. God. I swallow against the queasiness in my stomach and take a sip of Mountain Dew. In the back of the room there's a soda fountain stand like you'd see in a fast-food store with every soda anyone could want and beside it, a coffee bar. I figured the carbonation might help settle my stomach, but now I wonder if all the sugar isn't just making me feel more nauseous.

I put the cup back down on a coaster that says: *There are 10 types of people: those who understand binary and those who don't.*

Normally I'd crack a smile at a good programmer joke, but right now, not even a smirk.

Jackson and I work through dinner and long past the sun going down. Finally, my fingers feel like they're going to fall off, I'm getting a headache from the long hours staring at the monitor, and my stomach is growling with hunger.

Jackson finally looks over and takes notice of me. His eyebrows drop as shame covers his features. "I'm so sorry."

He pushes away from his desk. "This isn't what this weekend was supposed to be about at all. I swear I didn't bring you here to work you to death. We weren't supposed to be doing any work at all. It's just—" he cuts himself off mid-sentence and runs a hand through the back of his hair. His hair is already mussed from him doing this all afternoon. He has no idea he's even more attractive when it's sexily messed up like it is now. Too much like bed head.

I put on a smile and shush him. "It's fine. We both know how important this project is." Just for different reasons to each of us. I cringe internally. "You keep at it and I'll go make us some sandwiches."

"Really?" Jackson's eyebrows rise. "You aren't mad?"

"No." I look at him like he's crazy. Even if I wasn't awash in guilt, I wouldn't be mad that the weekend was turning out this way. I know how important his work is to him. He's having a major breakthrough.

"Have previous girlfriends been upset when you worked too much?" Then I realize how that sounded. Previous girlfriends. Like I'm counting myself as his current girlfriend.

"Don't answer that," I cut him off before he can say anything and turn for the door. "Sandwiches. I'll be back in a bit."

His kitchen is well stocked and I come back with ham and provolone sandwiches, filled with all the good stuff—lettuce, tomatoes, green onions, and avocados. It's all I can do not to groan in satisfaction when I bite into mine.

Jackson murmurs his thanks and sets it to the side, continuing to code instead of eating. I shake my head at him.

"Stopping for fuel is a necessity."

"When I finish this bit," he murmurs, eyes glued to the screen. Or screens, I should say, as his eyes flick back and forth between three screens. One has the active code he's writing for the new algorithm, the second has the log output and memory stack, and the third has a super zoomed in 3D wire frame of the drone itself rotating on the screen, certain sections highlighted.

It's pretty insane to watch this level of genius at work. I shake my head at him and take another glorious bite of my own sandwich. I'll bother him again if he hasn't eaten it in an hour. I finish my sandwich and wash it down with water.

No more Mountain Dew for me. I lace my fingers behind my head and stretch my arms, neck, and back, then return to my own work.

I stay at it for as long as I can, but when two a.m. rolls around, I have to call it quits. I'm fighting sleep and keep catching myself as my head is dropping, then jerk back up right before I face-plant into my keyboard.

Finally, I admit defeat. When I look over at Jackson, though, he doesn't look like he's running out of steam anytime soon. Which really ought to put me to shame. He's a decade older than me but he barely looks like he's flagging at all.

"I'm just going to go catch a quick catnap on the couch, then I'll be back."

Jackson jerks like he's startled by my voice. He probably is, he's so deep in it. Again that guilty expression comes over his face. He glances down at the bottom of the screen, no doubt taking note of the time. "Shit. Callie, I'm so sor—"

"Don't." I smile at him gently as I raise two fingers to his lips to cover his mouth. This man. My chest aches with things I can't name. Things I don't want to name.

I take a step backward. "You kick that code's ass. I'll be back in a little while."

"There are bedrooms upstairs. Just go to sleep for the night. I'll—"

"I'll be back in a little while," I say more firmly.

This time it's him who shakes his head, a smile cracking the edge of his lips. "I'll be here."

I laugh. "Oh, I doubt wild horses could drag you away from that keyboard right now."

His face goes apologetic. "I'm sor—" he tries again.

I'm out the door before he can finish. "I expect to hear about some impressive ass-kickage when I get back!" I yell over my shoulder.

Out in the living room, there's a large sectional couch that, while expensive looking, also seems like it was chosen for comfort more than appearance. I grab the throw blanket draped over the back and lay down. My entire body sinks into the form-shaping couch cushions.

I let out another low moan of pleased relief. My arms feel like jelly as I struggle to get the blanket to cover my body, but I finally manage it. I pull it up around my shoulders and tuck it into my face.

I'll sleep for a tiny bit and then get back to helping Jackson. Just a quick nap.

CHAPTER SIXTEEN

JACKSON

What did I do to deserve this gorgeous goddess of a woman?

I stare down at her where she's curled up on my couch, fast asleep. Fuck but she's beautiful. It's rare to see her like this—her face free of worry lines.

I frown and drop down to the floor, taking one of her feet in my hands and starting a slow massage. I'm not an idiot. I know there are things she's not telling me. I keep hoping that with time, she'll open up. That maybe this weekend...

Yeah well then you started coding and completely ignored her.

I duck my head and wince.

All I can do is try to make up for it now. I move to the other foot and rub my thumbs into her arches, kissing up her ankles.

She gives a little moan and shifts on the couch.

Maybe I should let her sleep. That would be the gentlemanly thing to do.

But no, that couch is lumpy and uncomfortable. The least I can do is take her upstairs to the bed where she'll be more comfortable.

To sleep.

Just to sleep.

I continue my massage and she blinks slowly, waking a few minutes later.

"What are you doing?" she mumbles, glancing down at me.

I smile. "I finished the code."

"But my part—" she scrambles to sit up but I urge her back down and then continue my massage, moving back to her other foot.

"You were almost there. I took what you had then finished it to put in the last piece of the puzzle."

"Did it work?" She sits up abruptly in spite of my ministrations. "Did it fix the problem?"

"It's compiling overnight." Then I look up at the skylight at the grayish sky, much lighter than the pitch black of night. "Well, over the morning anyway."

"What time is it?"

"A little after 5:30. I'll do the preliminary testing tomorrow. But the simulation results were promising. Callie," I grin, "you did it."

She scoffs and looks uneasy. "You were the one who coded everything."

"Which I couldn't have done without your idea."

She puts a hand to her forehead. Why doesn't she look more excited? I thought she'd want to celebrate with me?

Uh, maybe because she's running on two hours of sleep and your supposedly romantic getaway turned into an all-day workathon? I cringe.

"You've been up all night," she says, trying to tug her foot away from my hands. She's not looking at me anymore. Her eyes are fixed firmly on the wall as she says, "You should go get some sleep."

I should go get some sleep. Not *we*.

No. Fuck that. I'm not letting her pull away again. Not after how far we've come. I might have been an ass yesterday, ignoring her in favor of work, but I'll show her just how important she is to me.

"I think it's time for me to make up for neglecting what this weekend was supposed to be all about—*you*. Besides, you know what they say about all work and no play."

I let go of her foot but only to crawl up over her, skimming my body over hers the whole way. I'm not playing fair and I don't give a fuck. My next question comes out as a growl: "Does Mistress want to play?"

Her eyes snap to mine and within seconds, her breaths start to come in shorter, more heavily. She wants this. Wants me.

But then something else clouds over her eyes. Some conflict I don't understand. I don't think it's about me neglecting her for work, either.

It's something else. Even as her body relaxes into me, her nipples hardening into ripe little buds, the furrow between her eyebrows gets deeper. Goddammit, what *is* it?

"What's wrong?"

She squeezes her eyes shut and she presses her head back hard into the couch cushion. Enough. It's time to get to the bottom of this.

"Callie," I demand. "What's going on? Tell me."

She swallows and at the same time, she shifts beneath me, one of her legs falling open and wrapping around to pull me into her.

I hiss at the feel of her pulling me into her warmth and her eyes pop open. No doubt at feeling my hard length. What does she expect? Even touching her ankles had me hard as stone. This is what she does to me. I'm barely able to keep myself from popping wood at work. Does she know how embarrassing it is to be the CEO of a billion dollar company and having to scurry off to my private bathroom because I have a stiffy from walking by her cubicle? Jesus.

And that's nothing to having her hot and heaving beneath me. Still, nothing could prepare me for her next words.

"Is there a way to stay the Domme, but..." she trails off like she doesn't know how to ask for what she wants.

I put a knuckle under her chin to lift her face so she looks at me. "Hey. Never be afraid to ask anything. Not with me."

"Well," she tries again, swallowing. "Where I'm the Domme officially but you're the one doing some of the..." Her eyes drop. "...dominating?"

Jesus is she asking what I think she is?

It's a fight to keep my voice even. "We can do anything you want and you still stay the top. Even if it doesn't fall into the traditional roles. My job as your sub is to please and worship you in whatever way you want or need."

A shudder runs down her body at my words and I've never felt a more caveman desire to drag her up to my room and chain her to my bed. The things I would do to her if she'd let me—

"Then it would please your Mistress for you to spank her and get her off like you did the first time in the limo." Her eyes drop to the floor like she's already embodying taking on the role of submissive.

And my cock could officially break brick, I'm so fucking hard. Still, I don't want to scare her. So I take a breath and manage to get out, "Whatever Mistress wants." I even bow my head.

"Don't bullshit me," she laughs. "I know you're chomping at the bit." Then she wraps an arm around my back, locks it with the other she slipped around my chest, and uses the leverage to lift me up slightly. Then she wedges her knee between us and shoves me off of her.

Before I know it I'm toppling off the couch head-first.

Jesus! I barely manage to catch myself and somewhat direct my tumble to the floor. She's become positively dangerous after that self-defense class of hers.

"Just don't forget who's ultimately in charge." Her eyes are narrowed as she glares down at me.

I grin. "No, ma'am. Wouldn't think of it."

"Good," she says haughtily, sounding every inch the Mistress for a moment. "Then take me to a room where we can play."

But if she's letting me be dom for once, then my beast isn't going to pass up a moment of it.

Especially when a second later, I see the conflict enter her eyes again. She's not just asking me to top her on a whim. For some reason, she doesn't feel like she can be a good domme to me right now.

I think back to our very first lesson, that day I took her to the club. The dominant/submissive relationship is about *trust*.

I already know she's not willing to trust me with all her problems. But every opportunity I can take to demonstrate that I won't be like every other man in her life—that I'll *stay*, that I'll be someone she can actually *count on*, goddammit but I'm going to fight to prove myself to her.

So I don't wait for her to second guess her impulse. No, I grab her and throw her over my shoulder. When she shrieks, I smack her ass and the beast roars with approval.

I carry her up to my playroom, shoving open the door so hard it bangs into the wall. I don't care. I'm here to take what's mine.

I set her on her feet beside the large four poster bed the dominates the middle of the room. There's some of the other usual equipment around the room but all I care about is the bed. The frame is solid oak and connected to each bedpost is a short coil of chain and a padded cuff.

I'm about to order her on the bed when she snaps, "Strip and get on the bed."

My head snaps her direction but she's only glaring me down.

"You said I'm still the top," she reminds me darkly.

Yes. Fuck. It's a line I've never straddled before. In this power exchange, I have to remember that she ultimately needs to feel safe. So I'll do it her way.

For now.

Still, I can't help my jaw tightening as I bow my head and tug off my shirt, pants, and boxers and climb up on the bed.

Her eyes brighten. I think she likes the fact that submission is so difficult for me. I swear she revels in it.

And somehow that thought makes me harder. Jesus, being with her is a mind-fuck sometimes. One I wouldn't give up for the world.

She comes to where I sit on the bed and grabs my left ankle. She's sure to look me in the eye as she secures the cuff around it.

What will she do next? I never know. I just know I want to be with her for it, every step of the damn way.

She moves to my other ankle and secures the cuff around it as well. There's only a tiny bit of slack in the chains. She's got my legs forced open in an unnatural spread-eagled position and I have to force my breathing even.

Do I love being tied to the bed in this position, my cock completely vulnerable?

I can't imagine any guy would.

Still, I lean back on my elbows and meet Callie's gaze. I won't flinch or try to cover up. She'll only know she can trust me if she sees I'm willing to afford her the same.

She quickly averts her eyes though, dropping them to the floor as she yanks her sweater off, revealing a hot as fuck black lace bra. She shimmies out of her legging next and Jesus—she's got a matching barely there lace thong that's little more than a triangle of fabric covering her.

My cock strains toward her and my legs flex uselessly. Obviously I can't get to her, strapped down like I am. Well, she hasn't restrained my wrists yet, but I force myself not to reach for her. No need to remind her of that fact.

And thank Jesus, the next second she comes towards me, climbing up on the bed and then—

Jesus *fuck*—

She climbs up over my lap, bending over and arranging herself in spanking position. Her belly brushes the tip of my cock and I suck in a lungful of air at the contact.

Yes. Jesus. *Yes*.

I run a hand down her flank, stretching my jaw and reveling in the soft warmth of her skin. And then I swat her ass. Hard.

She lets out a little yelp and I wait. Will she retreat? *What's it gonna be, baby?*

Is she going to keep trying to top from the bottom or will she really let me take the lead? I'll do whatever she wants.

Her body goes tense and for a second I think she's going to run.

But then she relaxes, forehead dropping to the bed, arching her back so that her ass rises up in the air toward my hand.

That's right, baby. That's right.

She arches her back so that her ass rises up in the air, taunting me.

Oh baby. I don't need an invitation. My hand falls again on that sweet, sweet ass. She grunts but keeps wiggling her backside at me.

Is this a test of wills? Or is it like her fake smiles? Even here does she think she can put me in my place? Keep me behind glass so I can only look but not touch? Never *really* touch her? Never get to the *real* Calliope behind those walls she keeps so high around herself?

Because she's wrong. She's dead wrong.

She doesn't know it, but she's opened the gates the smallest bit and I'm going to do my damndest to ram my way in and bring light to the places she tries to keep hidden in darkness.

I continue the spanking, concentrating harder than even when I was coding earlier. Not every blow is hard. Some are light smacks that end in caresses between her legs.

Her attempts to excite and distract me by writhing in my lap aren't going to work. Doesn't she know by now how single-minded I can be when I have a goal?

I rain down more punishing blows and finally, finally, she starts to go pliant under my hands. Her eyes flutter closed and her features go lax.

I barely keep back the growl of satisfaction at the sight. Yes. Fuck yes. We're getting somewhere now. Peeling back the layers of bullshit and digging down to her truths.

Come on, Callie, baby. Give me your truth.

I tease between her thighs after landing another *smack* but pull back just as quickly. She moans in denied satisfaction and I grip both her pink ass cheeks in my hands before landing another spanking.

She's doing so good. I can feel her letting go. Giving into me.

And then all the sudden, it's like a switch flips.

She goes tense again beneath me. I don't know what happened, but I've lost her. "Harder," she says through a huffing breath. "And tell me what a bad girl I am. What a filthy, disgusting slut."

I recoil from her words. And then set about correcting her.

"You're my beautiful slut. Built so perfectly." I land a resounding smack in the center of her ass, right where it's pinkest.

I'm getting her truths all right. But Jesus. Is that what she really thinks of herself?

She twists, turning and glaring at me with a fury that goes beyond a little wordplay in a scene.

"I'm a disgusting cum bucket. Worthless except for my tits and ass."

I meet her gaze calmly. "Your body is a work of art and deserves to be worshiped."

Her mouth goes tight and she looks like steam is about to come out her ears, she's so pissed.

"I'm a filthy lying bitch," she growls, grinding herself down on my cock.

Oh, baby.

She's so desperate for any shred of control but that's not the way this game is played. Not tonight. Jesus, this has been a long time coming. This is what's been hiding in her head the whole time?

"Say it," she spits. "Say I'm a dirty cunt."

I keep my hands on her ass and start to massage them. No more spanking tonight. No, it'll all be about worship from here on out. "You're gorgeous. You're a goddess. You're—"

She leaps off of me. And before I can say another word, her hand comes flying at me and she slaps me hard across the face.

"I'm a disgusting whore!" she shouts. "Say it. Fucking say it!"

"Stiletto."

She freezes as I say the word. A second later she stumbles backward, a look of horror overtaking her face as she looks at me and down to her hand and then back to me like she's just realizing what she did. How far she went.

And then she looks like she's about to bolt.

But she takes a shuddering breath and comes back to the bed. She doesn't say a word and she doesn't look at me. She just begins uncuffing my left ankle. Her hands are trembling so badly, she can barely manage the buckle.

"Callie," I finally say gently as I bend to help her with the buckle.

I see her cringe but I finally trust that she's not going to run like a frightened animal. What I just witnessed—Jesus, finally, she finally let me in. She didn't mean to, that much is obvious. But it's part of what power exchange is about. Busting down barriers to intimacy.

"Tell me what's going on," I demand. Then I soften my voice. "Please."

Please Callie. Let me all the way in.

She looks lost in indecision. Actually, she looks tortured by it, her mind working a hundred miles an hour.

She looks down but I don't miss the tear that slides down her cheek. I reach over and catch it with my thumb, urging her face back toward me.

When I do, her features are devastated.

"Why wouldn't you just say it?" There's anguish, not accusation, in her voice. "You had no problem with the humiliation talk to the other sub. You encouraged me to use it." She looks at me and swipes angrily as the tears continue to fall. She quickly glances away as she works to free my second ankle.

"Vocal humiliation is a part of play because it's taboo," I explain, keeping my voice gentle. "Society says we're not supposed to say those things out loud, so when we do it in play, it turns us on."

"Exactly," she cuts in. "So why—"

I'm already shaking my head. "But you," I reach out and grab her hand. "I'm afraid you believe it about yourself. All those things you were saying. None of that's true. I won't say it to you."

She snatches her hand back and turns away from me.

Her body language says back off but I've gotten this far and I'm going to press my advantage. "Bad things have happened to you in the past, haven't they? You don't have to tell me what," I run a hand down her spine. "But you *will* allow me to help you through it. Now let's stop flirting with this switch. You need me to be in control tonight. So let me take it." My voice has the command of a dominant. "Get on the bed."

She could use her safe word right back and bring an end to this. I pray she won't, though. *Please, please, Callie. Be my brave girl.*

Her eyes dart every which way. And then she finally looks my way. "No bondage."

Just those two words and then her gaze drops to the floor.

I nod. I'm fine with limits especially when it means she's communicating with me. "On the bed."

Her chest moves up and down in clear anxiety, but she does as I ask. And I get it now. Why it thrills her so much to know that submission is difficult for me but that I do it anyway. It *is* more meaningful than if she just obeyed like a robot.

Her submission in this moment *means* something.

And I'm so damn proud of her. She has demons, it's clear, and she's facing them. With me. She's allowing me in.

I don't waste another second. I get on the bed and pull her into my lap again. It's a much more natural position now, though, without my legs spread awkwardly and cuffed to the bed.

I rub my hand down her warm, pink ass.

"Aw, there we are." I can't help the satisfaction that drips from my voice. "The most beautiful goddamn ass in all creation, made just for me."

I shift her and then lean over to kiss each of her sweet cheeks. I don't stop there, though. I shift her even more on the bed so that she's lying on her stomach and I drop to my knees. Her body jumps in shock when I begin tonguing the rim of her back entrance.

"Shh," I whisper, massaging her before delivering several stinging slaps again. Then I dive back in with my tongue, exploring her forbidden places.

She makes little whimpering noises as I wrap an arm around her waist to hold her in place while I continue thrusting my tongue up inside the tight rosette of her ass.

She shudders and writhes in my hold, like she's not sure if she wants to pull away or push back against me. Which only makes me tongue her deeper. I want her to know that nothing is wrong here. Nothing is forbidden between us. To know that I'm going to become familiar with every single inch and crevice of her.

I'm going to etch the memory of myself so deep in the very fabric of her body that she'll never be able to get me out. My hands. My tongue. My fingers. My cock.

I pull back from her ass only when her legs begin shaking. I grin when I see her pussy glistening with wetness.

"Look at this pretty, pretty cunt. You're juicing for me, aren't you, beautiful dirty girl?" I gather the moisture with my fingers, dipping them inside her pussy, rolling in a circle and then pulling back out. Then I drag my fingers teasingly, ever so teasingly back to her ass.

But, always wanting to keep her on her toes, then I deliver another stinging series of slaps.

I'm not spanking hard. It's more about sensation. And domination.

Her back arches in pleasure and Jesus, I don't know how much longer I can hold out. I reach down and squeeze the tip of my cock. *Not yet.*

I stand up and slide her more fully onto the bed, urging her up on her hands and knees. Then I lay down on the bed between her spread knees on my back and lift up, at the same time dragging her hips down until she's sitting on my face.

Oh *fuck.* Her scent. I seek out her clit and give a hard suck while I slip my finger inside her. I want to eat her out everywhere at once but before I move on, I tease the edge of my teeth along her clit.

She cries out and her stomach tenses, whole body jolting.

Jesus, she's at my mercy. I've got her right on the edge.

I grin and slide the finger I had inside her out and back toward her ass. I want her blind with sensory overload before I start questioning her again about what's going on. I want her stripped of all inhibitions so that she gives me the truth.

But as my forefinger starts to gently explore her back channel and I lap at her cunt for several more long moments to make absolutely *sure* she's lost in pleasure, I realize that—dammit. I've lost her.

Her moans and little gasps of pleasure have disappeared completely.

She hovers above me, all but frozen except for her hips that move restlessly back and forth against my face.

"Callie?" I say and she doesn't respond. "Callie, do you want to use your safeword?"

No response. Okay, so maybe she's embarrassed about liking ass play. Some women are and that's fine. I'll get her used to every sensation there is in the book.

My forefinger slipped up her ass easily and I slowly work in a second beside the first. She continues thrusting against my face so I take that as a sign she wants to keep going. I want her to know what it feels like to be absolutely devoured, worshiped in every sense of the word.

Her odd silence continues only another few seconds before she cries, "Oh God, *Jackson.*"

When I tilt my head slightly, I can see her looking down at me. Then a shudder moves down her body, her legs trembling so violently the bed is shaking.

Oh she's close. She's soooo close.

And she's the most goddamned beautiful thing I've ever witnessed in my life.

She's here, fully with me. And maybe for today that's enough. I don't need to know all her secrets for us to be as connected as two people can be. She'll tell me in time. Right now, this is enough. She trusts me with her body and I have to believe that it will eventually translate to trust in every other part of her life.

She mutters something unintelligible and then lifts all the way up to her knees, away from my mouth. Then she crawls down my body, straddling me and burying her face in my neck, inhaling.

Then— *oh Jesus.*

She's got my cock in hand and is guiding me inside her.

So tight. So fucking perfect. So tight. I'm thrusting because I can't not. It's Callie. Perfect Callie's pussy. Oh Jesus.

But no, dammit. I hiss through my teeth as she fully seats herself on top of me. I'm not ready to give up control yet so I grab her legs and then I sit up, my legs to the floor so she's not so much riding me as we're both equal partners in this.

She locks her legs around her back, squeezing me to her with everything she's got and damn if being wrapped up in her isn't the best thing I've ever felt in my whole life.

"*Fuuuuck,*" I groan, feeling my eyes roll back in my head. Still, it's not enough. I tangle my hand in the hair at the back of her neck and drag her to me, crushing my mouth to hers.

She cries out into my mouth, kissing me back just as hungrily and squeezing her walls around my cock. Oh fuck. Oh fuck she's the best thing I've ever—

I grip her hips to maneuver her up and down on my cock, fucking her with a tortuously slow rhythm. As much as I want to hammer her into next Tuesday, I want to savor this even fucking more.

And I want her to know that there's no part of her I won't be demanding, so I spit on my fingers and then stretch one hand back around to that sweet little puckered asshole of hers.

"Let me in, baby. Let me in. I want in everywhere. I want every filthy beautiful fucking part of you."

She shudders and buries her face in my neck again, breathing me in as I push two fingers in. I continue, relentlessly, in and out while she gloves me so tight. So tight, *Jesus*, so—

She whines and bites my shoulder hard.

"That's right. Let me know it. Give it to me. Give it all up to me."

Her nails dig into my back as she moves her hips back and forth, her whine growing higher pitched, more and more uncontrolled sounding.

"It's just you and me here. But I want everything. *Everything*," I demand, adding a third finger.

Does she feel me? Does she fucking feel me? Everywhere? I want to be her fucking everything. *Goddammit just let me, Callie. Let me in.*

I shift slightly and my cock angles, hitting even deeper inside her and she grinds against me and oh fuck—

"Jackson!" she screams, clutching me with every part of her body, her pussy contracting on my cock in a way that—

I pull out and shove to the hilt and cum harder than I ever have in my life.

Damn— Did I— I swear I just blacked out for a moment there.

When I come to, I find Callie blinking and looking at me in shock, panting, fingernails impaling my shoulder but I don't care. I don't fucking care. She's my goddamned nirvana. She's *my* everything. Jesus, maybe that's all I proved just now. That she's destroyed me.

I wrap my arms around her. Tight. I need to know she's real. I need her to be mine and I have the worst feeling that if I don't hold tight enough, she'll disappear.

But she can't. She can't.

Me before Callie… fuck, I can't even remember what that sad bastard's life was like. Except I can. I know what it's like to have Callie and then lose her. I'm not sure I could survive it twice.

I bury my face in her breasts. I just mean to hold her, but

goddammit, her nipples are so gorgeous and tempting, soon I'm kissing and licking and teasing and laughing. The next second, I collapse backwards on the bed, taking Callie with me, of course. Always taking her with me.

She's laughing too. I have no idea what we're laughing at but this is the moment I want to remember when I'm on my deathbed. Laughing and holding the woman I know I'll love into eternity.

We just lie like that for several minutes, laughing and holding one another. I keep my face buried in her breasts because this feeling, Jesus, it's so big. If I even look at her I know I'll want to blurt it out. How much I love her. How I want to marry her. Adopt Charlie. All of it. I want all of it with her.

It's only after a few minutes that I realize, shit, I didn't use a condom and she's just got my cum dripping out of her and making a mess on the sheets and her thighs.

I roll her so that her back is on the bed and get up. "Be back in a sec."

She throws an arm over her face and mutters something I can't hear.

"Did you say something?"

"No," she says too quickly.

She's already putting her walls back up. My heart sinks but only a little. Maybe I didn't demolish them completely today but I made inroads. And every single day I'll keep hammering until finally they give way and crumble completely.

I hurry to the bathroom and soak a rag in hot water, then come back and start to clean her thighs.

She looks down and then her eyes widen and she jerks to a sitting position. "Oh fuck!" Her eyes shoot to mine like she's just now realizing we didn't use a condom, too. "I'm on the pill. And I'm clean."

I just laugh. "I wasn't worried." I lean over and kiss her. "I'm clean, too. I would never endanger you if I wasn't."

"But you couldn't have known I was on the pill."

Well. I didn't think about that. Which is surprising because that would have been my first worry if it had been any one else. But even now, thinking about it. Jesus. Looking down at Callie. I already know I want her to be my forever. It would be a little soon but I wouldn't have minded if she weren't on the pill.

She's still sitting there looking really freaked out, though, so I don't say that out loud.

"My job description is to worship you." I hold up the warm towel and cock an eyebrow. "Can I get back to it now?"

She lies back on the bed again but doesn't look any less freaked out.

"Stay here," I say before jogging back to the bathroom to lay out the rag before returning. She's still there but she looks like she's not sure if this is the part where she should bolt or not. I'll be putting a stop to that.

"Move over."

Her brows furrow.

"Over," I say, adding command to my voice. She scoots over and I let out a breath of relief. With as vulnerable as things just got between us, there's always a chance she could react by trying to take two steps back.

I pull back the covers on the big bed and slide in beside her.

"Now here," I swirl my finger to demonstrate that she should roll back against my side.

"We're going to sleep here?" she lowers her voice, glancing around, "in the sex room?"

I laugh and drag her against me. Jesus she's adorable. And damn but I'm exhausted. The second she snuggles up warm beside me, my eyes drop shut like lead weights are attached to them.

"No windows," I murmur. "Best place in the house to sleep after I've pulled an all-nighter."

She pulls the silken sheet over us, one of her small hands coming up to cup my cheek that has a lot more than a five-o-clock shadows worth of stubble on it.

"Sleep," she whispers, and this time, I'm happy to obey her command.

CHAPTER SEVENTEEN

CALLIE

Hot kisses at the back of my neck wake me. It's dark. Completely dark. My whole body tenses, ready to scream and fight. Just as I make a fist and jerk my elbow forward so I can deliver a punishing gut-blow to whatever fucker got me in this vulnerable position, I smell it. Woods. Pine.
Jackson.
Memories of last night fled back in. I'm with Jackson. I'm *safe.*
"Babe?" he questions, his kisses pausing. He must've felt the tension tighten my body.
I turn my head and meet his mouth with mine. For about point two seconds I think about morning breath, but all thought is quickly swallowed up by sensation. The fear-followed-by-arousal is also disturbingly erotic.
I try to turn in Jackson's hold, but with one firm arm around my waist, he holds me still. "I want you like this, beautiful," he whispers. His hips move into me from behind and his long, thick erection nudges the backs of my thighs.

He slips one hand underneath my body and massages my breast. The other caresses slowly down my torso, dipping into my belly button before dropping lower, lower—

I moan and squirm beneath his ministrations as wetness seeps between my legs.

"Jackson..."

"Let me worship you," he whispers, going back to kissing and nipping the back of my neck.

It continues like that for several minutes with me growing wetter and wetter. The way he's holding me, I can barely grab him.

He's holding onto his power position from last night and I'm not sure how I like it. But oh— I melt against him as he begins rubbing in earnest at *that* spot.

I do so like what he's doing. It's— Oh God, right there, yes.

It's good but not enough.

"I need you in me," I rasp. "Get that cock in me. I need it hard. I need you in me so hard."

I try one more time to turn and loop a leg around his hip, but he just growls and grips the back of my right leg to part me for him.

I'm about to tell him *not like that*, but then he's filling me and the protest dies on my tongue. He spoons me as he thrusts deep up inside me, the position forcing a tight grip on his cock. He groans in appreciation and my head dips back on his shoulder.

Again, I breathe him in. Just like last night, I ground myself in his scent. When he first began probing my ass last night, I lost it for a few moments. I was back in that horrible room, men at my front and back, *violating*—

But then no. I inhaled. Just like I do now. Woods and pine and everything Jackson.

And it keeps me totally present. Here, with him, held so tight, one of his hands on my breast and the other moving back to tease at my clit.

No space for ghosts. Just him and me.

He makes my body new.

"Christ, your pussy's clutching me like a vise. Fuck. Never felt anything like it." He sucks on the back of my neck. Hard.

He's marking me. I'll have to wear my hair down to cover it. I love it. I want to claw and bite him to mark him as mine in return. Even the thought makes me wild.

I grasp what parts of him I can, reaching up a hand behind me and burying it in his hair, yanking him forward while twisting to kiss him. With my other hand, I cover his fingers rubbing at my cunt and we work it together.

His thrusts from behind turn almost violent. Both our bodies jolt with every stroke in, but he's holding me so tight, we stay glued together. I bite his lip and then suck it into my mouth to soothe it afterward. Our kisses grow even more ferocious.

"God. Fucking. Damn," he swears between each punishing thrust, sweat pouring from his brow.

Each time he hits that much deeper inside and *God*. The light and the high, it's so close, I'm half riding it already. But I want more, I'm a greedy bitch and I want more, I want it all, I want to ride and ride it—

"More. Please, Jackson. *Harder.*"

With a roar, he does. He pinches my nipple and goes at me like a battering ram from behind and then it hits so bright, so goddamn beautiful.

"*Fuuuuuuuuuuuuuuuuck!*" I scream as my body spasms and keeps spasming.

Over my shoulder I see Jackson's face contort in agonized pleasure. His eyes lock with mine and the high ramps up to another level because we're sharing this transcendent experience. We made it together. Him and me. Just him and me. Locked here forever.

Another spasm hits my body and I clutch his hand so tight I'm sure I'll leave those marks I wanted.

Jackson slackens first, his whole body slumping into me from behind. He wraps his arms around me so tight I almost can't breathe. One last aftershock rockets through me outward to the tips of my body. This time, when I try to turn around, Jackson doesn't fight me.

He pulls me just as close though, my breasts crushed to his chest, his head notched over mine, one of his legs swung over my hip. It's as if he's wrapping his entire body around me to cage me in like he's afraid I'll run or disappear at any moment.

Maybe that's what does it. Maybe it's the intensity of what we just experienced or the fact that I'm still left facing Gentry after all this.

Either way, stupid-ass tears start running down my cheeks. I bury my face in Jackson's neck. Pine. It's a smell that I'll associate with safety and pleasure for the rest of my life. He's helped me truly feel safe, even in the most vulnerable of situations. I smile through my tears.

One by one, he's helping me take back the positions Gentry and those animals stole from me. I didn't think I'd ever be able to enjoy that sexual position again—from behind.

Jackson's looking down at me. There are questions in his eyes that he doesn't ask. Damn him. He's too good. Too wonderful.

"You really should have some more flaws," I say through my teary smile.

His eyebrows quirk in confusion and he tilts his head sideways.

I just laugh at him and grab one of his hands. I kiss his fingers, then up to his knuckles, his palm, then to his thumb, which I pop in my mouth and suck. His sharp intake of breath gratifies me and my smile grows. I kiss up his forearm and as I do, I lift it to the corner of the bed. Once in position, it's a small matter to secure the padded cuff around his wrist.

This gets me another surprised breath from him. I grin at him like a cat with a bowl full of cream.

"You said it yourself. All work and no play…" I kiss and lick my way down the arm I've shackled over to his other arm, which I also secure.

I continue down to both his legs. There's no centimeter of Jackson Vale's body I won't have explored by the time I'm through with him. It's time he knows what it's like to feel worshiped.

And well, a little playful torture along the way won't go amiss either.

CHAPTER EIGHTEEN

CALLIE

The following week, it feels strange to be back in the real world. At least at first.

By Friday, I'd swear last weekend with Jackson was a bubble out of time, a wine-soaked dream I had after yet another lonely day chipping away at my never-ending fight to survive. Jackson's had to work so much on the new prototype, we've barely seen each other except in passing at the office. And anyway, surely nothing as perfect as last weekend could have actually existed?

No. I'm here dealing in cold, hard realities. I stare at the small one-and-a-half-inch cube of stacked mini computer chips with wires sticking out on two sides like spider legs.

"So," I ask, "the control-cube multi-rotor stack doesn't actually need to be altered with the new programming?"

Emmett Chen shakes his head. Emmett's been showing me around the machine shop whenever I've visited this past week. "Nope. The hardware will stay the same."

"Of course." I nod to myself. "It was the hardware that was holding

Jackson back the whole time." Then I realize how intimately I just said Jackson's name. "Mr. Vale, I mean. Holding Mr. Vale back."

Emmett nods, apparently not picking up on anything. "This is the best we've got for now. Eventually the state-of-the-art will catch up to Mr. Vale's initial vision, but in the meantime, we'll get a working competitive copter now that the algorithms are adjusted to the hardware limitations."

This time it's me who nods. Yup.

Thanks to yours truly opening her big fat mouth. Vale would have made it to the same conclusion eventually, or the hardware would have caught up to his initial vision. But probably not in the two-week time frame Gentry gave me. My heart sinks.

I look around the room filled with parts. What Emmett's just told me makes my job of corporate espionage that much easier.

If I go through with it. Which I *won't*.

But if I *did*...

There's plenty of hardware lying in easy access all around me. There are more than enough prototypes of the 'failed version' of the drone. I'd just need to have the new version of the program and know how to upload it to the control-cube.

I stare at the block of stacked chips and the wires that lead to various kinds of inputs. I turn back to Emmett. "So where do you hook these up to input the actual code to the—?"

"There you are."

I swing around, slack-jawed when I see Jackson striding through the doors straight toward me. I immediately jerk my hand holding the control-cube behind my back.

Because that's not suspicious. *Stupid*, Callie. I wince internally and drop the control-cube on the table behind me, hoping I'm being unobtrusive about it. Then I bring my hands back to my side, aiming for casual.

"What's up?" I try for breezy but I'm pretty sure I fail.

"I've been looking for you." He pauses then looks around. "Emmett had mentioned you were spending some time down here."

Shit shit shit shit shit.

"It's the way you did it, right?" I smile, careful not to make it too bright. Jackson picks up on too many nuances. Casual. Be fucking *casual*. "You wanted to learn your products from the bottom up. The other coders in the lab said you encourage everyone to come spend time down here so they can understand the product from every dimension."

His eyes soften. And I feel like the bitch that I am for lying straight to his face. I'm a horrible, horrible person and I will burn in hell.

No. Goddammit. No I *won't* because I will find a way around giving the prototype to Gentry. I stiffen my back, more determined than ever.

The softness leaves Jackson's face and my heart drops to my stomach. Shit. Shit, he's seeing right through me. He knows. I open my mouth to say something, I have no idea what, but he beats me to the chase.

"Your lawyer's been trying to get a hold of you."

"What?" My hand immediately reaches for my phone in my pocket. Which is flat. No phone there. I must have left it in my purse which is back up at my office.

"I forgot it in my purse." I look up at Jackson. "What do they want to talk to me about?"

"Alberto wouldn't tell me. But he said it's urgent."

Urgent? Urgent can't be good. What if Gentry decided I was out of time and released the video early? But no, that doesn't make sense. Then he wouldn't have any leverage over me. Then again, who the fuck knows what goes through that sociopath's mind?

I all but sprint from the room, down the short hallway and to the elevator. When it doesn't come right away, I'm about to go for the stairs, but then it pings.

I jolt inside and Jackson is on my heels. I frantically push at the *Close Door* button.

"Calm down, Callie. I'm sure everything's fine."

My eyes search his. "You said it was urgent. It was Alberto you talked to?" He's the main lawyer I've been working with on my case. "How'd he sound on the phone? Like it was I'm-gonna-lose-my-son urgent? Or, there's-been-a-delay-in-the-paperwork urgent?"

Jackson lifts his shoulders and looks helpless. "Yes, it was Alberto, but I don't know how he sounded. He just said for you to call him back as soon as you could."

"Give me your phone." Why didn't I think of this as soon as he found me? Stupid! I don't have to wait for the elevator.

As soon as he brings his phone out of his suitcoat pocket, I'm dialing the lawyer's number. He's probably got it saved somewhere, but I have it memorized. All I hear on the other end, though, is a *beep beep beep* noise.

"What the fuck?"

Jackson looks at the phone. "No reception in the elevator."

"Goddammit!" I slap at the wall and my foot starts tapping a frantic pace. It feels like all the stress I've managed to keep bottled the last week is finally escaping like a boiling tea kettle. And I feel like making that same high-pitched screaming noise the kettles do with every second it takes to get off this fucking elevator.

Finally, the interminable elevator ride ends and we're at the floor where my station is. I step off and head toward the wall of windows, pressing the call button again.

"Mr. Vale, good to hear from you as always."

"It's not Mr. Vale, it's Calliope Cruise. You have information regarding my son's custody case?"

"Oh," Alberto says. "Hi. Yes, I've been trying to call you."

"What about? I'm kind of going crazy here."

"There's been a development. David's lawyers just got some new testimony and it could be damaging to our case. Nothing that would lose us the case," he quickly amends. "But it won't be helpful either."

"Who's testimony could he get that could hurt us? Did he pay someone to perjure themselves?" I pace back and forth. "What the hell are they saying anyway? I swear, that bastard—"

"It's your parents."

Silence. "My..." I can't even finish the thought. I just... "What?"

Jackson, obviously frustrated at only hearing one end of the conversation, takes the phone from me and pushes a button. "Alberto, you're on speaker now. Can you please repeat what you just said?"

"David's lawyers have brought forward some new testimony that they'll be introducing at the upcoming trial. From Callie's parents."

Jackson's face mirrors my shock. Okay. So I didn't mishear Alberto.

"Do you have the transcripts?" My voice is little more than a whisper. "What did he get them to say?"

"You have to understand, Callie," Alberto starts, "it was most likely one of the investigators from David's lawyer's firm that went and spoke to them. They could've presented themselves as a neutral third party. Your parents didn't necessarily know that their words would be used to testify against you."

Didn't *necessarily* know.

"What do the transcripts say?" My voice is iron.

Alberto lets out a sigh. "They speak about the time when you showed up on their door pregnant. Your dad goes on record about how he discovered that you worked at Hooters for years. And he expresses...er, his disappointment over the entire situation and was less than complimentary about...um...your moral character."

I close my eyes and can't help the way my entire body slumps. Dad knew about Hooters? Yeah I worked there for years but I thought I'd hidden it from them. I worked forty-five minutes away, picked up all my paychecks and deposited them in a different bank than my parents used. Hell, I even used my friend Marcy's place as my home address to fill out any and all paperwork.

I wonder when he found out. Was it before I came home knocked up by my professor? Did it contribute to him saying I was little better than a prostitute? My parents said a lot of things at the time, but that was the comment that had landed like an arrow through the chest.

And because I'm an idiot, the hurt punches the old wound all over again. I wince and rub absently at my sternum. It might have been Mom taking me to all the pageants, but I was always Daddy's little girl. And then the sacrifices I made for him so he could keep that job at the bank, even if he never knew about his boss Mr. McIntyre's late-night visits to my room...

I hand Jackson his phone and turn away, ready to walk out of the room.

"What can we do to fight this?" Jackson asks.

"Callie," Alberto says, not knowing I moved away, "the best way I see for us to fight this is for you to go visit them and see if they'll testify on your behalf. They can explain they were tricked into saying things on the record and the judge will take that into consideration. We need them on our side so they can testify on behalf of your character."

I can't help the caustic quality to my laugh. "Didn't you read the transcript? You know exactly what my father thinks of me."

There's a short silence, and then Alberto asks, "How long has it been since you've seen your parents face-to-face?"

I shake my head, then realize he can't see it. "Three years."

As soon as my parents made it clear that neither I nor my baby was welcome, I swore I'd never step foot on their property again.

"There's never been a bigger incentive to reach out and reconcile," Alberto says. "What David's lawyers got on record were words no doubt taken completely out of context. Plus, they got nothing from your mother. We can fight this, and there's no better way than by getting it straight from the horse's mouth."

I lean against the nearest wall and look up at the ceiling. Shit. All of this boils down to one thing. The last thing in the world I want to do.

I have to visit my fucking parents.

CHAPTER NINETEEN

JACKSON

Finally logic wins out and I convince Callie to skip the six-hour drive up to Siskiyou County and let me charter a plane instead. It takes some doing, though.

"Six hours both ways," I remind her as we walk from her workstation toward the elevator at the end of the day. "I'm happy to go on a road trip with you, if that's what you want, but my friend, Deve, owns a bunch of planes that he charters out. He also owes me a favor so it'd be free."

She frowns, slowing down. "That doesn't sound very safe. Just borrowing a plane that your friend has."

I laugh even though she turns to glare at me.

"Oh, did I forget to mention that Deve is a founding partner of Excelsior Air Lines?"

She almost chokes on the sip she's taking from my water bottle. "Holy sh— Excelsior Air— Like the company that's building those commercial rocketships for tourist rides into outer space?"

I nod, amused by her shock.

"What'd you do for him so he owes you a favor?"

"A gentleman never tells," I joke as I press the down button to call the elevator. "So that's a yes? I'll pick you and your sister up at ten o'clock on Saturday morning and then we'll head to Deve's airfield. The ride to your parents' place should take a little less than an hour by plane."

The elevator arrives and we step on, moving to the back corner. Since we're on the top floor, it pauses at almost every floor on the way down to pick up passengers. I face Callie with my back to the rest of the box—I've learned if I don't, people will come up to me no matter where I am in the building with questions or to fanboy/girl over me, neither of which I have time or patience for at the moment. Every second with Callie is precious.

"So that's the plan?" I keep my eyes on her.

This is about more than a plane and both of us know it. I get the feeling she'd rather I not come with her to her parent's house but the little I know about them—kicking out their nineteen-year-old daughter for the sin of being seduced by her professor, a man who abused his position of power— And then now for them to testify on that fucker's behalf? I breathe out hard, barely containing my anger.

I don't want her heading into that situation without back up. Yes, her sister's coming too, but I've seen her fly off the handle at Callie before. I'm the only one I trust to be the support I suspect Callie will need.

"I..." Callie huffs out a breath then throws up her hands. "Okay. Fine."

I feel a little bad for steamrolling her into doing things my way. But only a little bit. Protecting her is ultimately more important.

But shit. I heave out a breath. Not at the expense of her feeling like she has no control.

When we get to the bottom of the elevator and everyone else leaves, I take her hand. "Hey. We can get there any way you want. But please. I really want to be there with you."

She looks up and meets my gaze. Then she smiles and squeezes my hand, going up on tiptoes to drop a light kiss on my lips before pressing her forehead to mine.

"We can take the plane. But if we die in a fiery explosion, I'm gonna be *so* pissed."

I laugh and grab her around the waist, swinging her in a small circle and depositing her outside the elevator, making her squeal.

"I don't know about this." I overhear Callie's sister Shannon ask, looking nervously around the narrow interior of the plane Deve lent us. "Doesn't it seem... a little... small? You know, I could still just drive up and meet you there."

I cover my smirk. I already let Callie know I have to work for the short flight. But I'm still sitting close enough to Callie and her sister that I can occasionally overhear them.

The plane is luxurious, something they've both been commenting on. Every seat is a plush lounge chair. But the plane itself is little larger than a bus, a fact which isn't going over well with either sister.

I offered to sit with Callie during take off but she assured me she'll be fine. Still, I glance her way as we leave the tarmac and she's clutching her Kindle in one hand, and her sister's hand with the other.

I grin and go back to my laptop.

Fifty minutes later, all projects are assigned and the tires of the plane squeal as we land on the tarmac at Siskiyou County Airport.

Callie didn't even know such an airport existed.

Looking out the window, I can see why. Calling it an airport is a stretch. It's more like one long landing strip and six hangers. Our plane taxis into one.

"How was your flight?" I ask after walking back to Callie's seat.

Her smile is wobbly. "I didn't have to use the barf bag, so we'll call it a win."

Shannon elbows her in the stomach. "What she means to say is that we appreciate you arranging the flight and it's so much nicer than driving in a car for seven hours."

"Suck up." Callie says under her breath and elbows her back.

I can't help my grin. Seeing Callie around her sister is a whole new side of her. Naturally, I find it just as charming as the rest of her.

She looks less than at ease as we grab our bags from the plane and walk out to the town car waiting for us on the tarmac.

I take her hand and she clutches mine back, face going paler and paler the closer we get to her parent's house. Which makes me more and more glad I insisted on coming.

I don't like the effect this place has on her. I thought her looking sick was just because of the plane ride, but if anything, she looks even more green in the gills when we pull into her parent's driveway.

"Callie," I whisper after her sister pushes the backdoor open and steps out. "You okay? Because we can turn this car around and leave right now."

"What?" She looks over at me, startled. "No, I'm fine." She flashes the plastic smile and I want to growl. I hate that smile.

The next second, though, she's let go of my hand and is scooting across the back seat, stepping out her sister's door.

I get out too and find her staring up at her childhood home, a look I can't read on her face. I glance at the house. It's nothing special. An oversized two-story house with pretentious white columns in front that lead up to a deck off an upstairs bedroom.

It looks exactly like all the other houses on the block except that some houses have brick columns while others have white columns with Corinthian flourishes. Oh and a few houses have circular driveways with fountains in front.

Callie follows my gaze. "My mom was always jealous of the houses with fountains."

"Mom finally got the landscaping she always wanted though," Shannon says, joining us.

I take in the thick grass that looks cut exactly to an inch and is an almost obnoxious green. I don't even want to think about the amount of water they have to waste to keep it that green, when I know for a fact that this area of California has been in a drought for years.

In front of the house, a small garden is hemmed in by big white stones. Little spherical bushes dot the garden at perfect intervals. A stone pathway leads to the front door and more little bushes line the walkway.

"Mom must be so proud," Callie murmurs.

I hurry around to grab the suitcases from the trunk and then join Callie and Shannon as they head up the path to the front door. I expect them to just head inside, but instead Shannon stops and rings the doorbell.

Didn't she live here as recently as... two years ago? Whenever I go home I always just walk in and call out Mom's name and I haven't lived there for a decade. But whatever. Different strokes for different folks, I guess.

Pachelbel's Canon echoes through the door.

"So she got the fancy doorbell too," Callie says. Her voice sounds odd. Detached and just... not Callie-like.

We all wait on the stoop for a good minute and a half before the door finally opens.

A blonde woman probably in her fifties answers the door and I have to fight the urge to recoil. She's wearing so much make-up and hair product she looks shellacked. She's obviously had a nose job but not by a very well-qualified doctor by the looks of it.

She smiles and it's even worse than Callie's fake smile. Her eyes glide right over Shannon, hover on Callie with a lingering top to bottom scan, and then land on me. Only then does she brighten.

"Welcome," she says with too much enthusiasm to be genuine. "Come in, come in." She backs up and holds the door open for us.

Callie shoots a quick glance at Shannon but she just shrugs and walks inside. With a look like she might throw up any moment, Callie follows. I grab the bags and follow, closing the door right behind us.

"Well don't just stand there," Callie's mom says, her voice still with that weird over-enthusiastic pitch. "Your father is catching up on some last-minute work in his study." She leans in to me and I have to work not to pull back at her overpowering perfume. "Any day now he's going to be promoted to branch manager, you know."

Callie stiffens beside me and I glance her way. Her mouth is pursed, jaw stiff. Something her mom just said ticked her off but I don't know what, or why.

She squeezes her eyes shut as her mother continues prattling on about updates they've made to the house. New white granite kitchen countertops. An infrared sauna they installed because, in her mother's words, "all my friends were getting one and they are just a necessity for clearing the body of toxins. It's really a can't-live-without item."

She looks between the three of us gravely. "Do you know how many toxins are building up in your body on a daily basis? I can email you some articles. Sitting for twenty minutes in my sauna is the equivalent of running two to three miles. You girls should really look into getting one. You could share it since you're living in the same apartment." Her face sours some at this.

"Hopefully that situation won't last for much longer," comes a man's voice from the other end of the living room. Her father, I presume. He's a tall man, dressed like he stepped right out of a K-mart catalogue in his khaki pants and polo shirt, sweater tied artfully over his shoulders. "If what you said on the phone is true and you've got a real job. It'd be nice to finally have a daughter we can be proud to claim."

What a fucking dick.

Now my back is as stiff as Callie's. I glance over at her but she's looking at Shannon, her brow furrowed. Shannon's face is carefully blank. Damn. I knew it would be bad but I guess I wasn't prepared for how screwed up this family dynamic would be.

"You must be Jackson Vale." Dad bypasses his two daughters with barely a glance and heads directly toward me, hand out.

I force a smile and grasp his hand to shake. If it's a little firmer than necessary, well, I can only contain the beast so much.

"I took a look at CubeThink's market shares when I heard Callie was coming up with you for the weekend," he says, nodding as if modestly impressed. "Not bad. Of course, all the easy money's been made in the market and we're in a bottoming process. But there's lots of cash on the sidelines and I really think we're constructive on the market. I'm cautiously optimistic. You?"

I feel Callie wince beside me. She knows as well as I do that everything her dad just said is total nonsense bullshit. I've seen his kind before. They like to sound smart so they can feel like they're more important than they are.

But really he's just a little man with a little life and he'll never be anything more. It's only because I can feel how uncomfortable Callie is, embarrassed by her father, that I don't call him out.

"I'm sure Jackson doesn't want to talk about that over lunch, Daddy," Callie says hurriedly.

He turns and gives her a stern look. "Your mother's getting lunch ready in the kitchen. Maybe you'd like to go help her with that while we talk business?" It's stated like a question but I hear the order underneath it.

And goddammit, I want to punch him in his smug, stupid face. He's such a blowhard but then he's going to stand there and try to demean his daughter? Tell her to go do women's work in the kitchen while the menfolk stand here and talk business?

Callie's chest heaves like she's three seconds from ripping him a new one, either that or she's about to start crying, when Shannon grabs her elbow and leads her toward the kitchen.

Her father immediately starts talking again but my eyes are on Callie. She glances back once before disappearing through the kitchen and I try to communicate as much as I can through the look. *Are you okay?*

She gives a quick nod, then jerks her head back toward her dad, like she wants me to focus on him. And I get it. He might be the biggest ass in three counties, but she needs him to recant his testimony, or better yet, testify on her behalf. So I suck it up and cater to his ego. Which is as big as the fucking state of California.

He goes on and on and *on* about his job as a mid-level manager at a local bank. About all his investments—aka, he plays in the stock market, mostly losing because he knows shit about managing money—and about how he's on the cusp of a great promotion, which he eventually lets slip he's been waiting for for over seven years now. He doesn't let me get a word in edgewise or ask me a single question.

How the fuck did Callie come out so great coming from parents like this?

Suffice to say, I'm more than glad when Callie comes back out carrying a silver platter of tiny cucumber sandwiches. Her back is straight and she walks with perfect poise.

About ten minutes later, the women have carried most of the food out and we're all sitting around the dining room table. The table is set with fancy china, silverware, crystal glasses—they've gone all out. Now awkward silence fills the room as we hand around a plate of dainty cucumber sandwich appetizers and Callie's mother brings out bowls of soup.

The soup is orange. A thick, *mystery* orange. I take a sip and try not to sputter. What the—

It's cold. Refrigerator cold. My eyes open wide but I manage to swallow it. I look to Callie only to find her eyes on Shannon. I follow her gaze. Shannon just shakes her head at Callie and dutifully swallows a large sip of the cold orange concoction. I swear, every second in this place gets weirder and weirder.

But fine. Whatever. We're here for a reason and it's time to get things back on track. Not that they've even asked about their grandson *once* but nope. Can't let myself think about that or I'll get pissed all over again.

"So Gerald," my voice breaks the silence, "has Callie told you about the impressive work she's doing at CubeThink?"

Callie stirs her soup with her spoon, biting her lip without looking at her father.

"Well, she definitely caught your eye," her dad says with a smirk I immediately want to knock off his face. "My daughter always has been a looker." He smiles at me, a sort of knowing-between-men kind of smile.

Son of a—

"She's quickly risen to a position as one of the top programmers in the company," I correct him, not caring about how clipped my tone is. My patience with this motherfucker is officially gone.

"I can just guess how that happened," her dad murmurs under his breath as he takes a spoonful of the soup before his face twists in disgust. "For God's sake, Martha, what is this?"

"It's pumpkin gazpacho, sweetie. I saw this recipe on a famous chef's Pinterest and knew I had to try it. Isn't it fabulous?"

Her father shoves the bowl away, the look of distaste not leaving his face. He grabs two of the quartered cucumber sandwiches and pops them in his mouth.

"Did you really just intimate that your daughter slept her way to her position?" I'm really fucking hoping I heard him wrong. "Right here at the dining room table in front of her. In front of your whole family?"

The clank of spoons against china stops. The entire room falls still and her father's cheeks flush. Good. He should be embarrassed. And fucking ashamed of himself.

"I— I," he blusters, "well I—"

"Because I know any well-mannered, cultured man would never say such a thing of his own daughter." I glare the man down. "Callie rises or falls on her own merits within my company. She's incredibly intelligent and talented. Just a week ago her out-of-the-box thinking and insight led to a breakthrough on a problem that had been holding back production for months. She's only a few classes away from graduating from Stanford University. May I ask where you yourself matriculated from?"

Her father sits up straighter in his chair, his features darkening along with the blush that's taken up residence in his cheeks. "I— I—" he stutters again before getting his bearings, "—I'm a proud graduate of National University."

"I'm not familiar with that institution." I smile affably even though the beast in me still wants to stalk to the end of the table, yank him up by his pretty as fuck shirt and drag him out to the yard where I can kick his ass.

"It's the premier college in the northernmost part of California," he says stiffly. Ha. *Northernmost part*. He's got to mean north of, and not including, Sacramento. The part of California where it's almost all forests, mountains, and tiny communities. The biggest town is Redding, a nice enough little place, but you blink a couple times and you've passed through it.

"Impressive," I say, just barely managing not to let all the condescension I feel for this self-involved windbag drip from my tone. Just *barely*. Because goddammit, we do still need him. "But certainly you're proud of your daughter who is only a few classes away from graduating from the number one college not only in California but the entire West Coast."

I look back to Callie and find her eyes shining. Like it's the first time in her life anyone's stood up for her. And I both hate that she's never had that before and love that I can be the one to give it to her. Jesus but she deserves so much more than these shit parents.

Her father makes a *hmph* noise and then clears his throat. "Well, when do you think you'll be graduating from Stanford, Calliope?" he finally asks.

Callie doesn't immediately answer. She's still staring at me. Her look has shifted though. If I'm not mistaken. Oh damn, the flare of her nostrils and the way her tongue flicks out to wet her bottom lip—is she thinking about what I think she's thinking about? My cock stiffens and I reach under the table to squeeze her knee.

"Callie?" I don't move my hand from her leg as I nod in her father's direction. "Your dad just asked when you think you'll graduate."

"Oh." She looks over at her father in surprise like she totally missed his question. I smirk to myself.

"Well, CubeThink has a tuition reimbursement program," she says, "so I've been planning to take one of my last few classes in the spring semester."

Her voice grows more confident with each word. We hadn't talked about her future but I love that that's her plan. Does she have any idea how proud I am of her? She's the strongest woman I've ever met. Nothing keeps her down for long.

"What's the title of your current position?" her father asks, finally looking at her. Really looking at her like she's worth his time and attention.

"Senior Software Engineer."

"Which means?" I prompt. "Tell him a little about what you do."

"Well," she starts a little hesitantly, "it means I'm working to design, build, and run the backend services powering the quadcopter drones we're building, including APIs and data pipelines." I get the feeling that if it had been anyone else, she wouldn't have gone into so much detail. But like always, she's smart. She needs her dad on her side and busting out the terminology he could never hope to understand can only work in her favor.

He nods thoughtfully, the kind of man not willing to let on that he has no clue what the hell she's talking about. "Nice," he says, nodding some more. "Well, I'm really glad to see that you've turned your life around and are finally living up to the potential your mother and I always saw in you growing up."

Callie pauses at that, her cheeks stained pink like she's not sure what to do with the praise. "Thanks, Dad. That means a lot."

Then her fake smile comes out, at a wattage the likes I've never seen before. She feels like she has to perform for these people. As if just being herself could never be enough. It pisses me the hell off.

"I think it's time for the main course," her mother says gaily. Then she snaps Shannon's name and she rises obediently to head into the kitchen. Callie rises to go help too but her Mom waves her to sit down.

"I'm happy to help—"

"No, sit, sit. We want to hear all about you," her mom says. "There's nothing going on in your sister's life anyway."

Shannon obviously hears this before she slips into the kitchen because I see her posture stiffen. Callie winces on her behalf but then Shannon's gone through the door. When she comes back in carrying a tray of plates like a waitress, her face is perfectly placid. Looks like Callie wasn't the only one who learned how to put on a false façade by living in this family.

Meanwhile, their mom and dad pepper Callie with questions about her new position, the project she and I are working on, and our budding relationship.

While completely ignoring Shannon. She finally sits down with her own plate and starts to eat quietly, not looking at anyone. Nobody looks her direction. Callie obviously notices too.

"Shannon's graphic design company has really been taking off this past year too," Callie finally says. "It's an incredibly competitive market, but she's really making a splash and gaining new clients every day." Callie smiles at Shannon. And for the first time since we all sat down at the table, it's a genuine one. "She works seven days a week sometimes to keep up with the orders."

"And yet she's still splitting the rent with her sister at the age of thirty-one and doesn't have any romantic prospects," their mother says, none too quietly as she sticks her fork into her quinoa, chicken, and kale casserole.

"Shan's got a boyfriend," Callie defends and a second later I feel her jolt, like she just got kicked under the table.

Callie looks up and Shannon is glaring at her.

Their mother's attention finally focuses on Shannon, though. "Why didn't you tell me? What does he do?"

Shannon's jaw hardens before turning to meet her mom's eyes. "It's not important, forget about it."

Their mother clucks her tongue and smooths out the napkin in her lap. "This is your problem. All you ever do is have a series of relationships you don't take seriously because you know they have no future. I just don't understand it. Why date someone if you can't see yourself growing old with them? You aren't a spring chicken anymore and it's long past time—"

"I just didn't want to deal with twenty questions." Shannon's obviously irritated but just as obviously trying to hide it. "Sunil and I have been dating for five months and yes, actually it is serious. He's thirty-five and owns his own thriving business."

"What kind of business?" their dad asks at the same time their mom asks, "what sort of name is Sunil?"

Can you hear a person's teeth grind from across the table? Maybe I'm just imagining it from the expression on Shannon's face, like she's barely holding on to her patience. "He owns a yoga studio downtown," she answers her dad and then pierces her mom with a glare. "It's an American name because he's American. Born here and everything."

Her mom waves a hand as if swatting a fly. "You know what I mean. That's an ethnic name. What kind?"

Callie puts a hand on her head, again looking mortified.

"A yoga studio?" their father asks dubiously. "That doesn't sound like a very solvent business. And two people who each own their own businesses dating…" He shakes his head. "Not a good idea. Do either of you even have insurance? A retirement plan? What kind of savings are you really able to establish if you're living month-to-month in that dump you girls share?"

"Oh Gerald, don't worry, Shanny's flings never last that long," their mom says with a flippant laugh, covering her mouth and leaning into me and her husband's side of the table with the pretense of whispering a secret. "We'll just hope the next one has more promise."

Callie keeps watching her sister like she's waiting for her to do something, waiting for her to stand up and walk out of the room any second at this shit they're pulling. But Shannon just sits there and continues eating, eyes glued on her plate.

Callie seems disappointed and at the same time, she follows Shannon's example, back straight, always keeping her mouth stuffed full of chicken and quinoa. And looking like she wishes she were anywhere but here.

And as much as I want to stand up and flip the table, tell her dad to go fuck himself, it's not what Callie needs right now. In fact, if her white knuckled grip on her fork is anything to go by, it's taking everything she has to hold herself together. Me showing just how pissed I am won't make it any easier on her.

And I swore to myself that I'd be whatever she needed on this trip and right now she needs calm and steady. She needs to not have to deal with her asshole parents. So for the next twenty minutes, I carry the conversation and to my relief, Callie begins relaxing beside me the more I regale her parents with stories of famous acquaintances and international travel. All the external shit I know will impress shallow idiots like them.

Shannon brings out key lime pie for dessert and Callie is tense again beside me.

"So Mom and Dad," she cuts in when there's the briefest lull in conversation, "can I show you some pictures of your grandson? Charlie's getting so big lately and he's the most adorable little kid. Really smart too." Another plastic smile. "He's definitely a Cruise."

She hurriedly brings out her phone and pulls up the most recent pics of her son. I get the briefest glimpse of the little boy flipping through a board book. He's looking up at the phone and the pic was snapped mid-giggle. Damn, he's a cute kid.

Callie's features are a mix of pained and loving as she looks at the phone before giving it to her mom. Her mom's eyes soften the smallest bit before she hands it over to her husband. He observes the phone for a moment and then nods once.

"His custody hearing is in a couple of weeks," Callie says tentatively. "It would mean a lot to me if you guys were there."

Her dad's quiet a long moment, still looking down at the picture on the phone.

I can feel the tension radiating off Callie. Jesus Christ. Why is this bastard making such a production out of this? He has the most fabulous daughter in the universe. What the hell is wrong with him?

Finally her dad hands the phone to me to give back to Callie. Then he looks Callie directly in the eye and gives another decisive nod. "We'll be there and speak on your behalf. You've really turned your life around and I can respect that. You might have made a mess of things a few years ago but everyone deserves a second chance. *One* chance, mind you," he holds up a single index finger and his eyebrows narrow in warning. "You only ever get one second chance with me."

Callie nods repeatedly, her eyes moist. "You won't be sorry, Daddy, I promise. I've turned my life around for good. I'm not that girl anymore. You'll see—" She cuts off mid-stream, her eyes dropping.

Then she picks up her fork and shoves a bite of pie in her mouth as if to forcibly stop herself from simpering any more to the father whose so obviously let her down so many times in the past.

But I got the glimpse of the girl she must have been. So desperate for a father's approval. This goddamned fucker. Because it's obvious he rarely gave it.

Callie shifts uncomfortably in her chair and then glances my way, cheeks going pink. Is she embarrassed for me to have witnessed that?

I smile encouragingly. She should know I would never judge her. The only judgement I have are for the people who should have loved her better.

She downs the rest of her pie like she can't get this horrible lunch over fast enough and I do the same.

As soon as I down the last bite she all but catapults off her chair. I expect her to take me up to the room where we'll be staying but oh no, the women have to do the cleanup.

Meanwhile Gerald claps me on the back and invites me to his, "man cave" downstairs in the basement. He actually calls it that. So I'm subjected to his company for another forty-five minutes. Now that he's given his blessing on the custody hearing, I know I have to play nice. So even though I'd rather bore a hole through my head, I put up with the pompous ass.

But forty-five minutes is all I can stand. He's just pulled out an album of his bi-annual fishing trips when I beg off, saying I want to go check on Callie.

When I get to the kitchen, her mother says she's gone upstairs with a headache. I doubt it was even an excuse. Even a short amount of time in these people's presence is enough to make anyone's head ache and we've been here for hours.

I walk into the room Shannon said was Callie's but I don't see her. I'm about to head back out to look for her elsewhere when a door I thought just led to a closet opens and she comes out fresh from the shower. With only a towel wrapped around her body.

She doesn't see me because the door opened outward, hiding me. But I can't go another second without my hands on her so I wrap my arms around her from behind, breathing in her fresh, clean scent.

"Save me," I whisper.

She yelps in surprise before turning around and smacking me on the arm. "You scared the shit out of me!"

The next second, though, her whole body immediately relaxes into me. She breathes in deep like it's the first deep breath she's been able to take in hours.

"I'm the one who needs saving." She face-dives into my chest. I try to focus on her words. Really I do. But all half of my brain can think is: *Naked under the towel. She's naked under the towel.*

"I can't handle them!" she goes on and I force myself to focus. "I don't remember them being like this. I swear. They've gotten all..."

She rams her forehead into my chest again, "I don't even know what to call it. They're just the *worst*. The whole time we were cleaning up, Mom was pecking at Shannon about her weight, what she was wearing, Sunil's family, her income, *his* income. I swear, it just never stops."

I hold her to my chest, massaging her scalp. "I know, baby. I'm so sorry. I'm so sorry." I can't say it enough times. Thinking about her bastard parents is enough to keep my libido in check, that's for damn sure.

She pulls her phone out of her pocket to check the time and then groans. "We haven't even been here for four hours yet and we're supposed to last the whole weekend? We got them to agree to come to the custody hearing, so we can go home now." I look up at him, an awkward angle since I'm so close. "Right?"

I just curl her into me. If she really wants to leave, God knows I'll call the towncar and we'll be gone this second. But it's probably not the wisest idea and she must know it too because she just sinks against my chest.

"Your mom said we should rest up for dinner," I tell her. "It'll be ready in an hour and a half. And that you should wear something nice because in her words it's a *formal dinner*."

"It's so fucking ridiculous." She wraps her arms around my middle and squeezes. "We just finished one meal and now we have to go back through that torture so soon. Again? I don't wanna," she whines in a mock childish voice.

The next second, though, she's all woman.

She grabs the front of my shirt and dips her head back, blinking up at me through her lashes. At the same time she grinds her hips against my groin. "An hour and a half, huh? I can think of a few ways to fill the time."

"Ha ha." I kiss her on the top of her head and pull away. But not before running my thumb along the top edge of the towel she has wrapped around herself. What can I say? She's fucking tempting. I just barely skim the top of her breast before pulling back. I can see her nipples harden through the towel. Still, if it's distraction she's after, giving in right away won't be any fun, now will it?

She lurches after me. "I wasn't kidding, you know."

I laugh darkly. "I know."

She frowns, her eyes narrowing. Then she reaches and undoes her towel where she secured it in a knot. With a satisfyingly dramatic sweep, it drops to the floor, leaving her moist-skinned and fully bared.

My cock goes stiff but I don't let anything show on my face. I try not to anyway but fuck. She's the most magnificent thing I've ever seen. Afterwards when I try to picture her I always think that no, she couldn't *really* have been that perfect but the next time I'm with her it's like, holy shit, she actually *is*.

She smiles like she sees exactly how much she affects me and takes a few steps backwards to the bed, crawling up and then lounging sideways on it, facing me.

She sucks on my middle finger, watching me the whole while. She releases the finger with a loud *pop* and then lazily trails it down her neck to outline her nipple, then she stretches and tugs at the taut peak.

My cock is straining in my pants but I stand still, enjoying the brief look of frustration that passes over her face at my lack of motion. I'm enjoying this little game too much.

Her eyes narrow in challenge. After circling her nipple several more times, she sends her hand further south to the smooth apex of her sex.

Aw *damn*. Even from here I can see how slick she is already. My cock pulses and I know precum is wetting my boxers.

And suddenly I don't know what I think either of us is getting out of this game. Screw delayed gratification. I stomp toward the bed, grasping my buckle and ripping it open as I go.

I have to have her. My vixen. Now. Fucking *now*. More than food or water or air.

She grins in triumph, watching me fumble with my belt.

With several more strong jerks, though, I get the belt free from my pants. She frowns when I don't immediately shove my pants and boxers down and instead advance toward the bed with the belt in my hand.

Her eyebrows shoot up, eyes on the belt, even as I see her bite her lip in interest.

"Don't get too excited," I laugh quietly as I approach. I fold the belt several times and then run the leather from her throat down between her breasts and further to her throbbing pussy. Then I lean in and trace the same path with my nose, inhaling as I go.

I can't help the low growl of approval that comes from my throat. "I can smell how much you want me."

But then she snatches the belt from my grasp.

"Don't forget who's in charge in these little games," she warns. "Last weekend was a one-off."

Not so fast. She's holding the top of the folded belt but I grab the bottom with a grip that challenges hers.

"Was it?" I use my commanding voice and see lust and anger warring in her eyes. I put a knee on the bed to crawl up between her legs. "I think you like to lose control and submit sometimes."

She opens her mouth like she's about to tell me off but I just smile wider and cut her off at the pass. "Only *sometimes*," I amend. "Don't worry. I haven't forgotten my place, Mistress. Unfortunately, since we're in your parents' house and we don't want them to find out how debauched the supposedly upstanding entrepreneur Jackson Vale is by finding him tied, gagged, and being spanked like a little bitch by their dominatrix daughter, I suggest you bite down on this so you don't make any noise while I eat the fuck out of your sweet pussy. Sound like a plan?"

I don't give her time to consider and she must decide there's not much to consider when presented with such an offer because she opens her jaw wide like a good little subbie. I shove the folded leather belt in her mouth and she bites down hard like she hopes to leave teeth marks. I grin darkly, hoping she does.

Then I shove her thighs open wide and dive in, eating and sucking and fingering and licking and massaging until she comes so many times we both lose count and she drifts into a satisfied, drowsy sleep.

And then I pull her close to my chest where she curls like a satisfied kitten. I breathe in her hair and memorize the feel of her skin against mine.

I meant what I said earlier. *Save me*. It came off flippant and I know she thought I just meant from her parents and this awkward weekend. But I meant so much more.

She's my salvation. One I never saw coming. One I don't deserve.

I blink and look up at the ceiling as I hold her tight to me. The fact that it was Bryce Gentry who brought her to me? The fact that I know he hurt her and that I think he did it because of me?

My eyes squeeze shut and my jaw clenches.

I'll protect her now. Slay every dragon. If it's the last thing I do, I'll bury that motherfucker Gentry in a hole so deep, he'll never see the light of day again.

And she'll never ever have to know my secret and shame.

CHAPTER TWENTY

CALLIE

"Time to wake up for dinner." Jackson shakes my shoulder gently.

I turn over into my pillow. "Sleep," I grumble back, attempting to pull the comforter up and around me so I can hide from the light.

"I don't think so, sleepyhead," Jackson says.

All right. That gets me up. "Did the words sleepyhead really just come out of your mouth?" I look up at him. He smacks me with a plush pillow. Oh my God. "Are you, Jackson Vale, starting what I think you're starting?" I raise my own pillow.

He looks confused for a second. I don't miss the opportunity. I attack, pillow raised high as I smack him over and over.

I can't stop laughing. The ever dignified Jackson, getting smacked with a pillow.

"What? Callie, this is—" A hit right in the face shuts up whatever comment he's about to make. Another laugh bellows out of me, complete with a snort at the end.

"That was a low blow," he says, red-faced. "Now stop it. Pillow fighting is completely indecorous—" I take another swing at him, but almost expertly, he ducks out of the way. Then he comes up swinging with two pillows that he must have grabbed when I wasn't looking. They come at me one after another.

"Take that!" he says, sounding about twelve years old.

"No fair," I laugh as I jerk out of the way when he takes another swing. "You have two and I only have one." I go low and try to sweep his legs but that just gets me clobbered on the back.

"That just proves I'm smarter and can make better usage of available resources than you," he says, going for a low-to-high swing that I block with my pillow. No problem for him because he's got the second pillow to smack me on the head with. I shriek in outrage and bounce off the bed, dancing out of the way before he can get me again.

I glance back at the head of the bed. Wait, shouldn't there be a fourth pillow? I don't try to be sneaky about it, I just make a break back for the bed. Jackson chases after me. He's a smart guy. Seeing my move, he must realize the same thing about the pillows. I don't see any on the side of the bed closest to us so I launch myself over the bed to look on the other side.

Aha! I've hit pay dirt.

The fourth pillow is on the ground tucked in the corner. I grab for it even as Jackson wallops me with pillows. Shocker that he seems to concentrate his blows on my ass. I roll my eyes and giggle. I never did manage to get dressed after the shower.

I grab the pillow from the floor. Now equally armed, I swing both pillows around and tackle Jackson to the bed until I've got him pinned underneath me, legs on either side of his chest. I rain down blow after blow on him with my pillows.

"Say uncle," I cry.

"Never!" He wriggles underneath me.

"Say it!"

"Not on your life."

"Fine, then say I'm the Queen of Awesome and you're my lowly slave."

I feel his laughter since I'm sitting on his chest, jostling me up and down on my perch. He reaches up and slides my pillows off his face. "I bow down, oh Queen of Awesome," he says with a wide grin. "I am but a lowly slave, always in service to her worshipfulness."

It's a light moment and his eyes are full of merriment, but I see something else there too as he holds my gaze. That *zing* that always seems to pass between us. Intensity. Rightness. The thing that turns a light moment deep and made me feel connected to him early on even when we hadn't spent much time together. I'm not freaked out or scared by it anymore like I was in the beginning, though.

This is Jackson. This is *my* Jackson. He's seen deep inside me to my needs and desires and wasn't frightened by what he saw there. We can meet each other in the dark. We're compatible there, just like we are in the other parts of our lives.

Neither of us are laughing or even smiling any more. Jackson's caught up in the moment with me. He reaches up and slides a loose piece of hair behind my ear.

"Calliope, I—"

A knock sounds at the door, interrupting whatever Jackson was about to say. I want to shout at whoever it is to go away. What is Jackson about to say?

"Callie?" It's Shannon's voice, none too quiet. She knocks again.

"I do believe she thinks she's committing *coitus interruptus*," Jackson whispers in my ear.

Jackson using that term sends me into a fresh wave of giggles. Obviously whatever we were in the middle of has been interrupted, and even though it wasn't *coitus*, I feel so frustrated it might as well have been. What had Jackson been about to say?

Maybe nothing. But maybe something.

I roll off of Jackson and grab my robe, a silky little nothing that doesn't leave a lot to the imagination. Shannon's still banging on the door with the fervor of an under-quota salesman.

I yank open the door, lean against the doorframe and run a hand through my hair to fluff it in a way that hopefully makes it look like I was just fucked.

"What?" I don't bother hiding my frustration.

Shan's eyes widen when she sees me. "How could you do *that* here? While we're all in the house? I had to tell Mom all the shrieking was because we saw a mouse up here. Which of course sent her into a tizzy about how we had to be wrong because her house would never have rodents and blah blah blah," Shannon stops and narrows her eyes at me, "Why are you grinning at me like that?"

"No reason, big sis." I throw my arms around her and hug her hard. Here she is, always trying to make peace, even when there's no real reason.

"Ugh, I don't want your sex sweat all over me." She tries to squirm out of my grasp but I hug her even harder.

"We were just having a pillow fight after I woke up from a nap, dork," I say, intentionally mussing her hair. No need to mention the numerous and mind-blowing orgasms before the nap. I didn't make a sound during those thanks to the belt, after all.

"Deity give me patience," she looks up at the ceiling, then back at me, "Will you ever grow up?" She finally manages to pull away from me and her hands immediately go to smoothing down her flat ironed hair.

"Not on your life," I pinch her in the belly.

She twists away and shakes her head at me. "Mom says dinner will be ready in fifteen and you know heads will roll if you aren't right on time." She glares at me but I can see some softness beneath it.

"You know you love me," I call as she walks away.

She sends me the one-fingered salute over her shoulder. We Cruise sisters are nothing if not a pair of dignified ladies.

Ten minutes later Jackson and I head downstairs, me in a modest but cute blue A-line dress and Jackson going all out by busting out a suit and tie. And day-um, does the man look *fine* in a suit. No doubt I'd have sticker shock if I knew how much the thing cost, but looking at how it fits his muscular body and that *ass*. Damn, that ass. I can't help but to reach down and discreetly give a squeeze as we descend the central stairwell.

"I want to get you alone and cuffed face down on a bed," I whisper in his ear as I take his arm. "I have plans for that ass."

Holding his arm like I am, I feel the slight shudder that goes through his body. He's as turned on by the thought as I am. At his request, I'm going commando and a draft slips up under the full skirt of my dress, hitting the moisture that's just spurted at the image conjured of Jackson spread out before me. My nails bite into the forearm of his jacket and Jackson looks my way, shooting me a knowing smile. Then he looks past me to the wall as we descend the stairs.

"So this is you, the Queen when she was but a pageant princess," he comments with a smile as we pass by a long row of pictures lining the stairway that I once heard Shannon refer to as The Callie Shrine Wall.

I can't say she's wrong. Some moms make scrapbooks. My mom created the Shrine Wall. You know how in TV and movies, serial killers sometimes have those creepy shrines to their victims with all kinds of photos of them all over the wall? Yeah. This wall is a little like that. Except the pictures are framed and they're all from my pageant days. Starting at seven years old all the way until I stopped at fifteen, it's a year-by-year chronicle of every pageant I entered. There are pictures, ribbons, sashes, hanging tiaras, all leading to the pièce de résistance— the giant shadow box of my glittering crown for Little Miss Siskiyou County that I won the year I quit. It's placed in a small inlet that Mom had some workmen cut into the wall, crafted specially to fit the crown.

"You're lovely," Jackson says.

I wince but when I glance over, he's not looking at the glossy pictures. Just at me, here, now, in the real world. I know I don't look my best.

I look from picture to picture and watch the way my pageant smile grows more brittle over the years. And how the external package becomes more, well... packaged. Spray tans. Glitter bronzer to highlight the cheeks—and, starting at eleven since I developed early— above and in between the breasts. And always, glossy hair. Glossy red lips. Eventually glossy eyes.

I turn away and jog down the rest of the stairs in spite of the fact that I'm wearing heels. These are only three inches high and I can easily maneuver in up to four-and-a-half—another skill I picked up from my pageant days, actually. Along with learning to invest all of my self-worth in my looks.

For fuck's sake, by the time I was ten I was accustomed to strange men leering at my body. I don't know who thought up the idea of having a swimsuit portion of a beauty pageant for twelve year olds, but they should be murdered. Slowly.

"Callie, you okay?"

Jackson's waiting for me at the bottom of the stairs, eyes concerned.

I smile but we can both feel the falseness in it. It's too reminiscent of the grinning girl on the wall behind us. I take Jackson's arm again and try to let him ground me.

I just need to shake off all the feelings the walk down memory lane brought on. That girl is long gone. I take a deep breath. I look up into Jackson's eyes and drop the grin. "I'm all right. Let's get this over with."

He lifts his right hand and squeezes mine where it drapes over his arm. All right. Let's get this done. One evening, then I just have to make nice tomorrow morning till lunch and we can leave. I can do this. *We* can do this.

I feel absolutely confident.

Until I turn the corner and see who's standing by my father.

Mr. McIntyre.

The man who sexually abused me for years.

CHAPTER TWENTY-ONE

CALLIE

"Callie. Jackson," Mom says brightly, though I see censure in her eyes for being late to come down. "We've been waiting for you. Look who took time out of his busy schedule to come by and dine with us."

I grip Jackson's arm, swallow hard, and do my damnedest not to let the dizziness suddenly assaulting me take me down.

Unlike Dad, Mr. McIntyre looks like he's aged a decade in the few years since I last saw him. And he was old when he first started fucking with me.

He's tall and rail-thin in a way that always reminded me of a skeleton. One with skin loosely stretched over it. Even just glancing at his face and the sagging skin at his jowls and ears makes my stomach sour.

I turn away so he's not in my line of sight anymore. Seriously, how much is a girl supposed to take? I already had to stand face-to-face with my blackmailing rapist last week and now here's my first abuser, standing and holding a bourbon with my father like nothing at all is wrong in the world.

I stopped doing pageants when a judge cornered me and told me the only way I'd retain my title as Little Miss Siskiyou County was to give him a quick blowjob in a closet.

I thought that by getting out of the pageant circle I'd be safe from all that—creepy men looking at me, the touches I didn't want when no one was looking, the comments when they thought no one else was in earshot.

But then there was Mr. McIntyre. Dad's business partner. At least that's how Dad talked about him. In reality, he was Dad's *boss*.

I learned that one night when Dad and Mom retired early after an especially long night of drinking Mr. McIntyre's special Kentucky bourbon. He so kindly offered to clean up since Mom had cooked.

Mom ordered me to help him before stumbling off to bed. I didn't think anything of it. Mr. McIntyre had been coming over for several months by then and had never been inappropriate before. Not even any lingering looks.

He started off by asking me about school. What grade I was in. What my favorite subject was. If I was thinking about colleges. The same sort of thing adults always asked.

Until he asked if I had a boyfriend. Even that was a question I'd been asked before, so it didn't seem weird. At first. It only started feeling off when I told him I didn't have one.

"I don't believe that," he scoffed, nudging me on the shoulder where I stood beside him drying dishes after he washed them. "Not with that body. I bet all the boys' pants get tight when you're around."

Yeah, my comfort level went from acceptable straight to zero at that point. Not that that was going to dissuade Creepy McCreepster.

"I mean, if I was a boy in your grade, I wouldn't get a single thing done. I'd be too busy staring at those huge tits of yours."

I dropped the plate I'd been drying back into the sudsy water and stepped away, but he must have been watching me closely because he seemed to anticipate my move.

He let go of the cup he'd been lackadaisically washing, caught me around the waist, and shoved me up against the counter with his body.

I opened my mouth to scream for my parents, but he quickly covered it with his soapy hand. And then came the oft-repeated threat that would keep me in check for the next three years.

"Yell and I'll fire your father like *that*." He snapped the fingers of his other hand. His cajoling voice was gone, replaced by one filled with malice.

"You want me to be your friend, not your enemy." He moved his wet, soapy hand to my breast, leaving what I knew would be a big wet handprint on the gauzy fabric when he pulled it away.

Which was a pattern, I'd find out later. He liked marking things. That turned out to be a blessing of sorts. Because he always needed the show of power, or, I don't know fucking why, he always wanted to see his release crudely painting my body.

He never penetrated me. It was just a lot of groping and then disgusting cleanup for me. On my face. My breasts. My ass. Then when he left, the showers that turned my skin lobster red until the hot water was gone.

And I put up with it. The thousands of justifications. It wasn't *actually* rape. If he ever tried to go that far, I'd scream, fight, and put a stop to it.

My dad's job was everything to him. And Mom. The money. Our lifestyle. Dad's reputation in the community. I couldn't be the one to pull the tablecloth out from underneath the house of cards.

Besides, if I ever told, Mr. McIntyre always said it would be my word against his—some stupid teenager against one of the most powerful men in the town. Who would people believe? Even if I did say something, could I really drag my family through that?

At the time, the answer was no. I didn't believe I was worth all the bother.

But now?

Fuck that shit.

I know *I am fucking worth it.*

I always was.

And that child-molesting bastard who has the gall to stand there smiling by my dad? Well he's one monster who doesn't get to get away with it.

Except... bitch shit cunt fuck cakes. I can't. Not right now, at least.

I'm trying to be the girl who thinks before just making impulsive decisions. If there's one thing I know about Jackson Vale, it's that he's protective. What would he do to McIntyre if he found out about the abuse right here, right now, with the bastard sitting in front of him?

I certainly don't want to protect my abuser. God knows I'd relish watching any beat down Jackson could give him. But how far would he go? And there are witnesses. I glance between my mom and dad. Even if they side with Jackson and me—

And are you so sure they would?

I ignore the insidious voice. I don't want Jackson getting in trouble and I wouldn't want my parents to have to perjure themselves if it came to it. After everything Jackson's done for me? I won't draw him into this bullshit. But that doesn't mean I have to suck it up either and force myself to sit through a meal across the table from my fucking abuser.

I go up on tiptoes and whisper in Jackson's ear, "I need to go chat with my mom for a second. I'll be right back."

When I pull back, I can see Jackson's more than just confused. He's concerned. He's always been too perceptive, damn him. I give him a gentle smile and squeeze his arm, then I turn away without giving him any more time to tease out what might be the matter.

I cross the dining room to where my mom is setting down the roast she started earlier in the day.

"Mom, can I talk to you about something in the kitchen?"

Her eyebrows narrow. "We need to sit down to eat. I've timed everything precisely so that it will all be the perfect temperature."

Time to change tactics. "That's what I wanted to talk to you about. I saw a dish still warming in the oven that we forgot to take out."

Before she can look out over the table to find the fictional dish I'm speaking of, I grab her arm and usher her back into the kitchen. As soon as the door shuts behind us, I start talking. "I need you to send Mr. McIntyre away. He sexually abused me for three years and I can't stand to be in the same room as him."

Mom's face blanches. She opens her mouth and then shuts it again, so I keep talking.

"On the nights he'd come over to eat, after you and Dad went to bed, he'd come to my room." Once I start, words spill out one after the other in a torrent I can't seem to stop. "He'd touch me, expose himself..." A shudder wracks my body. "...and other things."

There's a short moment of silence and then Mom's back straightens. I take a step forward, hoping for once she'll just take me in her arms and hold me. Unexpected tears spring in my eyes. The release of finally having told... it's so unexpected. After all these years, to finally tell Mom, I can't even—

She steps forward and I go to hug her. I just want to feel her arms around me and hear her telling me everything will be all right.

Instead, she grabs my upper arm in a bruising grip and jerks me to the other side of the kitchen island furthest from the door to the dining room. I stumble after her, wincing at the pain of her talon-like fingers on my arm.

"How dare you come back in this house and spit on our generosity with your filthy lies?"

I yank backward out of her grasp and stumble into the counter. What? No, this isn't how this is supposed to go.

The door to the dining room opens and Shannon slides in. "Is everything okay in here? Anything I can help with?"

"Get out of here," Mom snaps, voice icy.

Shannon doesn't obey, though. Her eyes shoot to me.

I can only stare at my mother, though. "It's true," I defend obstinately, my voice thin and oddly pitched.

"He sexually abused me for three years. He told me that he'd fire Dad if I ever told anyone. That's why I never said anything. But I'm *done* with that. I was just a child and he's a monster who preyed on me. Here. Under this roof." I gesture at the house around us.

Mom's face goes red. "Do you think we haven't found out about where you worked while you lived *under this roof*? Your friend Marcy started forwarding your mail here when she moved out of state for college."

Mom comes closer, eyebrows narrowed in fury. "I guess you used her address for that job you were rightly too ashamed for us to know about. But we received a tax statement from *Hooters*," her face twists in disgust at the name, "and it about killed your father to realize his daughter had been whoring herself out for what? Tips? Then the next thing we know you're prostituting yourself out to your professors and carrying one's bastard!"

She lowers her voice. "Do you realize how that makes us look? We worked hard to raise you as a beautiful, elegant girl and this is the thanks we get?"

I barely hear the last bit, because did she just say what I think she fucking said? I get right in her face, feeling like the vein in my forehead is going to explode, I'm so pissed.

"Don't you call my son a bastard ever again." I poke a finger hard into her sternum. "And if you were really a good mother, you'd believe me when I tell you that a pervert molested me from the age of sixteen to nineteen."

I shake my head at her in disbelief at the way she's responding. "You had to have noticed how I changed. Became more withdrawn. Stopped hanging out with my friends so much except for the nights he came over, when I would do anything to get out of the house. Except that you and Dad started forcing me to stay home those nights. Do you remember? Let me guess, that was at the request of Mr. McIntyre?"

Mom sputters. "You were a moody teenager. Besides, those were family dinners. You know your dad was trying to make Branch Manager. Bill is big on family values, so that's what we needed to show him."

Bill. Ugh. Even now, my mom speaks so cozily of my abuser.

I shake my head at her in astonishment. "It isn't that you don't see it, is it? It's that you *won't*." Again, my feet move me away from my mother. The woman who was supposed to love, watch over, and protect me. "You'll keep refusing to see how Mr. McIntyre always brought over that's special Kentucky bourbon—"

"He was just being polite," Mom breaks in. "That's the custom where he grew up.

"And was it custom to insist that you and Dad have two glasses while he barely drank any? What about the fact that he encouraged you to go to bed while he hung around afterward with your *teenage daughter*? That didn't strike anyone as strange? God," I laugh bitterly, "he barely even bother to be covert about the way he looked at me after the first year." I shake my head some more, my insides twisting like a pit of serpents.

How could a mother—?

For a split second, Charlie's face comes to mind.

That does it.

I lurch for the trashcan under the sink right in time to empty the contents of my stomach into it. Just the idea of Charlie ever encountering a monster like McIntyre has me heaving a second time until I'm coughing and sputtering, nothing left.

And no, I'm not pregnant or anything. I got my period during the week, it just finished up yesterday. There's just this much barf-worthy shit going on in my life and I've always had a low threshold hurl hair-trigger.

A soothing hand starts rubbing my back.

Mom—? Does she finally believe?

When I turn my head, I see Shannon instead. She's running water in the sink and the next second, she hands me a wet paper towel. I take it gratefully, meeting her eyes for a quick second. She's crying, tears running in streams down her cheeks.

"I'm so sorry," Shannon says. "I didn't know." Her voice breaks on the last word and more tears escape.

She believes me.

I nod over and over, my eyes watering as I wipe my mouth with the wet cloth she gave me. Shan takes my arm and helps me stand back up, which is good because I feel unsteady on my feet. I hate the way throwing up makes me feel like I've just been run over by a truck.

I don't have much more fight in me. I just want to go lay down somewhere for a long, long time.

The door opens and this time it's Jackson. His face goes from curious to alarmed in zero point two seconds when he sees me no doubt looking pale as hell, propped up by Shannon.

"What's happened?" he demands, voice clipped.

"It's nothing," my mother says, at the same time Shannon says, "Callie was just sick."

But Shannon doesn't stop there. "That man." Tears clog her voice. "He abused my sister for years. And none of us knew. None of us saw."

The bottom drops out of my stomach for the I don't know what time tonight. It happens fast. I see the words register. Utter rage fills Jackson's face. Killing rage. Oh fuck. Just what I was trying to avoid.

I launch myself at Jackson. My legs still aren't very steady, so it's not graceful. Jackson was turning toward the door to the dining room, but he has quick reflexes and catches me when I stumble into him.

That embrace I was looking for earlier from my mother? Jackson gives it to me a hundred fold. He wraps me so tight to his chest, I doubt there's a centimeter of space anywhere between us, collarbone to belly button.

And then his arms. So strong, they curl around my back, one of his huge hands cupping the back of my head until I feel so enveloped, so safe, that for the first time in half an hour, I feel like I might make it out of this night intact.

I know, I know. I'm supposed to be a strong woman. I can make it on my own and all that, blah, blah, blah. And I'm sure I could have and would have. I'd scrape myself up from this blow just like I have every other hit that's knocked me down in life.

But it sure is so much goddamn easier when you have a partner.

Partner. Holy shit. I never even let myself go there in my head before. But it's true. I want Jackson as my partner. Like, in life. Does that mean that I...? That I *lov*—?

I jerk out of the hug. "Get me out of here," I whisper to him. I'm not able to let go of him completely, no matter how freaked out I am by the realization I'd just had. I'm still holding onto the front lapels of his suit coat and I don't care how desperate I look. It's only half of the desperation I feel inside. This night. Too much. It's all too much. No wonder I'm having crazy thoughts.

Jackson doesn't say anything and while his face is still mottled with fury, there's also immense pain knitted on his features. Because of me.

Because you're poison to everything you touch. For the first time, I realize the voice in the back of my head often sounds an awful like my mother's. I cringe and cling tighter to Jackson.

"Please. I just want to leave." I plead with my eyes and his face softens, focus zeroing in on me.

"Of course," he says.

"No, you don't understand," my mother's voice butts in, conciliatory. "She's always been so overdramatic and excitable. Always making up stories for attention. I don't know why she's saying such terrible things. Mr. McIntyre is a prestigious man. He's the bank president and her father is quite close to being made Branch Manager. Why don't we all just calm down and go out and enjoy the lovely meal that I worked so hard to prepare—"

"You're unbelievable," I say.

I push away from Jackson and go straight into the dining room. Dad and Mr. McIntyre have already served themselves food, not waiting for the rest of us. There's a bottle of Kentucky bourbon in the center of the table and Dad's glass is half full. I know it's not because only a few fingers were poured, but because he's drunk the other half already.

"You all have certainly taken your time," Dad says, his annoyance clear.

I ignore him, walk straight over to Mr. McIntyre. "You're a pervert and a pedophile and just because I can't prove it doesn't mean it isn't true."

I spit in his shocked face, then grab the bottle of bourbon and hurl it at the wall. It smashes in a satisfying explosion of glass and brown liquid. It's amazing what stress relief smashing things is. This moment can't erase the bone-deep emotional scars this man inflicted, but I'm working on it, and fuck if this doesn't feel good in the meantime.

I planned not to even look back once, but when I get to the foyer I realize Jackson isn't beside me. I glance over my shoulder to call for him and get one last glimpse of McIntyre's wrinkled-ass face just in time to see Jackson's heavy fist land hard.

Even from where I'm standing, I hear the snapping of cartilage. And I've obviously become bloodthirsty, because the high-pitched squeal that comes from McIntyre's throat satisfies me somewhere deep, deep inside.

Shouts and screams about broken noses follow us as we step over the threshold and out the door, hand in hand.

Partners. That damn tricky word hits me again. It seems like I've finally hit on the word that describes the connection I've felt with

Jackson from the beginning. Working, living, playing, going through life side-by-side with this man as his partner. As a friend. As his lover. Is that possible for someone like me?

My breath hitches. Jackson either senses or hears it because he starts rubbing my back as we head toward his car. "I'm three seconds from heading back there and ripping the bastard into pieces. I'm rich enough. I could do it and hire a black market forensics team to make sure there's no evidence."

The night being what it has been, his inappropriate words make me giggle. "And what about my parents?"

He glances down at me. "That pair could so obviously be bought."

That thought sobers me. Because isn't that what's already happened? I was bought for the promise of a raise. Or at least it was enough for my parents to look the other way from red flags that should have tipped them off to a bad situation.

"Let's get out of here." All of the sudden, my energy is gone. Like back in the kitchen, and I just want to sleep for a week.

Right when I touch the passenger side door to the car though, the front door of the house opens.

I brace myself, ready for Dad to make some horrible speech about what a whore his daughter is. Instead, in the rectangle of light that appears from the open door, Shannon's slim silhouette appears. Words are being exchanged, that's obvious from the way she's gesturing with her hands, but we're too far away to hear.

The next thing I know, Shannon slams the door and walks toward us, bogged down by all of our luggage. Right. We forgot about bags in our dramatic exit. Jackson hurries forward and grabs his duffel bag and our two carry-ons from her. I stand there, mute.

Shannon just chose me over our parents.

Wow.

She's always been so adamant about keeping a relationship with Mom and Dad. And here she is, throwing it away for my sake? Just like that?

I go around to the back of the car where she's loading bags with Jackson. "Shan," I put a hand on her forearm. "You don't have to do this. It's my fight. Just between them and me."

She looks at me like I'm crazy. "You think I could continue to talk to them after everything I learned tonight? Oh my God, Callie, if I'd known... Lately things have been different but I was so horrible to you for so long..." She looks anguished and fresh tears streak her cheeks.

Jackson gently tugs the suitcase from her and she throws her arms around me again.

I stand there a bit uncomfortable.

All right already. Enough with the touchy-touchy feely-feels stuff. I'm ready for this day to be over. Done. *Finis*.

I nod gratefully into her shoulder and then pull away to climb into the car. I vaguely hear Jackson and Shannon's voices talking while they finish loading up the car and then Shannon climbs in the backseat and Jackson in the driver's side.

Shannon reaches up from the backseat and hands me a toothbrush, tube of toothpaste, and a bottle of water. I huff in surprise at her thoughtfulness. "Thanks."

I brush my teeth vigorously as Jackson pulls out of my parents' driveway, making a point of squealing the tires as he peals out. I hope it leaves dark rubber prints on their pristine driveway. At the same time, underneath the anger and weariness, already I can feel how raw I am.

No matter how much I intellectually understand why my parents are the way they are—they've become so accustomed to their lifestyle, it's just unthinkable for them to accept anything that might bring it all crumbling down... But still. I'm their *daughter*.

A tear escapes my eye and I try to swipe it away before anyone sees. It's not supposed to happen like this. In the TV specials, when you tell your parents about the horrible secret you've been keeping, they believe you. They support you. The entire message of those shows and books is just to get you to tell someone. It's a given that the parents will listen.

I turn my face away from Jackson and Shannon and watch scenery pass by out the window. There's not much to see since it's night out. That's fine with me. I'm good with losing myself in the darkness for a little bit. Numbing myself, inside and out. Not feeling. Not thinking. All of that takes so much energy and I'm tired. So tired.

I only look up once the lights of the small airstrip come into view. Jackson maneuvers the car down the small driving lane to the fourth hanger, the same one we landed at. We drive straight into the hangar and pull to a stop about twenty feet from the back of the plane.

All the lights in the plane are on and it looks ready to go. Jackson must have called or messaged at some point to get it prepped and ready, though I didn't catch him doing it. We weren't supposed to leave until late tomorrow afternoon.

I close my eyes and breathe out a long breath. Well, thank God Jackson took care of getting the plane prepped ahead of us. This means that in a little less than an hour, we'll be back in San Jose and another half hour after that, I could be curled up in my own bed. Perfect.

Then I can take all the time I need to process everything that's gone down. My parents. McIntyre. What Gentry's demanding of me. Then there were those unsettling thoughts I had about Jackson. Not to mention that Charlie's custody trial is now just two weeks away.

Christ. I scrub my hands down my face. Yeah. Sleep. Napping for a week is obviously not in the cards, but maybe a solid ten or eleven hours? With a Benadryl, I can probably swing that.

"Love you, Cals." I hear Shannon's voice from behind me and then the pressure of her hand on my shoulder. When I open my eyes, she's getting out of the car and heading toward the trunk.

Right. Back to the real world.

I reach to unlatch my seatbelt, but Jackson's large hand blocks me.

My eyebrows narrow in confusion as I look up at him.

"Shannon's going to take the plane back but you and I are driving the car."

"Huh?" I ask. Brain too tired to process over here.

"We're going to drive back to San Jose."

"But that would take six and a half hours." My eyebrows scrunch as I search out the clock on the dashboard. "And it's already eight o'clock at night. That doesn't make any sense." I reach to push open the door, but all the doors suddenly lock.

I try to push my own *door unlock* button, but apparently Jackson has the master lock because nothing moves mine. I turn back to him with a glare. "What the fuck? I'm exhausted. I've had a less than stellar weekend, and all I want to do is sleep. What I *don't* want to do is be stuck in a car for the next six hours."

"Me either," Jackson surprises me by saying. "That's why we'll be stopping an hour south of here to spend the night. If you're tired, take a nap." He leans over. "I'm betting sleep will be the last thing on either of our minds once we get there."

Even in the dim lighting of the hangar, I can see his eyes flare at this. I just stare at him, dumbfounded for a moment. Then he reaches out and cups my face before pulling me forward just enough to place a kiss on my forehead.

Before I can say another word, the trunk slams shut. Shannon gives a wave as she walks toward the plane and Jackson zooms out of the airport.

"Wake up sleeping beauty."

I blink blearily and look around. The car's pulling into the roundabout of a large hotel that doesn't tower so much as sprawl outward, its lights a beacon against the night sky.

Before I'm all the way awake, Jackson is out of the car and around to my side, opening my door for me. It's unnecessary—unlike Jackson, I don't usually have a driver opening doors for me—but I can't say something in my belly doesn't flutter at the gesture. Ridiculous. Belly flutters are for teenagers and girls who haven't been through all the shit I have.

I must still be half-asleep. That's all. I take Jackson's hand as I get out of the car only because it would be rude not to. I drop it as soon as I'm on my feet, though.

I just can't. Too much shit went down tonight. Sleeping was nice. If I dreamed, I can't remember any of it and that's how I like it. I don't care what Jackson says or what grand plans he has—all I want is to get into the room, make a beeline for the bed and pull the covers over my head. Asleep and numb are really working for me right now.

Jackson gets our bags from the trunk before heading inside.

Mutely, I follow a few steps behind him. Jackson keeps checking over his shoulder to make sure I'm there. I try to curve the edges of my mouth up but I'm not sure if it comes off as a smile or a grimace. Can't really be bothered to care either. But I don't miss the narrowing of Jackson's eyebrows that show his concern so I try harder at the smile. Even if it is the last thing I feel like doing right now.

The hotel is super nice inside. An intricate inlaid tile design runs down the middle of the floor. It has open ceilings and interesting architecture too. I didn't check to see what kind of hotel it was from the outside, but I shouldn't be surprised that for Jackson, it's only the best. Even out here in the wilds of northernmost California.

We don't head to the reception desk. Instead, the attendant on duty, a guy young enough to be just out of high school wearing dress pants, a shirt, and a tie, hurries over to us. He looks like he got into his father's closet and is playing dress up.

"Mr. Vale?" he questions.

Jackson nods. He pulls his wallet out of his pants and flashes his ID to the kid who nods profusely.

"Excellent, excellent. I'm William. But you can call me Will. My friends call me Will. Unless you prefer William. That's also perfectly fine. Whatever you like." The kid's face is absolutely plum red by this point, but Jackson just stands politely listening.

"Um," Will valiantly goes on, "That is to say, we are so honored to have such a VIP as you, Mr. Vale, visit our humble little establishment here. I mean, really, it's just incredible." His eyes are so bright they verge on gleaming. "My friends and I just entered a submission to ridiculousrobots.com, actually. When they find out I've met you, they'll just— Well, they'll never believe it, sir. Can I get a picture?"

"Sure," Jackson says affably, though his eyes flick to me in a *sorry* gesture.

Okay, well, this is actually kind of cute, seeing Jackson get fanboyed over like a celebrity. Not that I'll let him know I think that. I only roll my eyes but that just makes Jackson smile wider as the kid snaps the picture, arm thrown around Jackson like they're best friends.

"What does your robot do?" Jackson asks as he steps away from the kid.

"When you sit down on a chair, the pressure sensor sets off the machine that sings My Little Pony songs and projects a series of Truman Capote quotes with a laser pointer at the wall."

Jackson smiles and nods. "Perfectly nonsensical. Sounds like you guys really got the spirit of the thing right."

Will smiles like Jackson just made his year.

"Here are your two key cards and of course the rest has been taken care of by your man over the phone. Please, contact me here at the front desk if anything at all is out of place. Or if there's something to your disliking, I will personally fix the problem immediately."

Jackson takes the envelope with the key cards and then there's an awkward moment where the kid's still just standing there, a hair's breath away from breaching the etiquette of personal space. "Is there anything else?" Jackson finally asks.

Will's eye's go wide as an owl before shaking his head. "No. God no. I'm sorry. I didn't mean to keep you." He launches himself backward so violently, I'm afraid he's going to fall over, but he manages to stay on his feet.

For my part, I actually keep my laughter in until the elevator doors close, but then I lose it. "Oh my God," I say, holding my stomach, I'm giggling so hard. "Are people always like that around you?"

Jackson shakes his head. "I think I was just his first VIP." He doesn't look embarrassed. He's just smiling at me. He reaches out and traces my lips with his index finger. "I like this look on you."

My laughter slowly dies down at the intense look on his face. Especially when the finger at my lips pushes into my mouth. Oh fuck, that's hot. Fire zings straight through to my sex. Damn him. Somehow between the fanboy and Jackson's proximity, my plans for going straight to bed have gotten shot all to hell.

I could fight it or give in.

Two guesses as to which I go for?

Exactly.

I suck on his finger. He growls, then pushes it in deeper, hooking me like a fish in my cheek and pulling me closer. I let him.

His eyes go dark and his Dom face hits me with full force. I don't even know quite how to describe it. His features take on an intensity they don't normally have. The way he holds his body changes. Softness becomes edge. Command crackles in the air.

And I don't know why, but I need it tonight. It would be so easy to give into the numbness. I still feel it hovering there. Wanting to draw me back in. So I take the lifeline Jackson's offering me.

"Hands behind your back, eyes on me," he orders right as the elevator door pings and opens.

Reluctantly, I release his finger from my mouth and do as he says. Probably a good thing, since there's an older couple waiting when the elevator doors open. I hide a smile as I lock my hands behind my back and watch Jackson swiftly exit the elevator.

I keep just a few paces behind him, eyes glued to his spectacular ass. He said I had to look at him. He never specified where. I grin to myself.

He's not making it easy on me to keep up either. His stride is so long, I take two steps for every one of his. Finally, we make it to the room at the end of the hall and he uses the key card to let us inside.

I only get a glimpse of a luxurious suite before Jackson has the door closed. Then the world spins as he twirls me and slams me up against the wall.

His bulk is immediately up against me. I expect his mouth to immediately start devouring me but instead he simply leans in, nose in my hair, his cheek resting beside mine. Both of his hands cage me in on either side of my body and he just stands there, slowly moving his cheek and nose up and down the side of mine. Nuzzling me.

I blink rapidly and my body starts to tremble, overwhelmed by unexpected emotion.

I was prepared for animalistic sex. Clothes to be ripped off. Mouths on bodies and too much sensation for feeling or thought. That's what I wanted.

Not this. Not this.

As close as we are, I can feel his erection rubbing against my leg. He's certainly game. Time to get this train out of the station and moving along.

I reach down and grab his cock. "Fuck me." I give him a crude up and down stroke. I'm happy to take over Domme if he's not getting the job done.

But he immediately reaches down and snatches my wrist, pinning it up against the wall.

I gasp in righteous indignation. Especially when he continues moving at that slow pace, now slowly nuzzling the arm he has pinned, occasionally dropping the gentlest of kisses on my skin. When I try to make a move with my other hand, that one gets pinned as well.

"Don't move," he whispers as he pulls away from me and takes a quick step to his bag. I make a low growling noise of disapproval, but I stay where he's put me, like a pinned butterfly.

"That's perfect. You're perfect."

I see the satisfied approval in his eyes when he glances up from his bag at me, which makes a corresponding warmth flare in my chest. Jackson stands back up before I can think too much about anything. My eyebrows lift when I see what he's got in his hand. It's a small switchblade.

He pops the blade out and steps toward me, eyes dark. So dark. He runs the blunt edge down my cheek and I don't even blink. Blood play is a hard limit for both of us. So what's with the knife?

His eyes flare. "So much trust," he whispers, eyes moving back and forth between mine. He swallows hard, seeming moved by some emotion I can't name. And it's true. Usually this is the point where I should be freaking the fuck out. Second-guessing everything I thought I knew. But I don't. I know I'm safe with him.

Then he seems to master himself and he lowers the blade. I just keep my eyes on him, curious. He pulls out the bodice of my dress and his eyes flick up to mine again as he positions the knife-edge at the center of the fabric. His eyes stay on mine as the blade starts cutting down the center of the dress.

I swallow. He could have asked me to take the dress off. It would've only taken me a second. This is symbolic somehow, him divesting me of my clothes this way.

Seeing the glint of desire in his eyes, I can see he's enjoying himself and I can't deny the curl of pleasure this is giving me too. Especially when, halfway down the dress, he discards the knife, grabs the edges of the fabric and rips the rest himself. Oh fuck. So hot.

He repeats the process with every piece of clothing I have on. Bra. Panties. He jerks my body to him as he rips those off and I'm completely drenched. My hands fall from where I was holding up against the wall and land around his neck.

"Ah ah ah," he chastises, "did I say you could drop those hands?"

Obediently, I raise them back above my head, even though my muscles are beginning to ache. He's testing me and I will pass. I will love the burn. I bite my lip and thrust my breasts out. My nipples pucker and I can't help rubbing my thighs together.

But then, when I'm completely naked, he steps back and takes a slow perusal, head to toe. Goosebumps rise all over my skin under his careful scrutiny. Does he like what he sees?

His face gives nothing away. He's just standing there. Looking. And I start to feel cold. Exposed. Does he see areas he wishes were different? I think about what I saw when I was looking in the mirror earlier. The bags under my eyes.

Being back in my old room, it was so temping to go through the old routines. Spend twenty minutes laying down a base foundation including concealer and contouring. Then lash extensions and mascara. Smokey eye, red lips, all topped off with a liberal brushing of bronzer. The untouchable girl.

But I turned away in disgust before I could even open the little bottle of foundation. I grimace. Which means I've got to look pasty in this lighting. I shift from one foot to the other.

Jackson doesn't move. He just keeps looking me over.

What the fuck? It's been ninety full seconds of silence, him just standing there—and that's just since I started counting. Watching me. Categorizing defects, if he's like any other man I've met. David used to say that my thighs were too thick. I was pretty and everything, but he said he understood why I stopped doing pageants.

Do you know how long a minute and a half of silence actually feels with another person just staring at you? Even in pageants, the whole walking and posing process takes less time than this.

"Fuck, just take a picture already. Then you'll have all the time in the world to find all the flaws." Then, under my breath, I add, "And wank off to it, which is what I'm good for, right?"

"What did you just say?" His voice cracks like a whip.

But fuck him and his Dom shit. How dare he make me feel special one second and then remind me what I really am the next? Something to look at. Something to fuck. I *knew* it, I knew from the start this is how it would end up. "I'm just saying what we're both thinking."

"And what exactly is that?" Each word comes out through his teeth.

I drop my arms and cross them over my chest.

Fine. He wants to do this? Let's do this.

"That maybe this little visit home makes things clear. My mom might be a cunt, but fuck, it doesn't make her wrong." I shrug and give a shrill laugh. "She taught me how to put these assets to work," I grab my tits, "since I was a kid. So I just kept on doing it. Working at Hooters. Taking the job with Gentry—"

"Stop it," Jackson demands.

"You're fucking me," I say with a sneer. "So you obviously get it. Let's be honest. I fucked my way into this job, no matter how you try to spin it. You only prove my point every day—"

Jackson's hand slams over my mouth and a dangerous glint enters his eye. "You'll want to be very careful about what comes out of that mouth next. You are not only insulting me, but the woman I happen to care a very great deal for."

He moves so that his body covers mine, face hovering only an inch away from my face. His hand is still firmly on my mouth. "Your parents are worthless shitbags of human excrement who never deserved to breathe the same air space as you and I'm struggling not to go back and take an ax to that cock-sucker who abused you when you were just a kid."

His jaw is so rigid I think he might crack something when he continues, "I want to ram a white hot poker up all of their asses for making you question your worth, talent, beauty—" he finally removes his hand from my mouth and cradles the side of my head, "—and general fucking amazingness. As well as the strength that continues to blow me away more with every day that I know you. You pursue your dreams against all odds. You survived and thrived when any other person would have given up."

He grabs my hands and his eyes go glossy with emotion even as I see him struggling to keep it under control. He's cracked himself wide open for me and I can't imagine Jackson Vale doing that for anyone. "I was staring at you because I was taking you in, your beauty inside and out, all that makes you, you, and I couldn't stop looking because *I love you.*"

My breath hitches and I try to pull away but he doesn't let me.

"I know that scares the shit out of you but I don't care. You're not running. Not again. What I learned tonight was horrible but I was glad to learn it because I want to know everything about you. No secrets anymore. You are the strongest person I know and the only person I would ever submit to. I love you."

Slowly, he slides to his knees before me and I see all that he is offering me.

Not just his submission, but his life. A life together.

Jackson Vale is on his knees before me. It was surprisingly easy for me to trust him with my physical safety only moments ago, but then I was just as quick as always to pull back my belief in him. Yet here he is offering more than I ever, ever could have dreamed for. So much that my brain will explode if I think about it for a second longer.

So I focus instead on what I can handle—the man at my knees.

Yes.

That, I can deal with.

That, I can control.

With pleasure.

A wicked smile curves my lips.

"Crawl to the bed, slave." So, it's not exactly a reciprocal declaration of love. But ya know. I'm thinking on the fly here.

Jackson doesn't look up or bat the proverbial eye. He just starts crawling. My heart, which was beating so hard I thought some very un-Domme-like fainting might be on the agenda, finally starts calming down and I feel like I can breathe more regularly again.

I love you.

Wow. Okay. Yeah. So. Still registering that one. I look over at Jackson where he's on all fours at the foot of the bed.

"Take off your clothes," I snap in my bitchiest voice. He starts to comply and another wave of calm sweeps over me.

It really is like a wave. First my shoulders relax, then my arms, down to my stomach. Oh, except for my core. There, it's heating up. I rub my thighs together and feel a delicious twist. Oh hell to the fuck yes. This is exactly what the doctor ordered.

I squat down to my suitcase and rifle through the black bag I buried underneath all my other clothes. The one I highly doubted I'd be needing on this trip. Turns out I'll get to play with my new toys after all…

Over an hour later, I've decided that the penthouse suite is definitely worth it if only for the sturdy bed frame.

The cuffs were in Jackson's bag, not mine. I'm betting he's regretting packing them just about now. He's cuffed naked to the bed, spread-eagled in the most deliciously vulnerable position.

And of course I'm taking advantage of that vulnerability. Turns out, I'm a sadistic bitch.

Not sadistic as in dealing out pain with whips or burning wax or anything. Well, not too much pain. But I am discovering the exquisite fun of orgasm denial.

As in, you bring your man right to the *edge* of coming and then *BAM*, take it away. Blue balls in the extreme, except you get to play with the giant rigid cock.

I stare down with a loving smile at Jackson's massive boner, an elastic cock-ring fastened at the base around his dick and balls. A line of seven clothespins pinch the skin along the top of his cock like upside down mini-Eiffel towers.

Jackson jerks as I tap one lightly.

"Would you like me to take these off?" I gently swat each clothespin that runs down his long, beautiful engorged cock and grin evilly. His whole body goes taut as he tries not to show his discomfort. So macho, even now.

"Yes, Mistress," he breathes out through his teeth.

We've been at this for an hour and fifteen minutes and Jackson's eyes have gotten darker and darker until it seems like his pupils are blown. There's only a dim light on in the room and the further I push it, the more it feels like just him and me in the whole universe.

His gaze never wavers from where I sit hovering inches away from his cock. I lean over and lick the slit of his mushroom head. He groans and his hips thrust up off the bed in a spasm.

"Bad slave." I yank my mouth away and swat at his penis with a small riding crop I brought along. All the clothespins waver with the impact and he writhes.

I use the crop to tap individually up and down the line of clothespins. "Are you going to keep being such a naughty slave boy? Naughty slaves don't get to have their cocks jacked so hard every ounce of cum in their balls spurts out and then they pass out."

Jackson's eyes widen and shoot to mine before averting to look down again. Immediately, my crop shoots up toward his chin. I don't smack him with it, though. I gently touch underneath his jaw and lift his head so he's looking my way. "Look at your Mistress when she's talking to you."

Jackson and I will never have the kind of relationship where he's a boy licking at my boot heels. I'm not that kind of Mistress and he will never be that kind of man. It's not what I want from him either.

I run the tip of the crop down his strong corded neck and then further down the defined line between his pectoral muscles.

"So much strength." My eyes flash from his chiseled chest back up to his eyes at the same time as I grab his balls and squeeze mercilessly. I lean into his lips as the breath hisses out of his lungs, like I can catch it into mine. Taste his breath. Inhale him.

God I want this man inside me every way possible. Not just his cock in me. I want to eat him up. Consume him. Physically. Spiritually.

Everything. I want everything.

"You make me think crazy thoughts," I whisper to him, my face an inch from his. I search his eyes desperately, back and forth.

Maybe this wasn't such a good idea. I'm supposed to be mastering him.

And I am. I can see that I am. But there's something about all of this that takes our connection and sends it to an even deeper plane of intimacy. Him so in tune with my smallest movement. Me responding to his every twitch and breath.

"Like what?" His question is a breath. This close, I can see just the smallest ring of iris not consumed by his pupils. The darkest sea blue. A color that shouldn't exist in nature, it's too... extraordinary.

"All your secrets. Everything." I haven't moved. We're still so close. Sharing air.

But at my words, our magnificent connection—it breaks.

Jackson looks down. Ever since we began, his gaze has been locked on me like a laser. I've been his singular focus.

But here, right at the moment of ultimate joining, he's pulled back.

What the fuck? In my head, I run over everything I said. And light on a single word.

Secrets.

I pull back from him like he hit me. His eyes immediately jerk back to mine. But they're shadowed. Guilty.

The bastard is hiding something from me! Something big by the looks of it. How dare he?

Yeah but aren't you hiding Gentry's blackmail from him?

I tell that voice in my head to shut the hell up. I'm not the one who's been chasing a relationship and saying I love you... and... just... how fucking dare he?

I take the clothespins off his cock almost recklessly and Jackson strains against his cuffs, seeing my mood switch and apparently guessing the reason why. "Wait, Callie, I can explain—"

I glare at him like he's a piece of shit underneath my shoe. "If you address me as anything other than Mistress," I say, voice like a knife, "I will leave you cuffed to this bed and let you explain it to housekeeping in the morning when they find you like this."

He closes his mouth but a vein bulges at his neck and forehead. It's taking every ounce of self-control for him to listen and obey. Normally I'd be proud, but I'm too fucking pissed right now.

I smile at Jackson and his face goes on alert. As it should. He's learning quickly to be wary of Mistress' smiles.

I lean over his cock and take him in my mouth. I bob on the tip several times. In spite of myself, I savor the way the ridge of his head feels on my lips as I dip it in and out. My hand wraps firmly on his lower shaft, controlling his movement.

I peek up at him through my lashes. I know this is a huge turn on for him. It is for most men—it's such a porno move, it's all but programmed into their DNA to prep them to come on a dime.

And fuck if it doesn't make me wet as a little bitch. Sucking cock is supposed to be a job, but with Jackson, it does something to me. Even now, in this moment when I'm pissed as hell, bent over and mastering him with my mouth like this, the hand not holding his cock is gripped in the sheets so I don't start getting myself off. But fuck, I'm so goddamned hot for it.

Which makes me even more pissed. I take Jackson deeper in my throat and groan my own arousal, effectively giving him a hummer.

I feel his ass tense and his spine flex.

And I jerk him off so fast he's left gasping and fucking the air.

"What aren't you telling me, you fucking bastard?" I swat his thrusting dick with my crop and watch the look of absolute pained devastation on his face with complete dispassion.

Using a pair of rubber-tipped kitchen thongs, I hold his dick in place while I start to reattach a few clothespins, this time on the underside of his shaft. At the contact of the kitchen thongs, a dribble of cum drips out the tip of his cock. It looks like a little bit more than precum, but not nearly enough to be a full load.

I clip a pin right underneath the head and Jackson's entire body jolts. And not in pleasure.

I smile coldly up at him, only to find him watching the wall. I slap his thigh hard. "If you want to end the session, you say red or stiletto, you do not disrespect your Mistress by looking away or trying to zone out."

His eyes immediately shoot back to me.

"Tell me what you've been hiding," I command. "And if you lie to me, so help me God, we're finished. Not this session. But you and me.

Done." The words shock me as soon as they come out of my mouth, but at the same time I know I won't take them back.

A lie or omission of truth has been acknowledged between us. I refuse to go on in this relationship without truth. I don't care if that makes me a hypocrite because of what I'm not telling Jackson. That's different. I have no choice in the matter and it involves my son, which is a trump card in my book. This, whatever it is Jackson's not telling me, is between him and me.

Jackson doesn't look away from me but his mouth stays stubbornly shut. I don't break his gaze as I reach into my bag of clothespins, pull out the skin of his balls and attach a clip to it.

He flinches but only juts out his chin further. Stubborn fuck. I glare even harder as I do the same to the other side of his balls. Same reaction. Flinch but no giving in.

I arch an eyebrow. Fine. That's the way he wants to play it?

I walk to one of the other rooms of the suite and grab a chair from the little dining area. I yank it behind me none too gently as I come back. I prop it beside the bed, eye-level with Jackson's straining cock. Once there, I sit down, cross my arms, and continue glaring at him.

We sit locked in a stare down for five minutes—I'm watching the time out of the corner of my eye on the bedside clock.

Then, right after the five-minute mark, I get up and crawl back onto the bed.

"Tell me the secret you've been hiding. I want to hear *in detail* what it is you're so afraid to tell me."

Even while I watch him, I see it. He's terrified. Stripped as he is, literally and figuratively, his normal armor is absent. His eyes twitch and widen and his furtive swallow doesn't go unnoticed. I see everything. He looks so scared, almost lost. Whatever he's carrying is such a burden.

"You can talk to me." I gentle my approach and it isn't even a manipulation tactic. I rub up his thighs, massaging, wanting to sooth him. "I can see how this is torturing you. Let it go. Talk to me. Free yourself."

His eyebrows drop in agonized indecision before he finally shakes his head. "I can't," he whispers, his voice breaking. "You don't— I just can't—"

"You can." I urge, but he keeps shaking his head. And I start losing patience.

"You will." The chill returns to my voice.

This time his body jumps when I remove each clip.

"I can't, I can't," he starts repeating over and over, and I don't know if he means he can't take any more of what I'm doing to him or if he's talking about his precious secret. Either way, he always has a way out of this if he really wants to quit, and the word red hasn't crossed his lips.

Of course, with the ultimatum I tossed down, safe-wording would end a lot more than this play-session. Though 'play' is no longer applicable for what we're doing. The stakes have become too high. We're in an abyss here, going deep, deep down, and only Jackson can bring us out again.

If we make it out again, I have the feeling we'll be stronger than I ever imagined. That the paltry word 'partners' will seem silly in comparison to the rock-solid entity we could be. If...*if*.

Once all the clothespins have been disposed of, I drop my head again. I lick the long vein running underneath his shaft up to his thick head that's extra sensitive because of the clips. Jackson's entire body shudders, finally in pleasure.

I don't have to command him to look at me, this time. His eyes are locked on mine. When I drop my mouth over his shaft, I give him everything I have. I worship with my tongue. I suck and swallow. At the same time I plead with my eyes not to break us.

His face is agonized. Eyebrows low, mouth open, nostrils flared. His buttocks draw tight and his back starts to arch off the bed and again, I open my mouth wide and lift off him.

He roars in frustration but when he looks at me, it's not with accusation. It's still fear. Not just fear. Ten times worse than that, he's moved into a place of almost animal-like terror. Sweat mats his hair and there's water around his eyes even though he's not crying, exactly. Everywhere his muscles bulge—his arms, his neck, even his forehead. His eyes are huge as he tilts his head to the side as if in supplication.

"Please don't make me." His voice breaks. "You'll never forgive me."

For the second time tonight he breaks eye contact, his head slumping between his shoulders like an invisible weight is pressing him down from behind.

Oh God. It was too good to be true. I knew it. I knew it but I believed in him anyway. Stupid. I'm always the stupid, stupid girl never learning from her mistakes.

"What?" I pull away from the bed. "What is it? Just tell me!"

Jackson looks up at me, eyes full of regret and remorse. Oh God, I'm going to throw up. My hand goes to my stomach. "Tell me now or I walk," I demand. "What did you do?"

"It was Gentry," he says. I back away from him, shaking my head, tears pricking. Oh God, they haven't been working together, have they? I'll do more than throw up. I'll never be able to get anything down ever again. Or trust anyone. Anything.

"It was back when we were in college. I told you the games seemed harmless at first." Jackson's torso strains off the bed, arms pulling against his cuffs. His eyes beg me to understand.

I keep shaking my head. College? A small seed of hope starts to bloom. Maybe he's not going to confess partnering with Gentry recently in the horrors against me?

Jackson sounds no less tortured though. "He always had a different girl on his arm and three more who wanted to be with him. He was so *charismatic.*" Jackson spits the word like it's poison.

"So one night, we're all partying together." His eyes flick up to meet mine but then drop again. "Gentry had a girl hanging all over him, but like I said, that was nothing new. At the end of the night, though, he comes over to me and tells me the girl is actually into *me.*"

Jackson swallows hard and the moisture that was just a sheen earlier gathers at the rim of his eye. "He tells me she's kinky and that she's waiting, blindfolded, for me in his room. She thinks it's hot to call me the Dark Knight instead of my real name, so I should just go with it. And I do. It's not the first time he'd done that kind of thing. Gotten me girls." Jackson closes his eyes, face ashen.

I look at him in confusion. What does this story have to do with anything? Is he ashamed he couldn't get his own girls in college? It's not awesome and the fact that it was Gentry is... just *ugh*, but still, so what? Watching him as his eyes come back to me, though, so dark and lost, my stomach sinks. And then it hits me—*Gentry's a part of this story*. Of course something absolutely horrible happens next.

As Jackson goes on, every word only confirms my suspicions. "The girl was waiting there, just like Gentry said she would be. When I came in and sat beside her, she jumped me and started making out, immediately taking off my clothes. So I thought everything was cool." He chokes a little as he continues. "She said how hot it was to finally get to be with the Dark Knight. She said that over and over. How long she had wanted that. So we sleep together and I think we're all good." He squeezes his eyes shut.

"What happened?" I ask. I didn't realize it, but as he's been talking, I've walked closer so that now I'm by the bed again. I sit down beside Jackson and put my hand on his thigh.

"The morning happened." He looks up and meets my eyes. "I wake up and she's screaming that I raped her. The whole dorm floor freaks out and the next thing I know I'm in cuffs."

I suck in a shocked breath. "Gentry paid her off to say you raped her?"

He shakes his head. "God, I wish that's all it was." His voice hitches as he looks at me, eyes haunted. "No, to this day, she believes I raped her. And in a way, I did."

I jerk back from him.

"Gentry must have given her something, some kind of ruffie." Jackson's voice evens out to a monotone and his eyes drift to the wall. "She doesn't remember anything about the night before except that she went to the party wanting to sleep with Gentry. He was the only guy she'd wanted to sleep with all year. No one else. Then she woke up in his bed with me, some guy she didn't know at all other than having seen me once or twice at a party." Jackson's eyes flick briefly to me before going back to the wall.

"Gentry set us both up. He told her it was him who'd be meeting her in his room, and that he liked it kinky with the mask and the Dark Knight bullshit." Jackson's face pales, like he might be sick and when he meets my gaze this time, the tear that's been threatening finally falls down his cheek. "All my dad ever wanted was for me to be a good man. Instead I let Gentry make me a rapist."

Oh my God. The devastating reality of what he's lived with for all these years. Of what Gentry did to him. Of what happened to that girl.

Quickly I pull the key to the handcuffs out of my bra and undo the restraints at his wrists and ankles. Then I prop myself back on the headboard and pull Jackson into me. He collapses against me, head curled down against my breast and does something I wonder if he's ever allowed himself since it all happened. His entire body shakes silently. I imagine he's crying, but he's so quiet I can't tell. I stroke his enormous back and wrap as much of my body around him as I can.

Which is when I feel it. As fucked up as he must be about everything that went down years ago, I've gotten him so revved up over the past couple hours, he's still hard as a rock. His cock is engorged so much it's got to be almost to the point of pain. Then there's the matter of the ring I put around his cock and balls, only contributing to the issue.

I know what needs to be done.

"Get on all fours." It comes out in my harshest Domme voice.

In spite of everything, there's no hesitation. Jackson drops to the floor, his head sunk low between his shoulders, face to the ground.

"Did I say get on the ground? I said on all fours," I snap. "It should have been perfectly obvious I meant on the bed."

Jackson winces at the harsh tone of my voice, but gets back on the bed and on his knees. Never once does he look my way. He assumes the position on his knees with a military-like precision. Except for his head, which is bowed so low his forehead scrapes the bed.

I rear back and give his ass a hard smack. "Head up."

His head jerks up, eyes on the wall now.

"What do you say when I address you, slave?"

I give him another wallop.

His body doesn't even jerk with the impact. "Yes, Mistress." His voice sounds lifeless.

That is not acceptable.

I reach between his legs and grab his hanging cock. He lets out a groan that sounds more like a growl and I feel an answering roar of satisfaction in my chest.

And then he tries to pull away from my touch. "Mistress no. I'm a fucking monster. You heard— You know now—"

I grip his cock like a vise the further he tries to move until he half-crumples to the bed. "On your knees," I demand again.

This is not Jackson the business mogul, the self-confident dominant man everyone else in the world knows. This is my man stripped down and at his most vulnerable, maybe more than he's ever been before in his life. Well, at least a moment that he's shared with someone else.

I think of the morning he woke up to that girl screaming that he'd raped her. His confusion and terror and the horrible, horrible fear that somehow she was right and he'd done the unthinkable.

All my dad ever wanted was for me to be a good man. After a life being bumped around the foster care system, landing with his foster parents who eventually adopted him, changed everything for Jackson. Jackson was so close with his adopted dad—from the little he's told me before, I know it was the emptiness after his death that in part led to Jackson hanging out with Gentry in the first place.

And then to have the foundation of who you thought you were as a person and as a man questioned and ripped apart. How many years later and Jackson still calls himself a rapist and a monster—the opposite of the legacy his father wanted for him. And all this done by someone who was supposed to be a friend. Betrayal on top of devastation. Jackson didn't finish the story, I realize. He said he was taken away in cuffs. Obviously it all got settled somehow, though to him, that's not the important part of the story.

And I see it now—why Jackson really chose me. In the beginning he *did* want to save me from Gentry. But not because he saw me as some pitiable whore. He wanted to save me because he himself had been used, manipulated, and at least for a time, broken by Gentry. We'll both forever bear the scars of that bastard.

But it's not all Jackson and I have. We are so much more than the victims Gentry made us.

I reach out and put a hand on Jackson's flank, this time not a strike but a gentle touch. *We are more than victims*, I repeat it to myself to make sure it sticks. We've connected on so many deeper levels and become more than the game pieces Gentry tried to craft us into.

I rub Jackson's hips with both hands. His cock hangs huge like a horse between his legs and twitches with each deep massage even though my hands are nowhere near it.

I pause in my ministrations to open my bedside table drawer and pulled out an eye mask. Usually I like seeing his eyes, but for this, I want him completely lost in the sensory experience. I place the dark fabric over his head and make sure it's secure over his eyes so that he can't see anything. Once I'm satisfied, I go back to my bag and grab a couple other items. Then I return, drop the items by his feet and continue my massage.

I've tortured him long enough. Probably too long. I never intended this session to be so lengthy but then, of course I should have planned on Jackson's stubbornness.

Dripping some lube onto my fingers, I dip my forefinger into the pucker of his ass.

A low moan escapes me as my slippery, lubed-up finger presses up against the tight ring. The ass is so forbidden. I don't know why that immediately makes it ten times hotter, but it does and I go with it.

"Open up and let me in, you sexy fuck," I command.

At my words, his body relaxes and my finger instantly slips in. Oh God. It's so tight and hot.

I lift up on my knees and lean over his back even as a second finger joins the first. It's a slightly tighter fit, but I'm lubed up and determined. Leaning on him as I am, I can feel his shudder as it goes through him. I join him as he moans.

Slowly, ever so slowly, I push my fingers in and out. "I'm inside of you. Can you fucking feel me? Inside *you* this time."

"Yes, Mistress." His voice is little more than a croak.

"That's right," I coax. "Let it out. I don't want you to be quiet. I want to hear noise. I want you to be an animal underneath me. Don't analyze. Just fucking *feel*. That's a command."

"Yes, Mistress."

"Good." I pull back so I'm sitting more firmly planted on the bed and have better leverage with my fingers.

The key isn't to just push in and out, I know. Instead, I go in a little ways and then start pressing down on his prostate gland. The G-spot for men. That's where I start massaging back and forth, keeping firm pressure.

A shocked noise chokes out of Jackson's mouth and I smile. Good. I'll take that to mean I found the spot. I've heard you can make men come from this alone, but I'm not in the mood for experimenting.

I have a very specific goal here. I'm going to make Jackson Vale come harder than he ever has in his entire fucking life.

I continue with my fingers for just a moment longer before pulling out. Quickly, I lube up the prostate stimulator I grabbed from my bag. These things are supposed to be intense as hell for a man. Just what I'm looking for to push Jackson to the highest high possible.

"I'm not hearing you," I say. Grabbing his steel cock in one hand, I start jacking him off. I don't bother to be gentle. Hard as he is, I bet he wouldn't even feel gentle at this point. Once he's good and rutting against my hand, I work the toy in his ass. For a second I'm not sure he feels it either so I maneuver it and press down on his gland. Then I turn it to its most intense vibration setting and click it on.

His body lurches so hard, it's like I shocked him with a stun gun. The bed bounces and it takes my beauty pageant balance training not to be knocked off my knees and faceplant on the bed.

"Fuuuuuuuuuck!" Jackson roars.

This time it's me left panting, wetness all but spurting between my legs. His ass flexes in front of my eyes as he bucks into my hand. I do my best to keep up, rubbing up and down his shaft that's so thick, my fingers don't even touch where I'm wrapped around him.

The bed board bangs every time he lunges into my hand. I find a perch half-curved around his body so I don't fall onto the bed or lose my grip. With one hand, I work his cock and with the other, I press the vibrating prostate stimulator down mercilessly.

He continues yelling, but it's just grunting gibberish like he can't help but vocalizing, maybe just because I ordered him to. He's desperate. Wild. Uncontrolled.

Mine.

His whole body goes tight, he's flexed from his neck down to his outstretched toes. God, he's right on the edge of blowing.

"Say you're a good man," I demand. "Say it or you can't come." I squeeze the head of his dick, a trick to ruin orgasm even if he's right at the brink.

He growls through his teeth and throws back his head, shaking it *no*.

"Say it because your Mistress commands it and because it's fucking *true*," I shout at him. "Say it!"

"I'm a good man!" he shouts back.

"That's right! Now come!" I massage his cock the way I know he likes best, back and forth over the rim, paying special attention with my thumb to the vein right underneath the head. I rotate the stimulator down on his gland and put as much pressure as I can. I press my chest into his back and shout, "Mine!" into his ear.

Jackson gives one last thunderous bellow and then ropes of creamy cum explode all over my hand.

His whole body tenses as he comes, every muscle and vein straining and then the room that had been so filled with grunts and shouting just seconds ago is... suddenly very quiet. There's just both of us panting.

I expect Jackson to collapse after what I've just put him through, but he stays there, on his knees if slightly slumped. His back is sweat-slicked. Well, his entire body is. I push my hair back from my eyes and realize I'm wet with sweat too.

I slip the stimulator out of him and I'm about to say something to break the quiet... or no, I still need to be Domme for a little while longer, I should be in aftercare mode, checking in with him and making sure he's okay—

"Now you." Jackson's voice is so low it's half a growl.

He reaches over with his left hand and jerks back the comforter to reveal silken maroon sheets below. The next second, he rolls me so that my back is on the sheets. He kicks the comforter soiled with his release off the bed. Immediately, he's on top of me, bulging arms on both sides of my body.

His cock, which is somehow still hard after his explosive release, nudges at my slick entrance. I grin in readiness.

But then his right hand comes to my throat in a chokehold.

I jerk beneath him in surprise, immediately gasping for breath. He loosens his hold slightly so that I can manage the barest gasp. But once I've got it, his grip cinches tight again.

Then he enters me. He grinds his body low and deep so that the contact against my clit is fantastic. I blink rapidly. It's all so much—almost too much.

He thrusts several times. Oh God, it feels so good. I try to suck in air but Jackson's firm hand at my throat keeps me from getting in anything except the barest wheeze.

I stare at him. He's wearing his stern Dom face. His arm muscle glistens as he dominates me completely. I squelch around his cock because the sight is the most fucking erotic thing I've ever seen or even considered.

Except. I can't— Need breath—

And in a flash I'm back in the room. Arms holding me down. Men surrounding me. Inside me. I can't breathe! No, not again! Not again!

I grab the arm holding me down and struggle—

The grip immediately loosens and—

It's Jackson. I blink.

Of course it's Jackson. His dark eyes meet mine. The vulnerability when I broke him down earlier is still there, underneath the Dom.

"Do you trust me?"

Oh God. He has no idea what he's asking. I meet his searching gaze and take a deep breath in. Air. Precious air.

Together he's helped me take back so much of what they stole. Is it possible to gain this last territory? My very breath?

I take one last gulp of air. Then look him straight in the eye. "I trust you." My voice doesn't even tremble as I say it.

I release my death grip on his hand around my throat and lift my arms above my head in surrender. I don't miss the look that comes over his face either—relief but also empowerment, like I've just given him what he needs to truly be not just a Dom in this moment, but to be a man. A *good* man. I could tell him I believe it until I'm blue in the face, but maybe he'll never believe it until I prove it. Because if I thought he were in any way an actually violent man capable of rape, I would never trust him to do this. Can we both take back what Gentry stole from us in this one act?

Goddammit, I'm going to try. So no matter how fucking terrified I am of putting my very breath in someone else's hands—for Jackson and only Jackson—I'm not just going to *try*. I will do this.

My entire body trembles as his grip on my neck cinches tight again. "The most beautiful fucking thing I've ever seen," he murmurs as he begins to thrust inside me with torturous slowness. Every time he bottoms out, he swivels his hips around and around until I'm keening with pleasure. Against his grip at my throat, my cries only come out as choked half-whimpers.

Which makes the whole thing even more bizarrely fucking hot.

Jackson starts moving faster. He hisses through his teeth as his body fuses with mine, panting as he holds himself up with one arm beside my head, the other hand held unflinchingly against the base of my throat.

And God it feels—there's absolutely no more room in my head for reflection. I've moved to that place where it's all sensation. My eyes are on Jackson's. The world's becoming fuzzy at the edges as the pleasure ramps up and up and oohhhhhhh—

My back arches and I lift one leg to wrap around Jackson's hip. Closer. I need to be closer to him in any way I can. In every way. I'd do anything for him.

Everything narrows. Light shimmers around us. There's only him. All the feelings. Pleasure, but so much more. Oh God. Tears slip down my cheeks.

Him. Him. Him. Only him.

Spots dance in my vision as my climax lights me up. He notices, of course he does because he's in tune with me. We have become one.

He releases my throat and I take in a gulp of oxygen that's like lighter fluid on the flame of my orgasm. It erupts from within like a flash fire.

I pull Jackson down to me and sink my teeth in his shoulder as I screech out my pleasure. He pounds me with several more punishing thrusts as I ride out what's the longest orgasm of my life and then I feel his body shudder as he comes with me. I'm still spasming in aftershocks around him even after he's flipped us to the side and pulled me on top of him so that he's not crushing me.

"I—" I try, but then close my mouth because there are no words after what we just experienced. They aren't necessary anyway, I realize. We just communed in the deepest way two human beings possibly can.

Jackson's fingers play with my hair and for once, I'm the one who drops off to sleep first.

CHAPTER TWENTY-TWO

CALLIE

Things between Jackson and I stay good all week. Except for the fact that I still haven't told him that Gentry tried blackmailing me to steal his prototype. But, really, is there any need to at this point? Because I'm not doing it. Everything that happened last weekend made a few things very clear.

What Jackson and I have is too important to throw away. He told me he *loves* me. And after what Gentry did to him... God, there's no way I could betray him on Gentry's behalf. I just can't.

That video Gentry's threatening me with is despicable and yes, it might color the judge's opinion of me, but with my kick-ass lawyers, it won't be admissible in court. My lawyers. I have to remember I have the best. If I play it right, maybe Jackson doesn't ever even have to know about what's on that tape. God, the thought of him seeing me like that...

Maybe there's something else I could do so it won't even come to Gentry releasing the tape. Granted, I have less than a week to come up with a brilliant plan. Charlie's custody trial is next Thursday. Unfortunately, every pseudo-plan I've thought up so far gets shot down within half an hour of further research.

If I try to give Gentry fake code, he'll test it and realize it's crap within a day. Same thing if I give him an old version of the firmware. He'd quickly find the same problems with Falcon Six that we saw in our last demo.

I've thought about giving him the real version, but with some kind of virus that would infect his whole system and put the company out of commission for a few weeks. Problem is, I only know how to code some basic Trojans that are the kind of low-level thing that Gentry's malware detection software would pick up like *that*.

It's not like there's a Hackers 101 class at Stanford where you learn that kind of shit. Even if I spent every second in the next hundred hours or however much time I have left learning everything I can about how to sneak a virus into the firmware undetected, it's nothing that couldn't eventually be sorted.

And in the meantime, Gentry would know I was fucking with him and *voila*, the video still gets released.

My phone beeps with a reminder I have an unread text. From Gentry. I've been ignoring it for the last thirty minutes but I doubt he'll allow it for much longer. From the preview, I saw that he's asking when I want to meet to exchange the prototype for the blackmail video.

"Miss Cruise?"

I try to shake off thinking about it as I stand up and walk through the familiar reception office at Charlie's psychologist to see him for my weekly supervised visit. If there is any justice in this goddamn world, this will be the last time I have to be supervised just to see my own son. Although, knowing how slow the fucking court system takes to come to a decision, it will probably be at least another two months of this before the judge's ruling gets implemented.

Anger makes my jaw tense, but *no, calm the hell down, Callie*. Charlie's always been able to pick up on it if I'm upset and I only want him getting good vibes from me.

I take a second outside the door to grab several deep breaths and focus only on my little boy. The softness of his little-boy hair. The feel of his chubby little fingers when they curl around mine. Finally, when my heart rate is chilled out enough, I step inside.

Sometimes when I come in, Charlie is already playing with the blocks or the train set or coloring with the child psychologist, a friendly older woman.

When I open the door today, however, there's some strange man I don't recognize standing in one corner with a clipboard.

Charlie's on the ground in the center of the room, tearing pages out of a book. Ripped and crumpled pieces of paper circle him, as do a completely upended box of scattered colored pencils and crayons. Not to mention the red and blue scribbles all over one wall. Right at Charlie's level.

Oh shit. I really hope they've had other kids in here and it was one of the other kids who made most of this mess. I glare at the man with the clipboard in the corner. Who the fuck is this incompetent shit who's supposed to be watching over the kids who come through here?

"What's going on?" I march straight up to the aforementioned incompetent shit.

He looks up at me briefly before his eyes zero back in on Charlie.

I snap in front of his face. "Hey, I'm talking to you. Where's Martha?" I hope the name of the normal child psychologist will get me somewhere.

"I'm filling in today." An especially loud ripping sound comes from the ground behind us and Incompetent Shit looks down and scribbles away at the notepad attached to his clipboard.

I push the clipboard down and force him to see me. "Don't you think you should be paying more attention to the child in your care than taking notes? He was basically unsupervised before I got here."

The man looks at me with dispassionate eyes. "You were late."

"Wha—?" I grab my phone out of my pocket and check the time. It's two minutes after five, and considering how long I've been dealing with Incompetent Shit, I was *maybe* one minute late.

Screw this, I'm not getting anywhere and I'm missing time with my son. I turn around and go to sit with Charlie.

He starts to rip another page but I put my hands on his. "No," I say in firm Mom Voice. "This is not how we treat books."

Charlie's chin starts to tremble. I know what's coming next and brace for it.

"Aaaaaaaaaaa!"

Right on cue—the ear-splitting wail I was expecting. I see Incompetent Shit flinch in the corner and probably fail to hide my slight smirk. Charlie tries to reach for another book, but I pull it out of his hands as well.

"We treat books with respect. We do not rip out the pages."

"No fun! No fair! No fun!" Charlie throws himself on the ground and starts to absolutely freak out, pounding his fists and feet on the ground in a total toddler meltdown.

Oh Charlie. My baby, what is going on with you? I've seen this before, but only when he was a lot younger and once seven months ago when he missed his nap and was extremely overtired.

"Baby, you need to calm down. Take a deep breath. Breathe with mommy. One, two, three," I try to demonstrate breathing in and out.

He's not listening at all.

"Charlie. Charlie." I try several more times to gain his attention, but he's working himself more and more up. If he doesn't stop soon, I know from experience that he'll make himself throw up.

"Charlie, it's time to calm down or you'll have to do it in time out."

More nonstop freaking out.

"Okay, I need you to look at me." I put a hand to one side of his face and he turns and tries to bite me.

Screw that. This has gone far enough. I'm not mad at him. Shit is obviously going on with my sweet boy. He was not like this when he was under my care. He's three and this is not his fault. I want to murder my ex, but in the meantime, I need to take care of my baby. That does not, however, equal spoiling him and contributing to the problem.

I stand up and grab Charlie underneath his armpits, hiking him up with me.

"Charlie Bryan Cruise, you know this behavior is absolutely unacceptable and you've earned yourself a timeout."

His crying abates for just a moment and then continues louder than ever. He struggles and kicks and the only way not to lose my grip is to hold him firmly against my body.

I go to a corner of the room that is emptier than the others and I sit him down.

"Two-and-a-half-minute timeout and then we'll go clean up your mess," I say, addressing Charlie directly.

He immediately stands up and tries to run away from me. My mouth drops open. He *never* did that when he was with me. He knew timeout meant serious business. What has been going on at his father's house?

"Charlie Cruise, you have five seconds to get back in timeout or I'm adding a minute."

He starts scrambling even faster out of the time out area. He takes advantage of my shock and grabs one of the crayons, runs to the wall and starts to scribble on it before I can snatch him back up again. He's got a death-grip on the crayon. If I thought he was wailing before, it's nothing to the screeching that comes out after I finally pry the green crayon from his fingers and take him back to timeout.

I want to press my hands over my ears to shut out the noise, but I don't. A quick glance up shows the psychologist guy watching me with interest now. To him we are both fascinating specimens in a lab.

What a bastard. I should have made timeout in the corner right beside him to make sure Charlie's screeches give him the migraine I can feel pulsing behind my own eyes.

"Charlie, use your words with me. You know my expectations. We respect each other and the things around us. When we don't, there are consequences. If you don't stay in timeout, timeout starts all over again. You have choices and you need to make the right one."

"No! No! No!" As soon as I put him down in timeout, he's out again.

Charlie and I fight the timeout battle for more than half an hour, God, I lose track of time. But then he starts the ultimate freakout, banging his head against the ground so violently that I grab him up.

Dammit, I'm out of options. I flip him so that his back is to me and wrap my body around him, arms like a straightjacket over his, legs spidering over his so that all of his limbs are held down with all of mine. I have no idea how this looks to the psychologist monitoring us but I don't fucking care. The bastard would've just stood there doing nothing while my child injured himself.

"Shhh, shhh, Charlie, it's okay," I whisper in his ear, rocking him back and forth. "Mama's here. It's okay. It's okay now."

Charlie struggles and keeps wailing for about thirty more seconds, but then finally, *finally*, he relaxes into me and his cries turn into hiccups and gasps.

"It's okay, baby. Shh, it's okay," I keep cooing in his ear, relaxing my hold slightly so that now it's just a full-body hug. I move one of my hands so that I can run my fingers through his curls.

"Shhh, Mama's here." I can't stop saying it. Tears flow down my cheeks. Charlie shifts so that he's sideways and his head lies on my breast, so reminiscent of when I used to nurse him.

Within moments, his whole body goes completely lax. I keep running my fingers through his hair and rocking back and forth, back and forth. I hum some small broken melody, I don't even know what song, but it does the trick. Charlie's soft snore is the best music in the world. I hold him and tears continue down my cheeks in an endless silent fountain.

For a while, all is quiet. I calm down too and then just focus on the feel of Charlie in my arms. This beautiful little person who grew in my belly. He's got a big, long future ahead of him. And it's going to be a future full of bright things and happiness, I'm going to make goddamn sure of it. I want to squeeze him harder, but don't dare since he's sleeping so peacefully.

Instead, I inhale his little boy scent. At least they're keeping him bathed. My fingers clench a little and Charlie shifts, nuzzling into my neck.

"Shhh." Shit. It's something I vowed when David came back into the picture—that I would never let Charlie see my fury at his father. All the books say it's important for the child never to see the fighting between the parents but after today's display, it's going to be more difficult than ever.

My son is not okay. I don't know if he's getting the care he needs there or if it's just because he misses me or *what*. That's the bullshit of all this. I don't know anything. I'm his mother and I know nothing about my son's life other than this paltry two hours a week. One hundred and sixty-eight hours in a week and I'm only allowed two hours of my son's time. It's barely a blink and then it's over.

As if proving my point, right as Charlie settles back down, a loud, beeping alarm goes off.

Incompetent Shit ignores the furious shake of my head and how I'm gesturing at my sleeping toddler.

Instead, he says loudly, "Your visiting period is over. Time for the exchange with Charlie's legal guardian."

And then the fucker actually has the audacity to come over to where I'm sitting and physically pry Charlie away from me. There's a moment before Charlie is awake where I try to hold on. "You kidding? He's sleeping," I hiss. "You never wake up a sleeping toddler if you can help it."

The man's face goes hard. "Are you refusing to surrender your child? Because I know that your trial is upcoming and I'm happy to make note of your refusal—"

Fucker!

I let go of Charlie, hating myself as I do it because in this moment, the fucking system is forcing me to be a bad mother and I'm allowing it.

Exactly as I expect, Charlie's eyes pop open as soon as the stranger has hold of him. The wailing I managed to stop starts right up again. Except this time, Charlie's desperately reaching for me.

"Mama! Mama!" he calls, confused from just waking up. He catches on pretty fast though when the psychologist starts walking with him out of the room and I stay behind. His cries become shrieks. "Mama!! Mama, I want *Mama!!*"

The last thing I see is him twisting and kicking in the man's arms, fat tears rolling down his cheeks as he reaches for me with every ounce of his little might.

And all I can do is sit there and sob, knowing that if I go with my instincts, run and rip my own child out of that incompetent idiot's arms, I'm the one who'll be called the criminal.

I stay sitting on the floor with scattered toys all around me until long after I'm sure David or his wife have picked up Charlie. Meeting them in the lobby would not have done good things for my court case next week.

The psychologist doesn't come back either. Or maybe he took one look in the room, saw me still here, and hightailed it out of there like the coward he is.

After enough time, the fury burns away and I'm left with the absolute raw gulf of pain left behind after seeing what's happening to my child without me in his life. It's not just me selfishly wanting my son back.

He needs me. I've read the reports Jackson's lawyers have gotten me from his daycare teachers. His acting out is getting worse. He cries a lot and they've noted that his sleep schedule seems off. I've tried to tell myself over and over: *if we can just hold on a* little *longer until the trial, we'll make it. Charlie's still young. He'll forget and everything will be okay. It'll all be okay.*

But the truth is, I don't know if David and his wife are providing the stability Charlie needs at home or not. Maybe they don't know how or even want to deal with him when he's a handful like tonight.

Or maybe all of Charlie's behavior problems are a reaction to feeling abandoned by me—something I had absolutely zero control over, but how is a two-and-a-half-year-old supposed to understand that?

Bottom line: Charlie is *not* doing okay without me. He needs me.

My phone beeps in my pocket and I take it out to check my messages.

My phone beeps three times signaling a text right as I'm about to ring the bell.

GENTRY: Where is my prototype? We meet on Monday or I send this video wide and you lose your son in court on Thurs.

Mother fucking son of a bitch cunt—

I breathe out and count to three.

Double bottom line: I have to do whatever it takes to get my son back. Jackson's face flashes through my head. Him telling me he loves me. But it's quickly drowned out by the image of my screaming child being torn away from me. Jackson's a grown man and Charlie's two and a half. Just a baby, really.

There's still time to fix what I've broken. And yes, I might be damned to hell for it, but one thing hasn't will never change. I'll always do *whatever* it takes for my son.

My thumbs don't even fumble as I text back a quick message

My phone beeps three times signaling a text right as I'm about to ring the bell.

ME TO GENTRY: Done.

CHAPTER TWENTY-THREE

CALLIE

Which is how I end up in Jackson's office a little after midnight on Saturday night. I shut the door behind me and squeeze my eyes shut.

The thing is, I didn't even have to covertly steal his access card or anything like in the movies. Jackson gave the seven of us on the team working directly with him security clearance to come and go from his office since his terminal is the only one where the actual source code is kept. This computer is off grid, not connected to the internet so it's unhackable. It's the only real way to keep secrets secure these days.

Unless someone like me on the inside steals them.

The lights in his office are motion activated, so as soon as my converse-clad foot takes a step onto the plush carpet of his thick, ornamental rug, his whole corner office lights up.

I pause like I've been caught at something. Fuck. Fuck. *Fuck*.

Stop panicking. I'm only feeling like this because I am *actually* doing something wrong. To the outside, I look like I do every other time I come in here to tweak something on the code. If anyone knew why I was really here tonight, though...

If Jackson knew…

Nope. Can't think about that. Charlie. There's only Charlie. He's being threatened.

Mothers make sacrifices all the time. Sacrificing my happiness is nothing. Nothing.

And Jackson? What about his happiness? What will this betrayal do to him?

CHARLIE, I shout internally back at the other stupid voice. Charlie's an innocent. He hasn't been touched by any of this and he doesn't deserve to be.

I clench my jaw and sit down at Jackson's desk with renewed determination. Last night I went into the machine shop after hours. I've been spending so much time in there, no one even batted an eye. Nor did anyone notice when the big purse I always carry around had a slightly larger bulge as I left with one of the out-of-commission prototypes.

No one realized that all week I've been working on said out-of-commission prototype, switching out parts to make it work again. So that now it's a perfectly functioning prototype. I walked right out of the building with it, no one the wiser. They'll miss it eventually, but I imagine it won't matter by then. I'll be long gone.

The pang that hits my chest feels like a physical stab. I even put a hand over my heart and look down.

But there's no blood. No wound.

Not on the outside at least. I type in the password Jackson shared with me out of trust—what at first appears to be a completely nonsensical series of letters and numbers but is actually the consonants of his father's name, a mixture of asterisks, exclamation points, and the first letters of whatever song happens to be charting on the top 40 that week since he has to change it so often.

I type in the first letter of the *Twenty-One Pilots* song lyrics and then look back down at my chest.

It still aches like a bitch. But God, I don't even have the right to be hurting. I'm not the one who will really be left bleeding when this is all said and done.

I grit my teeth and forge on anyway.

I click on the encrypted file with the firmware to the prototype and you guessed it—I have the password for it too. I keep waiting for a password to be different. In the end for Jackson to have *not* trusted me. But the bastard fucking did. Goddamn idiot. Why would he make himself so vulnerable? Just because sometimes I'm his Domme? Stupid fucking bastard.

As I pop in the several terabyte memory stick and click *copy*, I'm struck by the extreme urge to throw up. Because here I am, what a bitch, trying to blame Jackson for being a good guy—the best guy.

His only flaw? Trusting me, a super fucked-up girl.

If there were only some other way...

There is no other way.

I stare at the comfortable carpet under my feet, only glancing up every once in a while to watch the status bar of the copy process. Sixty percent.

Jackson's face flashes through my mind. His many faces. The stoic one that seemed like his permanent expression when I first met him. The first time I saw him smile and the appearance of the dimple. How even then I knew I was in trouble.

Seventy percent copied. Eighty. Eighty-five—

I love you. I can see it so clearly in my mind's eye, the way he dropped to his knees before me. Offering me everything. And later, how vulnerable he made himself, looking at me with those eyes that pleaded as much as they demanded.

Ninety percent.

"Goddammit!" I whisper, fighting indecision. Am I going to go through with this or not? *Fuck.* How many times am I going to let myself be backed into a corner where I feel like I have no choices and get myself into something I regret forever?

"What are you doing in here, Callie?"

My head jerks up in guilty astonishment to see Jackson standing in his office door. He— How did he— I didn't even hear the—

"I'm... I'm just," Shit. Fuck. Think fast. "Um." Shit. Think *faster*. "I couldn't sleep and couldn't stop thinking about the project."

I glance at the screen. Ninety-five. One hundred percent copied. How am I going to explain this? I'm not, that's how. I click to shut the copy window, try to scroll to the section of code I've worked on before, and swivel the monitor for Jackson to see the now-innocuous screen. At the same time, I slip the memory stick out of the side port in what I hope is a distract-and-swap measure worthy enough for any amateur magician act.

"This part of the code here," I point with one finger while pocketing the drive with my other hand. I hop up on his desk and give the code my complete attention. Oh wow. In my crazy scrolling through the code, I actually landed near the part I was aiming for.

"I know that we reduced our calculation time from the initial model by a factor of three, but I wonder if we could push it even more. What if we considered the flight as a set of temporal marked point processes, constrained of course by the direction of travel. Then we could reduce the overall computation to a handful of functions."

My heartbeat thumps a mile a minute in my ears but I keep talking, almost as fast as my heart is racing. "Which we could learn through maximum likelihood estimates of the historical trajectories."

Jackson glances at the code on the screen but then his eyes come back to me. "It's a good idea."

I smile and hope he doesn't notice how strained it is. At any other moment, I'd be proud of his praise. I came up with the idea during my sleepless night last night. I was trying to figure a way out of my *real* problem and boom, all my mind could produce was ideas for ways to improve the very project I wish I could instead sabotage. Fucking classic.

"But are you sure that's all that's going on here?" Jackson's face looks troubled. "You could have talked to me about this on Monday. Besides, I thought you said you were tired and going to bed early. Isn't that why you said you didn't want to get together tonight?"

I feel myself twitch but force a smile. Shit. I thought I covered well enough. I walk around the desk and hop up on it. "I took a nap on the couch but then couldn't fall back asleep when I transferred to the bed. Couldn't turn my brain off."

I bring my legs around Jackson's waist. Oh God. I'm going to hell. It's official. Seducing my boyfriend to hide the fact that the drive in my pocket could betray his company and everything he's worked for. I force more brass into my smile. "Maybe I was hoping to catch you here because I know how much your head is on this project too."

I put my arms around his neck and drag him down to me, enveloping his lips in a kiss that quickly becomes devouring. His arms wrap around my waist and he pulls me to him, murmuring how much he needs me.

That pain that felt like a stab in my chest earlier burns with brand new agony.

By the time Monday comes around, I don't even bother eating lunch. Well, I mean I try, but after barely managing a few bites of a granola bar, I give up.

I step on the elevator I swore I would never ride again and hit the button for the top floor: the Gentry Tech offices.

My heart races like I imagine a rabbit's might right before a hungry jackal clamps its jaw down on its neck.

But no. I'm prepared this time. I reach in my oversized coat pocket.

Taser? Check.

I glance down at my shin-high Doc Martins.

Hunting knife? Check.

I flex my hands in their patent leather gloves.

Unobtrusive brass knuckles? Check.

I will not be caught unaware this time. No matter that I'm walking back into the mouth of the lion's den. I will *never* be a victim again.

The elevator opens to a familiar lobby. The receptionist desk is empty at this hour, though. A quick glance at my phone shows that I'm early. It's about four minutes before eleven p.m. The overnight security guard downstairs waved me straight past just like Gentry said he would. But this all seems too... simple.

I've been torturing myself over this ever since that day two-and-a-half weeks ago when Gentry told me what he wanted and yet, here I am. The glass to Gentry's office is clear instead of opaque. I can see that he's alone. No one else is waiting to jump out at me for a repeat of my last scarring encounter in these offices.

I'm still cautious as I head toward his office though, the rubber of my Doc Martins squeaking against the perfectly polished floor. I would have come in the baggiest sweats I owned except I want to be able to move if I need to. I settled for black stretchy jeans, cut-off at the knees, and a fitted dark blue hoodie. No makeup, hair in a low ponytail. This isn't a business meeting and I'm not going to try to pretty it up like one.

I shoulder the backpack I'm carrying with the prototype higher on my shoulder and push into Gentry's office with little-to-no finesse. If the damn door didn't have all kinds of mechanisms in place, it would have whacked into the opposite wall with a satisfying *thwack*. As it is, it only opens quietly and then hisses shut behind me.

Gentry's thumbing at his phone, appearing totally absorbed as he completely ignores me. It's such a petty power play, I just roll my eyes and cross my arms over my chest.

"Me and my prototype are happy to walk our asses right back outta this building if you're too busy for us." I toss a thumb over my shoulder in the direction of the elevator.

When Gentry continues staring at his phone's screen, I turn on my heel.

"Show me."

I allow only the briefest smile to flicker over my face before I make my features stone and turn back to face him. That's right. I'm going to set the tone of this meeting from the beginning. I'm the one in control. Not him, no matter how much he believes he is.

Calmly, I walked toward his desk, unzipping my backpack as I go. I pull out the prototype of the drone and set it on his desk. Gentry immediately snatches it up. His eyes avidly devour every bit of the twenty-two-inch prototype.

In this moment, I hate how intelligent he is. It's not fair. Why would God create intelligence only to deposit it in this waste of human tissue?

Gentry's eyes narrow as he looks back up at me. "Okay. Now where is the firmware that makes it fly? I want to look through the algorithms with a fine-toothed comb and see what he's done. I'll know if you're giving me shit code. You're a dumb bitch, don't think you can pull one over on me."

I look away if only because I can't bear to lock eyes with the man who raped and debased me. Even now he's trying to steal something else that's become so precious to me—Jackson.

The only way to get through this is to make myself cold and shut down everything—emotions, thought, physical response. I have to. Gentry can't see anything on my face. I won't give him an inch of power. Not one iota.

I reach for the bag again but Gentry eyes my gloves, then stands up and backs away. "Just put the bag on the desk." He eyes it like I've put a bomb in there or something. "There are contingencies in place. If anything happens to me, the video of you gets sent and you lose your son."

I scoff in disgust. "It would serve you right if I had a gun in here, you bastard." I bang my backpack on the table and step back. "But you think I would let you make me a murderer? You think I'd do that to my son?" I shake my head. "Front pocket."

I step back and resume my position, feet planted, arms crossed, and stare him down. Of course, I don't tell him I thought seriously about trying to stage his death as a self-defense kill.

If I attacked him, I know the fucker would have no qualms about hitting a woman. Then, as long as I let him get some hits in and rough me up a little, I could just kill the fucker with my bare hands—I know a suffocation hold that would do the trick—and if all else failed, I could use the knife.

But there are too many ways for it to go wrong. And it's too close to the custody hearing. I considered it in probably far too much detail. There were entire nights I spent lying awake planning just how I'd do it before I finally let the idea go. My hand clenches and the brass knuckles underneath my gloves dig into my skin.

Gentry retrieves the USB drive from the bag. Because he's been inactive from his console for more than five minutes, he has to not only put in his password again, but go through his overly anal biometric security measures to unlock his computer—not just the usual eye scan but also the newest in palm imaging technology. An infrared scanner reads his palm print and also penetrates inside to read and confirm the pattern of veins inside his palm.

On top of that, he whispers a password for voice recognition. I'm close enough to hear it: "Pandora six gorilla ten."

"You don't think all of that is a little overkill?" I tilt my head at him sideways. I remember always thinking it was so ridiculous when I used to work for him. "Oh, I forgot. You think your secrets are so special."

Gentry's nostrils flare. There he is. The barely civilized animal that he tries to hide in tailored suits. He fools so many people. He fooled me.

"I would think someone in your position would want to be careful." He holds up the memory stick he retrieved from the bag. "After all, you've already given me your bargaining chip."

"No," I sputter and take a step forward in spite of myself. "We had a deal. I gave you what you wanted. Now give me the video. And you swear it's the only copy, right?" I hate the desperation in my voice.

"We'll see," is all Gentry says. "First let's look at these algorithms." He moves to put the drive into the input slot on his computer and then stops, glancing up at me with a sardonic smirk. "On a computer that is *not* connected to my network, just in case you thought you could infect me with a virus or something equally stupid." He pulls out a laptop separate from his main computer.

I bite my lip and watch him insert the terabyte drive into one of the laptop's ports. I tap my foot impatiently. He looks surprised when nothing happens except the software loading.

"I'm not an idiot. I'm not trying to pull anything." I glare at him. "I only want to be free of you and get my son back home where he belongs."

Gentry doesn't respond. He just starts typing on the laptop and then flipping up and down through the code. His eyes widen at what he's seeing. Yeah. Because it's the real fucking deal. Everything he could never come up with on his own. The genius he has to steal from men and women greater than himself.

That's how he's made his entire career. He's smart, but never smart enough. He's just a bully that eventually turned into a monster. Or maybe he was a monster all along.

My stomach drops in disgust.

Gentry looks up at me. His eyes seem to lose focus for a second. And the bastard fucking grins. "What's it feel like to sell out your lover? What's betrayal taste like?"

"Just shut up and give me what you owe me," I snap, ready to be done with this.

"What the hell is going on here?"

It's roared from behind me and if I thought I felt nauseous a moment ago, it's nothing to now. I twirl and standing there in Gentry's doorway is the man I love.

Jackson.

CHAPTER TWENTY-FOUR

JACKSON

Callie looks absolutely devastated as her head swings my way. "No," she gasps. "You don't understand."

"Oh I fucking understand." I storm into the room. The beast inside me is roaring in fury and for once, I don't leash him. I look past Callie at Gentry and I let him fucking loose.

"It's not what it looks like, I swear," Callie cries but I ignore her.

I can't stand to look at her in this moment.

She continues pleading and when I brush past her, my shoulder bumping onto hers, she stumbles back and falls to the ground.

My chest clenches but still I don't look. I can't. I just fucking can't.

"No. Jackson." Tears choke her words. "Please, you have to listen to me."

"Always with your games," I spit at Gentry, stalking toward his desk. The beast is one with me and we both want blood. Gentry stands up and backs away from his desk.

"Look old friend," Gentry lifts his hands and smiles, "I don't know how you got past security, but you can't do anything to me. Our gentleman's bargain still stands. Anything happens to me and I release the tape of you raping that poor girl."

Callie gasps behind me through her choking sobs and that's it. There was little chance I'd ever have mercy on this fucker but now there's none.

I follow him, a lion on the hunt. Gentry always relied on manipulation and trickery to get his way, never brute strength. I tower over him in both height and mass. Manipulation can't save him now.

"Guess what, motherfucker?" I growl, my voice dripping with every ounce of menace I feel. This bastard wants to take everything from me? Time for him to know what that feels like. "It's called the statute of motherfucking limitations. You have nothing to hold over me anymore."

Gentry's eyes widen as if realizing that for the first time in his life he just might have to pay for his actions. I grin what I'm sure is an evil motherfucking grin as I lift my arm and swing with the force of a decade and a half of fury.

The beast roars in satisfaction as my fist makes contact with Gentry's nose. There's the crunch of cartilage and a high-pitched scream of pain from Gentry before he slumps to the floor.

I stare down at him a long moment, breathing hard.

Wait. He's unconscious? I only got one motherfucking blow and he's out?

I turn around to Callie. "Well that was disappointing," I deadpan. "Pussy went down with just one punch."

She grins as I hurry over and reach a hand down to help her off the floor. I don't stop when she's on her feet. I pull her into my arms, lifting her off the ground and swinging her in a circle. Then I kiss the hell out of her.

"Jesus, I was so worried letting you come up here alone with that psycho," I say between kisses.

"I was fine. I told you I had this."

I can't help kissing her again. "It about killed me, not going to you when you were crying. And when you fell."

She laughs, holding my face in her hands. "I did it just like we practiced. Nothing to worry about."

I shake my head in wonder. "God I love you."

She squeezes me to her. "Love you too."

I could hold her forever but she's quickly squirming out of my arms. "Okay, let me down, let me down. We gotta get to work. Let's nail this bastard to the wall."

I pull back and grin at her. "I like the way you think, babe." I let her down but not without a smack on her ass as I head around Gentry's desk to his computer.

Yeah, so that night back in my office when I caught Callie in there late when there was no godly reason for her to be there?

I'm not an idiot.

She tried spinning some BS about not being able to sleep and wanting to work on the code. Of course I knew better.

I suspected from the very first meeting that Gentry would try to use her to commit corporate espionage. It didn't take long for me to stop caring. I wanted her more and I knew that even if she went through with it, it wouldn't be of her own free will.

Because I know *exactly* how Bryce Gentry works.

Still, that didn't mean I was going to just give that bastard my life's work. No, I'd save her *and* my company.

So fucking arrogant.

Because I didn't save her at all, did I?

Remembering the night she revealed it all will haunt me forever.

"What are you doing in here, Callie?"

"I'm... I'm just... Um. I couldn't sleep and couldn't stop thinking about the code."

She slips a small USB drive in her pocket at the same time she shifts the monitor for me to look at what she's been supposedly working on. An obvious attempt at distraction.

Oh Callie. I rest my eyes back on her. "Are you sure that's all that's going on here? You could have talked to me about this on Monday." *Please, Callie. How many chances do I need to give you before you tell me the truth?*

I couldn't give her many more. My security liaison had made that clear this afternoon. He was losing patience with this farce.

He wanted to fire her the second he caught her on the camera in the machine shop stealing one of the old prototypes. I've been able to hold him off but I've got only one more week at most and then I'll have to call her out.

And risk losing her forever.

Because maybe being with me has only ever been about the blackmail. I don't know what Gentry had on her but I was sure it was something.

Blackmail is his M.O. He did it to me and countless others. I only knew about a handful but for as powerful and successful as his company has become, I knew he had to have a huge interconnected network of secrets he was holding over the most powerful players in the country, hell, in the world.

"Maybe I was hoping to catch you here because I know how much your head is on this project too." She smiles seductively but I see the apprehension in the lines around her eyes even as she kisses me and wraps her legs around me.

And I tell her the truth. No more bullshit. "I need you so much, you know that, don't you Callie? You're a part of my life now. I can't imagine it without you in it. I hope you feel the same."

"I do," she whispers and breaks the kiss to bury her face in my neck. She's usually liquid in my arms but right now her entire body is strung tight with tension.

Because she hates betraying me? Or because she's worried I'll catch her at it? I hold her even tighter.

I'd forgive her either way. I'd forgive her anything.

She stays like that a long time, face buried, and I hate it. Hate that she doesn't trust me. Hate that I don't know if she loves me back or if she ever could.

"Callie." I pull her back from me and shake her lightly. "Callie.

Stop. Whatever's running around in your head, just stop. Be with me in this moment."

Because if this is all we have, then I want her here with me.

Her and me.

The love of my life.

Because even if I'm not hers, she'll always be mine.

And finally, *finally*, she relaxes into me.

"Do you trust me?" I ask, trying to look her in the eye but hers are on the floor.

Such a simple question but so devastating. It's an echo of the question I asked that night when I held her very breath. I've hoped that her giving herself over completely to me that night meant that she was mine, forever and truly mine. But if she can't give me the truth now, the complete truth, maybe it means she never will.

Please Callie. Jesus, *please*. Believe in me. Believe in *us*.

And then she squeezes her eyes shut and murmurs, so quietly I barely hear it, "I won't let him make me a monster, too."

Then she stands up straight and meets my gaze firmly for the first time all night.

"I trust you so much, Jackson, that I'm going to trust you with my son. And he's my everything."

She swallows like she's fighting through a closed up throat to get out the words. "I'm trusting you with everything."

And then she tells me. She tells me about Gentry blackmailing her in order to force her to hand over the prototype we've been working on. She tells me Gentry has a video of her and that it would destroy her in court if it came to light.

She stops there, glossing over exactly what's *on* this damaging video. "But I hated it. Hated it the whole time. Jackson, please, you have to believe I never wanted to betray you. I—."

Her eyes drop again and I grab her hands and kiss her knuckles, bowled over at the fact she's finally trusted me even when the stakes were so high.

She breathes out a huge breath of relief, tears cresting in her eyes like she was afraid I'd reject her if she told me. She's so fucking brave. I pull her into my chest.

"I hate all of this," she says, swiping angrily at the tears falling down her cheeks before pressing her head back into my chest. "You must hate me."

"Of course not." Is she nuts? I stroke her hair. "Remember, I know better than anyone what Gentry is like. How he backs you into a corner. And this was about your *son*." Jesus if I think too long about Gentry blackmailing her with custody of her *son* I'll lose my shit so I focus on Callie. Just her.

"Still," she looks up at me, incredulous. "How are you just automatically being so cool about this?"

Oh, right. She thinks this is some huge revelation. I wipe a hand down my face and she pulls back from me.

"What?" I see the alarm that sweeps through her.

I offer a bleak smile. "I told you. I know how Gentry works. From the first meeting, I guessed Gentry wanted my prototype. Corporate espionage is almost a given with him."

"Guess you never expected the spy would be me, huh?" She gives a bitter laugh, swiping at another tear.

Then she must see it on my face.

"Oh my God." She yanks back from me. "You did. You knew all along it would be me. Is that why you hired me? So you could control who he used to spy?" She runs her hands through her hair.

"Christ, no!" My face twists in disgust. "Why do you always assume the worst? Even after all we've been through?"

Her eyebrows furrow and I feel bad for my strong words. Hypocritical too, because haven't I been tortured by similar thoughts? Jesus, why couldn't we just trust in each other? Well, *she* did. She came clean. She trusted me with her son.

I close the space between us and take her hands again. "I hired you because of your skill and because I wanted you away from that monster." Her body sags and I catch her in my arms again. This time I guide her over to one of the plush leather chairs by my desk and pull her into my lap, cradling her so that our faces are only inches apart.

"But after you resigned," I shake my head, the familiar pain lancing through my chest, "you were so different. I knew he'd done something." My eyes search hers. Will she trust me with this? With all of it?

Whatever's on that tape? I know Gentry often creates the scenarios he uses for blackmail.

"I know he destroys people and then manipulates them to do what he wants them to. It's his M.O." I run a thumb tenderly over her cheek. "And there are cameras in the machine shop. My security tech saw you."

Her eyes shoot to me, face full of shame but I hurry to silence whatever she's thinking with a kiss. "I know you." I hold her face in my hands and force her to look at me instead of dropping her head. There's no shame here. Not any more. "I know you wouldn't willingly steal from me if you had any other choice. He was obviously forcing you somehow."

Her eyes search mine, the pain in them so deep. Pain she's finally not masking from me. "I don't deserve you."

"Hush," I say, brushing her hair back from her forehead.

She smiles, her eyes falling shut. "I do that for Charlie. Brush his hair out of his eyes like that."

"It's what you do when you love someone. You take care of them."

Her eyes spring back open.

Shit. I haven't said it since that first night I confessed after her parent's house and I didn't mean to on a night like this. Especially when I have to ask what I do next.

"Tell me what's on the video he's using to blackmail you."

Her body stiffens and I hold her closer before she bolts.

"You can tell me," I coax, running a hand over her hair and undoing the pins, then combing my fingers through the length of it, scalp to tips. Jesus, every part of her is so soft. "You trusted me with your son. Trust me with this."

Her face crumbles and she looks away.

"Callie look at me and *tell* me," I demand.

She glares at me for a long moment but really, it's only tit for tat because she did the same to me the night she ferreted out my secrets. It's the give and take at the heart of the relationship we're building.

And eventually, she must decide the same. Because, even though her lip is trembling and her whole body starts to shake.

She tells me exactly what that monster did to her in that conference room the day she went to render her resignation. What those— Those— How they— Over and over, how they—

I almost get up to throw up at several points. It's only her warm and solid in my arms that grounds me.

I've never had to fight so hard to contain my beast. I imagined the worst—I *thought* I'd imagined the worst. But my imagination was nothing to that evil, *evil* fuck. I'll do more than bury him. Because even killing him wouldn't be enough at this point.

"So he recorded it and is blackmailing you with footage of your own violation?" I sum up, my voice a deadly quiet in the otherwise silent office.

"Yes." It's just a whisper, like that's all she can manage after such an emotionally exhausting retelling.

I hold her closer, look her dead in the eye, and make a vow I'll keep no matter the cost.

"We're going to bury that motherfucker."

CHAPTER TWENTY-FIVE

CALLIE

Right as I finish zip-tying Gentry's wrists, he starts coming to. I give the hard plastic tie an extra hard yank and he yelps. I smile with probably too much pleasure, but a girl's gotta get her thrills where she can.

"Look who's decided to wakey wakey," I sing-song to Jackson. I stand and give Gentry a nice kidney kick before stepping away. His ankles are similarly constrained, giving him a lovely hog-tied appearance. It's a good look on the bastard.

"You two are going to pay for this," Gentry yells, red-faced and spittle flying. "I have so much on the both of you! You'll lose everything you ever loved, I'll make fucking sure—"

The ball gag I shove in his mouth cuts off his rant into pure gibberish. He was so busy cussing us out he didn't even realize I was behind him readying it. I got it in with barely any effort. He jerks back and forth trying to get the rubber ball out but I calmly secure it behind his head.

"Ah," I smile serenely at Jackson, "that's better, isn't it sweetie? Silence really is golden."

Gentry thrashes on the ground, screaming in rage against the gag, but bound and restrained like he is, he just looks like a pathetic animal.

I know you really aren't supposed to kick things when they're down, but I'll make an exception in his case. I mean, I'm wearing the steel-toed boots and all... it's just a shame to waste them when there's rapist scum around.

I deliver another swift kick, this time to his balls. He emits a high-pitched screech, similar to the noise I imagine ten dying cats might make. I'm usually one who's all for a quiet work environment, but hearing the song of his suffering might just make up for it.

I head over to where Jackson sits at Gentry's console. "How's it going?"

He smiles up at me. "Just cracked his password."

I glance down at Gentry and see his eyes go wide.

"You thought you were so clever," I say in my most condescending voice, like a teacher might to an especially-dense kindergartener in the nineteen-fifties, you know, back when they didn't have to be nice to them. "You might have disabled any keystroke readers on your computer and have a super long nonsense password—how many digits is it, honey buns?"

"Twenty-four," Jackson helpfully informs me. Gentry's eyes ping-pong back and forth between Jackson and me.

"But guess what?" I bang on the glass wall behind Gentry's desk. "You remember what your company is spending all it's time attempting to develop?"

I give him a second but his blank stare tells me everything I need to know about the dude's nonexistent powers of deduction.

"*Drones.*" I roll my eyes at him and then smile at the window. "Say hello to Falcon Seven." Jackson pauses his typing on the keyboard, turns on the flashlight function on his phone, and holds it flush to the window behind Gentry's desk. The dim illumination is enough to see a CubeThink drone hovering just on the other side of the glass. "This is one of our prototypes." The *our* slips so easily off my tongue. "You know the one you'd have given your left nut to get your hands on? Well guess what? Falcon here can easily fly as high as the fifteenth story and look in the window over your shoulder to see what you typed in for your password."

Gentry's eyes, which were wide with confusion a moment ago, flinch again in fear. We've got this fucker running scared. Or well, tied up on the floor scared.

"And that's just the beginning. Want to grab him for the rest of the biometric measures, love muppet?" I ask Jackson.

He bows his head to me. "Your wish is my command."

Gentry starts to squirm as soon as Jackson comes his way. Jackson's easily got a hundred pounds on him, however, so there's little point. Jackson easily drags him over.

First is the iris scan. Gentry tries to yank his face out of Jackson's iron grip with little success and when that fails, to look everywhere but at the eye-scanner once Jackson pries his eyes open.

Ironically, however, Gentry got the top of the line equipment so it's able to grab an image of his iris with just the briefest flash of his eye. Getting Gentry's palm on the palm plate isn't a big deal either. Jackson gets him on his feet, back to the computer and forces his hand on the scanner.

I think Jackson wishes Gentry struggled more so he'd have an excuse to break his wrist. Alas, it's accomplished with little to no injury. Afterward, Jackson checks Gentry's wrist bindings, see's they're secure and then adds several more zip ties, probably just because it will make Gentry that much more uncomfortable.

Then Jackson drops him back to the floor. Bound like he is, Gentry can't catch his fall and I imagine we both enjoy his grunt of pain with probably a little too much relish.

Gentry's eyes narrow at us and he garbles more gibberish at us through the gag.

"Do you think he's telling us we won't get through his last little paltry security measure?" I ask Jackson.

"I don't know, dumpling," Jackson says with a wry smile.

Ha, I've been waiting for him to call me out on my sudden use of pet names. I grin even wider.

Jackson produces the small digital device with attached speaker from his coat pocket. "What was his vocal password?"

"I do believe it was..." I hesitate just for show, then give my pageant smile at the prone Gentry. "Pandora six gorilla ten. Bet you're regretting not sending me out of the room while you whispered that one, huh?"

Especially when Jackson types in the words and the speaker pronounces them in Gentry's slightly nasal, overly articulated voice.

The screen clears, all security measures passed.

How, one might ask, does Jackson have all this handy dandy equipment *and* Gentry's vocal pattern recorded and at the ready?

Well, it turns out Jackson's been planning Gentry's takedown long before I ever got involved. He already had hours upon hours of Gentry's recorded voice (from microphones at outdoor cafes, taxis, and everywhere and anywhere public that Jackson's team could get a mic on Gentry) and the software to scramble the syllables and make a simulation of Gentry's voice say whatever words Jackson wanted. He just needed the specific passcode, which Gentry changes on a regular but erratic basis every few days. And of course, he needed Gentry all alone, up here in his office.

Basically, we needed Gentry in his arrogance to set his own trap. We needed him to feel absolutely secure—setting the terms of the meet, on his home turf, while at the same time making himself absolutely vulnerable.

Jackson's fingers start flying and my teeth sink into my bottom lip. It all comes down to this. For all my Bond-villain-esque speeches, I've just been bluffing my way the fuck through this. If what we're looking for isn't on this computer's hard drive—say if Gentry keeps all the dirt he blackmails everybody with on a hard-drive in a lockbox at home or a safety deposit box in a bank—then we're fucked.

But we're counting on his ego. Counting on the idea that a man like Gentry would believe the safest place in the world is up here in his ivory tower with his name stamped on the side of the building. In this place where he thinks laws don't apply to him and he can get away with—

"Shit." Jackson's voice is a whisper and I jerk my attention back to the screen.

"Shit *good* or shit *bad*? What? Don't leave me hanging here!"

"Good," Jackson starts laughing. "Good for us at least. Very, very bad for the bastard over there on the floor."

"*What?*" I ask again, my eyes searching the document on the screen. "What am I looking at?"

"Bank statements. For Colin Wharton."

I look between Jackson's mirthful face and the screen. "I don't get it. Who's Colin Wharton?"

"Oh, he's just the government's point man who negotiated the US defense contract with Gentry Tech. Check out the rest of the documents in this folder," Jackson brings up several other files—pictures of a slightly overweight man in a dark, smoky room with his hand over his face, sitting at what looks like a poker table. More pictures of the same man walking down the lit-up Vegas strip at night.

Then there are bank statements showing large losses throughout the past three years. Then statements from the last few months—and guess what? Suddenly Mr. Wharton goes from being over a hundred thousand dollars in debt to almost one-fifty in the black.

Holy shit. If this means what I think it means, then Gentry dropped a cool quarter million on this guy to make the DoD contract happen. Now we just need the thread connecting Gentry to Wharton's money trail. Jackson opens all the other documents in the file, but there's nada linking Gentry directly.

Jackson opens another folder and double clicks a file. It doesn't open. Instead an encryption screen pops up. Jackson rubs his hands together and glances my way. "Child's play."

"You always thought you were such hot shit," Jackson looks past me to Gentry on the ground behind me, "but it was my homework you always cheated off of. You would never have passed Matrix Theory if it wasn't for me."

Jackson's eyes turn back to the screen. "Oh, you used a thousand-twenty-four bit encryption key. Isn't that cute?" Again, Jackson's fingers fly.

I sit back and watch him, alternately keeping an eye on Gentry. I might be enjoying rubbing his face in how we bested him, but I don't plan on making the mistake of underestimating him or letting him catch us off guard.

Occasionally I check the restraints, keeping my other hand on my Taser while Jackson works. But there's no way Gentry will be able to get free from that many zip ties. He's as immobile as a stuck pig.

"Got it," Jackson exults just ten minutes later while I snack on a Snickers bar I popped in my purse at the last minute. I couldn't eat anything all day, but now that we're here and Gentry is mostly neutralized, my appetite's come back with a vengeance.

"What is it?" I ask through a bite of nougat and caramel.

"Just a little thing called Gentry's Cayman bank account and routing numbers. As well as the cashe of blackmail information he's got on everybody he ever crossed." The easy smile drops from Jackson's face as his eyes flick back and forth over the screen. Lines strain around his mouth. "Including both of our videos."

Gentry starts moving especially vigorously on the floor and making all kinds of noises. We both ignore him. I put a hand on Jackson's shoulder and squeeze.

"Hey." I lift his chin so that he's looking at me. "We only do this if you're completely sure."

Jackson gives me an incredulous look. "Are you kidding? My video is nothing. You were the one who went to Natasha and made it possible for me to finally put it in the past where it belongs."

I smile, sit on his lap and gently kiss his lips. Yesterday we took the charter jet to Idaho and I went to visit Natasha, the woman Gentry tricked Jackson into having sex with. I told her why I was there and before she slammed the door in my face told her I was also Gentry's victim. I shared my story first, right there standing on her doorstep.

She let me in.

She has a good life now. We talked over tea. She has a boyfriend after being single for a long time. Understandably, it took her a good while before she was willing to trust any man. When I finally got around to talking about Gentry and Jackson, she was more willing to listen than I expected.

What's more, she believed me. I was astonished. Was it because of all that I had told her? I asked.

Gravely, she took a slow sip of tea and shook her head. No, she said. She'd believed for over a decade that Jackson had indeed raped her. It wasn't until Gentry himself came to her door and said that if the tape ever came to light, he would need her to testify against Jackson. Not in the legal system since the statute of limitations had passed and they couldn't officially prosecute, but in the court of public opinion. Gentry said he had extensive connections to national news outlets.

When Natasha said she wouldn't be comfortable with that, that she wanted to leave the past in the past, Gentry offered her a lot of money to do it. An *obscene* amount of money, she called it. She told him to leave and saw a change come over his face.

"I saw it then," she shivered. "What I had missed all those years ago in my stupid blind freshman crush. Other girls had warned me about him." She rubbed her arms up and down like she couldn't get warm enough. When she looked up at me again, her eyes were haunted. "He's a predator."

Luckily, her boyfriend had come home and kicked Gentry out. Natasha said she'd do whatever she could to help us. If Gentry released the video and tried to pass it off as rape, Natasha said she'd tell the truth of what she now knew really happened that night.

And as for my video? The video of those animals raping me. If Gentry's telling the truth—and I tend to believe he is in this regard—then us making this move against him will cause a chain reaction.

Copies of both Jackson's video and the video of my attack will be released to the public through a secondary relay, probably along with every other blackmail video Gentry has in his little digital vault of horrors.

I push Jackson's hands away from the keyboard and pull up Gentry's email program. I direct the email to the reporting department of the San Jose PD, attach the unedited video of my attack, take a deep breath, and hit *send*.

Hitting the send button releases a wave of relief so powerful I feel dizzy for a moment. I let out a shaky laugh and Jackson's arms tighten around my waist where I sit in his lap.

"Callie?" he sounds concerned.

I look at him and blink. "I'm free. He has no more power over me."

I thought in this moment I'd want to gloat over Gentry. To dance over his tied up body. To revel in the fact that he's going to prison for a long time for blackmailing and extorting the fucking Department of Defense to get a contract that he had no means of fulfilling. Then to imagine the nightly reaming up the ass he's likely to get by his fellow prisoners for being such a pretty boy who's pissed off a hell of a lot of influential people over the years. Maybe to kick him in the balls again and again and shout in his face that I'm no one's victim.

Instead, all I want to do is throw my arms around Jackson. So I do. "I'm free," I say again. Tears course down my cheeks.

"We're free," he whispers in my ear, squeezing me back just as tightly.

And we are.

Together.

CHAPTER TWENTY-SIX

CALLIE

So it turns out when you have a kick-ass legal team that's *actually* working on your side and an even doubly kick-ass private investigator who can dig up all kinds of shit on your ex and his shady-ass wife, you don't even have to go to trial.

You can sit down like civilized people with your two lawyers at a giant table and hate-stare each other down while your legal eagles do some serious shit-kicking on your behalf.

Example A:

My lawyer, Alberto, speaking to David's lawyer: "It has become clear during the discovery process that both of your clients have committed a host of felonies for which we have ample and irrefutable evidence. This evidence is all in the packets provided and includes but is not limited to: tampering with a judge, extortion," Alberto pauses to look over his glasses at the opposite side of the table where David and his wife Regina sit, *"really,* extorting her lawyer by paying for his wife to get into an experimental cancer trial, you people are despicable." He shakes his head.

Regina has the decency to look ashamed but David just stares at me, elbow indolently on the table.

Yeah. The mystery of why my lawyer dosed me with poppy seeds to make me fail my drug test is finally explained and it's horrible. He'll still lose his license to practice law. Which he fucking deserves because I've been separated from my son for four and a half months. But at the same time, I'm glad his wife is still in the experimental trial. David and his wife already paid for the whole thing.

Jackson squeezes my thigh underneath the table as Alberto flips a page. I glance over at him quickly and give a brief nod. The silent communication is enough. He told me before coming in that this was my show. He'd be here for support but wouldn't jump in unless I indicated he should. I love that he doesn't feel any macho need to try to run my life and trusts that between me and the lawyer, I got this.

Alberto continues on, "—conspiracy to commit fraud against the state of California, and you can see the rest listed." Alberto steeples his fingers. "Now. There's a *possibility* that we will not press charges on any of the counts. We simply require that Mr. Kinnock sign this document here," he produces an official looking paper, "signing the termination of his parental rights."

David sits back in his chair and stares at me like I just knocked all the breath out of him. "You can't take away my son." His eyebrows drop like I've betrayed him.

"Oh keep the kicked-puppy act for the naïve freshman and sophomore girls. That's not me anymore." I lean forward and stab a finger on the paper. "Sign it or get your ass dragged through the courts. Do some jail time and end up signing it in the end anyway."

My words are short and pointed. I have no patience for this overly-dramatic asshat and the show he's trying to put on here. "No judge in a *fair* courtroom is going to give a child to a criminal like you—"

David opens his mouth to object and I slice a hand through the air and continue, deadly calm and controlled, "—It turns out I learned a thing or two from you and guess what? From the tail I've had on your ass for the last two months, I figured out that you barely spend any time at home with this son you claim to care so much about."

I pull out a piece of paper from the folder and glare at the useless piece of shit in front of me. This pissed me off so bad when Alberto showed it to me, I had to go to the gym for an emergency heavy bag session or I was gonna put a hole through the wall.

"In fact, you haven't been spending many nights at home at all. Only two a week. What?" My words are cutting. "Trouble in paradise. Again?" I look between him and Regina. "You know what?"

I breathe out to calm myself down. He's not worth the energy. "That's not my problem. What I *do* care about is the fact that you left my son alone with a woman I don't know, who I *don't* trust, and who isn't kin to him."

David mumbles something I don't hear. I always hated it when he did that. I'd be making a point and he'd grumble something under his breath in disagreement. When we were together, I never pushed him on it. Screw that.

"What was that? You have something to say?"

He looks up at me, finally making eye contact. "*Our* son," he says passionately. "I said he's *our* son, not your son. And who's this guy?" He gestures at Jackson. "I don't know who he is and what if *I* don't want *him* around our son? Huh? Did you ever think of that?"

His outburst only makes me cooler and calmer.

"*He* is the man I love." I stare David down, seeing him for exactly the small creature that he is. "*He* is going to be the father you could never fucking dream of being because he knows what it means to be an actual fucking man." There really is something powerful about cursing when you're speaking in quiet, neutral tones. It has almost double the punch, though I've never noticed it before this moment. I slide the parental termination form an inch closer to David.

"Now sign this paper," I continue, my voice as calm as a glassy lake on a windless morning, "or I swear I will make it my life's fucking mission to pin every one of these charges at your door. And you think I'll do it discreetly?"

I raise my eyebrows. "Oh no. I'll make sure to email every student journalist at Stanford. Just imagine the headline: Deadbeat Philosophy Professor Extorts Lawyer of His Ex-Student (Ex-Lover, Current Baby-Mama)." I shake my head, "That reads more juicy than an episode of

Jerry Springer. I bet it will go over so swell. You know what my crack team here also informed me of?"

I lean even further across the table into David's space and if possible, my voice gets icier. "I learned that tenure doesn't mean your ass can't get fired. You can still be dismissed for violation of policy or law. And guess what? That lovely little list that Alberto here just read off a moment ago? That means you've violated both, multiple times over."

I lean back and stare David down. "The Dean is just a phone call away." I lift my cell phone out of my purse to make the point.

If there's one thing David values above all else, it's his profession. He's nothing without it, at least in his own eyes. He admitted as much to me one night when he got drunk and maudlin and spent the next week avoiding me because he was embarrassed about opening up.

Well, he says he loves his son. Let him prove it. I'm only asking him to give up everything for him. I grab the pen in front of me and slam it down on the papers of paternity termination. He can say no, tell me to fuck off, face the consequences of his actions, and fight for a relationship with his son.

After all, there's nothing I wouldn't do or give up for Charlie.

David takes four whole seconds fidgeting uncomfortably in his chair before he grabs the pen and signs his name.

I wasn't expecting the stab of disappointment.

It's not disappointment for myself. Fuck knows I have no shred of affection left for the man in front of me. But for Charlie. That his father was willing to give him up with so little hesitation. Yes, the ultimatum I gave him asked for everything and I knew what choice he would make.

"We did the best we could." I glance up in surprise to see Regina finally looking at me. These are the first words she's spoken the whole time.

"I did the best I could." Her hands are white-knuckled as she grips the edge of the table, tear-tracks visible on the thick makeup caked on her cheeks. "Maybe I can see him sometimes. I mean—" she chokes out. "I know you have no reason to— I have no rights, I know."

She swipes at her eyes and her nose drips. "But I love him. I love him." Her eyes beg me. They're a mother's eyes.

I grab the paper David signed and hand it to Alberto. I frown as I look at Regina, the woman who's been mother to my son for the past four months. I quickly do the calculation. He's so young, the months she's spent with him are almost a seventh of his life. I think of how emotional he was last time I saw him. Can I really just cut another mother figure out of his life?

At the same time, she was also an evil bitch to me. I cock my head to the side, taking in the huge diamond earrings that are weighing down her earlobes. "How much?"

She swipes at her eyes, eyebrows dropping. "What?"

I cock my head to the side. "You're very rich and I'm tired of being poor. How much is seeing Charlie worth to you?"

"You can't—" their lawyer starts to say but Regina cuts him off.

"Anything. Everything." There wasn't a moment's hesitation to her words and her eyes are wide with hope. She scoots her chair back and stands. "We'll go right now and add your name to my bank account. Whatever I have is yours."

And just like that, she passes the test that David failed. From everything I know of this woman, her wealth is her life. I push my own chair back. "Keep your money. We'll see about visitation, with me there, on a *trial basis*." I make sure to emphasize the last two words. She's still been part of some super shady shit. "Maybe we can all meet and play together in the park. Someday."

She nods over and over like a bobble-head, hands clasped.

"And I'll call you, not the other way around. Got it? You pull anything, any stalkerish shit, and it's done. No second chances. And I don't want to see *him*." I point in David's direction without looking at him. I don't need that man fucking with my little boy's heart. He starts to make some objection but Regina talks over him.

"I won't, I promise. I won't let him near." More tears pour down her cheeks as she shakes her head. "I won't do anything to screw it up. I just want to see him."

"Fine."

Without one last glance at David or Regina, I look to Jackson.

He holds out his hand to me. "Let's go get our son."

We clasp hands and the world is righted.

EPILOGUE

CALLIE

"Mom, check out our sand castle!"

I grin as I get up off the shaded umbrella chair where I've been lounging and reading. I walk the few paces to where Jackson and Charlie sit by a sandcastle that I have to admit, kicks all the other sandcastles' asses.

We've set up camp in a small area on Capitola Beach about twenty feet away from the surf. Well, we used to be twenty feet away. More like ten now. A wave crashes and the surf washes up far closer than it was when we first lay out our beach blankets and chairs a few hours ago.

I take a moment and soak it in—the sun warming my skin, the perfect cloudless sky, the crash of waves to my right. I didn't think perfect days were a thing people actually, like... got to have. I mean, maybe celebrities and really rich people and... okay, Jackson and I are pretty rich, but the happiness that settles all over me doesn't have a thing to do with what's in our bank account. We're on a public beach—there's noise and people all around us. My boys staked out a little piece of beach for their own to build on after we all swam and picnicked earlier. It's just... perfect.

My boys. My family. My life. I grin so wide I'm sure it's about to split my face.

Fucking happiness. Who knew?

"Mom, come on. Why are you just standing there? Take a picture. I wanna put it on my Instagram account!"

My eight-year-old has more Instagram followers than me. I am officially old. Yeah. I don't fucking care.

I laugh as I pull out my phone. "Say cheese."

Charlie rolls his eyes but then smiles anyway before I snap the pic. I stare at it for a moment. Jackson sits beside my son, laughing and still as chiseled and fucking gorgeous as ever at almost forty. That thing we always complain about where dudes manage to look hotter the older they get? Yeah. Not really minding it over here.

"Take another. Well, wait a sec till I fix this and then take it," Charlie's eyebrows furrow as he maneuvers a popsicle stick to perfect one of the turrets. Jackson just shakes his head and grins at me.

Watching them build the thing was freaking adorable. Jackson was trying to teach Charlie about engineering principles. Charlie was half-listening and half more interested in playing with seaweed along the surf. But toward the end, as it really took shape, Charlie got seriously into it. They've bonded so much over the past five years. Charlie was Jackson's mini-best man at our wedding two years ago. Talk about adorable Instagram pictures.

Charlie pulls the popsicle stick away. "Okay, ready Mom."

"No," Jackson says. "I think it's missing something."

Charlie's eyes narrow in concern, searching over the castle. "What?"

Jackson pops to his feet and in one bound, he has me lassoed around my waist. "We're missing the most beautiful woman on the beach."

Charlie rolls his eyes and makes a gagging noise like he always does when we're PDA-ing.

I laugh and screech a little when Jackson sweeps me off my feet, literally, and swings me in a circle before depositing me behind the sand castle. His long arm easily holds the camera out to get all three of us and the sand castle in the picture. I can see on the little screen that Charlie's making goofy faces instead of smiling so I tickle him.

Jackson snaps the shot right when Charlie's caught in an openmouthed laugh, showing off his biggest gap-toothed grin. Jackson and I frame him on either side, me laughing with Charlie, and Jackson looking at the both of us, his eyes so full of love.

We pull into the beach house around sunset.

"How was the beach today?" calls Regina as we tumble into the house.

"I swam in the ocean!" Charlie calls. "Like *really* out in the ocean. We went past the crashing waves part and then Dad held me up and we'd jump when the ocean would go like this." Jackson looks over Charlie's head at me. He told me once that it still gets him every time Charlie calls him *Dad*.

Charlie rolls his hand to mimic the swoop and swelling motion of the ocean water coming toward us before a wave crested. "One time it almost got over my head, but Dad lifted me up and we jumped—" Charlie jumps to demonstrate, "—and we just barely missed getting smashed by the giant wave. And there was seaweed everywhere and it was *yuck*, we were always pushing it out of the way and—"

"I made stir-fry," Regina breaks through Charlie's stream of chatter. Good thing too, because we both know Charlie could keep going without taking a breath for a half-hour straight. "Oh, but you two are headed out tonight, right?"

I nod at her. "You still good with keeping him the next couple days?"

She smiles at me, happy lines around her eyes. She wears less makeup these days but still looks wicked stylish. She's taken to beach-chic for this trip, lots of linens in muted pastels. Ever the lady.

Then I look around. "Where are Shannon and Sunil?"

Regina laughs. "They haven't gotten back from their meditation retreat session yet. Your sister was telling me all about it before they left. I've never seen anyone so excited about nine hours of sitting around with a bunch of people not saying anything and just..." she tosses her hands up, "...*sitting there.*"

I shake my head. I'm with Regina. My anal-retentive sister has become the most chill, hippie, and happy version of herself over the past few years, it's crazy.

I give Regina a hug and then head with Jackson to our bedroom to get cleaned up.

It's taken a long time for us to get to this point with Regina. It was baby steps at first, but it turned out to be the right choice not to cut her off from Charlie completely. He had a rough transition coming back home initially, but that was more because he was just having a rough time of it all around.

I ended up having Regina come stay with us a few days each week so Charlie wouldn't feel like it was a normal thing for people he loved to keep suddenly disappearing from his life. His behavior and disposition immediately improved.

And David? Yeah. Just like I'd suspected, Charlie'd barely seen enough of him to miss him.

That whole period in our life was capped off with Gentry going to jail for multiple life sentences. Jackson and I looked through the blackmail files we found on Gentry's computer and figured the only way to completely strip Gentry of power was to release it all to the press. There were high-ranking judges in there as well as any number of other powerful people he might have leveraged to influence the trial in his favor.

So we contacted the LA Times and the scandals that followed the release of the Gentry Files became so infamous, it was almost impossible to find a jury that wasn't biased against him. Not only was he blackmailing corrupt judges, city council members, and the district attorney's office, but mine wasn't the only sexual assault he'd videoed. Apparently it was a pastime of his, and in some of the other videos, his face was on-screen.

At his trial, the public wanted Gentry's blood and they got it. He was sentenced to four back-to-back life sentences and there would be no cozy white-collar prison wards for Bryce Gentry. No, he was thrown into Gen Pop at San Quentin. I've heard rapists aren't very popular in prison. I don't know what happened to him after that but occasionally I like to think of him there, getting his just desserts.

Eventually everything quieted down. Charlie settled and now we have one happy, healthy boy on our hands. I started going to therapy to continue working through everything that happened to me. More than that, though, I had Jackson. Every day he helps make me new.

I grin and hug Jackson once we get in our room.

"What's that for?" he asks, squeezing back.

"You," I say into his chest. "Our life." I lay my cheek against where his heart beats. "Everything."

He gives a soft laugh, squeezes me one more time, then lets me go. "Come on. We have to get going if we want to make our dinner reservation."

I follow him though, getting in his face and nipping at his bottom lip. "How about we skip the reservation and go straight to the other beach house we rented for the weekend." I run my hand up his inner thigh slowly and then grab his crotch in a tight clench.

He jolts and hisses between his teeth before grabbing me by my ass and grinding me into him.

"That depends. Who's going to be in charge tonight?"

As he looks down into my eyes, his take on a dark intensity.

I grin wickedly up at him and lick my top lip. "I don't even know which you like better anymore."

He only arches an eyebrow and produces a quarter from his pocket.

I laugh a low, throaty laugh. "How long have you been carrying that just waiting for this moment?"

"I'll never tell." He raises both eyebrows a couple times and looks so fucking adorable I want to devour him on the spot.

"Heads," I call.

"Tails it is," he says and pulls back slightly to flip the coin. He flips it expertly and catches it in his other hand. He's gotten some practice at this over the years, after all. Sometimes we go with whatever we're in the mood for, but then there are nights like tonight when there's no particular stress, need, or desire to work out and it's all fun and games.

He lifts his hand and reveals the results of the coin toss.

Heads.

I clap my hands and do a little jump up and down.

Don't judge me. I don't have to put on the Domme persona until we're in the scene.

Jackson rolls his eyes but then bows his head. "Mistress."

I bite my lip and grab his hands. "Okay, I was going to wait till the restaurant to do the whole big movie moment boom-box-on-a-shoulder kind of thing, but I seriously can't wait another fucking minute."

"Shh." He covers my mouth with his hand. "You owe a dollar in the swear jar."

I giggle and pull away from his hand. "Shut up. Charlie's not even in the room." Attempts to curb my swearing in front of the child have *mostly* succeeded. I can usually turn it off between the hours of seven a.m. to eight p.m.

"Besides, I have news. Big news." I grab Jackson's hands again and he suddenly sobers, eyes riveted to mine.

"Shut up."

I grin. "I took the test this morning. Three tests."

"Shut up."

"And then I took three more just to be sure."

"Don't fuck with me, Cals." His face is getting paler by the second and his grip on my hands white-knuckled.

"Now who needs to put a dollar in the swear jar?"

"Callie," he warns.

"You're going to be a daddy." I grin so hard tears leak out of my eyes.

Jackson shakes his head and blinks, like he's trying to shake something loose from his ears. "No way. No fucking way."

"Way," I laugh. "A bunch of pregnancy tests with pink lines, some plus signs and one happy face," I scrunch my eyebrows, because that was a weird one, "confirm that you and I have created an A+, gold star fetus right in here," I point to my stomach.

Jackson drops to his knees and presses his ear to my tummy. "In here?" He laughs through tears as he looks up at me.

I can barely see him from between my breasts, but holy shit, I've never seen another human being look so happy in all my life. I can't manage any more words so I just nod. Neither can he because he only stays there for a long, long moment, head bowed against my stomach and the new life we've created there.

When he finally looks up, there's nothing but worship in his eyes. "How may I please you, Mistress?"

HURT SO GOOD

Callie isn't the only woman Bryce Gentry tried to break, she was just the latest. Read the next book in the Break So Soft Series, Miranda and Dylan's story in HURT SO GOOD, for a story of dark desire, darker fantasies, and above all, true love.

Continue reading for a preview.

PREVIEW OF HURT SO GOOD: A DARK ROMANCE

CHAPTER 1

DYLAN

I stare over the rim of my glass of bourbon, watching the bombshell in the red dress work the room.

She's good, I'll give her that.

She flirts just enough with the men—only the important ones, I note—a touch of her hand on their shoulder, the brush of her hip, the flash of her smile. She's making them feel like they've gotten something from her but then she moves on before they can really get a taste.

And the more I watch her, a taste is exactly what I want of the woman.

I don't even know her name but my cock has been stiff for the last half hour as I've nursed my bourbon and watched her.

This is a bullshit mixer the Silicon Valley Robotics Symposium puts on every year, and it's made exactly for this kind of shit. To encourage the greasing of wheels that actually gets deals done. An open bar. A tight red dress. A word or two in the right ear.

The hotel ballroom is dimly lit while a band plays soft, unremarkable jazz on a small stage up front. Meanwhile, middle-aged men with flushed faces laugh too loudly at jokes and are a little too obvious about their hopes for getting laid. Because it's a tech conference though, there are about two guys to every woman, so their chances aren't good.

And then there's her. The woman in red.

I wonder what company the woman represents.

It doesn't matter. You aren't going to find out and you sure as fuck aren't getting a taste of her.

I frown and tip my glass back, draining the last of the bourbon. Don't know why the fuck I even stopped by here after my presentation. My brother, Darren, kept saying I needed to at least show my face or it would look rude after I gave the keynote speech. Considering he's also my business partner, I thought, *fine, I'll drop in for a few minutes and then get the hell out of here.*

Until I saw her.

Trouble is what she is. Trouble I don't need.

Which is why you're leaving. Right now.

I stand up and put the glass down on the bartop, then turn and—

Almost run straight into her. *Her.*

"Where you off to in such a hurry?" She flashes the same mega-watt smile she gave every other guy in the room and my eyes narrow. She thinks she's gonna run her game on me? It's insulting. Do I look like all the other desperate fucks in here?

I ignore her and reach for my coat and umbrella, then I move again to leave. I don't step around her, though. I step into her and our bodies do more than brush. We collide and I hear her quick intake of air as she rocks back on her heels.

I expect her to get pissed at the dick move. Which is for the best because I just need to get the hell out of here. Discipline has been my watchword for the last six years and I'm not about to blow it now.

But when I glance her way, her posture is completely different.

Her eyes have dropped to the floor and her head is bowed. Submissively. Her brunette hair shines in the dim light of the wall sconces and now that she's here up close I can see that she's younger than I first thought. Maybe only twenty-five? Twenty-six?

And then I see her tongue swipe out to lick her lips at the same time her chest heaves, ample cleavage rising and falling dramatically.

I'm captured by the sight and when a moment later she glances back up at me, the lust is clear in her eyes.

Who the fuck is this woman?

"Who are you?" I'm not a man who beats around the bush.

"Miranda Rose. With ProDynamics. And you're Dylan Lennox of The Lennox Brothers Corporation."

My eyebrow lifts. ProDynamics, huh? Rod Serrano, the CEO, has already put in his bid to have their Pro processors in our newest robotics motherboards we're pushing out. He keeps calling to get updates about his bid but I've been ignoring his inquiries.

Is putting this siren in my path his latest attempt to sway me into taking a meeting with him?

"Wow. Rod really does go all out," I sneer. Rod will find out along with everyone else when we make the announcement of which processing chip we're going with. But I already know I'm not interested in his processor. Processors like Intel has capitalized on—and like ProDynamics keeps producing—are the past. I'm more interested in the future.

The woman's eyes flare but she doesn't say anything. Fuck. She doesn't look pissed by my asshole attitude. She looks turned on. And her lust seems genuine.

Or she's just one hell of an actress.

Either way, no fucking way I'm letting my dick have any say in my business dealings. Jesus but I learned that the hard way, didn't I? I barely survived the scandal last time and only because I had the money to pay to make it go away quickly.

Never again.

So no matter how luscious Miranda Rose looks in that red dress and those fuck me heels, I continue pushing past her. My eyes shut briefly as I inhale her seductive scent but then I'm finally away from her.

I stride for the door and *almost* make it.

A red-faced Ken Kobayashi stops me feet from the door, clapping me on the back. "Dylan! Good to see you! Loved your talk. Come, have a drink with us." He gestures toward his table of big wigs from the Japanese tech sector who flew in for the conference.

I force a smile and shake him off. "Sorry, I'm heading out."

"No, man, you gotta come hang." Ken grew up in the states and we briefly knew each other in college. He's the opposite of every Asian stereotype—he always loved partying instead of studying, barely got by in his classes and only managed to get the position he has now because his daddy pulled strings for him in the family company.

Over his shoulder, I see Miranda heading out of the hotel ballroom, ass swaying sinfully in the red dress.

My cock stiffens again. Fuck, I need to get out of here and get home where I can take myself in hand and give in to all the fantasies crowding my brain before I embarrass myself in public.

"Great seeing you, Ken," I cut him off mid-sentence. I clap him on the back and then head out the same door she just left through. She's only about twenty feet ahead of me, strolling with those hips still swaying through the lobby and out a side exit to the garage.

I'm not intentionally following her.

... I don't think.

I'm just making sure she gets to her car safely. She'll never even know I'm here. It's the gentlemanly thing to do.

As if I could ever be accused of being gentlemanly. I know what this really is.

Just more fuel for tonight's fantasies.

For once, I'm giving in to the rush of what it feels like to stalk my prey.

CHAPTER 2

MIRANDA

My heels click clack on the stairs as I head up to the third floor of the parking garage.

Hairs tingle on the back of my neck, the same way they always do when I walk anywhere at night in the city.

It's not safe to be a woman alone.

The thought both thrills and terrifies me. Because I'm fucked up. I'm a seriously fucked up woman.

I bite my lip at the thought of the man in the bar.

Dylan Lennox.

His chiseled face and broad shoulders. Those eyes that captivated even as they dismissed me.

The man who followed me out of the hotel into the garage.

I don't hear his footsteps on the stairs behind me, though. Will he take the elevator? Or was he not following me after all?

He was leaving, too. He's probably just heading to his own car.

But he's Dylan Lennox. Surely he used valet parking.

I bite my lip as I reach the top of the staircase. I only offer one glance over at the elevator before pushing through the door to the open air of the top floor of the garage.

I parked at the very end of the row, at the corner of the rooftop. As I go, I force myself not to look back like I usually would. It's dark and I'm a woman alone. I'm supposed to be afraid.

And my breaths do come quicker with every step I take. I hurry, almost at a jog or as near to as I can in these heels.

My heartbeat only calms once I reach my car. A red Corvette, naturally. I'm so careful about the packaged product I want to project to the world as I make myself up each morning. The Corvette is all part of it.

Confident. Sexy. Desirable.

In control.

Everything I wish I actually was.

I reach in my tiny clutch purse and pull out my key, ready to push the button to open the door—

When I'm pushed from behind, my face crushed into the glass of the driver's side window.

"Spread your legs, bitch."

It's not Dylan.

The breath is heavy with the stench of cigarettes and the arm that cinches around my neck is merciless.

I let out a small cry before the arm tightens around my neck.

A foot kicks my legs apart. My ankle turns at the rough movement and I cry out again but it doesn't matter.

Nothing matters to the man at my back as he rips my dress up to my waist. I'm not wearing underwear because the dress was so tight that even the strings of a thong would have shown.

I cough and choke as tears rush my eyes.

Rough hands on my body. Hands squeezing my breasts as I cry out uselessly.

You'll take what I give you, you worthless whore. The memory and the present mingle interchangeably. *And you'll love it so much you come the more I hurt you. You'll beg me to hurt you even more.*

"Oh yeah, you're a hot little bitch, aren't you?" The man behind me breathes into my face, slobbering and then biting painfully at my ear. "You hot for me, whore?"

I shudder at the words as it all washes over me. Knowing the pain is coming. The humiliation. The helplessness.

Worthless whore. You want it over? Then beg for it. Beg for it, whore!

It starts to rise, just like it always did and I hate myself. I hate him for making me this way. I hate him and I—

"Get the fuck away from her!"

My eyes pop open wide as I wrench my head to the right.

Just in time to see Dylan Lennox barreling towards us.

Oh shit.

CHAPTER 3

DYLAN

I'll kill the fucker. It's the only thought I have as I tear into the guy and yank him off her. He goes down with little fight, throwing his arms over his face.

Miranda screams but all I can care about is the fact that I got him off her before he could. Before he could—

I roar in fury and bring my fist down on the fucker's face.

Once, then again, and—

I lift my fist to ram into his face again but arms wrap around me from behind. I look back in confusion.

It's Miranda. Dark mascara tear tracks line her cheeks from and she's shaking her head. "Stop. It's not what you think. Stop!"

What the fuck is she—

"He wasn't— He wasn't— I *wanted* it. We arranged this. Online. I knew he was going to be here."

She *wanted*—

I jerk back from both her and the guy I'm on top of. She tumbles backwards and the guy underneath me crawls away, dropping the condom he had clutched in his hand as he goes.

"You crazy fucks," he mutters as he crawls to his feet and limps away, hand to his bleeding face.

"You arranged for this." My voice is dead cold and my hands clench into fists. I still have the other fucker's blood on me. I'm sure I broke his nose.

Miranda just nods, her head down, sitting on the ground where she landed after I brushed her off me.

"You arrange for strangers to fucking rape you?"

Her head shoots up at this. "No! It's not... *that*. Not if I want it. We're consenting adults."

"Consenting—" I scoff, shaking my head. I can't fucking believe her. I drag my hands through my hair and turn away from her.

I rode the elevator up and then stood on the other side of the door for several long moments, warring with myself over whether or not to open it onto the roof. Just to peek. Just to double check she was fine getting to her car.

And when I lost the battle with myself and pushed open the door, only to find her struggling against that bastard and trying to scream...

"What the fuck is wrong with you?" I roar at her where she's still on the ground, dress up around her waist.

Jesus Christ, she's just exposed to the fucking world, not even trying to cover herself as she wipes at her eyes, only smearing the mascara worse.

I shouldn't have looked.

Fuck but I shouldn't have looked.

Because the sight of her there. Weeping. Broken. Legs splayed with one of her high heels broken, cunt bared...

It flips the switch I've managed for years to stifle. All the years of therapy, all the iron discipline.

Gone.

In a single moment, all of it, *gone*.

"Is this what you want?" I sneer, reaching down and grabbing her roughly by her upper arms, dragging her to her feet and then twirling her and slamming her face down on the hood of her Corvette.

I take both of her wrists and pin them behind her back. Then I bend over her from behind, just like that other bastard had her, and I jam my erection into her ass. "You want it like this? You want a stranger to fuck you?"

There's a distant voice shouting in the back of my head: *What the fuck are you doing? Let her go. Back away. Fucking* now. *This is a road you can never go down again.*

But then she bends her head to look at me, an awkward angle with the way I have her positioned. I can't read what's in her eyes. If it's lust or determination or what.

All I know is she doesn't look broken anymore.

"Yes, I want it," she whispers. "But only if you make it hurt."

My hand that's not holding her wrist is on my buckle the next instant. I rip it open and undo my slacks.

Fuuuuuuuuuuck, it feels good to free my cock. My tip immediately seeks her entrance. She's so hot. And wet. Dripping fucking wet.

She wants it.

And I haven't had it in so long. So fucking long.

Just this once. Just this once and then never again.

She *wants* it. It's not wrong if she wants it.

My hips surge forward and then I'm fucking her. It's not a decision. In this moment, I can't *not* be fucking her.

She cries out with the first in stroke. I don't ease her into it. And I'm a big motherfucker. Women have had trouble taking me in the past.

I pull back and then drive my hips forward again. Deeper. Fuck. I throw my head back and grip her wrists even tighter.

I'm not wearing a condom. Shit. It should worry me. But after six years without a woman, the only thing I can think is *fuck*, I can feel all of her. No barriers. Nothing between us. My nerve endings feel raw as if they're firing for the first time and the need to fuck her is this insane compulsion.

She clenches around me. Or maybe she's squeezing so tight because she's trying to keep me out? Is she regretting her decision?

The thought only makes me harder.

I put my hand on the back of her neck and shove her face harder into the hood of the car and I let my fantasies loose.

I followed her out of the bar. She was swinging that luscious ass so temptingly. Teasing all those bastards but then leaving them wanting.

Cock tease. My father's voice reverberates in my head. *Women who are cock teases need to be taught a lesson, son. A tease is a promise. It's our job to make sure they pay up.*

NO. I swore. I *swore* I'd never be anything like him.

Disgust chokes me.

But I fuck Miranda even harder. My hand pushes the side of her face against the hood. Fresh tears squeeze out of her eyes.

I'm horrified.

I'm fascinated.

She squeezes around me, tighter than my fist when I punish-fuck my hand for my sick fucking fantasies.

And I cum.

Deep and long and hard, I empty myself into her.

She squeezes tighter, tighter, milking me of every last drop, a high-pitched gasping wail escaping out her lips.

Fuck but she's cumming, too.

She really did want it.

I drag my cock out and then shove back in, rougher than I have yet, positively jackhammering into her and shoving her pelvis painfully against the hood of the Corvette.

So good. It's so good. So fuckin' good and I haven't had it in so long. My fantasies can't even compare—

Her nails scrabble against my arm where I hold her wrists and she shuts her eyes, pressing her forehead into the hood as her ass jerks and grinds against me. More pleasured whines escape her mouth. Jesus Christ, is she *still* cumming?

My cock jerks inside her, still hard even after I've cum.

She's fucking magnificent.

She frowns and I can see she's finally coming down and I shake my head because fuck that.

My cock still impaling her, I drop her wrists and reach around to her clit. I pinch it cruelly at the same time I spit on my forefinger.

I reach down and then ruthlessly shove it up her ass.

Her eyes shoot open and her mouth drops into a wide O. But a second later her face is transformed again as she's lost in another wave of pleasure.

Oh fuck. Oh fuck yeah, that's right.

I pinch harder and shove another finger up her ass. I'm not gentle about it, either.

"You like that," I growl. I drag my hips back and forth slowly, my cock still stiff in her cunt. "You like it when I fucking defile you."

I shove a third finger in her ass. Fucking invading her. A stranger finger fucking her ass, almost dry. It's gotta hurt. It's gotta hurt a lot.

When I look at her face, I'm not disappointed. There are more tears. Pain amidst her pleasured whimpers.

She's hurting. You're hurting her.

The horror hits. What the fuck am I doing?

But then her back arches. She thrashes against the car hood and it's not in pain. Or maybe it is, partially. But by the look on her face, it's more pleasure than pain.

I shove my fingers ruthlessly farther up her ass. Pull them out. Shove them back up again even harder.

Her forehead scrunches with the pain. But she thrusts her ass back against my hand.

And I start fucking her again. With both my cock and my fingers.

Mercilessly.

Pulling out.

Then hammering back in.

Out.

Jackknifing in again.

The car bounces on its shocks with my every thrust and Miranda lets out small grunts each time.

I pull my fingers out of her ass and move my hand up her body.

To her throat.

I curve my hand around her neck, thumb at her pulse point. Her heartbeat is thrumming like a frightened rabbit's as I continue to fuck her.

I fuck her and fuck her and fuck her.

How long has it been since I last came? Five minutes? Ten?

I squeeze my fingers around her throat and her breath hitches. I test the pressure and her rasping gasp makes pleasure spike down my spine.

She can still breathe, but barely.

I lean over her back and growl in her ear. "I could end it so easily. If I squeezed just a little harder. Is this how you like to play? You want the pain? You like the fucking danger of meeting strangers on rooftops where no one will hear you scream?"

She nods into my grip.

Fucking *nods*.

It infuriates me so much that I lose my fucking mind and squeeze harder for a couple of seconds just to teach her a damn lesson.

She needs to be scared fucking straight.

Almost the second my grip tightens, though, she comes. Fucking *comes*. Again.

"You stupid fucking idiot," I hiss in her ear, loosening my grip on her throat and moving my hand to cover her mouth.

I'm disgusted with myself the second I do it. But it also feels so fucking *right*. She can't scream now. I grip my hand over her mouth even harder, pulling her head back against my chest as I ram my dick into her cunt.

My fingers offer just enough clearance of her nose so she can breathe. The thought is a distant comfort.

It doesn't change the brutal scene.

Or how much I'm fucking getting off on it.

Because being back inside a slick cunt, having my hands on a woman again, like *this*, after so long, so many *years* without—Jesus *Christ*.

Her silky, dark hair is up in an elegant updo and I lean down and bite the back of her neck, roaring as I come again. Harder than the first time. So much harder.

My teeth sink into her sweet, soft flesh as the last of my cum pumps into her cunt that's squeezed like a vice around my cock.

She cries out against my hand and I roar into the nape of her neck in animal satisfaction.

And then—

Then...

I'm left heaving over her back, my mouth slack against her neck.

I blink and it's like coming back from a bout of insanity.

I pull my hand away from her mouth and jerk away from her, my cock finally slipping out of her.

I stumble backwards and my mouth drops open in horror at the scene before me.

Miranda is splayed face down on the hood of her car, legs awkwardly spread as cum drips down her leg and fuck—

I can see the bite mark on the back of her neck from five feet away. Did I draw blood?

She's blinking too and turning to look at me. Her face is a mess of mascara and tears. She looks fucking battered and broken.

By me.

Another voice rings out in my head. Not my father this time, but another monster even more insidious. *If you do it right, you can break them and they'll still beg you for more. That's when you'll know you're a god.*

"I'm sorry," I rasp, roughly jerking my pants up and shoving my dick back inside. "I'm so sorry."

She starts to shake her head but I hold up my hands and then I turn and fucking sprint toward the door.

Continue Reading HURT SO GOOD, available now.

Want to read an EXCLUSIVE, FREE NOVEL, Daddy's Sweet Girl, a dark stepfamily love story that is available only to my newsletter subscribers, along with news about upcoming releases, sales, exclusive giveaways, and more?

Get it here:
BookHip.com/MGTKPK

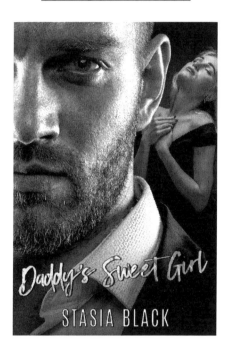

ALSO BY STASIA BLACK

MARRIAGE RAFFLE SERIES

Theirs to Protect

Theirs to Pleasure

Their Bride

Theirs to Defy

STUD RANCH STANDALONE SERIES

The Virgin and the Beast: a Beauty and the Beast Tale (prequel)

Hunter: a Snow White Romance

The Virgin Next Door: a Ménage Romance

BREAK SO SOFT SERIES

Cut So Deep

Break So Soft

Hurt So Good

ACKNOWLEDGMENTS

As always, I thank my gorgeous husband, lover of my heart, body, mind, and soul. I love *you* more. Haha, it's here in writing, so it must be true ;)

Thanks to some fabulous beta readers and their stellar feedback: Karina L., as always, you rock! Belinda D., thanks SO much again for your quick read of the series and your encouragement. Lindsay Johnston (sorry for being so evil and taking forever to get this book to you, won't happen again!). Aimee, zomg, what would I have done without your detailed edits? I will never understand why some words are hyphenated and others not, lol, and you are a genius and a God-send (or is it Godsend?)! And Kristin L. J. thank you so much for your edits —your eyes right at the end gave me just what I needed to nudge this to the next level so I knew it was absolutely perfect.

And thank you again, you gorgeous reader, you! Without you literally none of this would be possible. Thanks for taking a chance on a new author :) If you want to continue discovering sexy romantic stories that ride the motherf#@ing edge, I've got several more books coming out in the coming year.

ABOUT THE AUTHOR

Stasia grew up in Texas, recently spent a freezing five-year stint in Minnesota, and now is happily planted in sunny California, which she will never, ever leave.

She loves writing, reading, listening to podcasts, and has recently taken up biking after a twenty-year sabbatical (and has the bumps and bruises to prove it). She lives with her own personal cheerleader, aka, her handsome husband, and their teenage son. Wow. Typing that makes her feel old. And writing about herself in the third person makes her feel a little like a nutjob, but ahem! Where were we?

Stasia's drawn to romantic stories that don't take the easy way out. She wants to see beneath people's veneer and poke into their dark places, their twisted motives, and their deepest desires. Basically, she wants to create characters that make readers alternately laugh, cry ugly tears, want to toss their kindles across the room, and then declare they have a new FBB (forever book boyfriend).

Manufactured by Amazon.ca
Bolton, ON

33805265R00222